For Carolyn,
Un peu plus qu'hier, un peu moins que demain.

Acknowledgments

It's a pleasure to have the opportunity to express my sincere thanks to all those who, indirectly or directly, helped to produce this book and the first Carston story. They were generous with their time and their expertise and I hope I haven't distorted the information they gave me too hopelessly.

Specifically, they are:

My son Simon for explanations of financial affairs which I still don't understand;

Neil Donald for access to Aberdeen's nightlife and insights into the people who police it;

Elspeth Alexander for details of ceramics and glimpses into the fascinating world of auctions;

Gordon Murray for help with antiques;

Detective Superintendent Alexander Den of Grampian Police for invaluable information about procedures;

My editor, Kate Callaghan, for her perceptions, advice, and unfashionable faith in fiction;

And my wife, Carolyn, for just about everything else.

One

Friday afternoon, and Dawn and Jez were into one of their periodic fights. Floyd sat downstairs, rolling a cigarette and grinning at the insults they were screaming at one another. From what had been said so far, it seemed that Dawn thought Jez belonged in a museum, about halfway along the line of illustrations showing homo whatever's gradual elevation to the vertical. Jez, on the other hand, was surprised that Dawn knew what a museum was since she spent so much time on her back moaning "Oh yes, honey, yes," to whatever stranger had taken her fancy that particular day. Floyd wasn't given to speculation or any form of analytical thinking, but he got a lot of pleasure from the fact that two people who preached peace and love with such enthusiasm could be so relentlessly vicious with one another. It confirmed his contempt for the notion of love.

Floyd's cynicism was comprehensive. He believed in acquisition; acquisition without expenditure. He'd already spent four of his twenty-six years in prison for robbery with violence. More recently, he'd been working as a steward on a platform offshore. It had only lasted for three months because the two weeks on, two weeks off routine had been hard to take and the alternating cycle of alcohol abuse and enforced total abstinence wrecked his temper. A fight with a maintenance electrician who'd complained that his cabin hadn't been cleaned led to his dismissal. Since then, he'd done nothing. He'd been living in this squat for a couple of months and the others were beginning to find his perpetual sneering abrasive.

He heard footsteps clumping down the stairs: Dawn. She was only five feet two but somehow walked on her heels and made the floorboards shake far more than any of the rest of them. She came into the room, grabbed a magazine, and flopped angrily into a chair. Floyd lit his cigarette and waited as he heard Jez coming down too. Jez came in, looked at him, and stood in the doorway, undecided. He obviously didn't think the argument was over, but he didn't want an audience.

"Don't mind me," said Floyd. "I like violence."

"Shut up, Floyd," snapped Dawn.

"Now, now, darlin'. Peace an' love."

"Give it a rest, Floyd." This time it was Jez, grateful to have another target for his anger.

"Peace on earth, good ..." Floyd's taunt was interrupted by Dawn's voice. She was only just managing to control it.

"Keep your sick bloody comments to ..."

She in turn was interrupted, this time by a bang on the front door, which made her jump. She, Jez, and Floyd were the only ones in the house, but it couldn't be any of the others coming back; they all had keys, and the knock was wrong. Floyd sucked at his cigarette, looking at Jez, making it clear that he wasn't about to go and see who was there. Jez looked along the hallway and saw two silhouettes in the small frosted glass panel in the front door.

"Who is it?" he called.

"Scottish Gas, sir," said a man's voice. There was a pause. "A leak's been reported. We need to access the branch lines."

Jez went to the door and kept his foot hard against the base of it as he released the catch. In the last few weeks, they'd had a lot of hassle and he'd been squatting long enough to know the dangers. He'd want to see some proof of identity before he let them in.

He wasn't given the option. The instant that the catch slid free, his foot was forced away and he was flung back into the hall as the two men waiting on the step shoved forward. They stepped inside and closed the door quickly behind them. One of them was wearing jeans, a black T-shirt, and a blouson jacket made of some dark, tweedy material. His head was shaved and the loose skin around his jowls was gray with stubble and dirt. The other wore old blue cords, a navy blue jumper, and a black anorak. His hair was long, thinning at the crown and the temples, and dragged back into a ponytail. They were both big and their expressions told Jez right away that he was in trouble. He had no time even to shout. The one

2

with the shaved head leaned over him, grabbed him by the jumper, taking a handful of skin at the same time, and hauled him upright. He was slammed against the wall and the man jammed the baseball bat he was carrying hard across his neck and up under his chin.

"OK, you hippie bastard," he spat. "You're leavin', right? No arguin', no protestin'. You're out. Got it?" He jabbed the bat harder against Jez's throat to make his point. Jez clawed at it. The compression of his neck was making the blood bang in his ears. He couldn't speak. He couldn't even nod an answer. The man's breath was a hot, sour mixture of cigarette smoke and booze.

The other man was already at the doorway of the front room, an ax swinging freely in his right hand. As soon as he'd heard the noise in the hall, Floyd had gone to the window and started to open it. He stopped as the man appeared. Dawn scrambled to her feet. The man looked around. There wasn't much to see. The sofa and two armchairs were old Habitat designs with a green floral pattern. Between them stood a cheap coffee table. Beside the fireplace there was a small color television set on a homemade unit. On the shelf below it was a video recorder, underneath that a midi system, with tape and CD decks and a radio. Two speakers hung on hooks from the picture rail. There were five posters on the walls, but otherwise the room was simple and anonymous.

"What do you want?" said Dawn, who was now standing with the sofa between her and the man.

His eyes flicked to her and he brought the ax up to grip the top of the shaft in his left hand. His expression increased her fear. It was hard, dismissive; a face without compassion. His head twitched to indicate that the two of them should sit down. At the same time, the other man arrived, pushing Jez ahead of him with so much force that he sprawled face first onto the floor.

"On your arses, all of you," said the man with the bat, pointing at the floor in front of the sofa.

Jez was too hurt and confused to try to resist. He turned over and fell back against the sofa, his hands trying to ease some of the pain out of his neck. Dawn sat quickly beside him, looking at him for some sort of help. Only Floyd lingered at the window.

"Did ye no hear me, prickface?"

Floyd looked at the man just long enough to suggest that he wasn't as compliant as the others, then moved from the window and sat beside them.

"Right," said the man. "This is the score. You're on private property here. An' don't try to give me no shite about squattin'. This place doesna belong to you. So you're leavin'. Right?"

Dawn wanted to protest, but her fear tightened her throat. Jez's breath was still rasping heavily. Only Floyd was prepared to catch the man's eye.

"Right?" the man insisted.

Floyd didn't flinch. He'd seen enough trouble in the pubs and clubs around Aberdeen and Cairnburgh to know that these were pros. He also knew that weakness was what they were looking for. He raised his middle finger at the man. His defiance wouldn't save him, but he reckoned it might deflect the worst of what was coming onto Jez and Dawn.

It didn't. The man with the ax took two steps towards him and swung a boot into his side. Floyd rolled with the kick and lashed his arm up towards the man's groin. It made contact but did no harm. The man was angry now. He let the shaft of the ax slip through his fingers and clubbed it against Floyd's left temple. Floyd fell against Dawn, his vision blurred and blades of pain turning in his skull. Instinctively, Dawn put her arm around him. He retched dryly against her shoulder, then pushed her away.

"What's the matter with you bastard people?" shouted the man with the ax. It was the first time he'd spoken and his voice sounded as if it came from a badly scarred larynx. He kicked again, splitting the skin over Floyd's hip bone, and shifted the ax in his hand as if he were going to use the blade this time. Dawn turned her face away, leaning now to clutch Jez. The man swung the ax head into the TV screen. Glass splinters spewed onto the carpet and the set flew off its base, jerking at the various wires which connected it to other parts of the midi system. The man grabbed the wires, yanked them all free, and kicked the CD, tape deck, and amplifier out of the unit towards the fireplace. The video machine was on the floor. He buried the ax head in it. The loudspeaker leads were hanging free and the other man, almost carelessly, reached up and pulled

4

the speakers off the wall. One landed near his left foot. He swung the baseball bat at it, smashing it open and sending it hard into Jez's right shin.

"Now we'd be just as happy doin' that to your bloody heads," he said. "So it's up to you to look after yourselves. If you're no wantin' to end up a pile of mince, you'll be out of here before we come back. OK?"

Jez nodded.

The man pushed the end of the bat between Dawn's legs. "How 'bout Princess Di here?"

"Get away. Leave us alone," shouted Dawn, pushing her forearm against the bat and trying not to let her tears show. Roughly, the man pulled the bat away, then squatted in front of her, and pushed his free hand up under her skirt to grab at the flesh around her groin. He squeezed hard. He was too strong for her to push him off. His face was close to hers. The same sour breath which had washed across Jez in the hall was now warm on her cheeks.

"Lucky I don't fancy you, bitch, or I'd have fucked you rotten by now. So, d'you hear what I'm sayin' to you? You dinna belong here. You an' yer hippie pals better be on yer way, right?"

Dawn clamped her thighs around his arm and kept trying to force it away. He moved his head closer to hers, grinned, and licked his tongue around his lips. She shuddered with repulsion and the shaking took hold of her as she tried to control her sobs. Jez took his hand away from his throat and held it towards the man. "Alright, alright. Please leave her. Leave us alone. Please."

"Oh, not yet, son. It's no that simple," said the man. "See you, soon as we're away, you'll be boltin' the door and barricadin' yerselves in. So we'd be wastin' our time." He released his hold on Dawn and stood up. "No, no. Got to make our point, see?"

He flicked his head to the left to indicate that his partner should follow him and the two of them left the room. Jez put his arm round Dawn's shoulders. They heard the men running up the stairs. Floyd, his hand pressed against his head, stood up slowly and went to the door. There were crashes from the bedrooms. Without looking back at the others, Floyd stumbled down the hall and out into the street. He could still hear the noise the men were making. He crossed to the other pavement, slanting down towards the bushes and gate that gave access to the bottom end of Macaulay Park. He went through the gate and turned immediately left to crawl under the rhododendrons that bordered both the path and the street. He stopped and rolled over onto his back. The ground was cold and damp, but his head was on fire and he felt his shirt sticking to the blood that was running from the cut on his hip. Hotter than both was the anger he felt. Floyd hated being caught, hated having to take shit from anybody. He'd done his time in Peterhead Prison and even got respect from some of the hard men there. Running away and hiding in bushes like a kid was fucking insane. But what choice did he have? The bastards had surprised him. Maybe. But that wasn't the end of it. Nobody shamed him like that. It was that bastard Burchill, for sure; the guy that owned the place. He'd sent the two gorillas round. He ought to be made to pay for this. Floyd turned onto his side and pulled himself back towards the gate. The branches of the rhododendrons curved low enough to hide him still, but he had a clear view of the front of the squat. He waited.

Inside, Jez and Dawn had stood up but were reluctant to follow Floyd, partly from fear but also from a recognition that, once they left the house, the squat was finished. Not just for them but for the others who were away that afternoon. Their argument was forgotten as they stood together for protection against this new, very real threat. They heard the men coming downstairs and sat down on the sofa. The ax man was carrying Fran's radio cassette player and the man with the bat had a Walkman. He was the first to see that Floyd was missing. He swore and went quickly to the other rooms on the ground floor. When he came back, his anger was obvious.

"OK, you two. I'm sick of havin' to deal with wankers like you, so what you do is this. You pick up all the crap you've left lyin' about the place, you clean this place up, and then you piss off, right?" He kicked at the broken video recorder. "And when you see yer pal, tell him from me I still owe him one."

Dawn and Jez said nothing.

"D'you no hear me?" The man moved towards them.

"Yes, yes," said Jez quickly.

The man stopped and nodded. "Right then. We're no playin' games here." He paused and looked around. "That prick that's left. He'll find out. Now, if you or any of your pals are still here when I come back, you'll be in the hospital before you can say 'fuck off.' Got it?"

Jez and Dawn both nodded.

Lazily, almost without looking, the man brought his bat swinging down and across Jez's thighs. Jez shouted with pain, clutched at them, and leaned forward.

"Just so you remember," said the man.

He looked round again, made the same flicking motion with his head, and he and his partner walked out.

Floyd saw them leave the house and get into a black Nissan. He noted the registration number and watched as they drove past the gate and down towards the city center. His anger burned hotter all the time. He was sick of skulking around with that bunch of hippie losers in the flat, sick of being a target because of their soft "peace and love" shite. It was time to stir it up for them. Time to move on, too. But first, he needed financing. There were things to collect. He dragged himself up and headed for the pub at the end of the road. A few bevvies would take the pain away. Then he could go back to the squat, get what he needed, and show Burchill and the two bastards who'd just left that picking on him had been a mistake.

Detective Sergeant Ross tried to suppress the yawn he felt coming. It was only a partial success. The muscles of his jaw and neck tightened as he confined the strange satisfaction that yawns produce to his throat and the base of his skull. The effect was to drag a weird, flat grimace across the expression of interested concern he was trying to sustain. The man he was speaking to, an antiques dealer called Hilden, was too worried to notice.

"All these stories you read about Rembrandts in attics and Van Goghs being used as tea trays, you shouldn't set too much store by them," he was saying. "I've been at this for the best part of thirty years and I've never come across anything. It's alright for your Lovejoys, but the bread and butter's this." He waved a hand to indicate the piles of books and pieces of furniture which were crammed into his shop. Ross knew precious little about antiques and he certainly saw nothing among it all which impressed him.

"But it must add up to a fair bit when you put it all together," he said.

Hilden shook his head. "Eight, ten thousand pounds, maybe. It's not exactly Sotheby's, is it?" He picked up a heavy wine glass coated with dust. "Georgian. If I had six of them, they'd be worth nearly three hundred pounds. I've got three, one cracked, two with chips out of the brim. I'll be lucky to get fifty for the lot around here."

He put the glass back and pointed to a framed sketch propped against a marble-topped washstand. "See that? Joan Eardley. One of her Glasgow kids' drawings. They've gone right out of favor. The rest of her work, the oils, they fetch three, four, five thousand. For that? I might get maybe a hundred and fifty if I'm lucky."

Ross wondered whether the occasional application of a duster or vacuum cleaner might help trade to buck up, but what would he know? He made what he thought was an appropriate noise.

"That's why I don't understand it," Hilden went on. "Threatening to smash it all up. It's ludicrous."

"Could it be some sort of joke, d'you think?" asked Ross. "A try on?"

"Didn't sound like it. Hardly very funny anyway, is it?"

Ross took a few steps among the junk, taking care not to brush against any of the strange-looking teapots and vases that seemed to have been placed deliberately near the edge of the surfaces on which they were standing. He looked at the notes he'd been making in a small black book.

"So, from what you're saying, whoever it was doesn't know much about the antiques business. I mean, if they're asking for protection money and you've got nothing to protect, it all sounds a bit ... amateurish."

Hilden shrugged. "I don't know, sergeant. There's no way ... You may be right; they may know nothing about any of it. I wouldn't like to test them, though."

"You say 'they.' There was more than one of them, then?"

"Aye. Two. Then the phone call. He kept saying 'we'll do this' and 'we'll do that.'"

"And you didn't recognize them?"

Hilden shook his head. "I don't think so. I'm not a hundred percent certain ..."

"Local?"

Hilden nodded.

"Young? Old?"

The worried expression on Hilden's face intensified.

"Sorry. Just ... normal. Twenties, thirties, forties ... Don't know. I'm not very good at ..."

"Did they threaten you? You, personally, I mean. Not just to bust up your shop."

Hilden didn't answer right away. His eyes dropped to look at his hands, which he was kneading together in front of him. "Only if I contacted the police."

He was a small man, whose skin looked as dusty as the furnishings with which he spent his days. He was one of those bizarre people who comb their hair forward from a parting halfway up their neck to pretend they're not bald. Another sign of his nervousness was the way that his left hand kept going to the parting and wandering up and over the top of his head, teasing at the sparse hairs as if they were some precious filigree. Looking at him among the bric-a-brac, Ross felt a prickling of pity. There were people who seemed to move through the world apologetically, people whose trousers and sleeves were always too short, who wore clothes of ill-assorted tones, whose features had been assembled in such a way as to give them little chance of sexual or social success. Hilden was one of them. A natural victim.

"You were right to ring us, though," said Ross. "It must've taken a bit of courage, but in the end, it's the only way to handle things like this."

Hilden was shaking his head.

"You get fed up with it, that's all," he said, his voice hardly audible.

"Fed up with it?"

Hilden's left hand came away from his scalp and waved a gesture towards the shop window. "Aye. Everything. Out there. It's gone mad, hasn't it? Nothing but threats, violence, viciousness." He picked up a chipped Victorian jug from the table beside him. "No chance

9

of getting back to the good times. You knew where you were when this was made. Knew who was in charge."

"Aye," said Ross, "the folk wi' money."

Hilden managed a small smile. "Maybe. But even if you had none, you fitted. You had your place."

Ross looked at him. He seemed closed in on himself, trying to occupy the smallest possible space. Feeling grateful for a place at the bottom of the social heap seemed a strange source of comfort, but Ross could sense that, for Hilden, anonymity was appealing, a way of dodging the predators.

The antiques dealer looked at the jug, ran his finger round the rim, and put it back on the table. "What next, then?" he asked, sighing loudly.

Ross felt another yawn coming. He spoke quickly to deflect it. "Well, I suppose you've made sure the locks are secure so that they can't get in when you're not around." Another nod from Hilden. Ross turned to the shop's window. "And you'd see them coming a mile off if they came during the day."

"I don't even want to look."

His fear was obvious. Ross wanted to reassure him but knew that he was right to be frightened. If the caller was serious, Hilden might indeed be in trouble.

"Aye, of course." He looked around, searching for some comfort to offer. Nothing presented itself.

"Right, tell you what, I'll get one of our crime prevention boys to come round to give you some ideas. And I'll make sure the patrols keep an eye on the shop."

Hilden smiled weakly.

"We'd better get a proper statement from you, too, so if you could think about exactly what they said—when they came and on the phone—it might help us. You never know."

The more Ross said, the less impact he felt he was having. Hilden's vulnerability spread from him like thick ripples. The sergeant cut his losses.

"OK then. I'll be away now. If I were you, I'd lock up and get home for a wee dram. Wash the taste of all this out of your mouth."

Hilden smiled and pointed a finger at the ceiling. "I live upstairs,"

10

he said and his finger dropped back to caress the strands waving over his scalp.

"Great, Jim," Ross said to himself. "Why don't you just kick him in the balls and go?"

"Ah, sorry," he said aloud. "Still, not so far to go, eh?"

Now he was beginning to patronize the man. He moved to the door, his jacket swinging very close to a cheap china shepherdess, and stepped out into the short corridor that led to the street. Even that was piled with framed prints, more figurines, assorted glasses, and the general overflow from the shop. Ross stopped, turned, and tucked his notebook into his inside pocket.

"Don't worry, sir," he said, in a final attempt to reassure the man. "Now that we know about him, we'll do everything we can."

"Thank you," said Hilden and he held out his hand. Awkwardly, Ross shook it. He saw the slight creasing of Hilden's brows, which told him that his own grip had been too firm. He should have known. He went away up the street carrying the tactile memory of Hilden's hand with him. It was small, warm, and slightly damp, like a newly shaved mouse.

The bruises on Jez's thighs had deepened to black already and a purple bar ran across under his chin and up towards his left ear. His hand still stroked over it as he sat at the end of the sofa. Dawn was curled up beside him. There was no sign of Floyd. Will and Fran had got back at five. Liz came in at twenty past six. She was tall with dark, cropped hair, and a pair of blue-tinted glasses. Her jumper, skirt, and waistcoat were all in shades of dark green. There was no leader of the group, but she seemed always to dominate their discussions and hold them together. She looked at the solemn couple in the living room.

"OK, who died?" she asked.

Dawn gave her a quick résumé of the afternoon visit, her pain and fear obvious in both her words and the way she delivered them. Will and Fran came into the room just as she finished. Liz was saying, "We stay, of course."

Dawn nodded, slow and uncertain.

"What about when they come back?" asked Jez.

11

"What about it?" said Liz. "What did they break? Our stuff. The television, video, hi-fi. My bits of pottery. Fran's records. What did they take? My Walkman, Fran's radio."

She stopped, waiting for them to draw their conclusions. Jez spoke first.

"Aye. Didn't touch anything that came with the house. They could've pushed the front door in, but they knocked."

"Exactly. It's Burchill's version of bailiffs again, so they're not going to damage anything belonging to him. As long as we don't open the door, they won't try to get at us. They're not going to break it down because he'd have to pay to have it fixed."

"We've been expectin' it anyway, haven't we?" said Dawn in a small voice. "Ever since Burchill started up."

"Yes," said Liz. "It was bound to come."

David Burchill was a consultant engineer who'd made his killing by designing a downhole tool that told drillers both the angle of their well and the permeability of the rock strata through which it was being bored. This house, number twenty-eight Forbeshill Road, was one of several properties he'd bought in and around Cairnburgh with his first year's profits. It had been empty for almost two years prior to that because the previous resident had died intestate and the wrangling over its disposal was vicious and prolonged. In the end, the only solution acceptable to all concerned was to sell the property and its contents and divide the proceeds equally between them. Their haste to be done with it all was such that they accepted the first offer they received and Burchill got the house for a sum he'd intended to be a ludicrously low threshold from which to negotiate. He'd only lived in the property for a brief period and, for the past four months, he'd been on a contract in Nigeria. But now he was back in town and for some time he'd been trying to get his properties back on the market. Apparently he intended to relocate.

Will was at the window.

"So now this is a prison," he said.

"Don't be so melodramatic," said Liz. "We can still go out. Just have to be careful, that's all."

He came back and perched on the arm of Fran's chair. "Is it worth it?" he asked.

"Of course," said Liz.

"No, there's no 'of course' about it. We've got these bloody homicidal maniacs after us, and a property owner who's not scared to use them to get his investment back. You don't really think we can just sit in here and have wee chats until they go away and forget about it, do you?"

Liz smiled. "No, Will. But if we'd scuttled away the first time they tried to make us go, we'd never have managed to get anything done at all, would we? I'm just saying we chill out for a few days. See how he reacts. And look out for trouble."

Jez gave a humorless laugh. "Huh, you won't have to look out for it. It'll be here all on its own."

"Liz," said Dawn. "You didn't see those two guys. They were …"

For the second time that day, she was interrupted by a knock at the door. They all jumped, even though this time it was their knock, the signal they'd agreed on. But too loud.

"Floyd," said Jez.

"Maybe," said Liz. "Let's see."

They got up and went into the hall.

"I'll go and look out of my bedroom window," said Dawn.

As she ran up the stairs, Liz went to the front door and said, "Who's there?"

"Me, you stupid cow."

The voice was unmistakable. Nonetheless, they waited. Moments later, Dawn shouted down, "It's OK. It's Floyd."

Liz let him in and he looked at her and laughed before starting up the stairs, leaving in the air the sickly smells of cigarette smoke and beer. Liz locked the door and trailed back into the living room with the others. They said nothing, listening to the thuds and clinks he was making as he opened doors and walked back and forth. Soon, he made his way downstairs again and looked around the door. He had his coat on and was carrying a big black grip.

"Running away, Floyd?" said Liz.

"Havin' another bloody committee meeting, Liz?" he replied.

There was clearly little love lost between them. They glared their distaste at one another.

"You OK?" asked Dawn.

13

"Course I am. Why shouldn't I be?"

There was dried blood on the side of his face and a wide bruise running down his cheek from under his hair.

"Where've you been?"

"Out. What's it to you?"

"Floyd!" Liz's voice was hard and the contempt in her eyes was undisguised. "For Christ's sake, try not to be so bloody charming for a change. You were here. They hit you. We need to stay together to beat these guys."

The blaze in her eyes was matched by that in Floyd's as he turned on her. "Beat them, you silly cow? What're you gonna do then? Kick their balls in? Teach them a lesson? Gimme a break!" He looked around at the others. His words were slurred but his anger still bit through them. "You do this every time. Yak, yak. Talk about it and it'll sort itself out. You're in bloody fairyland." He turned his attention back to Liz. "These are pros. They're no just thugs he's brung in off the street. They know exactly what they're doin', how far they can go, how much they can hurt us. You don't stand a chance."

They were used to his hard negativity, but this time each of them knew that he had what could be called local knowledge of the subject. They'd all spent some time at society's margins, but only Floyd had tangled with its violence on a regular basis. Fran had flirted with prostitution when she'd first run away from Tam to Edinburgh to escape the groping, insistent hands of her father and uncle. Meeting Will in the Grassmarket and agreeing to try a summer in Aberdeen had saved her from the excesses that she could easily have been sucked into. Will himself had managed to avoid the fists and feet that were a part of life on the road. He'd slept rough since he was sixteen, an innate laziness making him choose the streets rather than classrooms. He had no great faith in people, but eight years of job-hunting around the central belt and the north of England had taught him that lots of them were to be pitied rather than feared.

Dawn's father was a headmaster. Despite having been trained in the liberal sixties, he'd retained a very old-fashioned attitude towards discipline. His only daughter had had to submit to such embarrassments as school uniforms and nine o'clock curfews on

Saturday nights until she left to become a student of languages at Aberdeen University. There, she was surprised to find that most of her fellow students were already, at the age of nineteen, planning career structures and pension schemes, seemingly unaware of the jobs void they'd be plunging into. When she came back from her compulsory year in France, the courses seemed even less relevant and she dropped out, working on and off in the Edinburgh Fringe office and trying to get involved with theater at the Tron in Glasgow and Edinburgh's Traverse. But she was one of far too many. She'd met Jez during a demonstration at Faslane and they'd come east together a couple of years ago.

Liz was some five years older than the others. Her father was an army colonel and had often told her how much he'd have liked a son. He'd applauded the revolution of the eighties until it began to extend to regimental cutbacks. The bewildering gap this created in his system of values soured even further a domestic atmosphere in which Liz had always been made to feel like an intruder. At the age of twenty-two, she suddenly became aware of herself as a comfortable, middle-class Scot on the verge of getting engaged to a financial consultant, and wondered how she'd wallowed for so long in such a loveless void. She'd moved away from her parents' detached, three-story house in Glenrothes and traveled around Scotland taking various temping jobs and searching for something she couldn't define. For a while, the hopelessness of what she was doing had threatened to drag her into the desolation that beckons most runaways but in the end, her intelligence and a sort of bloody-mindedness had helped her to survive and get involved in living again. For the others, the squat was a convenient escape; for her it was a statement of principle.

Even among a group of people for whom ambition was a totally foreign concept, Jez was noticeable for his irresolution. His life had been unrelievedly prosaic. The breakup of his parents' marriage was civilized, reasoned, and totally amicable. Jez had stayed with his mother. When a stepfather appeared, he turned out to be caring, considerate, and eager to make sure that Jez had all the space he needed. One day, bored with the posters on his wall and the music he was playing on his CD, Jez had simply taken all the money out

15

of his building society account and left for London. The money lasted just under seven weeks, but by then he'd been accepted into a little clutch of people, most of whom were rent boys. He stayed with them on the streets for a while, then boredom set in again, so he moved on. He went from London to Bristol, then, via Manchester and Newcastle, to Edinburgh. Cairnburgh just happened to be the place he and Dawn had been dropped off when they last hitched a ride. Dawn was part of the reason he'd stayed.

As usual, Floyd's sneers stirred a bitterness into the mood. They'd been threatened before, but this was the first time that it had translated into actual assault. Their intuition that he was right meant that, more than ever, they needed one another's reassurance. Lazy speculation about principles was one thing; broken bones and bleeding flesh called for different strengths.

Jez went to the kitchen to make coffee.

"You know, Floyd, it'd make a helluva difference if you were on our side for a change," said Dawn.

Floyd had simply been waiting for another chance to spit some more of his venom at them.

"You're as bad as she is," he said, flicking a thumb to indicate Liz. "'On our side.' It's not bloody hockey, or darts."

"I know it's bloody not." The shrillness of Dawn's shout surprised them all. "We all know that. I was here, remember. I saw them. But it makes it a bloody sight worse if you go on with your snide, stupid, negative bloody remarks."

She was working herself into one of her rages. Floyd was recovering from his surprise and starting to enjoy the effect he'd had.

"Christ. Little Miss Muffet's found …"

"Shut up, you … you fucking idiot," she yelled. "If you can't find anything to say that's positive, just keep your stupid mouth shut."

Floyd smiled and looked round at the others. There was no need for him to say anything. The edge of Dawn's voice had cut into all of them, embarrassing them, splitting through the thin veil that hid their fears and insecurities. Jez came back from the kitchen, went to her, and put his arm around her shoulders. She shrugged it away.

"You selfish bastard," said Will, looking straight at Floyd, who held his stare, the smile still on his lips. Will's anger was as obvious

16

as Dawn's had been, but he didn't shout. Instead, his tone was unnaturally flat, cold, and without inflexions.

"One day, if those guys don't beat the shit out of you, I will."

Floyd's smile disappeared, but only because he formed his lips into a pout to blow a kiss at Will.

"Anytime, Willie," he said and walked down the corridor and out of the front door, leaving it gaping wide.

It was guilt which eventually drove Detective Chief Inspector Carston to do some housework. The place wasn't particularly dirty. In the five days his wife Kath had been away at a photography course in Inverness, he'd done nothing but eat and sleep there. Kath liked to feed her feminist leanings by encouraging the idea that he was almost totally dependent upon her for anything connected with the home and so, on the very rare occasions when he was left to fend for himself, she always stuck instructional notes on cupboard doors, the freezer, the fridge, the central heating boiler, and at various other strategic locations. Carston admitted privately that there was some justification for her actions. He never noticed dirt, dust, chipped mugs, and all the other things that periodically exasperated her. His washing-up technique tended to remove grease and food stains only to replace them with some other smears that he was at a loss to explain. Being alone in the house should have meant freedom from such considerations but, paradoxically, it simply increased his awareness of his deficiencies and kept him looking for evidence of his own domestic inadequacy.

This time the guilt was triggered by "Coronation Street." He never watched it, had no idea who the characters were, and yet here he was, staring at the screen, with a week's worth of newspapers in the pile beside him, scraping the last folds of pasta from a bowl of lasagna. The word "sloth" eased into his mind. He immediately felt the need to accumulate some credit points to counteract his own suspicion that he really was just a slob. He switched off the TV, took the dirty bowl into the kitchen, and fetched the hoover from the bathroom cupboard. A yellow sticker fell off it. He picked it up. It read "If by any chance you use it, empty the bag each time."

"No," he said.

Twelve minutes later, he was sweating slightly and feeling martyred. He'd plugged the hoover into an extension cable in the back bedroom and gradually snaked his way through to the double room at the front. As he finished that and turned left into the bathroom, the flex pulled tight and he heard a crash. He switched off and went to the back bedroom to find books and two broken vases spread over the carpet. By pulling the cable to its limit, he'd dragged it against the leg of the small table on which they'd been arranged. It was a sign. He cleared up the broken pottery, replaced the books, put the hoover away, took it out again and emptied the bag, put it away a second time, and, with something like relief, set out for the station.

As usual, he walked. Not in deference to Superintendent Ridley's new directive concerning the savings that could be made by restricting the use of the cars in the garage pool, but because it was the only exercise he got. Cairnburgh was quiet. The final Christmas rush hadn't yet got going and the days were still being cropped of more and more of their light. One of the constantly repeated pleasures Carston experienced living in Cairnburgh was the wonderful light of northeast Scotland as it stretched itself farther and farther into spring and summer evenings. But there was a price to be paid; this slide from October onwards when, earlier each afternoon, night began its crawl across the sky, making everything and everyone turn inwards.

He avoided the shortest route because that would take him through the town center. He liked people and activity but not the fact that the row of shoe shops, banks, building societies, and stores that he'd have to pass were cloned from a thousand other high streets from Wick to Penzance. For a man in his forties, he was remarkably old-fashioned about civic anonymity. Even though the sign on every local corner shop was donated by some fag manufacturer or American drinks company, he still preferred the shops' intimations of specific customers with individual needs and a place in a unique community. It was almost eight-thirty when he pushed through the swing doors into the station.

"Evenin', sir," said the desk sergeant.

"Evening, Sandy. What's on?"

Sandy Dwyer flicked through some sheets of paper beside him. "Not much. Two cars nicked in Hutcheon Street. Kids breaking windows around Lombard Gardens. Pile-up on the Elgin Road ... Aye, and one for your lot to look at. Spurle's in there with it now."

"What time did Jim get back from that antiques place ... er ... Nostalgia?"

"He didn't, sir. Phoned in to say that he was going to see two more of them and that he'd go straight home after that. One of them was up near where he lives."

"Yep. Makes sense," said Carston.

He went through the door beside the desk, along the corridor and into the CID squad room. DC Spurle was bent over a typewriter keyboard, obviously looking for a letter.

"Top row left," said Carston.

Spurle looked up, his expression a question mark. Carston pointed at the typewriter.

"Top row left."

Spurle shook his head.

"That's where the E is," said Carston. "Statistically, it's the one we use most often. Chances were, that was the one you were looking for ... I thought I'd take a flyer."

Secretly, Spurle got very pissed off with Carston's smartarse comments and ideas. He thought they were alright if you were on some crap telly programme like "Have I Got News For You" but bloody stupid when you were trying to work.

Carston stopped beside Spurle's chair and looked at what he was typing. "Sergeant Dwyer said there was something came in for us tonight. Is that it?"

"Aye, sir." Spurle took three A4 sheets off his desk and sat back as he handed them over. Carston flicked through them.

"I don't believe this. Checkered skipper butterflies! What the bloody hell are they?"

"Butterflies, sir."

Carston looked at him. Spurle shrugged.

"So what've they got to do with us?"

"This guy's been trappin' them up around Loch Kirrian and sellin' them."

"In December?"

"No, sir. It was this summer."

"So what?"

"He's no got a license."

"And ...?"

"The wee buggers are rare. Protected species. Wildlife and Countryside Act 1981."

"I still don't see why we're involved."

"The uniform boys need some evidence."

"Bloody hell!"

"Aye, sir."

"And you got stuck with it."

Spurle shrugged again. Carston gave the sheets back to him, shook his head, and went through to his own office. In fact, the idea of having to deal with butterflies was fairly attractive when set against the rival claims of broken padlocks on warehouses or battered wives and kids. But it was still work and the load never got any lighter. Just the opposite, as pressure groups got more articulate and the media looked for new nerve ends to scrape across, the number and complexity of misdemeanors seemed to grow.

The small glow of holiness he felt at being in the office outside working hours cooled very quickly when he looked through the papers that were waiting for him. Prominent among them were the neat columns of Superintendent Ridley's proofs that good policing was fundamentally a question of economics. His schemes for manpower reduction and transport rationalization would apparently save £18,000 in less than six months. This would no doubt mean another surge up the management ladder for Ridley even if the people of Cairnburgh had to be left a little more exposed to achieve it. But that was the way things worked now. Leslie Donald, one of Carston's neighbors who was an anesthetist at the town's Laidlaw memorial hospital, had told him that the road to medical productivity lay in getting patients to die as quickly as possible. The figures this generated showed a rapid throughput and an admirable bed availability ratio. Life was becoming a science fiction story conceived by an accountant.

The phone rang. During the day, Carston avoided answering it

20

as much as possible. Tonight, though, it was a welcome distraction from the ravings of Ridley.

"Carston."

"Aye. Sorry to grab you right away, sir." It was Sandy Dwyer. "There's a guy on the line says he's been threatened. I thought you'd maybe want a word."

"Another antiques dealer?"

"No, sir."

"What's wrong with Spurle, then?"

"I don't think so, sir. It's yon squat. Down in Forbeshill Road."

"Ah. See what you mean. OK. Put him through." Carston understood Sandy's reluctance to let Spurle loose on squatters. The constable's attitude to policing seemed to have been learned from Waffen SS handbooks. On top of that, in interpersonal relationships, he had the sensitivity of a cheese grater. And anyway, Carston was genuinely interested. Twenty-eight Forbeshill Road had already figured in various West Grampian files. As part of the battle to evict the squatters on behalf of David Burchill, two members of the West Grampian drugs squad had wasted a week trying to prove that the place was being used to make Ecstasy and neighbors had been canvassed (unsuccessfully) to file complaints. Burchill himself was living in his main place up on Inverdee Crescent and pestering the police almost daily for help in repossessing his property. Carston had not yet had any direct dealings with him, but he was familiar with the amount of time his colleagues were having to waste being polite in the face of his persistence. Burchill delivered frequent, tedious sermons to them on citizens' rights, abuses of welfare, and the role of the force in the protection of property. And, of course, his complaints were given extra weight by the fact that he belonged to the same lodge as the Assistant Chief Constable.

"Hullo?" The caller didn't identify himself.

"Hullo. This is Detective Chief Inspector Carston. How can I help you?"

"Get off your arse for a start."

Carston was thrown. Sandy had said the caller was being threatened, but his tone was that of an aggressor.

"Sorry?"

"Look, I've already told the other guy. If you don't do something about it, somebody's going to get badly hurt."

"I'm afraid I haven't been given the whole picture yet. Would you mind ..."

"There were two guys there this afternoon. Worked the place over. Us too. Told us to fuck off or else, then showed us what they meant."

"You mean you were assaulted?"

The answering laugh was unpleasant.

"Yes, that's right, man. 'Assaulted.' Thumped with a fuckin' baseball bat and an ax, that's all. And they're comin' back. So what you gonna do?"

Despite the American twang, the accent was Scottish. It was obvious, too, that the man had been drinking.

"We'll need to get some more details from ..."

"Fuck that. Like what?"

"Well, your name to begin with."

"Look, pal, I'm tellin' you just the once. There's two guys. They're heavies. Done it before. They've been round to frighten us and I know fuckin' well they're gonna be back. An' if they find anybody in, they'll cream 'em. That's the details. An' if you don't do nothin' about it, ye're a bunch o' black bastards."

The words were spat down the line and it immediately went dead. Carston took a breath and dialed the front desk.

"Our friend's just rung off, Sandy. Any idea who he was?"

"No, sir. He just piled straight in."

"Did he give you any details at all?"

"No. Just that he'd been threatened and wanted to speak to CID."

"Didn't say where he was?"

"No."

"How're you fixed for bodies?"

"Tight. I've had to send two cars to that pile-up. I s'pose I could get Cunningham to come up from Canal Road to ..."

"No. It's OK. You've got enough on. I'll see to it. Just log the call and leave it with me."

He put the receiver back and drummed his fingers on the desk. It was hardly the sort of thing that needed the attention of a DCI, but if he sent Spurle on his own, he'd probably preempt the assault and save the "heavies" the trouble. On the other hand, the caller had sounded angry enough to be serious. He couldn't ignore it. He got up and went back through to the squad room. Once again, Spurle was peering at his keyboard. It was amazing that he ever completed any of his reports.

"OK, Spurle. Get your coat. You're coming with me."

Spurle hesitated only briefly then, glad to be released, got up and took his coat from the back of the door.

"Where to, sir?"

"Forbeshill Road."

Spurle paused and looked at him. "Number twenty-eight?" Carston nodded.

"About time we sorted out those bastards," said Spurle, his face setting into a grin of satisfaction.

Around ten o'clock, the center of Cairnburgh was well into its usual Friday and Saturday night metamorphosis. The shoppers, family groups, schoolkids, and office workers who'd occupied it during the day had vanished and were being replaced by individuals and groups of what seemed like a different species. The shops had become dark facades, breached at intervals by glowing, pulsing holes through which streamed an arterial surge of noise and night people. Along the pavements wandered predatory groups of men drinking from cans, eating chips, swearing, and trying to sound like characters from American movies. In the town's only nightclub, Macy's, etched by blue strobe lighting and energized by a beat which shook the air around them, were women of astonishing elegance. They wove, cool and controlling, inside the music, their glamor belonging to the night, generating an exoticism never seen in the streets in day-time.

Fran was an exception. She wore little makeup and her loose cotton dress floated incongruously alongside the shining sheaths of the other dancers. But she knew how to move and her slow hips and dipping shoulders drew as many greedy glances as the weaving of the glittering panthers surrounding her. She was dancing with Will and oblivious to everything but the music. They weren't

23

regulars, but on the rare occasions when they had money to spare, this was the way Fran liked to spend it. Will didn't mind. He was there as a sort of minder, although his first instinct was always to avoid trouble. He was easy in Fran's company and they'd never yet had any problems. The clubbing was self-indulgent, but it drew them into the company of strangers and nobody asked them any questions. They'd lived in the squat with Dawn, Jez, Liz, and, more recently, Floyd, for the past seven months. For all the heady coherence of the club's dancers and watchers, if they'd known the truth about Fran and Will, they'd have instantly stigmatized them as aliens, social leeches, or just scum. The oil-rich younger generation of northeast Scotland was partying towards the millennium, but they were dragging some deeply ingrained attitudes with them.

Up in the High Street, self-expression was equally changeless. A girl in a short yellow dress and a coat far too thin for the early December night, waited patiently at the curb while her boyfriend finished being sick in the gutter; small queues formed and re-formed at the taxi ranks; chip papers blew, and two friends laughed and wrestled in the doorway of the Odeon cinema. They shouted insults at one another in accents that would have been unintelligible to an outsider, except when they resorted as they did, fairly frequently, to the word "motherfucker." This was a relatively recent import and had not yet been sufficiently distorted to disappear into the general swirl of the local dialect.

And everywhere, unfocused, brooding, was a sense of threat.

Isobel Beattie felt it very strongly. She was in her early forties and didn't belong among these aimless wanderers. She lived above her antiques shop in Victoria Street and was walking home from a meeting she'd had with a BP engineering manager who was looking for some Hans Sloane plates for a Christmas present for his wife. Beattie's expertise lay in ceramics, especially the porcelain from Chelsea and Bow. This new commission was far from easy but, apart from the percentage she'd make, the challenge of tracking down the peculiarly English plates with their precise botanical illustrations created in her a feeling that was somehow elemental, like the thrill of the chase or the exercise of substantial power. She hurried along, her gaze resolutely fixed on the pavement, unwilling to risk eye contact with anyone and fearful of the potential hazards she was having to negotiate. In auction rooms and at antique fairs, she was icily controlled, but this was feral. She crossed the street and, when she heard the chants of "Rangers! Rangers!" was even more glad to be moving away from the danger area. Bands of young males, alcohol, and territorial dominance were already ingredients far too potent for her to deal with; if football fever was being stirred in too, she wanted to be far away before it boiled over.

The two people at the head of the queue waiting to get into Macy's were asleep. They'd been drinking since six o'clock. Next in line was a girl who'd been told that sophistication meant sucking at a lemon before sipping her Tequila Sunrise. She'd had eight so far and was puking over the railings, a quarter of a lemon still clutched in her left hand. Neil and Frank, the regular doormen, were standing quietly, secure in the knowledge that they were sober and that their reflexes would keep them ahead of most of the people crowding on the pavement and steps outside. They also knew that Mark was halfway down the stairs and Big Tam was at the bottom. They were a team. Each watched out for the others and the first sign of a problem for any of them would bring them all together to stamp on it, sometimes literally, before it developed.

Neil was a deterrent in his own right. He was just under six feet tall and had enormous shoulders and a chest that filled the doorway. But the real menace in his appearance came from the scar which ran from his left eyebrow down across his nose to the right-hand side of his lip and on into his chin and neck. It was the legacy of another night's work and the inspired creativity of a drunk with a grudge. The drunk had been ejected by Neil and, as they always do, had threatened to come back and deal with him. This one, though, had kept his promise. He'd brought with him two Stanley knife blades, which he'd held together, separated only by a 10p coin. The two parallel wounds this inflicted made it impossible for the surgeon to sew the edges together properly. Effectively, the drunk had taken a couple of millimeters of face away and left Neil with a permanent diagonal of puckered flesh to remind him of the down side of the job.

Like Beattie, he and Frank heard the trouble arriving. At this time of night, football chants were like a primed detonator. It wasn't a Saturday. There'd been no match. The trumpeting of tribal affiliation was a signal that the night's drinking was shaping into a direct challenge. There were twelve of them. They wore no scarves or other emblems that indicated any connection with football and they spread themselves across the pavement, looking for confrontation. As they got nearer, some of the people waiting on the steps of Macy's crossed the street. Neil shouted a warning to Mark and stepped back into the doorway with Frank. The group arrived at the bottom of the steps and began to push their way through. They had no interest in the club or in dancing, but the need to dominate was strong. And once the men in the queue were provoked, the fact that there were women watching meant that their strutting machismo was under threat, so they had to respond. One minute there were a couple of isolated face-offs between individual group members, the next a generalized aggression had been unleashed. Ring-pulls, specially saved for such an occasion, were slashed across cheeks, fists with keys protruding through the fingers were jabbed at eyes and lips, boots cracked against shins and up into thighs and groins. Some couples were locked together and fell to roll among the thrashing feet. Women, at first held by the excitement of the initial exchanges, were soon running from their growing ferocity. Some of the men had enough sense to see that their pride could turn out to be costly and they, too, spun out of the pack and away down the street. The rest were locked into the flailing, snarling mess that was now boiling around the foot of the steps.

While the fighting stayed on the pavement, Neil and Frank stayed put. Out there, it was a problem for the police. They'd only have to react if it spilled in through the doorway. Neil called again to Mark, who came to the top of the stairs and stood just behind his two mates. But when the fight surged up towards them as some of those who'd been queuing looked for refuge inside the club, they were quickly forced back down the stairs by the sheer numbers that battered against them. One man lashed at Neil's head with a bottle. Neil caught his arm, brought it down hard, and heard the wrist crack as it dislocated. He spun the man around, his arm now

26

forced up behind his back, and used him to push against those who were still shoving forward down the stairs. Frank had another of them in a double armlock and swung him against the rest like a flail. With Mark adding his weight to the barrier they'd made across the stairs and Big Tam arriving as a final prop, they managed to stop the rush before it reached the doorway into the club.

The screaming and banging cut through the music. The DJ cranked the volume up and a barman called the police. Some of the men inside went to the door and saw the crush of bodies locked in the narrow stairway. As others crowded behind them, they were pushed out to join the four doormen, and their impetus helped to force the intruders back out onto the street. Will and Fran had stopped dancing and gone to sit at the side of the club farthest away from the door. They said nothing. This wasn't the first time they'd experienced violence here, and they'd been victims in plenty of places too often already.

A few hundred yards away, in Victoria Street, Beattie had gratefully bolted her door behind her, taken off her coat, and gone up the stairs to her flat. Inside, she breathed deeply and noticed that her hands were shaking. She sat down and clasped them together. Her eyes fell on the tea set that was arranged on the table beside her. Gradually, her breathing started to slow and she felt relaxation creeping across her shoulders and down her back. She turned on the desk lamp and picked up a cup. She looked hard at a triangle on the bottom of it, then turned it to follow the molded decorations which flowed around its bottom rim and up its handle. The basic color was a translucent milky white with a soft glaze. At three points, the surface was raised into the shape of a flower. She held it up against the light and smiled at the pinholes and crescents she could see as she turned the cup carefully against the glare. Her passion for her collection of Chelsea ware was as fierce as that of the nearby fighters for their football club. The sound of sirens outside jabbed a reminder of her previous alarm into her mind, but the soft pink glaze of one of the flowers drew her eyes back again and everything but the cup disappeared.

By the time the pressure from those down in the club had forced the fighters back onto the pavement, the man whose wrist Neil had dislocated had passed out from the pain caused by the constant leverage on his arm. Others had had their anger diffused by the panic they began to feel when they were caught in the stairway and the breath was being crushed out of them. When the police cars arrived, most of the fighting had stopped and only those stupid enough to try to prolong it were taken into custody. Neil, Frank, Mark, and Big Tam were unhurt. They stood together at the top of the steps, still feeling the buzz of the job they'd done, ready for more action. One of the football fans, a fat ginger-haired guy in a Tennents' Lager tee-shirt, looked up at them, pointed a finger, and said, "Ah'll be back, ya bastards!" As the police grabbed him and dragged him towards one of their cars, Neil raised a cupped hand and shook it back and forth at him in the familiar loose-wristed "wanker" sign.

Downstairs, Fran was trying to get back into the oblivion of dancing. It was hard. She felt simultaneously angry and sad. It shouldn't be like this. Why were there always people ready to destroy? Despite the heat in the club, the air felt chill and sour. She felt a depression creeping into her. It seemed that nowadays, even the simplest of pleasures always got spoiled.

Two

David Burchill drummed the fingers of his right hand against his jeans. The evening was beginning to wear on and he hated wasting time that he should be devoting to activities that used more hormones than sitting at the wheel of his Mercedes waiting for pillocks to answer the phone. Impatiently, he smoothed nonexistent creases out of his shirt and flicked at specks on his jacket. The jeans were by Gianni Versace, the shirt by Nicole Farhi (a hundred and sixty quid's worth), and the jacket was a Paul Smith special. He'd read the magazines, knew the value of labels. In fact, he was something of a celebrity. There were plenty of others around the area who'd made money from oil and, before that, from farming or fishing. Apparently, Porsches were thicker on the ground around Aberdeen than anywhere else in the UK. But most of those who had earned fortunes preferred to perpetuate the myth of northeastern miserliness by keeping a low profile. Not Burchill. He was flash. He'd fathered three illegitimate children, put two small but potentially dangerous competitors in the engineering field out of business, and, despite having only recently got back in town and being intent on leaving as soon as possible, was now captain-elect of the Royal Cairnburgh Golf Club.

There was still no answer. He jabbed fiercely at his mobile phone to call up another number. He was lighting a cigarette when he got a reply.

"Benny Mitchell."

"Where the fuck have you been?"

"Mr. Burchill?"

"I've been trying to get that dozy sod Simpson. Where is he?"

"I dunno."

"Well?"

"Well what?"

Burchill took the phone away from his ear and lifted his eyes up in exasperation. He took a deep drag on his cigarette and forced himself to control his response.

"Well, did you go? Have you done it?"

"Course we have. I don't think you'll be getting any more trouble from there. Barry was ..."

"Never mind that. I don't want details. I'm on a mobile, you berk. You were supposed to phone me. I needed to know, didn't I?"

"Aye, I know. Barry was supposed to be doin' that. Last I heard, he said he was givin' you a bell."

"Well he didn't."

"Anyway, it's OK. Wrapped up."

"It better be."

"Trust me, Mr. Burchill."

"Fuck off."

Burchill hit the "end" button and slipped the phone inside his jacket. The call had told him what he needed to know, but it hadn't reassured him. One of the problems of living in a backwater was that there were no professionals. Mitchell and Simpson had done other jobs for him, but there'd always been residuals, untidy things that needed further attention. When he'd worked in Houston, he'd had seven different telephone numbers he could call to get troubles ironed out. He'd only ever used one, but the job had been done immediately and there'd never been any comebacks.

He'd made his money by means which were entirely legitimate, but he found that keeping and increasing it sometimes meant using strategies which bypassed legal strictures. Tax, for example, was a continuing nightmare and forced him more and more frequently into dealing in actual cash. The problem was that this sometimes came in very large chunks. In the USA, he'd learned the basic principles of money laundering, but now the Criminal Justice Act was making even that more difficult. One of its clauses obliged banks and building societies in England and Wales to report any suspicious movements of large sums of money. Since it had come into force, Burchill had been compelled to find new outlets, and his attentions had turned to art, antiques, and the gem trade. But, as with everything else in this town, dealers' minds were small and he was constantly struggling to drag others into the fast lane of his operations. Every day in Cairnburgh, he found himself picking his frustrated way around more and more creeping irritations.

He threw his cigarette out of the window and banged the gear lever forward.

"If you use sheep-shaggers, all you get is fucked up sheep," he said through gritted teeth as he released the handbrake. The car squealed its way up the street, its howling tires warning his neighbors that Mr. Burchill was going out for the evening and would probably not be back until the late early hours. But when he did come home, they'd be sure to hear him.

Carston had been impressed with the precautions the squatters had taken. Mistrustful of yet another strange knock late at night, they'd insisted on having his identification passed through the letters slot in the door and studied it long and hard before they'd let him in. The release sequence of bolts and deadlocks which followed indicated a level of security that he wished more of his fellow citizens would emulate. For their part, Liz, Dawn, and Jez were surprised to hear that the afternoon's incident had been reported and suspected that, rather than being intent on gathering information, Carston and especially Spurle were there as part of the overall plan to evict them.

Carston looked around the living room. It was clean except for the pieces of broken equipment, which they'd tidied into a heap under the window.

"Nice place you've got," he said with a smile.

Nobody answered.

"I mean it," he insisted. "You're looking after it. Good to see."

"You from the hygiene department, then?" asked Liz.

Carston grinned, then pointed at the heap. "They do that?"

"Why?" said Liz.

"Destruction of property. It's a crime. They can be charged. It's evidence, if you like."

"But we're not bringing charges. Nobody's made a complaint."

"Somebody did, darlin'," said Spurle. "That's why we're here."

Liz ignored him. "Look, Inspector, none of us called you. I don't know who did, but we can manage. There's been no damage to the property, so Mr. Burchill can relax. That stuff's all ours."

Carston strolled over and, using his handkerchief, picked up some of the pieces. On the dusty shattered side of one of the loudspeakers, he saw the smudged imprint of three letters. They could have been the beginning of a word except that the only upper case letter was the third in the sequence. They were obviously inverted, a mirror image. He bent and looked at the other speaker. It was intact and there were no markings on it. He held the broken one towards the group.

"How did this get broken?" he asked.

Jez looked at Liz then said, "One of them pulled it off the wall."

"Ah."

"He smashed it with a baseball bat," Dawn added.

"Thank you," said Carston. "D'you mind if I take this with me?"

"Help yourself," said Liz.

Carston wrapped the hankie round the piece of wood and handed it to Spurle, who tucked it into an inside pocket of his overcoat.

"What else is missing?"

He hardly had time to finish the question when Liz's voice cut sharply across him.

"Look, what's all this about? We're not complaining, we don't want any help. So why stick around? We'll handle this."

Spurle stepped across and poked his face straight into hers.

"We don't give a fart about any of that, darlin'. It's no your place to tell us what ye want or no ..."

Carston placed a hand on his arm. Hardly able to disguise his disgust. Spurle backed off.

"Whoever it was who called me seemed to think that you could be in real danger. If it wasn't one of you, it was certainly somebody who knew that you'd had a visit. All I'm concerned with is to stop any real trouble happening."

"Aye, the polis is well known fer their kindness to squatters," said Liz, her accent abruptly dropping several grades down the social scale.

32

"Shut it," said Spurle.

Carston felt his own anger rising. For all that he tried to keep his mind open among a bunch of colleagues who'd find the Monday Club too liberal, he'd never managed to accept the principle of squatting. Commandeering a house or flat, taking advantage of equipment and facilities which someone else had paid for, seemed like just another form of robbery. He needed Ross with him, not Spurle. Spurle's barely controlled aggression seemed too appropriate at the moment, very easy to justify. Ross stuck to the facts and rarely wandered off into the speculative tangents that too often drew Carston's attention. He looked squarely at Liz.

"Your attitude to the police is of no consequence," he said slowly, irritating himself by sounding so pompous. "What does concern me is that violence has been threatened. Part of my job is to stop that sort of thing happening." He paused, then added, despite himself, "Whether the people who've been threatened deserve it or not."

Liz's smile both showed up his mistake and reinforced his reason for making it. He turned away to bring himself back under control. The ringing of a telephone helped to cover his confusion. It also increased his irritation. How come the squatters had a phone? Why was it connected? Who paid the bills? And who the hell would want to ring them anyway? It implied a degree of social normality that didn't fit with any of his preconceptions about squatting. Liz's voice broke into his thoughts.

"Can I answer that or are we all under arrest?"

Carston looked back at her and his anger grew as he saw the smile still playing on her lips. He flicked a hand at her and she went out into the hall. His growing temper turned back onto himself; it was a long time since he'd acted in such an unprofessional way. Maybe it was some sort of contagion from Spurle. It was time to take control again.

"Right," he said, measuring his tone very carefully, "what we'll do now is get a full description of what happened and of the people responsible. We'll take statements from those who were here and we'll leave on one side any thoughts about the attitude of policemen to squatters or the attitude of squatters to everybody else. Is that OK?"

There was no answer.

"Right, Constable," he went on. "Statements from all of them. One at a time. In the kitchen."

It was already past eleven o'clock. The thought of an hour with these wasters did nothing to lighten Spurle's mood. He went to the door, turned, and spat "First" at them before going through to the kitchen. Dawn and Jez looked at one another. Jez sighed.

"I'll go," he said. "The kettle's boiled. I'll make some tea while I'm there."

His words gave Carston a little lift of satisfaction. Being alone in a room with Spurle for a while would soon wipe all thoughts of normal, domestic pursuits from the kid's mind.

The following morning, the two cleaners whose job it was to collect and stow away the debris of each evening at Macy's were faced with an even less enviable task than usual. Bottles and broken glasses were always hazards and tended to spread from behind the bar across the dance floor. The walls of the lavatories were always coated with vomit, and sticky residues of spilled alcohol provided an uninterrupted medium for bacterial culture from the bar up the stairs and even down the steps onto the High Street. But today there was the added ingredient of blood, most of it dried but some of it still sticky where it had pooled. Last night's fight had been brief enough but still sufficiently savage to splash it over the railings and steps and down into the recess below them, where the bags of rubbish were stored for collection on Tuesdays and Fridays. Jessie, whose job it was to see to the steps, knew all about HIV and the dangers of blood which might have come from what she called druggies. She was wearing thick rubber gloves and scrubbing very carefully at the stains. Rosie, the other cleaner, was at the door wiping the handle and the brass fittings around the knob and the letterbox. She was suddenly aware of a stillness at the bottom of the steps. She looked down at Jessie. She was standing on the pavement, motionless, staring at something.

"What's up, Jess?"

Jessie gave a little shake of her head and pointed at the recess. Rosie was frightened. Something was up. She went down to stand

34

beside Jessie and followed her gaze. A man was lying among the cardboard boxes. They could only see his legs and the bottom half of a black grip.

"Bloody disgustin', i'n't it?" said Jessie. "They'll sleep anywhere. Drunken buggers."

"I don't know," said Rosie, the small crackle of fear still chilling the back of her neck. "He seems a bit … well …"

"Ah'll soon sort him out," said Jessie, her disgust at the blood she'd been cleaning finding a focus. She leaned forward and pulled back the pieces of cardboard which were covering him. "Come on, you drunken pig," she shouted. "Some of us have got …"

Her words choked in her throat and behind her Rosie began to shake and whimper. From the shoulders upwards, the man was all blood. His hair was set in a dark brown tangled mat of it. Sticking out of the side of his mangled face was the bottom half of a broken beer glass.

The telephone hauled Ross from fathoms down in sleep. For almost a month now, Mhairi, his baby daughter, had started crying at about ten-thirty every night and stubbornly refused to give up until around two in the morning. The doctor had shown no sympathy when, during one of his visits, the bleary-eyed father had asked for help.

"Three-month colic," he'd said. "Come the New Year she'll be fine. You'll have forgotten all about it."

The only thing that seemed to soothe the baby was being rocked against his shoulder to the rhythm of a tune that he'd recently found out was from a Mozart opera. He knew nothing about opera, wasn't a fan, but that particular theme and rhythm seemed to do the trick. The problem was that the spell wore off as soon as he stopped humming and tried to put her back in her cot. So he and his wife, Jean, took it in turns to walk several miles around the spare bedroom each night with Mhairi and Wolfgang. Last night, it had been his turn and, when the ringing woke him, it took several moments before he could contribute coherently to the conversation.

"Mhairi again?" asked Carston, when Ross had eventually begun to make sense.

35

"Uh-huh. What time is it?"

"Just after eight. Sorry. I wouldn't've troubled you on a Saturday, but they've found a young guy carved up in the High Street."

That was enough to blow away the last fogs from Ross's mind.

"On my way," he said. "Where is it?"

"Macy's. But don't bother to come here. There's nobody in the club and the team have nearly finished. I'll see you at the station. Get on to the fiscal's office, will you? See what the chances are of ordering an autopsy."

"Right."

Jean was already in the kitchen with their elder daughter Kirsty. He washed, shaved, and hurried down to them.

"Sorry you were woken up," said Jean. "I tried to get to the phone but I had my hands full."

"It's OK, love. It was the boss. I've got to go in."

She put her arms round his neck and hugged him close. "Shame," she said.

The word was for him, not her. She knew that he did everything he could to protect their home life against the job's encroachments. She'd prefer him to be in some other line but had known from their earliest days that she was stuck with a career policeman. Before too long he'd be promoted and she hoped that perhaps he'd shift into a branch that kept relatively normal hours. She never complained. As soon as possible, she wanted to get back to her own career in teaching, and she knew that Jim would be just as understanding when that happened. He kissed her full on the mouth, a lover's kiss, not the dry marital peck that so often replaced it.

"Stop it, Daddy," said Kirsty.

"You're just jealous," he said, picking her up and nuzzling into her fine, sweet-smelling hair.

He put her back in her chair, grabbed a piece of bread, scraped marmalade onto it, and took it with him as he went out to the car. He was still humming the Mozart.

Outside Macy's, the blue and white police tapes marking off the area were clattering in a cold breeze. Photographs and video had been taken, two officers were working over every inch of the steps and the pavement around and under them, and two others waited for Brian McIntosh, the police surgeon, to finish his examination. He was kneeling among the cardboard boxes, looking closely at the lacerated neck and face of the dead man. Despite the impatient mutterings of the uniformed constable who'd been posted to keep the curious passersby moving on, a clutch kept forming, dispersing, and re-forming on the pavement. There was nothing for them to see because the bit that interested them, the gruesome bit, was shielded by screens, but the fascination of blood and the fact that life was suddenly made more real because it looked like a scene from the television drew them irresistibly.

Carston stood at the bottom of the steps and looked round the screen as McIntosh probed. He'd already seen his fair share of corpses in similar conditions. Usually, it was hypothermia which got them, sometimes the result of lying uncovered in an oblivion bought by alcohol. Some had fallen and knocked themselves senseless before the cold had taken over. Others had drowned in their own vomit. With all of them, the variations in the manner of their dying had been the only divergence from a depressingly inevitable trajectory. The dead man was young and, from the look of his clothes, not exactly affluent. The jeans, trainers, checkered shirt, and dark blue jumper were all cheap. The blouson jacket, on the other hand, was a Hugo Boss and so had probably come via Oxfam. From where Carston stood, it looked as if most of the blood had come from his head. From the chest down, he looked like just another cardboard-kipping dropout, one of the growing army of folk left behind in the gallop towards TESSAs, PEPs, and the National Lottery.

McIntosh stood up, stretched, and took a last look over the body. The two constables started unrolling their body bag. McIntosh stepped carefully out to where Carston was waiting.

"Just the sort of thing you like, Jack," he said.

"Meaning?"

"Complications."

"Like what?"

"Well, hypostasis is fully established ..."

"Brian, you're doing it again."

"What?" said McIntosh, all innocence.

"Talking like a text book. I think I know what hypostasis is, but I'm very simple-minded and I'd prefer you treat me accordingly."

It was always the same. McIntosh wasn't one of those playful forensic medics who performed eviscerations with one hand while eating a bacon sandwich with the other, but he always tended to be indiscriminate in his use of the terminology of his trade. Carston's protests were fairly frequent.

McIntosh raised an eyebrow and scratched at his beard. "Ah, right. He's certainly been dead for more than six hours. It's been a cold night, so the post mortem temperature drop must have been speeded up a lot. Usually, it's about one degree centigrade an hour. He's not exactly a fat individual, either."

"So you can't get very close?"

"Closer than usual. He hasn't been dead all that long. My guess would be between nine o'clock yesterday evening and midnight."

"Doesn't sound very complicated."

McIntosh scratched some more and smiled.

"Ah, no. That's something else. The distribution of lividity around the usual pressure points, his buttocks, shoulder blades, places like that. I haven't had a chance to have a proper look, but I'm pretty sure he was lying face down somewhere else for a while before he was dumped here. There's a dual distribution, you see."

"No," said Carston.

McIntosh stopped scratching and looked at him.

"I don't see," Carston explained.

"Gravity," said McIntosh. "Blood settling when it stops flowing. Darkens up the skin. If there's a pressure point, though, there's not much of it, so it stays white. In his case, the most severe lividity's on his chest and the front of his shoulders. But there's more on the back, too, from lying in there."

Carston remembered now that he'd had the condition explained to him before. More than once, too. It was his resistance to the terminology that was getting in the way again.

"Interesting," he said.

McIntosh chuckled.

"Thought you'd like it. It gets better, though."

38

He paused, enjoying the impatience he saw on Carston's face as he waited for him to go on.

"Can we get on, sir?" asked one of the men with the bag.

"Hang on," said Carston before turning back to McIntosh to ask, "Well?"

"The glass sticking out of his face."

"What about it?"

"It's just decoration."

Carston looked again at the body.

"It's chewed up his face a bit. But he was long dead before that was done."

"You sure? Seems a weird thing to do."

"You and I know there are some weird folk about, Jack. That glass has cut up the flesh, but there's not much bleeding. Looks to me as if he was hit on the side of the head. That's what killed him. He's all yours now, though. I've been on to Grampian. You're lucky, things are a bit slack for them at the moment. They'll start him this morning. I'll get up there right away."

"Thanks, Brian. Jim's phoning the fiscal."

In cases of suspicious death, autopsies were ordered by the procurator fiscal on advice from the police. There had to be two doctors present and McIntosh was usually one of them when the West Grampian force was involved. Carston envied the facilities available to his colleagues in Aberdeen. As well as their very sophisticated mortuary and its facilities, they had extensive forensic labs for biological and chemical analysis. They'd recently added a new identification bureau to it all, too. They were getting prints off polythene bags, newspapers, plastics, and using all sorts of new techniques to build a comprehensive database. Smaller forces from all over Scotland were starting to consult them with inquiries on fingerprints, photography, and document analysis. Sometimes it meant delays for his own West Grampian investigations because they had no labs of their own and had to rely on Aberdeen for both autopsies and forensic analysis, but usually his own contacts and, more especially, those of Brian McIntosh, helped him to jump the queue.

"What I'd really appreciate is a quick identification," he said as McIntosh pulled his coat tighter and tucked his scarf into it.

"Donnelly," said McIntosh.

"What?"

"That's his name. Donnelly. Driving license was in his wallet. It's been bagged up. It's on its way to your place."

Carston shook his head and gave a deep, deliberate sigh. "Nobody tells me anything," he said.

McIntosh laughed and walked to his car.

"Take care, Jack."

"You too, Brian."

Carston turned back to the recess where the constables were getting impatient in the cold wind. Before he'd left the station, he'd already got Sandy Dwyer to get in touch with the night shift to get notes from the patrols which had been called to Macy's. He'd also detailed two DCs to interview the people who'd been arrested after the fight. Not that he expected much to come out of that. A quick visit to the cells had revealed a collection of figures like those in medieval paintings of purgatory. This new information confirmed what he already suspected—that the death had nothing at all to do with the fight. Nonetheless, the concomitance of the two manifestations of violence was curious. Coincidences happened all the time, of course, but when they formed part of one of his investigations, he didn't trust them.

He stepped across to the body and squatted beside it. The head was angled to the right and the glass was sticking out of it almost vertically. He could see what McIntosh meant about it. The rips it had created in the face and jaw were deep but looked like gouges in some sort of pasty clay rather than tears in once living flesh. He leaned over farther. The right side of the face was shadowed, but he could see that it was dark, except for a pale flash across the top of the cheek and another large patch on the forehead. Those were presumably the pressure points McIntosh had been talking about. Carston replayed the scene for himself. The body had been lying somewhere for a while after death. Then it was brought here, taken out of a car, and dumped among the boxes. The glass was grabbed and twisted into the face, forcing the head to turn. Some of the cardboard was then scattered over the man's chest and head and the culprit or culprits had left him there and driven off. How long would it have taken? Two minutes? It was an extraordinarily risky thing to do. There were always people about in the High Street. Macy's didn't close until three and then the staff had to clear up before leaving. That left a one-and-a-half- or two-hour window before the various early shifts started walking about, getting their buses, and generally filling the street with potential witnesses. But why move the body at all? Why choose such a public spot? And why the seemingly gratuitous mutilation?

As he stood up and motioned for the two constables to carry on, he realized that he was whistling to himself and smiled as he acknowledged McIntosh's perceptiveness. He got into his car and set off for the station. The doctor was right; Carston did enjoy complications. No doubt Superintendent Ridley could put all this into a calculator and establish the relevant probability ratio. Carston preferred to amble along the twisting pathways of human motive and intent. He never lost sight of his destination and didn't hang about, but there was nothing wrong with enjoying the scenery on the way.

Like Ross, Burchill was also dragged rudely into his morning by a phone. It was the mobile, which he'd forgotten to switch off when he'd come in. He, too, had spent an active night, part of it in a hotel room with two girls in their late teens. Around two o'clock, one of them had begun to cry too loudly from the pain his appetites were causing her and the other started getting anxious, so he'd given them two hundred pounds each and sent them home in a taxi. He'd arrived home between four and five and, for a change, had woken none of his neighbors. Dr. King in number twenty-one had just got back from a call-out and was parking his own car as Burchill turned into the crescent. The doctor was pleasantly surprised to note that the Mercedes purred slowly if somewhat crookedly into its carport and that its driver managed to shut the door without slamming it.

Burchill tried to ignore the phone but, even on its low setting, the warbling probed into him. At last, swearing violently, he got up, took the phone from his pocket, hit a button and shouted, "Who is it?"

"Barry Simpson, boss."

"What? What the hell d'*you* want? It's nine o'clock. You'd better have a bloody good reason for waking me up."

"Benny said ye phoned last night."

Burchill's mouth tasted foul. He belched. It brought bile to the back of his throat.

"Listen, you dozy bastard. If I phoned him last night, that means there's no need for you to phone me this morning, is there?"

"Aye, there is, boss. I've just been at that guy Hilden's ..."

Anger had woken Burchill enough for him to cut sharply across Simpson's words.

"I don't want to know. Nothing to do with me."

"But ..."

"Shut it. If you've got problems, you sort them out with your pal. Don't bring 'em to me. Specially not this time of day, right?"

"Boss ..."

"Right?"

"Right."

There was a pause as Mitchell waited and Burchill tried to think what his reason for phoning might be. Nothing came to him. He couldn't imagine what sort of problems might have occurred. His instructions about Hilden and the house in Forbeshill Road had been straightforward and he'd given them the money upfront. He certainly didn't want any of their crap being flung back in his direction. If there was anything funny happening, he'd hear about it soon enough. He had plenty of other things to think about.

"Right. No more calls, OK?" he said. "Whatever you've got on your mind, keep it to yourself. I'll be in touch next week sometime. And I don't want to hear from you or your mate before then. Now then, tell me you understand me."

"Aye, sure. I understand ye."

"So put your bloody phone away and let me get some sleep." He disconnected the call, switched off the mobile, and threw it onto the bed, then went down to the kitchen and poured a glass of orange juice. The cold made him shudder and the sharpness of the citric acid joined the bile to scour down inside his throat. He couldn't afford to prolong the association with these two amateurs. If they'd done their job properly, as they claimed, there should be no more need for them. But the phone call suggested that somehow they'd screwed up. The only thing to do was wait a day or two, see what happened, then, if necessary, make fresh plans. There was an outfit in Edinburgh he could call on. Maybe that's what he should have done from the start. They weren't known around the town. They could have come up, done the business, and disappeared, no questions asked. The antiques market down there was livelier too. As he yawned and stretched, he wondered what the hell had made him rely on two guys who wouldn't make it as extras in a Michael Winner movie. The need to tie up the remainder of his concerns in Cairnburgh was making him hurry, distorting his judgment. He was making mistakes. He picked up the wall phone and dialed a number. When the person at the other end answered, Burchill spoke in a tone and accent several steps away from those he'd used with Simpson.

"Good morning. Mrs. Beattie? ... Good. It's David Burchill ... Yes, yes. Pity about the winter greens otherwise I'd have been teeing off already." He listened and laughed. "Good idea. I'll try it myself one day ... Not today, though. I've got a meeting later on this morning ... Yes, I know. Still, have to make ends meet. Look, sorry to ring you so early with this but I'm looking for another of your bargains ... That's right. Maybe some Meissen or Sèvres? ... No, I know it's not like popping round to Sainsbury's." His tone was still light but his left hand was in his groin, massaging gently. "Well, say something like ten, twelve, fourteen thousand? ... Yes. In that sort of region ... Well, you know how it is—a thing of beauty..." He listened, laughed again and said, "Right. I can leave it with you then? ... Good. Let me know when you've found something. Maybe we can talk about it over dinner one evening ... Yes, I'd like that. Thank you again. Goodbye."

Beattie rang off. Burchill held the phone in front of his face, took a deep breath between clenched teeth, and clutched hard at his groin. "I could really fuck you, *Ms.* Beattie," he said. Then he hung the phone on its rest, yawned, set his alarm for eleven, and went back to bed.

◆◆◆

43

When Carston got back, Ross had already set up an incident room and collated the notes from the night shift and the details of the interviews with the people being detained. He'd looked through them but nothing suggested the likelihood of any of them being involved in a murder. To all of them, police and detainees alike, it had been just another Friday evening rumble, with consequences even milder than usual: the dislocated wrist, a few stitches, lots of swearing, and plenty of sore heads. The savagery of the killing was of a different order to the almost prosaic violence they all described.

Ross had pinned a chart on the wall opposite the window. On it he'd listed the personnel available and the lines of inquiry that had to be followed. As well as their own squad—Fraser, Spurle, McNeil, and the new recruits Bellman and Thom—he'd be able to call on some limited uniformed help for the legwork. They wouldn't be needed right away because until they found out more about who Donnelly was and where he lived they only had the staff of Macy's to talk to and a general call to put out to anyone who'd been thereabouts at any time between three and six.

Carston saw the preparations and secretly thanked whichever God of Reason and Organization had delegated Ross to be his assistant. He had a slight twinge of nostalgia for the larger forces he'd worked in, where teams of up to a hundred had been available for all the necessary chores of investigation, but he knew that the degree of tight control and the flexibility he and Ross had in their work more than made up for pure numbers. He looked quickly over the various headings, nodded his combined approval and thanks, then got everyone to sit down and gave them the details of what he'd seen at Macy's. At the name Donnelly, Spurle said, "Oh, shit, no."

Carston stopped. "Got a problem?"

"Is that Floyd Donnelly?"

"Dunno. Dr. McIntosh just said Donnelly. There's a driving licenge in his wallet. It's been sent here, apparently, with the rest of his stuff."

As Carston was speaking, Ross produced a polythene bag from a basket.

"I bet it is him," said Spurle.

44

"Well? You going to share it with us?" said Ross, looking through the items in the bag.

"It's one of yon bloody hippies." He looked at Carston. "Last night. Forbeshill Road, sir."

Carston hadn't yet begun to reflect on the time they'd spent in the squat and they'd only talked vaguely about the statements that Spurle had taken. When the morning's news had come, everything else had dropped to the bottom of the schedules.

"And?" said Ross impatiently.

"Me an' the guvnor went there last night. Some guys was puttin' a squeeze on them. One of the ones in the flat when the guys come was this Floyd Donnelly."

"What time was this?" asked Ross.

Spurle looked at Carston. "We must've went there about tennish and left near midnight." Carston nodded his agreement.

"Was he there?"

"No," said Carston. "Dr. McIntosh reckons that was about the time he was being stiffed."

"Could be he went lookin' for the guys who'd came round," said Spurle. "The other two reckoned he squared up to them. Said he was goin' to get 'em, stupid wee bugger."

Ross held up a driving license. "Bingo. Darren Floyd Donnelly."

Carston reached out a hand and took it. A twitch of excitement cut through his tiredness.

"It must've been him. The phone call," he said.

"Sir?"

"Last night, about nine o'clock. It'll be in Sandy's log. The man who phoned. He told me about the assault. He said, 'They worked us over.' There were only three of them in the flat, the two we spoke to and this Floyd Donnelly."

"So he phoned you, then went off and got himself killed."

"Seems like it."

"What was he like on the phone?"

"Upset, angry, abusive. Drunk, too."

"So he could've gone lookin' for 'em," said Spurle.

"It's a good place to start, isn't it?" said Ross. "He could've found them but not been as handy as he thought."

Carston shook his head.

"Yes, Jim. But this sticking a glass in his face after he's dead. Just for fun? That doesn't sound like a normal punch-up."

"The sooner we find them, the sooner we'll know."

"Yes, you're right. Two of the squatters are supposed to be coming in to look at some mug shots today. They probably won't bother, though." He looked at Spurle. "Best if you go over and fetch them."

"Now, sir?"

"Yeah. No sense in hanging about. Take McNeil with you." Spurle gave a snort. "What for, sir? They're no goin' to resist."

By way of answer, Carston simply pointed a finger at him.

"We'll need two of them to identify him, too," said Ross. "Get that sorted at the same time."

"Right, sarge," said McNeil. She was already on her feet. She was the only female in the squad and used to being treated as a piece of furniture, but her speed of thought and sharpness of tongue were always a match for Spurle's lumpen brutishness and Fraser's testosterone-fueled quips. Bellman and Thom hadn't been in the squad long enough yet to take the initiative in goading her, but they generally provided a sniggering accompaniment to their colleagues' dreary chauvinism.

"Don't worry, Spurle. I'll look after you," she said as she pulled on a deliberately sexless navy blue overcoat.

"What's that mean? Blow job?" said Spurle.

"Spurle!" barked Carston, but the DC had anticipated the rebuke and was already out through the door, shoving it closed behind him as McNeil followed. She caught it with her left hand, smiled at the others, tapped her temple with her forefinger, and left for a trip which would clearly be very short on warmth, chivalry, and comradeship.

Carston got genuinely angry about the way McNeil was treated. Time and time again, she'd proved how good she was at the job, but there seemed to be something in the minds of the rest of them that prevented them seeing past the fact that she had breasts. The smiles that they were hiding now betrayed the pleasure the exchange had given them.

"Christ!" said Carston. "When are you bloody lot going to get out of nappies? Send 'em away, Jim, for Christ's sake. It's like being in a bloody primary school."

Ross looked at his chart.

"Right. Bellman, Thom. For you it's Macy's. Get the home numbers of the manager and all his staff. Get on to all of them and get them to the club by ..." He looked at his watch. "Say, half-eleven, twelve. Tell them I'll be there to talk about last night."

"Some of them may have day jobs, sarge," said Bellman.

"Well, find out where and go and interview them there then."

"What sort of things do we ask them?" asked Thom.

"Anything. Everything. What happened? Was anything different? Did they know this guy Donnelly? Did they see anything of the fight? ... Use your initiative." His reply was articulated slowly, painfully, as if he were speaking to someone with an IQ in single figures. The two young DCs felt the scorn which was pulsing from both him and Carston. They needed to get clear to reassert themselves, to use one another to prove that they were right and that their guvnors were wrong. But they still hadn't moved.

"Think you can manage that?" asked Ross.

Thom nodded as they both got up quickly and went out. Neither of them had any idea where they were going to start finding out who the manager of Macy's was, but they needed to be away from the pressure.

"Where the bloody hell do they get the intake these days?" said Carston.

"Never mind, sir," said Fraser. "Ye've still got me."

Carston laughed in spite of himself. "What've we got for Sherlock, Jim?" he said.

Ross put the wallet and other things back into the polythene bag. "Well, somebody'd better find out something about this guy Donnelly." He threw the bag to Fraser, who caught it in one hand. "There you go. See what you can dig up."

Fraser took the bag to a desk and began to look through the things it carried. Carston beckoned to Ross and the two of them went through to his own office. There, he clicked the switch on the new coffee machine. For years he'd resisted their appeal, but in the end, the granular and powdered stuff had begun to taste and look too much like sewage.

"We're going to have to do something about the way Spurle niggles away at McNeil," he said as he flopped into his chair.

"Can't think what, short of castration," said Ross.

"When's she taking her sergeant's exam?"

"Not for a couple of months yet."

Carston shook his head. "No doubt she'll last that long. She takes so much crap from them, Jim. I don't suppose another few weeks'll hurt. Now then, what about this Donnelly thing?"

Ross sat on the edge of the desk. Before he could answer, the phone rang. Carston waved a hand for him to answer it.

"DCI Carston's office."

"Jim? It's Tom."

Tom Sawdon was another of the duty sergeants.

"What's up, Tom?"

"Apparently you went to see some antiques dealers yesterday?"

"That's right."

"Well, one of them—a guy called Hilden ..."

"Aye."

"Seems he's just checked in to casualty."

"Eh? What happened?"

"Not sure yet. Somebody broke into his shop. Knocked him around. Smashed up some of his stuff."

"Oh shit! Do we know who it was? Has anybody talked to him?"

"Not yet."

"OK. Where is he now?"

"The Laidlaw. Still in casualty."

"OK. Cheers, Tom."

He put the phone down. Carston was waiting to hear what it was about. Ross explained quickly. Carston understood his concern.

"You'd better get over there, then."

"What about Donnelly?"

Carston shook his head. "Not much we can do until we've got the basics sorted. There's certainly time for you to go and find out what you can from this Hilden bloke."

"Aye. I'm no sure how pleased he'll be to see me, though."

"Why?"

"They told him they'd only hurt him if he contacted us."

Carston made a face. "Rather you than me, then."

"Aye," said Ross. "How did Dixon of Dock Green get such a cushy bloody number?"

He went out and Carston's smile faded as his eyes came to rest once again on more of Ridley's charts and spreadsheets. He pushed them aside, pulled a fresh pad from his drawer and wrote "Donnelly" on it.

Ross hated hospitals. He hated the flowers that people brought which nobody really wanted. He hated the chairs and trolleys carrying failing bodies, the resolutely cheerful nurses who'd grown mental calluses to protect them from the pains which they saw too often and were helpless to alleviate. And most of all he hated the smell, a nauseous hygienic wash which smothered everything and just reminded him of the enormities that needed masking in such places. In the cubicle where they'd put Hilden, it was even fresher, a mixture of new bandages and disinfectant. Hilden's head was covered with dazzling white wrappings. The bits of his face which were still visible showed that the bruising from his beating had spread all over it. As he moved to sit beside the bed, Ross noted incongruously that the bandages and pillows which framed him made him less pitiable than the clothes he usually wore. The bald head with its absurd coiffure had been covered and, while the striped nylon shirt wasn't exactly Noel Coward, it was closer to normality than the short-sleeved jackets that characterized his usual wretched appearance. Ross noticed that his expression, too, had changed. During their conversation the previous day, he'd been wary of eye contact, dropping his gaze to look at the floor or at the items around his shop. This morning, there was less submission. He looked straight at Ross and seemed to challenge him with his stare.

"D'you want to talk about it?" asked Ross, uncertain for a change how to approach the interview.

"What's to say?" said Hilden. "It was talking that made them do this."

49

Still his eyes accused.

"How many of them were there?"

Hilden turned his head away in exasperation and immediately winced.

"One. But you needn't think I'm bringing charges. Next time, they'll kill me."

Ross remembered the pathetic little man he'd spoken to amidst the dust and junk of his life and understood his resentment.

"I know why you're saying that, Mr. Hilden, but if we catch them, there can't be a next time."

"If," said Hilden with a surprising degree of irony.

"When did it happen?"

"Last night."

"What? When did you come here then?"

"This morning."

Ross said nothing. Hilden knew why but was not giving in to him today.

"I was hurting, sore, scared out of my wits," he said. "I just wanted to lie down."

"But ..."

"And I didn't want to bother folk. They get enough to do here. Especially Friday nights."

"All the same, sir ..."

"No, Sergeant. You don't realize. You don't know." He stopped, apparently uncertain of what he wanted to say. When he spoke again, the defiance had left his voice. "Sorry. I just ... I didn't realize how bad it was. Didn't know I needed stitches." He turned slowly to look directly at Ross again. "I was absolutely terrified. I just wanted to ... I didn't know ..." He spread his hands, giving up on the explanation. Ross felt the helpless pity surge inside himself again. "Aye, sir. It must have been a helluva shock ... I'm sorry."

Hilden fell back again. Ross leaned towards him, his voice when he spoke very soft.

"I'll still need to ask you a couple of things." Hilden didn't move but the muscles in his jaw clenched tighter.

"What time did it happen?"

"Does it matter?"

"It might."

"I don't know. Ten, half-past, something like that."

"Did you recognize him at all? Was he one of the ones who came before?"

There was a long pause, then, "No comment."

His voice had hardened again. The changes in him were remarkable. In his anger at being let down by the police, at having exposed himself unnecessarily (as he now seemed to think) to the punishment for having talked to Ross, he was accusing, almost aggressive. Ross's underlying tiredness made it difficult for him to adjust to the new tone.

"Mr. Hilden, we can't just let an assault go."

Hilden turned angrily.

"What d'you mean, 'we'? I was the one he beat up. It was my stuff he smashed up ..."

He stopped as the pain in his head jabbed a warning at him. He fell back again, breathing deeply. Ross waited and kept his voice low when he spoke again.

"Look, if you wouldn't mind, I think it'd be an idea if we had a look at your shop. We need to see the damage. See whether ..."

He stopped as Hilden turned quickly towards him once more.

"I do mind. I mind a lot. It's because ... Oh, I wish I'd never ..."

The effort was too much again. There were tears in his eyes. He brought a hand up to his chest and pressed on it to help control his breathing.

"Sergeant," he said at last, "I know it's not your fault. I'm sorry to lose my temper but ... like you said, it's been something of a shock."

Ross waited, uncertain of what to do and unwilling to provoke another mini-crisis. Hilden tried to smile. "Perhaps later. They're letting me go home again soon. It's not as bad as it looks. Maybe when I've had time to ..."

He stopped. Ross recognized that it was a cue.

"Aye. Better if you get some rest. I'll ... I'll get in touch later today, shall I?"

"If you like."

Hilden's eyes were closed. He nodded his head slowly.

51

Ross got up and looked at him again before turning to leave. Hilden's voice made him turn back again.

"I still don't want to get involved. I couldn't take another beating like this."

Ross nodded uselessly and went out. He felt guilty.

Three

Fraser had been dealt the easiest job. From his first inquiries about Floyd, he'd found that he had a record and so he could simply sit at the computer and get all the details downloaded from the central database. Less than an hour after the briefing session, he took the results of his research to Carston's office.

"'scuse me, sir?"

"Yes, what is it?"

Fraser handed him a green folder.

"Donnelly."

Carston was impressed.

"Bloody hell, that was quick."

"He's got form. Robbery with violence. Did four years in Peterhead."

"Ah. Still, nice job. Thanks."

"What now, sir?"

Carston thought for a moment. It was Saturday and Fraser had a wife at home, but there was no question of anybody getting any time off this early in an investigation. Fraser knew that, too.

"First of all, look out the local rogues' gallery mug shots. Those two squatters'll be here soon to go through them. Get the muggers and GBH files. Then have a look through the guys who were picked up at the fight last night. Some of them had bits of form. See if any of them connect with this Donnelly at all."

Fraser went off again, happy to be doing some button pushing for a change instead of dragging about on a cold, gray December morning. Carston flicked through the stuff on Floyd. It was the usual depressing picture of a young man bright enough to find more conventional ways of earning money but preferring the faster, easier route of petty thieving. It was when he'd been interrupted by a householder that pettiness had escalated to a more serious level. He'd knocked her down with the heavy-duty torch he was carrying, then set about her with the steel bar he'd used to prize open her window. The attack was totally gratuitous and, according to the prosecution, had been prolonged more for the pleasure it seemed to give him than to facilitate the robbery. The manner of his own death was therefore a simple extension of his attitude to life. Secretly, Carston admired its symmetry but knew that such admiration belonged in the same shameful category as Donnelly's aggressions.

Ross came in as he was closing the file.

"Any of your coffee going?" he asked. "It's bloody freezing out there today."

Carston waved a hand at the machine.

"Help yourself. I'll have one too."

As they drank, Ross filled him in on the details of the assault on Hilden. Carston asked a couple of questions but realized that they'd have to wait until the man was ready to help them.

"You can't help feeling sorry for him but it's a bloody nuisance, too," said Ross.

"What is?"

"This sort of … meekness there is about him all the time. Frightened of his own shadow."

"He's got every reason to be scared, Jim."

"Aye, I know, but it could get in our way. Hold us up."

"How d'you mean?"

"Well, for a start, I'm pretty sure he knows who it was."

"Oh?"

"Aye. I could sort of see it. There was a … I don't know, hesitation … And I mean, why say 'no comment' when I asked him?"

Carston shrugged.

"Have you been in touch with the other dealers you talked to? Asked if they've had a visit, too?"

"Not yet. I was going to do that now."

"Yes, just as well. Better warn them to be careful anyway."

"Aye."

Carston thought for a moment. When he spoke again, he sounded puzzled, concerned even.

"D'you really think somebody's trying to run a protection racket here?"

"Looks like it."

Carston shook his head slowly.

"But scruffy little antique shops? All a bit amateurish, isn't it?"

"I wouldn't be fooled by the scruffiness. There's plenty of bundles of used tenners stuffed inside drawers in some of these places."

Carston was surprised. "I didn't know you were into antiques."

"I'm not. Don't know a thing about it. But I know some of the people. Don't know what checkbooks are, half of them."

"Money's not illegal yet, Jim."

"I know, but tax-dodging is. You want to see the black economy? Have a look in the auction rooms on Monday nights and Tuesdays. Like Irishmen at a horse fair."

"OK, but protection money? London maybe, or Glasgow. But Cairnburgh?"

Ross got up to add some more milk to his coffee.

"You know, for somebody who's been around as much as you have, sir," he said, "you're a bit naïve."

"Eh?"

"Aye. Have you never tried leaving your car on any of the housing schemes in Edinburgh or Glasgow?"

Carston knew what he was talking about. You no sooner locked your door than there was a kid there asking for a couple of quid to make sure the paintwork didn't get scratched.

"OK, OK." he agreed. "But on this sort of scale, out in the open, organized."

Ross sat down again. "Aye, I know. They'll never get away with it. We'll have 'em before Christmas."

"Yes. Meantime, we don't want any more accidents like Hilden."

"Aye. I feel bad about that."

"Not your fault, Jim. What could you do? Give him a while to cool off, then try him again. There's plenty to occupy us with this Donnelly business anyway."

"What's the latest?"

Carston brought Ross up to date on the murdered man's identity and criminal record and Ross agreed that, in such a context, violent death was unsurprising. Unlike that which sometimes erupted bloodily into the lives of ordinary people, this had always been part of the script for someone with Donnelly's habits and connections.

"Suit you down to the ground, Jim, wouldn't it? To find out it was one of his fellow villains who'd done it."

"Why d'you say that?"

"Stands to reason. Keep it neat, tidy. Logical."

"Aye, and you'd prefer it to be some voodoo priest whose Tarot cards told him to sacrifice a Scot on a Friday."

Carston smiled. "Nah. Too easy."

There was a knock on the door and it was opened immediately. Thom's young, red face appeared round it.

"Er, 'scuse me, sarge. The staff at Macy's. They'll be there by half past eleven like you asked."

"All of them?"

"No. There's two girls works in Asda, and the barman and two of the bouncers are students. Me and Bellman are off to see them now."

"OK. Check in as soon as you get back."

"Right, sarge. Cheers."

He ducked quickly away without waiting for any reply. He was very aware of his inexperience and Carston made him uncomfortable. He knew that taking Spurle for his role model had been a mistake, but the coarseness and the comments Spurle made about all his superiors behind their backs made him an easy focal point for anyone with a beginner's insecurity. What he needed to do was get some results to let Carston and Ross know that he was worth the trouble.

Carston smiled as the door closed. "Christ, you haven't half frightened him, Jim." He put down his empty cup and pushed it away across his desk. "Never mind. It's all getting them ready for performance-related pay."

Ross laughed. Despite their differences, he and Carston were of one mind in most matters concerning police procedures. The latest suggestion, from whatever quango or think-tank regulated affairs from its Whitehall bunker, was that all officers up to the rank of superintendent would be appraised before they were awarded any pay increments. There was even talk of them being able to earn bonuses. One afternoon, over a sandwich lunch in the Dolphin, Carston and Ross had speculated on the effects of offering a results bonus to Spurle and his equivalents in forces up and down the country. In less than a month, the jails would be chock-a-block and arresting procedures would become as indiscriminate as vacuum cleaners.

"Spurle and McNeil should be back soon," said Ross. "D'you want me here when you're talking to these squatters?"

"Don't think so. Depends what they have to say. They're only looking at photos."

"OK," said Ross, putting his mug on the desk and taking a small notebook from his pocket. "I'll phone these dealers then, get that out of the way."

As he stood up, Carston took a photograph from the file in front of him and handed it across.

"Better take this with you. That Donnelly character. You might need it down at that club."

"Aye. Right," said Ross.

He went out and Carston sat back in his chair. Suddenly, unaccountably, Kath had come into his mind. She'd been away six days now and he was beginning to miss her quite badly. Not for any specific reason that he could pinpoint, but just because there was a layer, a dimension missing from his days. They'd spent very little time apart in the eighteen years they'd been married. There'd been plenty of late nights and unsocial hours, of course, but she'd almost always been there when he eventually did get home. As he thought about her now, he was ashamed to recognize a small surge of resentment at her continued absence. He knew she'd ring that evening; she always did. Inexplicably, he felt that he actually needed to be there when she did. The feeling was so strong that it surprised him.

"You're getting old, Jack," he said to himself.

◆◆◆

Spurle was driving. Despite the fact that McNeil had been through the same course and passed the same exams as he had, whenever they went out together, he always took the wheel. McNeil was beside him and Dawn, Liz, and Jez were crammed into the backseat. There'd been little in the way of conversation. On the way to the squat, Spurle and McNeil had naturally talked about the murder. Spurle was already convinced it was the work of the two visitors with the baseball bat and the ax. McNeil agreed that that was probably too much of a coincidence to be discounted. She lapsed into silence when Spurle started developing the theme that whoever was responsible was doing everybody a favor by getting rid of wasters.

None of their passengers had any desire to talk to them. Their contact with Spurle the previous evening had confirmed all their preconceptions about the police force and, paradoxically, the fact that a woman could be part of such an organization made McNeil seem even more of an aberration in their eyes. In a way, their blindness matched that of Spurle.

At the station, they checked in at the desk and went through to the squad room. Fraser had stacked two box-files on a desk in the corner. Each one contained about forty A4-sized cards with ten photographs on each. It threatened to be a trying morning for everybody. Spurle pointed at the two chairs behind the desk. "One of youse'll have to stand," he said.

"No," said Liz, "I don't want to look at your snaps. That's not what I'm here for. I wasn't there when they came, so I didn't see them—remember?"

Spurle hadn't really listened when they'd fetched their three passengers from Forbeshill Road and hadn't therefore registered the fact that Liz and Jez had agreed to identify the body. McNeil anticipated his reaction and was quick enough to head it off.

"Yes. If you'd like to come with me, I'll take you through to DCI Carston."

As Dawn sat down, Liz followed McNeil out of the door again, holding Spurle's gaze all the way, challenging him.

"Bloody dyke," he muttered as she disappeared.

Carston greeted Liz with a bigger smile than he normally put on for visitors. He was still aware of the ambivalence of his feelings about her and her friends and anxious not to let them show. He invited her and Jez to sit down, offered them coffee, which they both declined, and explained what would be needed of them. They listened, neither one showing any reactions at any of his information. Carston's attention was particularly taken by Liz. He felt her coldness and, despite himself, began to wonder about her. Emotionally, identification of a corpse was never easy. He'd seen men and women alike faint as the gray faces of the people they'd known in life were revealed; uncontrollable shaking and throat-stopping tears were commonplace and even the thin-lipped expressions of those who managed to harness their reactions were often stretched over an inner turmoil that would need releasing in some other way when they'd left the station. The prospect of having to face such trauma seemed to make no impression at all on this woman, who looked straight at him all the time, nodding occasionally and giving a faint impression that she was both watchful and, at the same time, humoring him.

"And you knew Mr. Donnelly for …?" Carston waited for her to complete his sentence.

"About two months."

"As a … fellow tenant."

Liz laughed. "That's right."

"Would you call him a friend, then?"

"No."

There'd been no hesitation before she answered. It was discon-certing, but intriguing too.

"How about you, sir?"

Jez shook his head. "No. He was no friend of mine."

"I take it you realize that it means driving into Aberdeen?" said Carston.

Liz nodded.

"Well, there are things I have to do there, so I'll take you in. DC McNeil will come with us, of course. If you like we can leave straight away."

Liz stood up. Carston had no option but to follow suit. He took refuge in turning to McNeil.

"Er … Take …" He realized that even though this was the second time he'd met the squatters, he hadn't even asked their names. He looked at them, waiting for them to supply them. Jez looked out of the window. Liz stood by the door, keeping her silence. It had the opposite effect from the one she was hoping for. Carston smiled. He preferred unpredictability. Conversations which followed the rules were tedious. "Right," he went on, turning back to McNeil. "I'll see you at the car. Tell DC Spurle you're coming with me. I'll just nip in and let Sergeant Ross know we're off."

Ross was on the telephone when he went through, talking to one of the people on his list of antique dealers. He excused himself and held his hand over the mouthpiece as Carston told him he'd be away for most of the day.

"How about tonight's briefing?"

"Oh, I'll be back for that. If I'm not, start without me."

"OK."

"We'll need a team to go over Donnelly's place, see what they can find."

"I'll get it organized."

"And it wouldn't hurt to do a rundown on the squatters, see if we've got anything on any of them."

Ross nodded and made a note.

"And check on Spurle as soon as you can, will you? Maybe find a WPC to put with him; the squatter he's in with's a woman."

Ross nodded again. "Aye, OK. If she recognizes anybody, d'you want them picked up?"

"Yes. Don't let on what for, though."

Ross opened his eyes wide. "You don't think they might guess?"

"Not if you're subtle," replied Carston. "Think you can manage that?"

"No. I'm only a sergeant."

"See you later."

He left Ross to his calls and went down the stairs and out to the car park at the side of the station. McNeil, Jez, and Liz arrived almost at once and, with McNeil driving, they set off for Aberdeen. They decided to pick up the Deeside road, then branch left at Banchory onto the B977. It was a trip of just under thirty miles and

60

Carston was quite intrigued to find out what sort of conversation they'd manage in the next forty-five minutes or so.

At eleven-thirty, Burchill was in his office on the fourth floor of Burchdrill PLC. He'd deliberately chosen Saturday morning for the meeting. He had to be there to see to one or two things and inconveniencing others always added spice to his days. CML, the agency that handled his marketing, had suggested making a video to send to Singapore to spread the word among the companies drilling in Indonesia and the Pacific Basin. He'd agreed and was listening to the ideas of a freelance scriptwriter on how best to package the message. The man was obviously keen to get the job and had already offered four very varied treatments, ranging from one using full computer animation to one based puzzlingly on a parody of Charles Laughton's portrayal of Quasimodo. Burchill saw the CML's rep was impressed. That was no surprise; the writer was handing out ideas which should have been coming from the agency in the first place. They'd commission the script, book a video company and a facilities house to do all the grafting, do bugger-all themselves, and then bang eighteen to twenty percent on top of the budget for their trouble.

"I mean, I know the product's already been proved and the statistics speak for themselves, but viewers still want to be entertained," the writer was saying. "We can't just give them information and expect them to take it or leave it."

CML's man nodded. Burchill gave no reaction to either of them. The writer took it as encouragement to go on.

"So, if we start by disorienting them, infiltrating their expectations, the data can ..."

"Where'd you get that ring?" asked Burchill, in a tone that implied he hadn't been listening. The writer stopped and looked at his hand as if he hadn't realized there was a ring there. On the third finger of his right hand was a big silver band with a checkered black and white pattern running around its center.

"My girlfriend," he said.

"Looks like something somebody knocked up on a bench in our fabrication shop," said Burchill.

There was a silence. Then the CML rep laughed and the writer managed a grin.

"Yeah," he said, a blush suddenly covering his cheeks. "But if I didn't wear it, she'd ..."

He finished with a shrug. Burchill looked out of the window, his credentials as hard-nosed buyer reinforced. As the rep and the writer took up their sales pitch again, he laughed inside at the power his money and his success had given him. He let the two men drone on for another ten minutes, giving no reactions to any of their suggestions and contributing nothing to any discussions. In the end, knowing that if he asked for alternatives he'd just have to go through it all again, he told the rep that it was his job to decide what worked best in the marketplace and that he should talk to his finance director before finalizing anything. Without getting up, he shook hands with the two men and left them to make their way out of his office as he turned his attention to the letters in a tray on his desk.

The phone call from Beattie came as a pleasant surprise.

"How nice to hear from you so soon," he said. "You haven't found what I was after already, have you?"

"I may have. I'm not sure. Perhaps we could meet to discuss it."

"Delighted." He looked at his watch. Today it was a Tag Heuer, unnecessarily large and studded with dials and functions he'd never use. "What are you doing for lunch?"

He heard a page being turned.

"Nothing special. It's that urgent, is it?"

"Not necessarily. I just like the thought of having lunch with you."

It was as well he couldn't see the look of disgust which Beattie directed at the mouthpiece of her phone.

"Alright then," she said, her voice betraying none of her dislike of him. "Where?"

"How about somewhere out of town? They say the Raemoir at Banchory's very good."

"No, I can't take more than an hour. I've got calls booked to an agent at Christie's this afternoon and I need to do some sums before I talk to him."

"Christie's. Is that where you're thinking of getting whatever it is you've got in mind for me?"

She granted him a little laugh, knowing from past experience that men found its music attractive. "Somewhere much more discreet than that."

"Sounds great," said Burchill, charmed by the laugh. "OK, where do we eat?"

"How about Cullen Lodge?"

"Fine. I'll pick you up at …"

"No, no. I'm seeing a client in town first. I'll meet you there at … say twelve-thirty."

"Look forward to it."

"Bye."

Burchill put the phone back and leaned away from the desk, looking out at the crackling blue of the sky. It looked like a day made for golf, but he knew that the late morning sunshine that was flooding across Grampian's fields and hills had no heat and would anyway begin to die by three in the afternon. No, given the choice of how to spend the rest of such a day, he knew that he'd opt for the lunch at Cullen Lodge followed by an afternoon in one of its suites looking out across the Cairngorms, fucking Isobel Beattie. Hard. Over and over again.

By the time Ross left the station to go to Macy's, the incident room was not a pleasant place to be. Dawn was just starting on the photos from the second box-file and, at frequent intervals, Spurle was making her aware of his impatience. WDC Ellis, the probation-ary woman constable that Ross had borrowed from Sandy Dwyer to ride shotgun, had little experience of the procedures involved but shared Spurle's opinion of squatters and so kept on echoing his expressions of dissatisfaction. Far from pleasing him, this only served to increase his frustrations. She was young and female and so, by definition, fit for only one thing. Hearing her second his opin-ions somehow devalued them and when Fraser came in and offered to take over, he grabbed at the chance and went to get a beer and a sandwich in the Dolphin.

"Fancy a cup of tea or something?" asked Fraser, needing to talk after a morning spent with only himself for company.

"I'd prefer coffee," said Dawn.

Fraser looked at Ellis and flicked his head to indicate that that was her job.

"I'll have tea," he said.

As she went out, he perched on the edge of the desk.

"How's it goin'?"

"Boring," said Dawn. "They all look the same. And they all look guilty. Who takes these photos?"

"Depends. Some of them come from Aberdeen, Dundee. Some of 'em are ours." He pointed to one of a bald man with enormous eyebrows. "That one's come off the computer. Been sent up from down south somewhere. You can tell, it's sort o' fuzzy."

She carried on flicking through the cards, the portraits seeming to resemble one another more and more closely, like variations on an identikit theme. The tea and coffee were produced and drunk and Fraser, in an expansive mood, kept setting off on little conversational asides to make the process less tedious for everyone. One of his diversions was meteorological and surprised Dawn so much that she stopped studying the photos for a while.

"O' course, it's all tropospheric," he said.

Dawn looked at this hulking man who could easily have passed for a heavyweight wrestler and was taken aback by his smiling earnestness.

"What is?" she asked.

"Weather. The troposphere's the lower layer of the atmosphere. That's where it all happens."

"Is it?"

"Aye. Ah've got my wee weather station at home. Been keepin' records fer the past five wiks."

Dawn almost laughed. "A weather station?"

"Aye. That's what it's called. Got it from a catalog. Rainfall, thermometer, wind speed, wind direction. It's all recorded."

"Very impressive."

"Aye. And there's a wind chill chart an' a'. Eleven quid it cost me. Worth every penny."

As he went on to talk wisely about the terminal velocity of different drops of rain, WDC Ellis was as fascinated as Dawn by his apparent expertise in such a specialized area. She hadn't been at the station long enough to know that Fraser was an ardent buyer of gimmicks from the types of catalogs that slid out of the *Radio Times* and other weekly magazines. His enthusiasms were varied but usually short-lived. The one exception was gloriously demonstrated when digression about the interrelated effects of solar radiation and thermal convection caused him to mention measurements taken in Brittany. Dawn had spent her year abroad as a language student in Rennes and she said so. Even Ellis knew the effect this would have.

"*Ah, vraiment?*" said Fraser, his previous smile swallowed up by a beam as broad as the weather fronts he'd been parading for her. "*Alors, vous parlez français?*"

There was no concession made to the fact that French requires an accent different from that of Aberdeenshire, but his delight provoked an automatic response of "*Bien sûr*" from Dawn. And that ensured that further examination of the photographs was postponed for almost twenty minutes.

Fraser had learned rudimentary French at night school the previous year in order to get the most out of a holiday in France. For a change, it was a passion he managed to sustain and he'd practiced it diligently on everyone until Carston, under pressure from the rest of the squad, had had to order him to stick to English at work. The holiday had taken him to Normandy and he and his wife had eventually driven down as far as Tours. The sun had shone, the wine had flowed, the food had been gorgeous and, by some fluke, they'd been made welcome everywhere. The result was that he'd come back an unapologetic Francophile. At the slightest opportunity he slipped into his version of French and, in the Five Nations championship, his allegiance was first to Scotland, then to France.

Dawn was amused and even charmed by his enthusiasm and they happily swapped experiences of French drivers, regional foods, and Gallic bloody-mindedness.

Ellis could contribute even less to the exchanges than she'd been able to before and began to feel that she was in some sort of work-warp which she might have to explain to her sergeant. She tried, as discreetly as possible, to bring attention back to the photographs. Dawn started glancing through them again, still managing to react sufficiently to Fraser's observations to keep them multiplying. It was just as he was expanding on French attitudes to pets and expressing his amazement at the quantities of dogshit that they seemed to tolerate on their streets that she suddenly cut in.

"Hey. This is him. The one with the baseball bat. At least, I think it is."

The others looked at the photo. Their first vague impression was of a pair of scowling eyes under a scruffy thatch of hair. Dawn looked more closely, trying to imagine the head shaved. The dark jowls were unmistakable. "Yes, definitely. That's him."

Fraser was disappointed at the interruption but pleased at the reason for it. He turned the card round to get a closer look.

"Huh! Barry bloody Simpson. Should've known."

He picked up the other cards and flicked through them until he came to another photograph. It showed an individual with a neck like a bull and lank, dark hair falling over his ears.

"How 'bout this one?" he said, turning the photo back for Dawn to look at it. She stared and nodded.

"Yeah. That's the other one."

"*Quelle surprise!*" said Fraser. "Benny Mitchell. They're always together. OK. That's a good job you've done. If we bring 'em in and organize an identity parade, will you be able to pick 'em out?"

Dawn looked down at her hands.

"It's OK. They winna ken it's you," said Fraser.

"If I've got to, I guess that's it," said Dawn.

"It's your duty really."

Dawn and Fraser stopped and looked at Ellis, who'd offered up this little pearl. She blushed and wished that Spurle would come back. At least with him, you knew where you were.

Without the strobe lights and the spinning effects, the interior of Macy's was like the storeroom of an old tenement. The black walls looked dusty and stained, the floor was scuffed and there were chips out of most of the chairs and tables that were scattered around the place. The sweet smell of old, spilled alcohol and the dry, flat smell of last night's tobacco hung together and caught at Ross's throat. The whole atmosphere was light years away from the romance that would nonetheless come throbbing back when the beat started and the lights flashed again.

The manager of the club was anxious to be helpful but hedged too many of his answers to Ross's questions with disclaimers and protestations of his own innocence and that of his clientele. He managed to make Macy's sound like a 1950s youth club frequented by people as familiar with altars and pews as they were with his bar and its stools. The discovery of a corpse literally under his doorstep was first unbelievable and, second, a deliberate attempt to ruin innocent pleasures. Ross couldn't help thinking that, to carry the man's remarks to their logical conclusion, he should perhaps arrest Floyd's body and charge it with behavior likely to cause a breach of the peace.

The two doormen who were there (he'd quickly been corrected when he called them bouncers) were much closer to the truth of what Macy's represented. They knew most of their regulars and had never seen Floyd before. They talked calmly, objectively about the fight.

"Nothin' special about it," said Neil. "Just like the others."

"D'you get that many then?"

"Nah. Once in a while. It's usually quiet, though. No bother here. Not like down the Transom. Back o' Canal Street."

"Aye."

Ross had heard of it. Called itself a club but doubled as boxing ring and brothel, depending on who was there.

"So what was different about last night?"

Big Tam shrugged. "No idea. Just happened."

"Aye," said Neil. "One minute there's folk just queuein' to get in, next the animals arrive and there's a punch-up."

Ross held up Floyd's photo again.

"And you didn't see this guy anywhere? You don't think he was part of it?"

Neil shook his head.

"Nae idea. I didna see everybody, but he's nae one of our regulars and he certainly wasna in the queue."

"Could he have been with the Rangers guys?"

Again the shake of the head.

"Coulda, but I dinna think so."

Their answers were quiet, considered, and somehow made their physical presence seem even bigger. Ross himself was not small. He'd once played lock forward for the East of Scotland police, but the size and strength of Neil and Big Tam were of a different sort. They were loose, relaxed; somehow gave the impression of feeling good about themselves. Neil's scar was testimony to the violence that was part of his nightly experiences, but apart from that, there was no menace, no threat from either of them.

"D'you like the job?" asked Ross, from a general curiosity not connected with his inquiries.

The response was instant and very positive from both of them.

"The fights and things, they don't bother you?"

"Nah," said Neil. "Like I said, they don't happen all that often."

"But there's always the chance one will."

Big Tam smiled.

"Gives you a buzz."

Neil nodded.

"Aye. It's different. We know we can handle it. It's the team, see."

Ross waited.

"We trust each other. Work for each other. Always lookin' out for each other's backs."

"Aye," said Big Tam. "You soon ken wi' new guys whether they're any good."

"How?"

Neil thought.

"If a guy's got his hands in his pockets, he's no ready. You get rid o' him."

Big Tam was nodding all the time.

"Aye. In this game, that's no good to anybody. He's a liability."

Ross was getting even more interested. The rules of this game seemed very unambiguous.

"So what's the biggest problem? I mean, where does most of the trouble come from?"

The two men looked at each other and shrugged.

"Hard to say really," said Neil.

"Booze? Drugs?"

"Ah no. Soon as you think there's any drugs goin' about, you stamp on that."

Ross was surprised at the vehemence in Neil's words.

"That's real trouble. But you can spot 'em a mile off."

"Aye," agreed Big Tam. "Whether they've been on it already or they're lookin' for it, it's obvious. And we just kick 'em out. No questions."

Ross marveled at the precision of this tiny world with its specially drawn boundaries and clear moral distinctions.

"What about the hard men? The ones that want to have a go just because you're there?"

Neil smiled.

"Oh yeah, you get plenty o' them." A short laugh broke through his words. "They soon find out."

"But what if they're carrying?"

"What d'you mean, guns?"

"No, no. Knives, stuff like that."

As he spoke, Ross was suddenly more aware of Neil's scar. A grin on Neil's face suggested that he was, too.

"You usually see them coming," said Big Tam. "Tell you what they've got nowadays—baseball bats. In their cars. Sometimes you put them outside and they're all ... 'See you, I'll be back for you, you bastard!' Stuff like that."

"They all say that," said Neil, still grinning.

"Aye. Sometimes they do, though," Big Tam went on. "They go and fetch their bat and come back swinging."

"So how do you handle that?"

Neil laughed again.

"Make sure there's no home runs."

The remark wasn't bravado. It came out of the same cool confidence that marked everything else they'd said. These were no bone-headed stereotypes, cuffing and clubbing their fellows for pleasure. The more Ross talked to them, the more it was obvious that they really did see this as a worthwhile job. It paid well, it gave them a special status among the club and pub goers, and, yes, there was the buzz of being the upfront, acknowledged hard man. The agency they worked for was based in Aberdeen and covered most of the clubs there as well as those in the smaller towns around it. Neil and Big Tam reckoned that Macy's was one of the easier places to be.

"So last night must've been a bit of a shock?"

"Why?"

"Well, finding a body."

"Oh, aye, that."

The two men nodded slowly. Then Neil shook his head.

"Tell you what, sergeant, I'd be very surprised if that was anything to do with what went on here."

"Oh?"

"Aye. We'd've seen somethin'. You couldna push a guy under the steps like that wi' us about the place. No way."

Big Tam was nodding again.

"Aye. That musta happened after we were away."

Ross was suddenly caught by a yawn.

"Tirin' work in the polis, is it?" asked Big Tam.

Ross got up and smiled.

"No. I've got a baby girl. Takes more out o' me than any criminal."

Neil had been infected by the yawn. He stretched his long arms, the muscles bunching in his shoulders.

"Aye, it's babies that keep us awake, too," he said. "Trouble is, they're all over eighteen."

The three of them laughed and Ross left to go back to the station feeling that he'd had a brief glimpse into a way of life that lay totally outside his experience.

Isobel Beattie looked gorgeous. The cold air had whipped redness into her cheeks and a sparkle into her blue eyes. Her lips shone from the perfumed lip salve she'd put on before getting out of her car and her fair hair had been blown into tangles which she'd simply teased at with her fingers. The effect was a careful balance of accident and control. She settled into the wing-backed Victorian chair and lifted her gin and tonic to Burchill.

"Cheers," he said.

She sipped, put the glass back on the table, crossed her legs, and arranged the folds of her black wraparound skirt. It fell to her

70

ankles but emphasized rather than concealed the shapes beneath it. Burchill felt the genuine pleasure and excitement that always stirred in him when he was with a female. With the ones he paid for, it was a quick, hot greed that often spilled into anger when he began to satisfy it. But with classy women who were involved with other men or who were, at least in theory, unattainable, it spread slowly through him with the even coursing of his blood.

She arched her head slightly forward and let her eyes drift across the view through the window beside which they were sitting. It was a long bay window which gave onto an open garden of rose beds. Lots of the bushes still had daubs of color on them as their blooms defied December. Around them were textured borders crammed with leafy shrubs judiciously selected for a winter display. At the end of the curving lawn, a hedge of dwarf conifers sealed off the grounds of Cullen Lodge and drew a golden line under the stretch of blue hills which folded up towards the highest peaks of the Cairngorms. The spines of snow scratched up their sides into a sky whose blue was already beginning to grow paler.

"Beautiful place, isn't it?" said Burchill.

She nodded, her eyes still wandering over the scene. "Mmm."

"Wonder how much it'd be if they ever put it on the market."

Beattie smiled and shook her head slowly.

"More than I could afford."

Burchill said nothing, hoping that she'd pick up the implication that he, on the other hand, was very capable of making an offer.

A woman, whose voice suggested that she was probably one of the owners rather than a mere employee, came, smilingly, up to them and handed them two menus.

"I'll just let you have a look at these. We've also got some specials today, a salmon en croûte starter, and two plats du jour: rack of lamb with flageolet beans and monkfish in a Choron sauce."

"Choron," said Beattie, with obvious pleasure. "You don't often hear that. Most places are satisfied with a straight béarnaise."

The woman was pleased by the implied compliment.

"Do you use cream as well as tomato?" Beattie went on.

"Yes. My husband finds it's a good balance for the tarragon."

"Sounds wonderful."

71

The woman bent towards her, dropping her voice to a conspiratorial murmur.

"It's absolutely delicious."

Beattie smiled and opened her menu. The woman went away, content to have a discriminating customer and confident of being able to satisfy her.

Burchill, on the other hand, was discomfited. After the phone call from Beattie, he'd rushed home and showered, then taken great care to choose the things in which he'd envelop himself. He started with Heritage de Guerlain eau de toilette, then (unfortunately, given their combined pungency), Paco Rabanne aftershave. The pale blue shirt was by Turnbull and Asser, with a mustard-colored Stefano Ricci tie. His ebony trousers were from Comme des Garçons and his navy wool jacket from Agnès B. As a final flourish he'd added the Cartier sunglasses which were now lying carelessly on the table in front of him. All in all, he reckoned that the ensemble was bloody impressive. The trouble was that you could do that sort of thing with clothes; the labels themselves were eloquent. No need to add anything. But food and drink were a bastard. There weren't any rules. He couldn't just learn a recipe book or memorize all the good years for claret or guess when a burgundy would be a better bet, or even when white was better than red. Christ, when you saw Agnès B on a label, you knew it was good gear, but what the bloody hell was *béarnaise* or *béchamel*? And what did you do with them, spread them on bread or dunk your turbot in them? It didn't matter if it was only the waitress who knew because she didn't count, but Beattie sounded as if she'd spent her bloody life chatting to Raymond Blanc.

Her ease with gastronomic sophistication had a slightly suppressant effect on his desire. Fantasies of drinking champagne from her navel were briefly replaced by the desire to humiliate her. Fortunately for both of them, she was keen to get straight down to the business which lay beneath their meeting.

"Now then, this little investment you've got in mind. We could go the scenic or the direct route for it."

Burchill was not quite ready to get into linguistic gameplaying. He merely looked at her. She kept her gaze steadily on the distant hills.

"The scenic route could take a while. I've got accounts with the major houses, of course, but I don't always get every catalog. They know it's mostly the ceramics that tempt me. Anyway, catalogs are pretty pricey nowadays; they save them for the really big spenders." She took another slow sip of her gin and tonic, letting the rim of the glass rest on her lower lip for a moment before continuing. "Then again, even when it gets to the auction, it's not really the sort of thing you're looking for."

"What do you mean?" Burchill was interested, despite himself.

Beattie put her glass down. As she leaned forward, the movement of her breasts inside her blouse suggested she wasn't wearing a bra. Burchill's interest increased and took a new direction.

"Well, flapping paddle numbers about, paying amounts that may be miles out either way. If I read you right, you've got a fixed sum in mind and you just want to pay it upfront, without too much need for paperwork."

"I think you read me right," said Burchill, trying to seed the words with ambiguity.

"So the ideal is to find a seller who's as wary of the whole auction system as you are."

"And you know one?"

Her answer began with a little arpeggio of laughter. He thought again of her missing bra.

"I know lots and lots. I mean, why risk paying one percent insurance, another one percent for an illustration in the catalog, ten percent commission? And worry all the time whether your piece is going to make its reserve?" She turned towards him, her head tilting to rest against the wing of the chair. "A cautionary tale. There was one old dowager down in the Wirral, last spring. She took some of the family silver along to a museum and offered it to them as a private treaty sale. They offered her fifteen thousand."

"Not bad."

"Yes, but she thought, reasonably enough, that if it was worth that much, she could probably get a lot more. So she took it down to London. The trouble is, the auctioneers put it in the wrong sale. Guess what it fetched?"

Burchill shrugged.

"Two and a half thousand," said Beattie.

"Christ!"

"Exactly. And that's not the only story. So, if you come across a seller who knows the business, especially one who's got a bit of cash flow problem, there's room for a little maneuvering."

"And you've found one?"

She smiled and sat back in her chair again. "Maybe."

It was Burchill's turn to lean across. "You're not playing hard to get, are you, Isobel?"

She showed no reaction to his use of her Christian name but it annoyed her.

"I phoned around a little after our talk. Apparently, there's a retired lieutenant colonel just outside Elgin who's looking to sell a couple of pieces of jewelry. Nineteenth-century."

"Any good?"

"Ah. That's why I'm 'playing hard to get' as you put it. I haven't had the chance to go up and look at it yet. There are two particular pieces he described which sound interesting. He's asking thirteen thousand for them. Says a dealer friend of his valued them at that. I think I might get them for less, though. It just depends what they're like."

"Well, they're in my ball park," said Burchill, splaying himself back in his chair.

"How much of a hurry are you in?"

They both knew they were now talking around things which were on the fringes of legality and their tone reflected the hesitancy they both felt. For Burchill, money was his whole power base and, because of the indulgences it allowed him, had become fused in his mind with most of his impulses. For Beattie, it was a tool. The commissions she could make from people like him would not be parasitized by accountants. They would allow her to acquire more of the cups and bowls and urns and vases that gave her so much delight. And playing the system against itself was quite fun anyway.

"I don't want to hang about," said Burchill, after a pause for thought.

"Right. I'll arrange to go and see him tomorrow."

"D'you want the cash to take with you?"

74

She shook her head.

"There's still lots of ground to cover before we get that far."

Despite the smudge of superiority in her smile, this time Burchill didn't mind revealing his lack of sophistication. According to him, the antiques business was crawling with homosexuals. Ignorance of its procedures was an affirmation of virility. Names like Meissen, Spode, Chippendale impressed him, but he couldn't tell a chaise lounge from a three-piece suite. This whole process was simply a means to an end. As long as the money got tied up and disappeared from his accounts, he was content.

"Not your line though really, is it?" he said.

"Well, I have certain favorite things. I think I've mentioned them before."

"Yes. Something about anchors, wasn't it? Raised ones? Or were they red? Or gold or something?"

Beattie lifted her glass to him. "Remarkable, Mr. Burchill."

"David."

Her hesitation was minimal. "David."

She took another sip. "Raised and red and gold. Correct on every count."

"You were going to tell me where I could get hold of …"

He was interrupted by the woman, who was back but standing at a distance convenient for discreet hovering, ready to take their orders. Beattie opted for a small portion of the monkfish and Burchill, to see what the fuss was about, did the same. He then looked quickly at the wine list, saw one priced at eighty-five pounds a bottle and pointed to it. The woman looked at the list, then at him, but he'd already turned away and she had no option but to go and fetch the excellent Pommard Le Clos Blanc, a 1985 *premier cru* whose delicacy would be totally overwhelmed by the general robustness of a sauce containing tarragon vinegar and black pepper. In its battle with the flavors of the monkfish, it would probably end up tasting like an eighty-five pound bottle of diesel oil.

Four

As McNeil negotiated the Hazethead roundabout at the western edge of Aberdeen, and began the drive along Queen's Road, Liz pointed to the houses on the left and said, "There. See what I mean? What puts the owners there in a different league? It's obscene."

The houses she was referring to were certainly very impressive. For the most part, they were detached and very large. They were all granite and clearly intended to be more than just places to keep out the cold and rain. The people who'd built them or had them built were fixed firmly in this world. They'd probably dropped significant sums in the collection plate each Sunday, but their real intimations of immortality were expressed by these imposing blocks. The stone was hard, massive, elegant; made to defy the full harshness the northeast could produce but also to lend its permanence to the commercial success of those who quarried and used it, and impress it on those who passed by.

Liz's remark had not come out of the blue. It was merely a footnote to what had been a fairly wide-ranging discussion. It had started some ten miles out of Cairnburgh as they joined the road between Aboyne and Banchory. Before then, various comments had been made but they'd been confined to the front seats and neither Liz nor Jez showed any inclination to open up. But Carston had never been a fan of small talk and he'd turned round, said so and asked, "person to person," as he was careful to put it, how their two passengers could justify squatting. He'd quickly added that his curiosity was born of his own ignorance and inability to come to terms with the ethics of claiming rights over something which belonged to someone else. At first, there was more silence as Jez just gave a laugh and Liz looked at Carston as if she had difficulty

76

believing what he was saying. But his face refused to become that of an enemy. It was slightly tanned and had lots of laughter lines around the eyes. There were gray streaks in the brown hair and gravity was just beginning to pull the cheeks downwards. But Carston was still handsome and, more important to Liz, his expression was open and seemed to express genuine curiosity and an honest expectation of an answer. Most of his dealings with her had been fairly gentle and she realized that her own preconceptions about fascist policemen might be as mistaken as his about squatters.

"Know much about recycling?" she asked.

It was Carston's turn to have to think about answering. The question had thrown him.

"A bit." He thought some more. Liz waited. "Paper, bottles, cans," he went on. "I know they're pretty hot on it in Dundee." Her eyes were hidden behind the tinted glasses. He wished he could see them to get some clue as to what she wanted to hear. "OK," he said at last. "I give up. Why d'you ask?"

"D'you approve?"

"Of course."

"Right. Of course. Taking something somebody else doesn't want and, instead of wasting it, using it."

Carston suddenly saw the point. He wrinkled his nose to signal not disgust but the opinion that her argument seemed specious.

"So that's what squatting is, is it? Recycling houses."

"Got it in one, Chief Inspector."

"But they haven't exactly been discarded, have they?"

"What do you call a house that's empty for months?"

Carston shook his head but didn't get time to reply.

"Nowadays, most of them have been repossessed. Some poor sod's defaulted on the mortgage, so they kick him out on his arse, and the building's not a home anymore, it's just something in a ledger."

"Not your place, though. That belongs to Mr. Burchill," said Carston, feeling as he did so that he wasn't really confronting the issue they'd raised.

Liz looked out at the trees.

"I thought you were interested in ethics," she said.

Carston had wanted to avoid small talk and he wasn't being disappointed. He accepted the invitation to go back to generalities and as he multiplied his questions, looking for the flaws in their stance, Liz and Jez built a case for squatting that, theoretically, began to look more than reasonable. They stressed how careful they were to do nothing that contravened any law. They never broke into a house but looked instead for a window that was already open.

"Surprising how often you find them in places the owners are supposed to be so keen on protecting," said Liz with a lightness that was nonetheless thick with sarcasm.

"And try checking our accounts," said Jez, who'd been enlivened by the topic. "Phone, electricity, gas, water, all paid for."

"We even tart up the bloody places," added Liz. "Friends of mine in Glasgow completely rewired a semi and installed central heating in the bedrooms."

This was a bit too holy for McNeil.

"So you're sort of Samaritans for bricks and mortar, are you?" she said.

Carston was surprised at the depth of scorn she put into her tone. Liz wasn't thrown.

"No. We've just got a different handle on things."

"Like what?"

"Like not getting in cowboy builders who'll rip off us, the VAT man, their suppliers, the guys working for them, and Uncle Tom Cobley and all," said Liz evenly. "You want criminals? That's where to look."

McNeil snorted her scorn again. But Liz was launched.

"Read what they said at the 1992 Earth Summit in Rio. Recycling, saving energy, cutting down on all this bloody consuming we do. It's disgusting."

Her fervor was impressive, but as soon as Carston heard it shaping into a manifesto, his interest flagged a little. He'd heard too many justifications for too many untenable attitudes, political and personal. As Liz offered the eco-logic of self-help techniques as a solution to global problems, she shriveled in his esteem. The intelligent individual he'd been talking to a moment ago had become a mere hippie. In a few short statements of principle, she'd validated all Spurle's synonyms for waster.

He listened still as McNeil took up the challenges and was fascinated by the conviction which fueled both her comments and those of Liz and Jez. There were only a few years between the two women and yet they lived in seemingly alien worlds. McNeil, engaged to an interior decorator with his own business, was sternly ambitious. Marriage and kids didn't yet have a place in her plans; helping people did. That's why Carston had been surprised by the venom in her reactions. She had compassion, understanding, an insight into people, especially women, that gave her work an edge missing from Spurle, Fraser, and the rest. Liz seemed to reject all the values by which McNeil lived and yet she too claimed compassion as her motivation. And, again surprising Carston, in the end, it was she who offered conciliation.

"We'll never talk the same language," she said. "You bought into it, sister. I'm not being snide. I just mean you … I don't know, found a way through. I didn't. I could've warmed my bum on a seat in the bank, joined the Abbey National, things like that. Christ, I almost got engaged to a stockbroker. But it's sick. Pretending things haven't changed, pretending to kids that if they're good boys and girls they'll get all the things Mummy and Daddy have. It's crap. When Mummy and Daddy were kids, there were jobs. Not now."

Her voice was quiet. The strident edge it had had when she was pontificating had gone. The individual had beaten her way back up through the stereotype.

"The papers talk about the lost generation; it's true. Everybody's wanting to make them into clones. But they don't belong. It's not the same place. There's no work and there never will be. That's the truth. You were asking about ethics." Her remarks were now directed at Carston. "The old ones don't fit anymore. Where's the morality in bunches of folk wrapped up in cardboard under a bridge while houses stay empty and get damp because the owners are in one of their other places in Mustique? Why d'you think so many kids take Kurt Cobain's way out?"

Carston had heard the name but couldn't remember its context. And anyway, he wasn't sure how to counter the generalities of what she was saying. The argument wasn't specious anymore, but it wasn't unanswerable either. The problem was that he didn't know what the answer was.

It was shortly after the silence that followed these remarks that Liz quoted the Queen's Road monsters to illustrate her point. Carston looked at the richness of the houses and gardens and noted the types of car that were parked in some of the driveways. There was something in what she said. Some of these cars cost as much as a small flat and were probably a bloody sight more expensive to run. That wasn't the point, though. But then, what was? The silence that persisted in the car all the way to the Queen Street headquarters of the Grampian police seemed to leave Liz and Jez triumphant. Carston determined to be better prepared if the subject came up again.

Inside, he identified himself to the woman working at the front desk and she phoned through to tell someone in CID that he'd arrived. As they waited, a small man in a very dirty raincoat kept insisting to another of the women on duty that she should witness what he was writing.

"Look. Look here. John R. Finnie will pay six pounds a week, starting tomorrow. That's Wednesday. See?"

"Aye. Right y'are, John," said the woman.

He held up a piece of paper. "See that?" He put the paper back on the counter and continued writing. "… will pay six pounds …" He broke off again to look up at the woman. "Ah'm no a criminal, ken? Why'm ah havin' tae …?" Once again he stopped, before turning his attention back to the paper and his biro. "… pay six pounds a week …"

A door to the left opened and a tall, slim man with dark gray hair came out, holding his hand towards Carston.

"Afternoon, Jack."

"Hi Dennis. How's it going?"

Dennis Paskett had been with Grampian CID for many years and had helped Carston a lot in his first months with West Grampian. Not that Carston needed any teaching about the methods and practices of detection, but the transfer to a small force in the northeast when he was only just getting used to the Scottish system meant adjustments and re-education in some basics. Dennis had always been at the end of a phone and had crammed nearly twenty years of experience into a series of quick, accessible lessons. He wasn't exactly a friend; his opinions were a bit too fixed for Carston to feel completely comfortable with him over a jar in the pub, but you were never in any doubt where you stood with him.

Carston introduced McNeil and the others and he led them down to the basement. At the door of the mortuary, he said, "I'll leave you to it, Jack. You won't want me in the way. Give us a shout when you've finished."

Carston nodded and they went into the viewing area. It was a small room with a curtained window in one of its walls.

"I have to remind you," said Carston. "This could cause you some distress. When you're ready, we'll just draw the curtains and I'd just like you, if you can, to identify the person you see. It'll just be his face."

Liz showed no sign of anxiety at the prospect of what was about to happen. Jez was less at ease. His fingers were playing with the hem of the long sweater he was wearing and his eyes were lowered. Carston had a clear impression that he wasn't looking forward to the experience.

"It's very important that you both identify him," said Carston. "One's not enough."

"Shall we get on with it?" said Liz.

"Yes. Right. We're just waiting for the doctor."

The pathologist had supervised the transfer of Floyd's body from the refrigerator in the reception area to the viewing area and had lined up the trolley so that the lacerations caused by the glass were on the side facing away from the curtained window. He pulled down the sheet until only the neck and face were visible and went through to where Carston and his group were waiting.

"All ready," he said and Carston nodded.

The doctor went to the window and drew back the curtain. Carston didn't look through at Floyd but kept his eyes firmly on Liz and Jez. He'd been at far too many gatherings of this sort but recognized that they sometimes caused reactions that made the process of detection much easier. Guilt took lots of forms, and often this confrontation with the fact of the death triggered responses that were equivocal, and sometimes as good as a confession. On this occasion, he had no reason to be looking for guilt, but his mind was open.

In Liz's face he saw no perceptible change whatsoever. She looked long and straight at the pale profile on the trolley. It was strange. She'd been living in the same house as Donnelly, his corpse couldn't simply be an inert phenomenon. It must surely have caused some sort of shock. And yet nothing showed. She was still staring at the body when she said, in a voice scoured of expression, "That's Floyd." Carston waited.

"Mr. …?" he said at last, irritated with himself for still not having found out their names.

Jez had hardly been able to bring himself to look. When the curtain went back, he kept his eyes down. They traveled back and forth over the base of the wall and the tiled floor. Carston's question forced him to look up. His eyes flicked to Floyd's face and immediately widened and were briefly held there. After about four seconds, he nodded and said, "Aye. It's Floyd." Carston noticed that the fingers picked even more nervously at his sweater and that the crack in the voice showed that he didn't have Liz's control. He nodded again at the doctor, who pulled the curtain back in place.

As they went back upstairs to deal with the other formalities, Carston continued to let Liz and Jez think about what they'd seen. Jez was silent but, as soon as they were back on the ground floor, Liz said to McNeil, "I thought people always got offered cups of tea and stuff in police stations."

McNeil looked at Carston.

"Yes, good idea," he said. "DC McNeil'll get that organized for you. I've just got to nip over to Nelson Street labs to see whether they've got anything for me. I won't be more than an hour. That OK?"

"I'll need a doughnut, too, then," said Liz. There was no smile as she said it and Carston felt that, somehow, she was seeking to disrupt his observations. He expected anything from breakdown to indifference, but when people who'd just identified a body made jokes, they were usually accompanied by other signs of betrayal like laughter or nervous tics around the mouth. Liz continued to seem completely unmoved by the experience, indifferent to the extreme she'd just touched.

At the counter, the same individual in the dirty mac was still in conversation with the exasperated receptionist. "Ah was born in 1938. Now, you tak' that away from 1995 an ye'll ken how auld ah am, see?"

"All yours, McNeil," said Carston. He looked at his watch. "I'll take the car. See you back here about two-thirty."

That gave him just over an hour to pick up whatever early crumbs of assistance were going at the forensic labs where everything had been sent. All the items that were collected at the locus or taken off the victim (and the suspect, if you were lucky) were known collectively as productions. Today, though, Carston didn't hold out much hope of success. The place where Floyd had been dumped was usually cluttered with dustbins, so they were likely to find anything and everything in and on his clothes. The chance of some distinguishing element leaping out as specific to victim, perpetrator, or the place where he'd been killed was remote. Before leaving, he went back down to the mortuary and into the reception area where Floyd's body was just being wheeled back in.

He knew that Brian McIntosh had been and gone and that the preliminary autopsy had been done.

"Anything, doc?" he asked the pathologist.

The doctor spread his hands. "Nothing special yet. He was covered in all sorts of garbage, as you can imagine."

Carston nodded.

"Cause of death was just one blow to the side of his head. There's a pretty severe laceration there. Bit of patterning, too. That might be useful."

"Why?"

"Well, don't get excited, it's not much, but there's a sort of cross-hatching at the edges of the split. I'll let you have a photo of it before you go. Could have come from whatever he was hit with. It's not very clear, though."

"Could it have been a baseball bat?" asked Carston, suddenly remembering the markings that had been left on the broken loud-speaker in Forbeshill Road.

The doctor shook his head at once.

"No. Something with a square edge. An ornament maybe, base of a lamp, leg of a chair, I don't know. Something like that anyway. It's a clean cut. The scalp's split. There's a crushing at the edges and hairs are bent into the wound."

"And he was hit just the once?"

"Yep, just the once. Well, apart from contusions on his hip and some other bruising on his face, but they were done earlier, a few hours before he was killed. The head wound's a relatively mild impact injury, but the fractures radiating from the point of contact have burst blood vessels over a pretty wide area. That's what did the damage."

"What about the glass stuck into his face?"

"Couldn't tell you what that's all about. Inflicted post mortem, but you knew that. Couple of hours after he died, at least. There's plenty of glass all over him. We've sent some samples over to Nelson Street, just in case."

"OK, doc, thanks. I'm on my way over there now."

"Don't expect miracles, Chief Inspector. We'd probably find glass all over you if we looked. It's surprisingly common. Anyway the lab haven't had any of it long. I shouldn't think they've done anything yet."

"I know," said Carston. "But I'm an optimist."

"Big mistake," said the doctor with a smile. "I'll leave the photo at reception for you."

"Thanks. Bye."

He drove out of the car park, up Queen Street, and turned right along the front of Marischal College. Once again, the power of granite struck him. The great slab of the facade reared up to dominate Broad Street. Rows of high, vertical windows splashed regular patches of reflected sky along its front and, at the top, absurd, exuberant crenellations stretched upwards. This was Victorian money talking, another reminder that this merchant city had been proud of itself for a long time and wasn't afraid to show it.

As he drove the short distance to Nelson Street, he thought about what he'd said to the pathologist. It was true, he was an optimist. The things people did depressed him if he allowed them to and he was cynical about the perfectibility of human beings, but he had always enjoyed life and there were always enough examples of resilience to reassure him. The doctor's news about how Donnelly had been killed was also interesting. If it was just the one blow, and not a very heavy one at that, it perhaps wasn't a cut-and-dried case of him having a fight with the thugs who'd visited the squat. Surely they'd've done a bit more damage. And anyway, it was hard to see why, as if it were an afterthought, they'd given him a pint glass as a facial ornament. Carston smiled at his own cussedness. He was actually feeling a little glow of pleasure at the thought that the crime might offer some resistance to quick solutions. Not many of his colleagues shared his preference. Superintendent Ridley, for example, would be appalled. He like straightforward "black ink crimes." These were crimes that got reported and, because that put them on record, they got more resources allocated to them. If you solved them, it showed up in the statistics and made detection rates look good. Ridley would actually prefer it if difficult or unusual criminal events went unnoticed. Rapes, muggings, and the variegated forms of assault practiced by Cairnburghers on one another were much more numerous than the charge sheets suggested but, as long as no one said anything about them, Ridley could balance his books and the clear-up rate looked terrific.

At Mounthooly roundabout, a couple of women students ran across in front of his car. He wagged a finger at them as they looked back at him, knowing he'd had to brake. One of them, a redhead, blew him a kiss and followed it with a huge, happy smile. He felt the usual nudge of hopeless lust and wished that Kath were back from Inverness. He had no idea how much longer she was planning to be there, but it disturbed him that his body was now beginning to miss her as much as he was. Once again, he felt the need for this day to be over and for him to be talking to her on the phone.

Before he'd left Macy's, Ross had rung the hospital. As Neil and Big Tam had spoken in such matter-of-fact tones about dispensing and defusing violence, the image of Hilden's bandaged face had come into his head more than once. He still felt responsible for the man's condition and needed to talk to him as much for his own good as for Hilden's. The accident and emergencies secretary told him that Hilden had already gone home. There were no complications with any of his injuries and no need for observation of any sort, so they'd been glad to shuffle him off to make space for the next in line.

Ross drove to the station, picked up the photographs of Simpson and Mitchell, and went straight to Hilden's shop. He felt as if he'd already had a long day, and the yawns were beginning to build up again. He allowed himself to think briefly of getting home for the evening, reading Kirsty her story, and dozing in front of the telly. He switched off the cosy images before they progressed to the midnight shift with Mhairi and Mozart.

Not unnaturally, the shop was closed and he had to wait several minutes before Hilden, his face still almost obscured by bandages, came down to let him in. Right away, Ross saw the evidence of the previous night's visit. The corridor, which was narrow enough to begin with, had been reduced to a single swathe about two feet wide which had been swept between heaps of broken ornaments, torn papers, and splintered pieces of furniture. None of the objects had been spared. The attacker had reduced everything to rubble, spelling out his message with cruel efficiency. Hilden had cleaned up and simply stacked the pieces on either side of the passageway.

Ross saw that Hilden was looking at him, waiting for a reaction. There was no point in trying to hide his first impulse.

"This is obviously where it happened."

Hilden looked around and nodded.

"I wish you hadn't cleaned up."

"It was a shambles," Hilden mumbled.

"Aye, but there may have been things that could've helped us put away the guy responsible."

Hilden was strangely still for a moment, then he lifted his hand and pointed at an old sword lying on top of one of the piles. Ross looked at it, then back at Hilden, waiting.

"He used that," said Hilden at last, his voice tiny, almost apologetic.

"In the assault?" asked Ross, after a pause. "He hit you with that?"

Hilden nodded. Ross bent to look more closely at the weapon.

86

The guard around the hilt was broken but still fairly ornate. The blade had no edge and was more like a square steel rod. On it, there were clear signs of dried blood.

"D'you mind if I take it away with me?"

Hilden was still nodding.

"You do mind?"

The nod changed to a shake.

"We'll see if we can get any prints from it. Did you notice whether he was wearing gloves?"

"No. I couldn't say. It was …"

He stopped and, once again, Ross was aware of the pity he provoked. The thought of this feeble, harmless individual being beaten with a sword was depressing; it added a personal dimension to his professional desire to catch the perpetrator. He noticed Hilden shift uncomfortably and was suddenly aware that he'd been staring at him.

"Sorry," he said. "I was just … er. Shall we go through to the shop?"

Gratefully, Hilden turned and went inside. As Ross followed him, he felt slightly better when he saw that, as far as he could tell, nothing much there had changed. The visitor had made his point in the corridor and by the beating he'd given Hilden and, since destroying all his stock would put him out of business and therefore make protection superfluous, he'd left what were presumably the most saleable of his items intact. It was, very obviously, a clear unambiguous warning.

"How are you?" asked Ross, his guilt still prodding at him.

"Oh fine. Peak condition," said Hilden.

Ross rode the sarcasm.

"Did he come in here at all?"

Hilden shook his head. His hand went up to touch the bandage and unconsciously sketched the gesture of arranging the unseen strands of hair over his skull.

"No."

"Any idea how much damage he's done?"

Another shake of the head. "Couple of thousand maybe."

"Still, the insurance'll cover it, won't it?"

Immediately, Ross knew that again he'd said the wrong thing. Hilden's face turned to look at a couple of inkwells on a shelf beside him. He was very still.

"Mr. Hilden? ... You are insured, aren't you?"

The shake of Hilden's head was almost imperceptible.

"Why not?"

Hilden turned to him. "Oh sergeant, really. You don't belong to this world, do you? Look at this. I told you it's hardly worth anything. It's no goldmine. Sometimes things get a bit hard and ... well, insurance premiums come a bit low on the list of priorities."

"But all the same ..."

"I know. It's a false economy. But what can I do?"

Again, Ross pitied the man. He lived his quiet lonely life among relics; not the glorious relics of Fabergé, Delft, or Robert Adam, but the clay, wood, and plastic of domestic ephemera. He was right; it was a world Ross didn't understand. A yawn began deep in his chest. To mask it, he took out the two photographs he'd brought.

"You said the man came just after ten, didn't you?"

"Something like that. I can't be exact about it." Hilden had become wary again.

"I'd like you to look at these."

Hilden reached out and took the photos. Ross lost his fight against the yawn and apologized for the long sigh it produced. Hilden was looking at the two faces. The stillness continued. Ross was certain that he recognized the men.

"Why did you bring these particular photos?" asked Hilden.

"D'you recognize them, then?"

The answer came quickly. "No. But why these? Did you have these people in mind when we were talking yesterday?"

Ross was interested. Something was going on here. "Does that mean they're the ones who came to see you before?"

No response.

"Mr. Hilden, was it one of these who did it?"

Hilden's tone was surprisingly firm. "Why these?"

Ross gave in. "We had a complaint about another assault yesterday. We think these men may have something to do with it."

"Have you arrested them?"

"Not yet. It may not be a question of arresting them. But we certainly do want to talk to them."

Hilden became silent again as he continued to study the photographs. At last, he handed them back to Ross.

"Well? Do you recognize them?"

Hilden's hand was once more caressing his bandaged scalp. He shook his head.

Ross couldn't fathom Hilden's reactions. He was positive that he'd recognized one or both of the men. Surely there should be some satisfaction that his tormentors could be identified and picked up, that the threat would probably be lifted, or at least that the police would know the people he'd need protecting from. But looking at the photos seemed only to have pushed him deeper inside his gloom.

"Look, if we do find the men who did this, would you be prepared to identify them if we organized a parade?" asked Ross.

Hilden didn't move. His eyes were fixed on his hands, which were back in his lap, folded, unmoving.

"Mr. Hilden."

"I told them," said Hilden.

"Sorry?"

"I told them. On the phone. After you'd been. I thought about it and told them."

Ross was instantly alert. The yawns retreated far away.

"I'm sorry. You phoned somebody? Told somebody?"

Hilden lifted his head and gave a slight nod. His gaze dropped back to his hands.

"Who? Who did you phone?"

No reaction at first, then an almost tearful admission. "The ones who threatened me."

"You phoned them? What for?"

A tremble had started in Hilden's hands.

"I … I told them I'd seen you."

"What?"

The words began to come more quickly. "I thought it'd frighten them off. If they knew I'd told you about them, they'd keep away. They wouldn't risk it. I don't know. I didn't know what to do. I was … afraid. I wanted them to know you knew."

He stopped. Ross hadn't absorbed the information sufficiently to reply immediately. It was too bizarre. Hilden's head turned slowly. He looked straight at Ross.

"I told them you were giving me protection."

Ross's tone was gentle when he eventually replied. "But why? They said they'd hurt you if you told us. You knew that. Why go and tell them?"

"I thought it would be better. I thought if they knew you were here, they'd … they'd keep away. I … I obviously thought wrong, didn't I?"

"Well, it does look like it, doesn't it?" Ross tried to keep his words reasonable. "It was a bit of a strange thing to do. Almost as if you were … well, boasting to them."

"God, no. I certainly wasn't doing that. I was just … Well, I wasn't thinking straight. I'm sorry."

"Did you really think they wouldn't come?"

"Yes, I did. I really thought that. I thought that they might not want to risk coming if the police were there."

Ross still couldn't really cope with the information. He'd need the leisure to think about it and talk with Carston. He'd have some fancy theories which would probably turn out to be crap, but at least it would give Ross a context for his own speculations. He took out a notebook.

"I suppose we'd better get all the details and then we'll see where we go next."

Hilden pointed at the ceiling. "Would you like to come upstairs? It's not wonderful but it's a bit more comfortable than here."

Ross noticed that his eyes had filled with tears. It embarrassed him.

"Fine. Whatever you like," he said, trying to pretend that he hadn't noticed.

"We could maybe have a cup of tea."

"Not for me, thanks, but you go ahead. We can chat while you're making it."

Hilden brushed at his eyes, smiled, and led the way out of the shop, past the piles of broken ornaments and up a dark staircase with brown walls and what had once been a blue carpet. Ross followed, notebook ready. All he wanted now was to get the whole interview over. The dreariness and the pathos of this man were getting to him; he needed to get outside into the cold shining air and stretch into a long, satisfying yawn.

The whole team was back in the incident room by five-thirty. Although they were technically not much farther ahead than they'd been at the morning's briefing, there was an unspoken feeling that they'd all made some progress. Simpson and Mitchell had been identified and, although nothing as yet tied them to Donnelly, the fact that positive leads had been turned up less than twenty-four hours after the killing was cause for some quiet self-congratulation. Carston listened as each of the squad in turn gave details of what their particular day had produced.

Much of what they had to say simply served to close off some lines of inquiry. Fraser, for example, had checked the people who'd been arrested at Macy's very thoroughly. Only two of them had previous records and neither of those could be linked even tenuously with Donnelly. Bellman and Thom had been to Asda to talk to the two women who worked at the club and then to the student flats in Treadle Street to see the barman and the other two bouncers. None of them had anything useful to say about the fight. When Ross added the information he'd got from Neil, Big Tam, and the others, it all seemed to converge in the conclusion that there was no connection between the fight and Donnelly's murder.

"But," said Carston, when that opinion was eventually articulated, "we still don't rule it out. There may still be something we haven't come across yet. Put it on the back burner, but don't forget it altogether."

He went on to tell them about his conversation with the pathologist and the forensic scientists at the lab. As the doctor had suggested, there was little that the lab could tell him, as they hadn't had time to get very far with their searches and analyses. While he'd been there, they'd done nothing but confirm that there were traces of just about everything on Donnelly's clothes, mainly on the back where he'd been lying among the rubbish, and that they were interested in the plentiful glass fragments.

"Why? What's special about them?" asked Fraser.

"Size," said Carston. "Apparently, we've all got bits of glass in our clothes, but the odds against any of them weighing more than a milligram are pretty long."

"So?"

"So, if there are lots of them that are bigger, it's unusual. Could be significant."

"It's obvious that it's significant, isn't it?" said Spurle. "He had a pint glass stickin' out of his face."

"It might be more than that," said Carston. "We'll just have to wait for their report. They reckoned another couple of days."

He took a photograph from an envelope he was holding. "Another interesting thing," he went on. "I'll stick this on the board. It's the wound that killed Donnelly. Interesting markings along the edges. If we can match them up, we've got the weapon."

"Simple as that, eh sir?" said Fraser.

"Yes, apparently. According to the pathologist ..." He paused to unfold a note which had been attached to the photograph and read from it, "it's an 'impact abrasion with no relative movement' ... er ... 'Loose underlying connective tissue' ... um ... 'differential movement of the skin at the edges of the instrument.'" He stopped and held the note for them to see, shrugging away his instinctive irritation at the terminology.

"Aye, that simple," Fraser repeated, totally baffled.

"What it boils down to is that we've got a sort of negative image of the thing they hit him with," said Ross.

"Right," said Carston, folding his notebook to a fresh page. "Now then, what about Mitchell and Simpson?"

"Haven't been able to find them yet," said Spurle. "Me an' Fraser went round soon as we'd took they squatters home."

"And?"

"There was nobody in at Mitchell's place and Simpson's missis thinks he's maybe at the football. But she's nae sure."

"What football? Where?"

"She doesna ken. The Dons is playin' Motherwell or one of they other Glasgow teams today. She thinks he maybe went down there wi' Benny Mitchell."

"Might be worth asking Strathclyde to pick him up for us," suggested Ross.

"She's nae even sure he's there, though, sarge," said Fraser.

"No," said Carston. "Strathclyde have got enough on without having to put men out looking through a football crowd for people who may not even be there. Let's wait till they get back."

"It's taking a chance, sir," said Ross.

"What choice have we got?" said Carston. "We don't have the people to sit around at their place waiting for them to arrive." He turned to Spurle. "What did you tell his wife?"

"Just that we was wantin' to speak to him, that's all."

"And to tell him to get in touch when he got back," added Fraser.

"OK. Let's hope she does. What about last night? Did you ask her about that? Where he was?"

"Aye," said Fraser. "She doesna ken. He wasna back afore she went to bed. That was after midnight."

"Aye, then this morning," Spurle went on, "he got a phone call early and went out. He hasna been back since."

"Right, he's the one we're looking for," said Carston. "Now, anybody dig up anything on the squatters?"

"Yes, sir," said Bellman. He, in turn, flicked open his notebook. "Four o' them have been in trouble before."

Carston looked at Ross and raised his eyebrows; suddenly, all sorts of things seemed to be opening up.

"Elizabeth Munro. Nearly two years ago. Fined for shoplifting. And Dawn Rennie, Jeremy Brown, and William Campbell were picked up demonstrating outside the Shell building in Aberdeen in October last year."

"Another peaceful protest?" said Fraser.

"Aye," said Spurle. "One o' the Grampian boys had to have sixteen stitches in his head."

"Anything about violence in their charges?" Carston asked Bellman.

The constable shook his head. "No, sir. Just demonstratin'."

"OK." Carston turned to Ross. "How about you, Jim?"

Ross had been the last to arrive at the briefing and hadn't therefore had time to bring Carston up to date on his talk with Hilden.

"I think our man was quite busy last night," he said.

"Oh?" said Carston.

"Aye. I've been to see Hilden. Took the photos with me. He wouldn't ID Simpson, but I'm bloody sure he recognized the photos. I'll bet it was them who turned his place over."

"Is that a guess?"

"Maybe. But I've brought a sword back with me. The guy used it on Hilden. It's maybe got his prints on it."

There was a buzz around the room. Carston felt a pulse of excitement, too.

"A sword? Bit drastic, isn't it?"

"He didn't stab him. Used it more to sort of whip him. It's got no blade to speak of."

"Just as well," said Carston. "Anything else?"

"Not really. But it's Simpson and Mitchell's M.O., isn't it? And his shop's no far from the squat. I wondered whether they were maybe working a beat there. If it was Simpson, he was at the shop around ten or a bit later. By the time he'd finished with Hilden, he might have been ready for some more action. Wouldn't take him long to get to Forbeshill."

"We don't know where Donnelly was murdered yet."

"I know," said Ross, "but it'll help if we can show that Simpson was near where he lived."

Carston nodded.

"And around the right sort of time, too," he said. "Good, Jim. Well done. The sooner we have a chat with these two, the better. Fraser, Spurle, get over to Simpson's place first thing in the morning."

The expressions on the two men's faces showed what they thought of that.

"First thing," insisted Carston. He turned to Bellman and Thom. "And you two, same thing. Mitchell's place. Bring 'em straight back in when you've got 'em. I'll be here."

If he was having to get up, too, there was no argument. Not that they'd have dared try one.

"Now, what else have we got?" he went on. "What came up at Donnelly's, McNeil?"

"Nothing much, sir. There was one thing, though. He'd been nicking gear."

When they'd driven Liz and Jez back to the squat, a team was already there looking through Floyd's room. Carston had left McNeil with them so that she could report anything they came across directly back to him.

"What sort of gear?"

"Nobody seems to know. At least, they don't know where it's from. It's just bits and pieces he's nicked. There's things he's taken from the house, too."

"Like what?"

"There was a canteen of cutlery in his cupboard. No cutlery, though, just the box."

"How did they know it was from the house?"

"The girl Liz said she thought it was. There was dust all over it too, like it had been stored somewhere."

"Nicking stuff, eh? I thought they didn't do anything illegal."

"They don't. This was Donnelly."

"Did you check the attic?"

"Aye. No sign of any cutlery there, and things had been shifted about, disturbed. I'd guess Donnelly's been up there a few times."

"Anybody told Burchill about it yet?"

McNeil smiled. It lifted her mouth more at one side than the other. "No, sir. I thought that might be better comin' from yourself."

"Why?"

"You're a man, sir. And a chief inspector."

Carston couldn't help smiling with her.

"You're getting as bad as these buggers," he said.

"Excuse me, sir. I'd rather you didna swear in front of a lady," said Fraser.

"Eff you," said Carston. He looked at McNeil again. "OK. I'll give him a ring. Did the squatters have anything to say about Donnelly nicking stuff from the house?"

She shook her head.

"Not much. The girl Liz said it was just another way of recycling."

"Huh! That's her bloody answer for everything. So much for keeping the right side of the law, eh?"

He looked at the notes in front of him, then round the room. "OK. Anything else?"

95

Heads shook.

"Right. Have a wonderful evening. But make sure you're up early in the morning."

As the others began shuffling papers and getting ready to go, Ross followed Carston through to his office. Without a word, he folded a paper filter into the holder on the coffee machine and started spooning coffee grounds into it. When he'd poured in the water, he sat heavily in the chair beside the desk. Carston looked up from the notes he was still checking through.

"Tired, Jim?"

Ross nodded and rubbed his eyes.

"Fancy a pint instead of that stuff?" said Carston.

Ross thought, then suddenly heaved himself up again.

"Aye. Good idea. Then I'll away home."

He switched off the coffee and went to grab his coat from the door of the incident room. Carston put the notes into the shiny black leather briefcase which Kath had given him for his birthday and which he hated. Less than ten minutes later, they were sitting at a table in the pub down the road.

"You been watching Perry Mason re-runs?" asked Carston when they'd taken their first cold mouthful of lager.

"Why?"

"Your little bombshell about Hilden and the sword. Very impressive."

"Thought you'd like it. I saved the best, though."

As Carston listened in growing bewilderment, Ross told him about Hilden's confession that he'd brought the damage on himself by the phone call he'd made.

"Bloody hell," said Carston. "What was he thinking about?"

"I don't think he was. He's shit scared of them. Even when I was there the first time he didn't know where he was, what to say. He just wanted it all to go away."

"Hardly the way to go about it, ringing a mugger to tell him you've shopped him."

"Why do you think he did it? You're the psychology freak," said Ross.

Carston thought for a moment. "I don't know. What are the

96

options? First, panic. Maybe he's afraid they've seen you in his shop and he wants to preempt them, wants to brazen it out."

Ross made no response. He lifted his glass and drank again, shivering at the chill along his throat.

"Or else, like he said, he hoped it'd keep them off him."

Ross nodded and waited. Carston thought some more.

"Maybe he didn't phone to tell them he'd spoken to you. Maybe he phoned to try to come to some arrangement about paying them or maybe he tried to get them to back off."

"What, and they said no and he just …"

"Well, yes. Maybe just blurted it out. Panic again."

"Maybe."

"But beyond that, I can't for the life of me think why else he'd do such a bloody silly thing. Then again, why tell you about it?"

"Aye. I wondered about that, too. Makes no difference to the way we'll handle things. Just makes him look a bigger bloody fool."

Carston clicked his fingers.

"Maybe that's it. D'you suppose he was just wanting you to feel sorrier for him?"

Ross gave a humorless little laugh.

"He'd have a job. He's a pathetic enough wee bugger as it is."

"Well, maybe that's it. Makes himself vulnerable and hopes that'll make us look after him a bit better."

Ross's head was shaking slowly. The image of Hilden came into his mind. "You havena seen him yet, have you?"

"No."

"He doesna have to make himself vulnerable. He already is. And it's no act."

They talked around the problem a bit more but nothing came up to persuade Carston that it was anything other than what Hilden himself had said. He'd simply been trying to scare Simpson off and it had backfired. But it was an intriguing little alleyway off their main concern and Carston knew he'd come back to it again.

"What d'you suppose they're on about up at the lab?" asked Ross.

"What d'you mean?"

"This fascination with glass."

"Oh yes. Dunno. There was plenty of it about apparently."

"Aye. Like Spurle said, no great surprise if he's had a pint mug shoved into his features."

"That's what I thought, but you know what they're like. Easily excited."

"And how were our wee trespassers when they saw their pal on the trolley?"

This was another area that Carston wanted to think about.

"Interesting," he said. "The girl, Liz she's called, the one who seems to be the boss—"

"No good telling me that. I've never met 'em."

"No, well ... Amazing. She didn't bat an eye. Cold as you like. On the surface anyway."

"They are sometimes."

Carston shook his head.

"No. Colder than that. No reaction at all. Either she's a complete weirdo or she can just switch herself off. I mean, this was a guy who'd been living in the same place as her and ... just nothing."

"How about the other one?"

"He didn't like it. Scared, I'd say."

"Of what?"

"Hard to say. The whole idea. Dead bodies, murder, violence, I don't know. He had a job to cope with it. He was very quiet the rest of the afternoon."

Ross nodded and the two of them drank again and looked around the bar.

"Could they have had something to do with it?" asked Ross at last.

"Who? The squatters? Well, yeah, they could. What makes you ask?"

"Don't know really. My money's on Mitchell and Simpson, but I can't figure why they have to take him to Macy's and stick a glass in him."

"Why would anybody?"

"Unless they're weird. And you reckon your squatters are." Carston sucked in a breath, held it a moment, then let it out as he shook his head.

"Trouble is, I was with them around the time Brian McIntosh said Donnelly must have been killed. Well, three of them anyway. And it's hard to see any motive other than the obvious one. Violence, plain and simple. I mean, nobody there liked him, but there was no suggestion they felt strongly enough to want to get rid of him."

"So what did they say about him?"

"From what I could make out, Donnelly was a complete outsider at their place. Had nothing to do with the rest of them, nothing in common with them. None of them ever went out with him. None of them knew where he went. Liz admitted that she thought he was a 'complete wee shit,' but otherwise he was nothing to them." He took another swig. "One funny thing, though."

"What?"

"The two who weren't there when Spurle and I went last night, I asked about them. Seems they were at Macy's."

"Eh?"

"Yes. The Liz woman told me."

"What did they say about it?"

"Don't know. I haven't talked to them yet. I'll leave it till tomorrow. Or maybe go round there tonight."

Ross looked at him.

"Kath still away, is she?"

Carston nodded. With the evening stretching ahead, he preferred not to think about Kath. On the one hand, he was eager for her phone call; on the other, he didn't much fancy the gaps on either side of it.

"You could come over to our place."

It was an unusual offer. Carston and Ross tended to stay well apart when they were away from work. Kath was quite friendly with Jean, but their socializing was confined to the daytime. Carston wondered whether the fact that he was missing Kath was beginning to show.

"Thanks, Jim, but I couldn't do that. There's a row of polythene boxes in my freezer with meals and days scribbled on them. Lunch, Monday. Dinner, Monday. Things like that. If I didn't eat them in the order instructed, I'd probably be severely punished."

He wasn't entirely joking. Before her infrequent trips away, Kath always spent a day organising the meals he'd have in her absence. She bought in some Marks and Spencer's ready-to-cook packs, cooked and froze her own sauces for pasta, and left detailed notes on defrosting, cooking, days, and times. As long as Carston could read, he wouldn't starve.

They talked around the case a little more, agreeing that, in a very short time, they'd done pretty well. As they finished their drinks and got up to leave, Carston noticed Ross stifling yet another yawn and said, "I don't see any need for you to come in in the morning."

"But we're bringing Mitchell and Simpson in."

"Yes, but that won't be till later and we'll have to go through a few of the formalities first. Stay with Jean. I'll give you a shout if I need you."

"OK. I'll probably look in in the afternoon anyway."

"Might see you then."

Outside, they went their separate ways, Ross to spaghetti bolognaise, *Fungus the Bogeyman*, and, later, peripatetic Mozart, Carston to a polythene tray wrapped in cling film and labeled, "Dinner. Saturday."

Five

It was nine o'clock and, when the phone rang, Carston had just poured another glass of Cahors. It was his fourth. The other three had washed down the leek and Roquefort bake he'd found, appropriately labeled, in the freezer.

"Carston here."

"Mrs. Carston here."

"Hullo, love. How are you?"

"Fine. How about you?"

He resisted the first impulse, which was to tell her he was cracking up and wouldn't get better until she was back.

"Great. So, what have you been up to?"

Kath immediately launched on a detailed description of the people and things she'd encountered in the twenty-four hours since her last call. Each day seemed to have brought fresh interest. The course had been very successful and her portfolio had just about doubled in size. She'd learned new darkroom techniques for processes like solarization, posterization, and bas-relief, and her subject range had begun to take in macro studies as well as her preferred portraits and landscapes. As he listened to her enthusing about a tutor called Philip something, a very small but nonetheless noticeable resentment began to grumble inside him, fueled by the wine.

"Glad you're having such a wonderful time," he said.

There was a short silence. Kath had picked up his tone.

"Are you drinking, Jack?"

"Not to excess."

"Are you jealous, then?"

"Should I be?"

Kath laughed. "You have been drinking. Well, I'm very flattered."

Carston's resentment evolved to a tiny flush of annoyance.

"Why?" he asked.

"Because, whatever you say, you are jealous. And as soon as I'm away, you have to dive into a bottle."

Carston recognized the tone, heard the laughter in her voice, and knew the teasing was affectionate.

"That's ridiculous," he said. "I've only had two or three."

"Glasses?"

"Bottles."

Kath laughed and talked some more about the projects she'd been working on, including an idyllic trip to the west coast to take moody black-and-white shots of the hills and sea lochs of Wester Ross.

"We must go there, Jack," she said. "It's beautiful. The most beautiful place I've ever seen."

"Better than Deeside?"

"Better than everywhere."

The thought that she wanted him to share the pleasures she was having was warm and reassuring. He felt guilty about the childish spat of annoyance he'd felt earlier.

"I miss you," he said, simply.

"Yes, I know. Well, can you wait another … sixteen hours?"

"What?"

"My train gets back to Aberdeen four o'clock tomorrow afternoon. Can you meet me?"

Carston felt ridiculously pleased.

"Of course," he said. "Why didn't you say so before?"

"You didn't ask."

"Know what you are?"

"What?"

"A thrawn besom."

"A what?"

"A thrawn besom."

"What's that?"

"Dunno. Apparently, it's what Fraser called his wife when she said she didn't want to go to the Christmas dance this year."

They were into the normal lightness of contact which both found

102

so reassuring. It was silly, often childish, but it traced comforting patterns of intimacy over the cold, selfish events which made up so much of Carston's work. He listened now with interest and pleasure as Kath told him more about the people she'd met on her course, including a retired university professor from Aberdeen who related everything they did to a medieval French cleric.

"Did they have cameras in France then?" asked Carston.

"Well, he doesn't go that far, but he seems to think that this bloke would've invented them if he'd had time."

He laughed and listened on as she described a woman whose wardrobe looked as if it had been gathered from things that Oxfam had rejected but whose pictures were stunning, a couple who spoke of nothing but their grandson, and a young student from Manchester who never spoke at all. In turn, he told her about Floyd Donnelly, the squatters, and his own uncertainty about the rights and wrongs of their case. He asked her who Kurt Cobain was and was pleased when she didn't know either. Then, as he recounted the conversation he'd had with Liz, he was surprised to hear her voice reactions which echoed his own. Usually, she was quick to outline the liberal standpoint on everything, but this time even she admitted to some ambivalence. Clearly it was a question that had no easy answers.

They talked on, about things of no consequence whatsoever, about food and weather and acquaintances in Cairnburgh. Eventually, towards the end of their chat, when questions of ethics had been comprehensively displaced by what Kath was calling "arthritic eroticism," she suggested that they should say goodnight before his blood pressure reached critical levels. Reluctantly, he agreed and, after a final, relatively restrained paragraph of endearments, he put the phone down, poured a fifth glass of wine, and turned on the television, the demands of Donnelly and the rest all but forgotten.

In death, Floyd was managing to be even more disruptive than he'd been in life. The upheaval which the past thirty-six hours had brought to the squatters had shaken them all very severely. Visits to and from the police had altered their profile and redefined their relation to the town they were living in in a way that none of them welcomed. As usual, the fragmentation was at its most obvious when Liz was absent. Late on Saturday evening, only Dawn and Jez were in. Since returning from Aberdeen, Jez had said very little. The sight of Floyd's bloodless face had stayed in his mind. He'd only taken the briefest of looks when Carston asked him to confirm Liz's identification, but the image had registered like a snapshot and kept returning despite his attempts to erase it. Dawn was telling him about her identification of Simpson and Mitchell.

"They want us to pick them out from an identity parade when they get them."

Jez made no sign that he'd heard. Dawn was used to his moroseness. It was a recurrent state, but usually he eased out of it after a while; its persistence this evening was irritating. She tried again.

"D'you know what? The guy at the station, the policeman? When he heard I'd done languages, he wanted to speak French all the time. Can you believe that? A Cairnburgh bobby?"

Jez looked at her, a dark, unfathomable stare.

"I s'pose you liked that."

"What d'you mean?"

Jez turned away again.

"Come on. What?" Dawn insisted.

His gaze came back to her, held her eyes as if he were inspecting her.

"Speaking French. Reminiscing about the good old days."

"Oh, not that shite again," said Dawn. She got up and went through to the kitchen to get a beer from the fridge.

She'd once told him about a boyfriend she'd had for just a few weeks while she was in Rennes. He'd seemed to take the news as nonchalantly as she'd offered it, which had led her to tell him of other little encounters she'd had. To her, they were of no consequence, but in Jez they settled and grew until, at last, he'd invented a whole French past for her, in which she was straddled and ridden by a succession of men, young boys, and, for all he knew, women. Each time the subject came up, it unleashed dark discomforts in him. As on all the previous occasions, he sank deep into a familiar cavern of silence. The unspoken intention was to make it clear to Dawn that he was hurt; the actual effect was to exasperate her so much that she neither could nor wanted to offer him the reassurance he needed. While she drank her beer and flicked angrily through a magazine, he sat still and lost in his mind's shadows, feeling acres of space between them.

The silence lasted until just after nine, when Will got back with Fran. As they came through to the front room, neither of them remarked on the deafening stillness, partly because the mood was a familiar one with Dawn and Jez and partly because they had their own concerns. Fran had gone for a walk in the park that afternoon and, when she hadn't got back by eight-thirty, Will had gone looking for her. He'd found her huddled in the dark by the small fountain near the bare twigs of the rose garden. She was sitting on the edge, looking at the faintly gleaming water, and had only noticed him when he touched her on the shoulder. When he'd asked her what was wrong, she'd just shaken her head slowly, got up, and started walking with him back to the house.

"Anybody want tea or coffee?" asked Will.

Jez shook his head, Dawn lifted her beer can to indicate that she was taken care of and Fran gave him a little nod of her head before walking to the window and looking out at the darkness. She saw herself as a black silhouette picked out by a rim of light from the room. By turning her head slightly, she brought detail into the planes of her left cheek, her lips, and the edge of her nose. She looked at the shapes in the glass and felt detached from them, as if the reflection were nothing to do with her, as if it had been etched onto a photographic plate and hung outside in the night. She turned into the room and went to sit on the floor with her back resting against the sofa. When Will came back with two mugs of instant coffee, none of the other three had moved. He handed one mug to Fran, ran his hand along the side of her head, and sat on the sofa behind her. When she spoke, her voice was very quiet but it took Dawn and Jez by surprise.

"I think I might ... go somewhere."

"Where?" asked Will.

Fran shrugged. "Don't know. Away. Down south maybe."

"Why?" asked Dawn.

The answer was slow in coming.

"This ... All this ... Floyd. I don't know."

Will stroked her head again. He didn't know what to say. He'd already tried to talk about it all with her, but she'd retreated from him. She was like the old Fran, the one he'd first met in the Grassmarket. In those days, booze, joints, and sex had all been part of a loveless routine which filled the spaces. Her laughter had been quick and shallow, her reactions to everyone around her defiant, and, at twenty-two, she'd already begun the countdown towards her own dying. Will's concern had gradually made itself evident to her and, once she began really to believe that he was reaching for someone inside the automaton she'd become, the desperation had been progressively shuffled off and they'd both found that there were still some pleasures to be had in life. Now, as she leaned her head back against his stroking fingers, he could see her left profile and noticed, with some anxiety, the deadness of her expression, the tightness of features that suggested she was walling herself up against everything once more. Will would do anything to shield her but was afraid that she was moving too far away.

"Yes. I've been feeling the same way really," said Dawn. "It's only going to get worse, isn't it?"

"What?" asked Will.

Dawn gestured with the hand holding the can. "Everything. Identifying those guys, getting involved in trials, being witnesses, all that shit."

"Do we have to?" asked Will.

Dawn shrugged. "Dunno, but we seem to be in pretty deep. I can't see them letting us off the hook."

Will nodded. "Aye. And how long before Burchill's on our backs again?"

"Bloody Floyd. He was always trouble," said Dawn.

"Not now," said Jez. Dawn and Will both looked at him, their interest triggered by the hollowness of his voice. He looked back at them, then dropped his eyes away again.

"People don't look like people when they're dead," he went on. "All that shit about 'to sleep, perchance to dream,' forget it. There's no more Floyd. Just that gray lump."

Will felt a slight shiver run through Fran. He looked down at her. Her expression hadn't changed but her dead eyes were spilling tears. His hand dropped to her shoulder. He leaned forward and began gently to massage the side of her neck.

"Are you saying you're sorry he's gone?" asked Dawn, glad to lead Jez away from his previous obsession.

"No."

"Right then. Poetic bloody justice, that's all it is. You saw the way he provoked those thugs. He brought it on himself." There was a self-righteousness about Dawn's words and expression that revealed the middle-class conformist she would one day become. She swigged at her beer and pushed her thick black hair back from her forehead. "If they hadn't done it, one of us would have in the end."

Fran dabbed at her cheeks. Will and Jez looked quickly at Dawn.

"Don't be bloody stupid," said Jez. "It's murder we're talking about, Dawn."

"So?"

Jez looked away in exasperation. Will's hand was still on Fran's neck.

"He was always a candidate," went on Dawn, her voice fiercer. "He asked for it, time and time again."

"Not murder," Jez insisted.

"Oh no? Not even when you thought he was fucking me?"

Jez was suddenly angry again.

"Oh, for Christ's sake, Dawn. Why does it always come back to that? Why can't you see what's bloody happened here? It's because … your cunt's between your ears, that's the trouble. Whenever there's a man involved, you just …"

He stopped. Fran had begun to shake her head and sob. The noise was coming from a misery that was deeper than mere compassion for Floyd. Like the others, she had felt the tremblings of their world since Floyd had joined them and the ragged breaches which had been opened in it by the various recent intrusions. For a long time, they'd been living their untroubled lives, menaced only by the occasional incursions from Burchill's representatives; now the demons of the real world had reasserted themselves. The idyll was over and here they were, thrashing out against one another. There was no escape from it.

Will pushed himself down to sit beside her, cradling her head into his chest, his eyes flashing anger at Dawn and Jez for the pain they'd unleashed. Jez slumped back, his own anger still curdling inside him, circling around a combination of self-contempt and the desire to repay Dawn for the hurts she'd caused him. Dawn felt her own tears beginning to well but suppressed them fiercely, determined to distance herself from any sign of weakness. The people she was looking at were losers; she didn't want to be part of their defeat.

As they drove to Simpson's house at seven the next morning. Spurle and Fraser's moods were at variance. Fraser was describing the new bedside alarm that had arrived in last Thursday's post and Spurle's resentment at the early start was growing in inverse ratio to his partner's enthusiasm.

"Large format see-through LCD screen," recited Fraser. "Shows the time in twelve or twenty-four hour format. There's an optional hourly chime, the alarm's got a snooze function, a fifty-nine minute countdown timer ..."

"What the fuck's a 'snooze function'?" Spurle interrupted.

"Lets you kip on for ten minutes, then the alarm goes again."

"Fuckin' great."

"It's a calendar, automatically set till 2099 ..."

"Ah s'pose ye'll send it back then?"

Fraser's mood was good enough to accommodate the sarcasm. He delivered what he thought was the coup de grâce. "And it gives you the ambient temperature in a choice of Fahrenheit or centigrade."

"Just what ye need when ye wake up at six o'clock," muttered Spurle. "How much d'you pay fer that crap?"

"Nineteen ninety-five."

Spurle shook his head and swung the car into the side of the road outside Simpson's door. He got out and leaned (literally) on the doorbell. They heard the repeated bing-bonging echoing just inside the hallway.

When Simpson's wife arrived and half-opened the door, she was pulling a housecoat over a nightdress that must once have been white. She squinted at them through red, gritty eyes.

"What is it this time?" she asked.

"Yer old man in?" asked Spurle, pushing past her into the hall.

She followed him. "No. He went to see you."

"What? When?"

"When he come home last night. Ah tellt him ye was wantin' to see him. He said he was goin' round to the station."

Spurle punched his fist against the wall.

"Bastard!" he said.

"What time was this, love?" asked Fraser.

The woman folded her arms and shrugged her shoulders simultaneously. "Dinna ken. Musta bin eleven, twelve o'clock. Ah was away to mah bed."

"He told you he was comin' round to see us that time o' night an' you believed him?" said Spurle.

"That's what he said."

"Aye. An' you didna think to ring us up to tell us."

"What for?"

Spurle held a pointing finger under her nose. "If he's done a runner, missus, ye're in trouble. An accessory, that's what you are. An accessory, and a bloody liability."

He turned and stamped out of the house. Fraser was still standing at the door.

"Are you sure he's no hidin' himself away here?" he said to the woman, who was unimpressed by Spurle's threat.

"Of course not. What would he want to do that for?" Fraser believed her and anyway, they had no legal right to search the place.

"OK, love. Tell ye what, though, if he comes back again, don't say nothin' to him. Just give us a ring instead. Will ye do that?"

"What's he done?"

"Maybe nothin'. That's why we want to have a wee chat with him. So will ye give us a ring?"

The woman nodded. "Aye. OK."

"Good. Thanks," said Fraser, turning to leave.

The woman's voice stopped him. She pointed at Spurle in the car.

"If ye have to come back, can ye no bring somebody else instead o' him?"

Fraser smiled. "Ah, he's OK. Just a bit mental, that's all." They drove straight back to the station and Spurle's mood was made darker by the fact that Bellman and Thom had got a result. Their trip to Mitchell's place hadn't been wasted. They'd brought him back and he was now in interview room one with the two of them and Carston.

Even this early, Carston's mind was cranked up to its usual sharpness. When he'd got up at six, the fogs in his skull and stomach reminded him of his often repeated determination not to drink too much wine, but they began to dissipate quickly when he remembered that he'd be seeing Kath that afternoon. It was the anticipation of this pleasure that kept his questions quick, light, and telling.

"OK, Benny. Let's move on. Where's Bazza?"

Mitchell looked blank.

"Come on. You were with him in Forbeshill Road Friday afternoon. Being nasty to some squatters."

Mitchell shook his head.

"Ah, you weren't? OK, your double was. We've got two witnesses who've put you there. And there's another one who swears you and your mate came to see him in his antiques shop."

His only objective basis for saying this was that a clear set of Simpson's prints had been found on the hilt of the sword which Ross had brought from Hilden's shop. Two others, on the blade, were from his left forefinger. There was nothing to suggest that Mitchell was involved in any way, but Carston's main aim was to unsettle his man. The speed of his accusations and the confidence with which he delivered them had their effect. Mitchell's hesitation before shaking his head again made it very clear that he was lying.

"Right then," said Carston. "Let's talk about the football."

Mitchell looked at him, a frown making his face even less pleasant.

"You know. The football. Yesterday. The Dons."

"What about it?" Mitchell's voice was harsh, rasping, grated to a croak by tens of thousands of cigarettes.

"Was it good?"

"No. The usual crap."

"Yeah. Lost their way a bit, haven't they? How about Barry?"

"What about him?"

"Did he like it?"

"How do ah know?"

"Eh?"

"He wasna there."

"Oh, I'm sorry. I thought you went down together."

"No. We were s'posed to, but he never showed. What're we talkin' about the football for anyway?"

"We're not. We're talking about you and your mate and some GBH. And maybe something else, too."

"Like what?"

"Ah. We'll get to that later. Let's start from the top." He looked at a notebook. "What were you doing on Thursday afternoon at … er … two twenty-four?"

"No idea."

"So you weren't anywhere near Nostalgia?"

"No."

"But you know what I'm talking about? You know where Nostalgia is?"

"Er … Ah'm no sure. Is it no some sort o' shop?"

Carston looked again at the book.

"How about Friday afternoon, four seventeen?"

"How about it?"

"You weren't leaving fingerprints anywhere near the hall, living room and three bedrooms of twenty-eight Forbeshill Road?"

Mitchell shook his head. Carston held up a broken piece of wood.

"And you didn't see your mate Barry break this loudspeaker with his baseball bat?"

Another shake of the head, but slow, uncertain. Mitchell was beginning to wonder how much evidence they had and whether he should cut his losses and go along with them. Carston held the wood closer to him.

"Funny, that. See the letters? M O H. They're backwards but they look the same both ways. Funny sort of letter-style, isn't it? Sort of jazzy. Only place I've seen them is in adverts. For American baseball gear. HomeRun, it's called." He clicked his fingers, as if he'd just had an idea. "Wait a minute. Your mate's bat's like that, isn't it? That's a HomeRun, too."

The speed of it all had taken Mitchell way out of his depth.

"OK," he said. "What's going on?"

"Helping us with our inquiries, aren't you? At least, until we've sifted through all the forensics. Could get a bit nastier then."

Mitchell made a decision.

"Listen. We were sent round to frighten them, that's all. Aye, OK, Barry broke the speaker, but it was nothin' serious."

Carston nodded understandingly. "Mr. Burchill's idea, was it'?"

Mitchell said nothing, but his eyes gave him away.

"Right, so now you're saying you did go to Forbeshill Road, are you?"

Mitchell nodded.

"To … put the frighteners on them."

"Aye, that's it. That's all."

Carston dropped the piece of wood and, like a conjurer, produced a photograph of Floyd which he put on the table.

"Was he there?"

He watched carefully as Mitchell looked at the photo then nodded. He gave no sign other than that he recognized the face. His expressions so far had betrayed him so comprehensively that Carston was fairly sure that he didn't know that Floyd had been killed. The opinion was confirmed by Mitchell's next words.

"He was a smartarse," he said. "Ah … tapped him. To shut him up."

"Where?"

"The side of the head." Mitchell's hand tapped his own temple. "Just a wee reminder, like."

Carston had already asked Brian McIntosh whether the blow that had killed Floyd could have had a delayed effect. McIntosh didn't think so. The location that Mitchell was now indicating coincided with the other bruising that had been found. It was unlikely that what he had just said was a confession of murder.

"OK," said Carston, making it seem as if "tapping" someone on the head was acceptable and merited no censure. "Now what about Nostalgia? You want to reconsider that?"

112

Mitchell thought for a moment, then nodded.

"OK. Ah was there. Wi' Barry. But we didna do nothin'. Just spoke to the guy."

"Mr. Hilden."

"Aye."

"And what did you speak about? Antiques? The weather?"

Again, Mitchell hesitated before making up his mind. Bellman and Thom were fascinated by the speed of what was happening.

"There's this guy," said Mitchell at last. "Hilden owes him a lot o' cash. We were sent round to collect it."

"Ah, I see. And there was no GBH there. Just a bit of debt collecting."

"That's right."

"Who for? ... You said 'this guy.' Which guy?"

As Carston asked the question, he didn't expect an answer. He didn't get one.

"Right. You were just collecting."

He sat back in his chair.

"There was no threatening to break the place up unless he paid you a bit of protection money?"

Again, Mitchell's quick reaction to his suggestion made Carston feel uncertain whether he genuinely knew the reason for the questions.

"Look, are you tryin' to fit me up for somethin'?"

"Mr. Mitchell! Do I look like a bent copper?"

Carston's ease and confidence had completely disoriented Mitchell. It was too early in the morning, after a long night of McEwans Export, and the suggestions that there were more sinister charges waiting to be made unnerved him even more. Carston knew that he wasn't telling everything. Whenever Burchill's name cropped up, for instance, a veil fell over his face. And there were other secrets that he wasn't ready to reveal. But the relentlessness of the questions quickly drew out of him a fairly full description of the events in the squat and what had happened on the visit to Hilden's shop. He really didn't seem to know where Simpson was; he hadn't seen him since they'd gone for a drink after leaving the squat on Friday. That evening, Mitchell had gone home to eat, then gone to the Red Rum Casino, down by the canal, where he'd stayed until three in the morning. The place had been full and he was sure that the manager, staff, and plenty of customers would confirm his alibi, though he still didn't know why he needed one.

The more he talked, the more expansive he became. Carston was annoyed to hear him articulate the same sort of feelings about squatters that he himself had. According to both Mitchell and Simpson, they were bloody parasites. Certainly not worth getting done for. And anyway, the errand was just to frighten them away from the place. On top of that, the bloke they were doing it for didn't pay them enough to make it worth taking any risks. Again he stopped short of naming the individual concerned, and Carston, who knew very well that it had to be Burchill, was impressed at the hold he obviously had over his hired hands.

"OK, Mr. Mitchell," he said at last. "You've been very cooperative and we're grateful for all your help. Now, I'm afraid I can't just let things like threatening people, demanding money with menaces, causing damage to property … things like that, I just can't let them go, but we'll leave it at that for the moment and see whether we can't come to some arrangement sometime in the future. What do you think?"

Mitchell was being made to feel like a good citizen for a change. Carston knew that he was taking a small risk by making such an offer, but he was trusting his instincts that he had read his man correctly. Mitchell was only too glad to get away from the pressure for a while so that he'd have time to sort himself out.

"Aye, OK," he said.

"Right. So, we'll just get a statement from you. Then you can get back to bed."

Thom had been taking general notes of the interview. Carston got up and said, "Right, constable. He's all yours. Just run over what you've written with Mr. Mitchell, fill in some details, and get it typed up and signed."

He went out to the incident room. McNeil had arrived and was sitting at a desk reading some papers from a file. Spurle and Fraser were making notes on a report.

"Right," said Carston. "McNeil, in a minute, you're coming round to that squat with me again. The rest of you, we want Barry Simpson. Spurle, you and Bellman make a list of all his mates, associates, all the villains he's knocked around with. Go and talk to them. He's got to be staying with somebody."

He pointed at Fraser. "You, get the names of those dealers who've been threatened. As soon as Thom's finished with Mitchell, take him with you and go and find out if any of them have been contacted. If he's done a runner, he'll need cash. He may have tried to hustle them a bit. If any of you get a sniff, let me know right away. McNeil, have a quick look back over the file on the squat, see what sort of complaints Burchill has put in, the dates, investigations, any other incidents. Then sort out a car. Give me a shout when you're ready."

He went out and, as the others started their various jobs, their actions showed that his briskness had been transmitted to all of them. Even Spurle was moving with a little more purpose than he had been earlier. He still found time, though, to say to McNeil, "Drive carefully. And no hand-jobs on the way."

McNeil didn't even look at him. "You're the hand-job expert," she said.

In his office, Carston was toying with the idea of calling Ross. In spite of saying he could have a lie-in, the things Mitchell had said had brought a definite focus to the inquiries. Getting hold of Simpson was a matter of some urgency. He looked at his watch. It was still only twenty past eight. Even if he got Ross to come in, there was nothing much he could do beyond what was already being done. He decided to leave the call until later. With any luck, some trace of Simpson would have turned up and they'd be getting a case together.

He poured a half cup of the coffee he'd made when he'd first come in and stood at the window as he sipped it. On the opposite pavement, a fat, red-haired girl in khaki trousers and a flak jacket wandered along, scuffing her feet. Her hair was that frizzy-textured ginger-red which would never allow her to be anything other than a paid-up member of the Celtic fringe, but, thought Carston, she probably didn't care. The ungainly way she moved suggested that her self-image wasn't formed from visions of catwalks and that she'd

115

be more at home in the anonymity of some agricultural production line.

"Bloody hell," he said out loud, ashamed of himself for entertaining such sub-Spurle prejudices. He blew a kiss at the shuffling creature's back and turned to sit at his desk.

He flicked through the notes he'd made in his notebook. Even though he wanted very much to speak to Simpson, he wasn't convinced that that would be the end of it. Once again, he ran over the possibilities he'd considered. The fight was probably irrelevant, but Simpson's visit to the squat surely wasn't coincidental. Logic suggested that there was some connection there. It was difficult at the moment to imagine that any of the other squatters were responsible. He'd looked through the transcripts of Spurle's interviews with them and picked out some of their opinions on Donnelly. They'd all taken the same line. "Gets on our tits most of the time." "He's never been the same as the rest of us." "Always been a problem." "Just a pain in the arse." "Didn't belong here. He was a bastard." It all added up to a highly unpopular flatmate, but there was nothing to suggest that any of them had a motive to kill him. And, on the face of it, none of them seemed capable of murder, although Carston knew better than to set much store by that sort of observation. Mitchell's information put Simpson very much in the frame, but nothing explained the glass in the face or the choice of dumping place.

These were the aspects of the crime that fascinated Carston. The choice of spot was perhaps easier to explain. It must have been deliberate; anybody in a panic and wanting to get rid of a body would hardly choose the main street. So they must have thought about it, planned it, and waited for the right time to act. The question was, why there? Carston reckoned there were maybe two answers to it. First, the amount of rubbish lying about would confuse attempts by forensics to identify any traces of the place where Donnelly had actually been killed. This suggested that the person who'd done it was thinking fairly clearly and knew something about detection procedures. They were either just being careful to make his job more difficult or there was something specific that they wanted to obscure. Next, the club was anonymous, frequented by lots of people but with no special meaning for any one group except those who worked there. And, as Friday night had proved, it was also a place where violence was a regular ingredient. Every way you looked at it, if you wanted to create a more or less acceptable context for the extraordinary phenomenon of a mutilated corpse, dumping it among the rubbish at Macy's was as good a way as any of doing it.

The mutilation seemed to pose different problems. It wasn't extensive enough to be an attempt literally to deface the victim, nor was it consistent with the patterns normally associated with that type of perversion. Wounds deliberately inflicted post mortem were usually confined to genital areas, women's breasts, or the abdominal cavity. The face was sometimes slashed but rarely in isolation and, when it was, the cutting was generally more selective and concentrated on specific organs, mostly the eyes. This twisting of the broken glass seemed totally gratuitous and hard to reconcile with any notion of perverse pleasure. So if that option was discarded, what was left? Well, either the simple idea of deliberately introducing an unexplained element that would mislead investigators or, once again, the need to cover up something else. The murder weapon had already left its patterns on the skull; what if there'd been others, easily identifiable, on the face? Grabbing a nearby glass and scooping down through them would obliterate them. Once again, if Carston's reasoning was sound, the implication was that the murderer was thinking clearly and aware of the need to cover his traces. None of this actually ruled Simpson out, but none of his previous crimes had shown much evidence of lucid thinking or indeed any thinking at all.

He flicked over another page and swore under his breath. The name "Burchill" was scribbled on its own at the top. He'd been putting off contacting him about the things that had gone missing from the attic in Forbeshill Road, but knew that he'd soon have to bite the bullet. Part of the problem was that he knew that Burchill was the source of a lot of what was happening. He'd sent Simpson and Mitchell to the flat and, if they were there on that errand for him, they might just as easily do him another favor at Hilden's place. He looked at his watch. Nearly half past eight. If Burchill wasn't up yet, he bloody well ought to be. He looked up his number in the directory and punched it into his phone. It rang for a long time; long enough for him to start feeling relief at the thought that the conversation could be postponed until he had a bit more evidence to implicate the man. Then the receiver at the other end was picked up.

"Who is it?" barked Burchill, his cracking voice betraying the fact that he'd been woken up.

"Good morning, sir," said Carston, quietly pleased to be the cause of his discomfort. "DCI Carston, West Grampian Police."

"What the bloody hell do you want?"

"It's about some property of yours, sir. In your Forbeshill Road residence."

"Not that bloody place again. What about it?" Carston allowed his voice to ease into a parody of police-speak.

"Well, as you are no doubt aware, we've been conducting fairly extensive investigations there on your behalf for some appreciable time now …"

"Bollocks."

"… and there has recently been a development which may prove to be significant and which does in fact require your personal attention."

"What the bloody hell are you on about?"

Carston decided to check how much Burchill knew about what had been going on. He dropped out of the parody.

"I'm afraid there's been some trouble there, sir."

There was a pause. Long enough to be very noticeable. "There's always bloody trouble there," Burchill went on at last. "If you'd got your fingers out, it would have been sorted ages ago."

"Yes, well, this time it's rather more serious, I'm afraid."

"How?"

The sudden change to a monosyllable had been preceded by another pause. Burchill was obviously waking up and Carston fancied that he had suddenly become more wary.

"Assault," he said, wanting to give Burchill as little as possible to work with. Again, the reply was preceded by a definite hesitation.

"What sort of assault?"

"Serious."

"But … I mean, who was assaulted?"

"One of the squatters."

"Serves the bugger right. He shouldn't have been where he didn't belong."

Carston let a pause grow. He noticed that Burchill had assumed the victim was male and hadn't asked who'd done the assaulting.

"So … why're you phoning me about it?"

"Well, it is your property."

"Yes, but assault … that's got nothing to do with me. Or is somebody saying it has?"

Carston ignored the question. "There's also a suggestion that some property's gone missing."

"What?" Burchill's hesitation had gone.

"Yes. From the attic. We need you to have a look and confirm if things have in fact been taken."

"If they have, I want those bastards charged. I've told your lot so many bloody times …"

"Well, perhaps we'd better establish that there has actually been a crime before we start making accusations, eh?"

"Don't you think living in my house rent-free and uninvited counts as a crime then?"

"Not according to the law, sir."

Burchill then spent some time telling Carston what he thought about the law and its failure to protect those who were actually contributing something to society and shielding "thieves and sodding gypsies" as he put it. Carston found that, once again, a person with whom he otherwise had nothing in common was articulating some of his own thinking about the youngsters living in Forbeshill Road. The fact that the whole package was wrapped in the sort of ideology that got standing ovations at Tory Party conferences, however, made him determine to look more closely at his attitudes in future.

From his moral high ground, Burchill began eventually to dictate terms to Carston. The original invitation to visit the house and look through the things in the attic was turned round to become an insistence on his owner's right to enter the property at any time and the corresponding duty of the police to enforce that right. Carston had disliked Burchill from the first time he'd heard about him; as he ranted on, the feeling grew and made his contributions to the dialogue shorter and shorter. In the end, he arranged for them to meet at the house at nine-thirty and replaced the receiver before the name of the Assistant Chief Constable could be made part of the whole equation.

He was angry. First with Burchill for being such a rude, self-opinionated bastard and then with himself for allowing himself to be affected by him. He finished the cold dregs of his coffee and rang for McNeil to bring through the stuff she'd raked out so far on the squat. She arrived with a thin folder and flicked through the sheets in it.

"There's no much, sir. All a bit repetitive. Burchill just kept hasslin' us. We've done everythin' by the book. There's nothin' there. Apart from the times Bellman picked up on, they've done nothin'. Certainly nothin' to do with the flat. Stayed well inside the law."

She closed the folder and put it on his desk.

"OK, we'll be off soon. Before we go, though, just see what else you can find out about Burchill."

"What sort of things?"

"Anything you like. If nothing turns up, too bad. I'll be out in a minute."

He began looking through the folder. It all confirmed what McNeil had said. There was nothing there. Burchill had pushed his citizen's rights to the limit and beyond. He'd tried everything to get the squatters out, looking for weaknesses and exploiting them. The variations he'd come up with could easily be seen as obsessive. It would be no surprise at all to find that he'd taken his complaints elsewhere, to people whose methods weren't circumscribed by the need to stay within the law. And the intemperate terminology he frequently used convinced Carston that, as well as doing things by proxy, he was quite capable of getting personally involved with it all.

He was reading the last file when there was a knock at the door and Thom came in with Mitchell.

"That's it, sir," said Thom. "All signed and sealed."

"That was quick. Everything to your satisfaction, Mr. Mitchell?"

Mitchell just nodded.

"Good. Thanks for your help. Away you go, then."

Mitchell didn't move. He seemed uncertain. Carston looked at him.

"Was there something else?"

"Am ah no gettin' a lift home?"

Carston smiled.

"As you go out, look at the notice outside. It says 'Police' not 'Taxi.' Close the door behind you, will you?"

Simpson didn't want to get up. His head was sore and his eyes felt as if they were bulging out of his face to get away from the hot sand that someone had poured into his sockets. He'd realized on Saturday morning that he'd need money to get away for a while, so he'd spent the afternoon going round some of his antique shops collecting what he could from the people he'd threatened. The protection business was his baby. Benny helped him out with it and took his whack, but he was the one who'd set it up. Combining it with the jobs they'd had to do for Burchill gave him some extra clout, and if some of the punters believed that Burchill was behind it, so much the better. The truth, though, was that it was all his own creation. It was made easier by the fact that he despised most of the people he dealt with. He came across them at Enderby's, the auctioneers where he worked part-time, and soon knew which ones would keep quiet and pay up. Half of them were as wary of the police as he was and, anyway, they all knew him well enough not to risk messing with him.

Yesterday afternoon, as he'd moved from shop to shop, his desperation had given his threats a sharper edge and produced a quick response from most of them. By four, he'd been to all the ones who were open, so he'd kept out of the way until the evening and then gone to a pub on the other side of the canal, where they didn't know him. He eventually went home just after midnight to pick up his things. He was already drunk and when his bitching wife told him that the police were looking for him, he was glad he was

121

already so far ahead of the game. There was no time now for reflection, no time to work out alibis and get backup for them. If he waited for morning, he'd be buggered. So he chucked some clothes in a bag, grabbed the three-quarters full bottle of whisky, took the four remaining cans of export from the shelf in the kitchen cupboard, and left. By two o'clock, the booze had all gone and he was sound asleep.

This morning, he was paying for it. The single bar of the electric fire he'd had on all night was useless. He was freezing cold under the three bits of sacking he'd found in the back room. He pulled them around him and sat up. His head hammered even harder and he swore out loud. He looked slowly around. The room was almost bare. At one end there was a long table in front of a tall, upright desk. Inside the door, a row of waste bins curved round towards a big basket. On the table were some old newspapers and a telephone. He knew they might come here looking for him, but there was nowhere else to go. He reckoned he was OK for one more night, but he'd have to be out early in the morning and if he wasn't well away from Cairnburgh by Monday evening, he'd be completely fucked.

After holding his head for a few minutes and failing to make it feel any better, he stood up and went to the table. It was early, but he didn't have the time to hang around. He had to get the rest of his cash organized. He picked up the phone, screwed up his eyes with the effort of remembering a number, then dialed. Altogether, he phoned eleven people. All but three of them protested, but each one that did was silenced with threats of comprehensive destruction, guarantees that this was the last demand he'd ever be making, or a combination of the two. Of the other three, two acceded to his demands with no form of resistance or protest while the other one told him to piss off. Simpson was angry that this had had to happen on a Sunday. It meant waiting till the banks opened the next morning before he could collect. It also gave the punters time to change their minds and contact the filth. But he had no choice. It would just mean being extra careful when he went to collect. He went back to the electric fire, pulled the pieces of sacking tighter around him, and lay down again, the drums still booming in his head.

Six

At Forbeshill Road, Carston had to go through the same rigorous inspection procedure as on his first visit before they let him and McNeil in. It was Liz who eventually opened the door. She was still wearing the blue glasses and Carston noted how, as well as hiding her eyes, the color itself seemed to add to the impression of coldness and distance that had been so striking a part of her on both their previous meetings. They followed her through to the front room, where Fran was sitting in one of the chairs. Jez and Dawn were in the kitchen and Will had still to surface.

"Coffee, Detective Chief Inspector?" asked Liz, drawing out his title with a smile and in a tone that made it clear that the charm had a satirical intent.

"What a lovely idea," he replied, mimicking her buttery smoothness.

Liz's smile broadened.

"Not for me," said McNeil, not giving Liz the chance to adopt the same sort of condescension with her. As far as she was concerned, their respective positions had been drawn up during the ride to Aberdeen and she was wary of anything masquerading as normal contact.

Liz went to the kitchen, leaving them in a sort of hapless silence with Fran, who had looked at them when they'd come in but then turned back to the newspaper she was reading. It was McNeil who took the initiative.

"I don't believe we've met you yet. I'm Julie McNeil. This is Detective Chief Inspector Carston."

Fran looked up and nodded, then went back to her paper.

"We've spoken to the others and ..."

"Will's upstairs. Still in bed," said Fran. "Better wait for him, hadn't you?"

"Why?" asked Carston.

Fran shrugged, her eyes still on the paper.

"We just wanted a few words about last Friday. You were at Macy's, weren't you?"

Fran let the paper fall into her lap, gave a deep sigh, then got up and went out.

"Another little charmer," said McNeil.

Carston shook his head. "You expect too much of people."

They heard Fran's footsteps on the stairs and the clinking of crockery in the kitchen. Carston noticed once again that the place was spotless. Just as well. Burchill was due in less than an hour and he'd be looking for the tiniest sign of damage so that he could press charges and get the eviction he wanted. McNeil was studying the posters on the wall and Carston was looking out of the window when Liz came back in.

"Won't be long," she said. "Jez'll bring it through in a minute."

Carston turned, gave her a huge, warm smile, and sat down opposite the chair on which Fran had left her paper.

"I'm sorry to disturb you again, Ms. Munro," he said. Before they'd left the station, he'd consulted Bellman's notes to remind himself of their names. He was pleased with the result. Liz was obviously thrown by the use of her surname. She pulled at the sleeve of her sweater to hide it, then looked up at him.

"You can call me Liz."

"I'd prefer not to," said Carston, forced once again into a stuffiness he detested.

"OK, then. Stanley, if you prefer."

"Ms. Stanley?"

"No, just Stanley. I prefer it to Munro and if you don't like Liz ..."

"Police inquiries aren't frivolous wee games," said McNeil, her animosity towards Liz transparent once again. "We need proper identification for everybody who's givin' us any evidence."

"Gosh, how impressive," said Liz. "Well, Police Constable whoever-you-are, I think you'll find it's easier to have the chats you want if you call us by our names. Nobody here's Mr. or Ms. anything.

I'm Liz, Dawn and Jez are in the kitchen, that was Fran who just went upstairs and, when she comes down, she'll probably have Will with her."

As McNeil was about to reply, Carston lifted a hand to stop her.

"Excellent," he said. "And I'm Detective Chief Inspector Carston and this is DC McNeil. You can use our full names and titles if you like."

"Of course. Wouldn't dream of kicking your crutches away," replied Liz.

"And I expect Mr. Burchill will also prefer the more formal mode of address when he gets here," added Carston, stretching another unctuous smile across his face.

It had the effect he'd hoped for. For a moment, Liz's self-assurance stalled. She looked away from him to compose herself.

"Should have known it," she said at last. "You're just here as an advance party. Eviction, that's all it is, isn't it?"

Carston shook his head. "Absolutely not. We just wanted a word with … Fran and … Will. And I've also asked Mr. Burchill to come and look at the stuff stored in his attic. As you know, Mr. Donnelly … sorry, I mean Floyd … has been removing things from the house and disposing of them. We need to know the extent of the losses and what sort of things are involved. Mr. Burchill's the only one who can tell us that."

"And slap some sort of charge on the rest of us."

"Not unless you've all been at it."

"We haven't. Floyd was … different."

"Didn't like him, did you?"

"No. He was a pain in the arse. But I'd still prefer his company to Burchill's."

As she spoke, she moved Fran's paper aside and sat facing Carston. She lay across the chair, her weight over to the right and her thighs slightly parted in what he felt sure was a deliberate provocation. In the course of their previous meetings, he hadn't really had time or the chance to look at her properly. The infuriating blue shades had always kept her counsel. Now, though, he noted the sheen on her skin, the lines of her breasts and hips under the sweater and denim skirt, and the smile at the corners of her mouth

125

as she watched his gaze sliding over her. She had the focused, anchored confidence that belongs more naturally with women than with men. In males, it's often too close to a challenge; females have nothing to prove. For all that she was some twenty years younger, Carston felt that she was in control. It was attractive and he felt a shiver of sexual interest, allowing himself mentally to peel back the clothing that masked her and imagine her responses to his hands and … Bloody hell! It was just as well that Kath would soon be back.

Noises on the stairs saved him from further moral degeneration. Fran had dragged Will out of bed and the pair of them were on their way. Before they arrived, Jez came in with mugs of coffee on a tray. He put the tray down, took two of the mugs, and sat on the floor beside the fireplace. Dawn came in and sat beside him. Liz was still looking directly at Carston. She waved a hand towards the mugs still on the tray.

"Help yourself."

Carston took the smallest, then, to McNeil's disgust, handed another to Liz. As he sat down again, Fran and Will came in. Will was wary, his stance closed, defensive. His eyes moved from Carston to McNeil and back again. The arm he put across Fran's shoulders as she sat beside him on the sofa was possessive and protective.

"You must be Will," said Carston. Will stared at him and gave a barely perceptible nod.

"We just wanted to have a word about the other night. At Macy's."

"What about it?"

Carston found himself yet again fighting back his own prejudices. Pubs, cinemas, nightclubs were places where what the Americans would call "regular" people went. Squatting implied such a comprehensive inversion of values that it seemed perverse for the people who did it to behave so ordinarily and socialize in the same way. Was there really such a difference between paying rent and buying a pint? McNeil, focused as ever, didn't waste time in speculations.

"Your friend turned up there dead with his face mutilated, that's what. How did that grab you?"

Will looked at her, his eyebrows drawn into a frown as if he didn't understand either the question or the manner in which it was put. When he spoke, he was calm, quiet.

"We were just dancing. We stopped when there was that fight. Then we danced some more and came home."

"What time?"

"One, half past."

"You came straight back here?"

"Aye."

"Was anyone else up when you got home?"

They all looked at each other. Dawn said, "I heard them come in."

"What time was that?"

"No idea. Why? Are they suspects?"

Dawn smiled at Jez. Carston ignored the provocation.

"You didn't see Mr. Donnelly at any stage of the evening?" he asked.

"Floyd? At Macy's? No way," said Will.

"Why d'you say that?"

"According to Floyd, the only people who went to Macy's were poofs and wankers."

Will's explanation was unstressed, revealing nothing of what he himself thought of the opinion or of the person who had held it. Carston was interested.

"So you're saying that Floyd never went there."

"Not that I know."

"How often do you go?"

Will looked at Fran. She was looking down at the black and gray trainers on her feet. His fingers moved gently on her shoulder.

"When we can afford it."

"And Friday night ... did you notice anything different, anything unusual?"

Will shook his head.

"Not even the fight?" asked McNeil.

Again the shake of the head.

"It happens now and then. Not usually in the club. The bouncers have got that sorted."

"D'you know them well, the bouncers?" asked Carston.

"Pretty well. They're usually the same ones. They're OK."

127

"And the way they handled the fight, that was normal, was it?"
Will thought for a moment.

"I don't know how they handled it. We heard it on the stairs. Some people went to look. We just sat down till it was finished."

"And then started dancing again," said McNeil, "as if nothing had happened."

"No." It was Fran's voice, low and with a hint of a break, like a child on the edge of tears.

McNeil was about to ask another question when Carston looked at her and gave a quick shake of his head. They waited. Will's fingers massaged at Fran's shoulder.

"It was different. Something had happened, hadn't it? The usual bloody nonsense." Fran stopped and looked down at the floor again.

"What do you mean, 'usual'? I thought you said it didn't happen very often," said Carston.

"Not in the club it doesn't. But outside, all over the place. There's always somebody proving something. They can't just ... have a good time."

"Who are you talking about?"

Briefly, there was a flash of temper from Fran.

"Christ, you're a bloody policeman. What a stupid bloody question. Your cells are probably full of them."

"Yes, but who in particular?" Carston's tone was patient. Fran raised her hands slightly, shrugged her shoulders, shook her head as if to suggest that there were lots of answers to the question. In the end, she was still again and the temper had gone as she said, "Men."

"Any particular ones?" asked McNeil, her tone more sympathetic than before. Fran's changes of mood were disturbing her. The girl was wound up, unaware of the fact that she was sending out distress signals. In some of the counseling work she'd done, McNeil had seen and heard them too often. Fran made no attempt to answer. She'd retreated from them again. Will's arm hugged her tighter. She showed no sign of noticing.

"Why are you asking that?" said Liz. "You know very well who starts all the fights—guys out on the piss, hard men, BNP, wog-bashers, queer-bashers, take your pick."

"What a pity you're not in the police force," said Carston. "I'm sure it'd do wonders for our clear-up rate." He turned his attention back to Will. "Were any of the people at the club the sort who might start fights? Or get involved?"

"Who knows?" said Will. "The guys on the door wouldna let them in if they thought they might start any trouble. So ..." He ended with another shrug.

As they continued to talk, the conversation went over the same ground again and again. There was nothing about Macy's or its clientele that offered any insights. It had been another night's oblivion among lights and sounds with few individuals stamping themselves on the awareness of those who were there. Everybody had been having a good time, forgetting what was waiting for them in the morning at their colleges, their workplaces, or in their homes. Fran added nothing to what she'd said. She was turning around some inner weariness where their questions had no relevance. Will spoke for the two of them and kept on confirming that they'd been an anonymous fragment of the collective pleasure and that the fight had fractured the mood. It was barren ground and Liz kept on telling them so.

Through all the exchanges, the squatters were fiercely unified. They were clearly used to having to defend themselves and having to rely on one another. Their solidarity was impressive and tinged with none of the defiance that often characterizes groups who feel they're under attack. Carston noticed, too, how none of them expressed any regret at any stage about what had happened to Floyd Donnelly. He had lived with them but obviously didn't belong. They treated his death as a fact. Only Fran seemed troubled by it and Carston felt that it was death itself, rather than Floyd's dive into it, which caused the reaction.

At twenty past nine, they heard a sudden squealing of brakes outside, a car door banging, the sound of a key being tried unsuccessfully in the front door, then a furious hammering which echoed through the hall to them. David Burchill had arrived.

When Liz let him in, his intentions were instantly clear. He shoved past her and began a systematic inspection of each room. From the kitchen he went across the hall to the front room, where

Carston and the others were waiting. Pausing only to register their presence, he went on upstairs and they heard doors and drawers being opened and shut. Carston told McNeil to wait with the others and he went up to find Burchill. He was in Liz's room. It was clean, the bed was made, and there were very few objects or ornaments on the various surfaces. Behind the door was a heavy green coat. Burchill had opened a wardrobe. It contained very little, perhaps three dresses and four or five skirts. On shelves at the side there were jumpers, jeans, and trousers folded tidily. Liz was obviously not extravagant where clothes were concerned. Burchill turned to look at Carston as he heard him arrive.

"I want them out," he said.

"You know I can't do that, sir. We've been through it before. The ..."

"Don't give me that shit about the law again. This is my sodding house. I want access to it."

He didn't wait for a reply but strode out to continue his inspection. Patiently, Carston followed him, half inclined to reprimand him for intruding into the privacy of people's bedrooms. The other ones were less tidy than Liz's but were still so clean that Burchill could find nothing to complain about. Outside the bathroom, he reached up to pull on the release cord that held the ladder to the attic.

"I'd be grateful if you'd be a bit careful going up there," warned Carston.

Burchill paused.

"We've had a team going over it. They've taken prints and so on, but it'd be best not to disturb things too much in case something comes up and we need to look again."

Burchill pulled hard on the cord.

"Wouldn't be necessary if you did your job right in the first place," he said. "Or if you'd cleared the buggers out when I asked you."

The loft ladder folded down as the trap door in the ceiling lifted on its counterweights.

"Still, wouldn't hurt to take care, would it?" said Carston, deciding that feigning imperviousness to the barbs would be the wisest tactic and might even have the added advantage of irritating Burchill further. "I'll come up with you. Perhaps you could tell me what should be there. And if anything's missing."

Burchill was already at the top of the steps. Carston followed him as he disappeared into the darkness. Burchill switched on the light, a single, unshaded 60 watt bulb, to reveal a typical attic. Rolls of carpet, boxes, and heaps of junk had all been pushed out round the edges of the space. In one corner, there was what looked like a nest of old newspapers. They were stacked in such a way that they were like walls around a central hollow. Carston looked inside and saw an old-style child's car seat, a kite, and two rusty woks. Between the farthest wall of papers and the roof, there were two dolls and a punctured football. From McNeil's inquiries into Burchill's activities, Carston knew that he'd never even acknowledge the children he'd fathered let alone have them living with him, so most of this stuff would probably have belonged to the previous owner. Everything was thickly coated with dust, but lots of footprints and criss-crossing patterns on the floor showed that there'd actually been plenty of traffic here in recent days, most of it, of course, the police team. Burchill was standing at the left-hand side of the space, looking at the things that were piled there.

"Shit, they've been robbing me blind," he said.

Carston went to stand beside him.

"So there are things missing, are there?" he asked.

Burchill turned his head to look at him. "I thought you were a detective," he said.

Carston looked over the boxes and cases against the wall. Burchill was right. Even Spurle would have seen the paler squares in the dust on the wall which indicated where other, now missing containers had been stacked, and the dust-free surfaces of the top layer of boxes indicated that, until recently, they'd been protected by other things.

"They could have been shifted somewhere else," he said defensively.

"Where?" asked Burchill, spreading his hands to encompass the whole of the attic. "The rest of this stuff's all crap. Everything that had any sort of value was stacked here."

"What sort of things?"

"My lawyer's got a note of it all. Some of it came with the house. But there was some bloody good gear. Couple of Tiffany vases, for a start. And there was a box of cutlery on top. American stuff." The label suddenly came into his head. "Saccarrappa, Maine. Hundred and fifty years old. I don't see any sign of that."

"You're a collector, are you?"

"I've got some stuff," Burchill said, his tone becoming momentarily guarded.

"I'm just a bit surprised that you should leave valuable things like that up here as if they were just junk."

"I didn't know my house was going to be commandeered by a bunch of fucking gypsies, did I?"

"No, but the point is …"

"The point is, this gear's worth a lot of money and those bastards downstairs have been shifting it."

Carston nodded.

"Well, as I said to you before, we need to know exactly what's disappeared before we can begin any meaningful investigations."

Burchill turned to face him square on, having to bend slightly to avoid banging his head on the slope of the roof.

"Meaningful investigations? Where the bloody hell are you coming from?" he said. "Things are missing. That's enough surely? D'you always need to find out exactly what's been nicked before you get your finger out?"

"No, but we do need evidence before we lock people up. It may be old-fashioned but that's the way the law works."

"Very funny."

Burchill looked around the attic once more.

"Well, you'd better get the law working double quick this time because I'm pressing charges. And I want these bastards out."

Without waiting for a reply, he went back to the trap door and began to climb down the ladder. Carston followed him, looking once more around the attic before turning off the light.

The tableau in the front room was more or less as Carston had left it. Will was on the sofa with Fran, his arm still around her shoulders. Jez and Dawn were on the floor beside the fireplace. Liz was back in her chair and McNeil stood just inside the door.

Strangely, when Burchill came into the room, it was he who seemed like an intruder. In spite of their edginess, the squatters sat around in relaxed enough poses, their Sunday morning gear right for the room they were in. Burchill's Calvin Klein trousers and Romeo Gigli sweater screamed their inappropriateness. He stood in the doorway, McNeil on one side, Carston on the other. Liz was directly opposite him. Carston realized that it was intentional on her part. She'd angled the chair slightly to achieve it. The others were marginalized by this direct confrontation. Burchill's choice was silence, retreat, or a face-to-face with her. He pointed a finger at her, then flicked his thumb towards the door.

"You're on your way out," he said. "Trespassing's one thing, robbery's another."

To Carston's surprise, Liz took off her blue shades and held them in her lap. Her eyes were lowered for a moment, then she raised them and seemed to clamp them onto Burchill's. Her face showed no expression. The movements were all slow but they implied great power.

"I was ready to let you do yourselves a favor before, let you just move out," said Burchill. "Not any more. I'm bringing charges. You're going to pay for all the hassle you've caused me."

"What's missing?" asked Liz, surprising both Burchill and Carston with the direction she was taking.

"You know bloody well what's missing. You took it."

"That's slander, Mr. Burchill. In front of impeccable witnesses, too."

Carston knew that he should intervene and try to regularize the exchange, but he was keen to find out what might come out of it. Neither of them seemed to care about him or McNeil being there.

"Listen, wise-arse, even the plod can't miss the fact that you haven't been letting anybody in here for months. The stuff didn't walk out on its own. And you're the only ones who've been here. You've been ripping me off for too bloody long."

"No, Mr. Burchill. We haven't been ripping you off. We've been looking after this place, stopping it rotting, keeping out the damp ..."

"Bullshit! Don't give me any crap about ..."

133

"And none of us here has been anywhere near your antiques or whatever else it is you've got stashed away up there."

"Hear that?" said Burchill, triumphantly, turning to Carston. "How does she know there's antiques up there unless she's seen them?"

Carston looked at Liz, knowing the answer to the question already. She nodded to him, allowing a small smile to dance briefly across her lips.

"Your colleagues, I'm afraid. Told us what they were looking for. Very chatty."

Burchill looked from her to Carston.

"Bloody marvelous," he said. "What is this, a branch of your nick now? Special constables, this lot, are they?"

His frustration and temper grew as he tried harder and harder to establish some sort of dominance over Liz. None of the others contributed anything, but her calm self-possession was enough to reduce him to progressively more meaningless threats.

McNeil was desperate for Carston to take control of it all because she could see the reports that Burchill would be putting in to his pal the Assistant Chief Constable, but Carston had long since dismissed Burchill from his reckonings and was marveling at the control being exercised by Liz. Her mind was sharp, her tongue lethal, and her reading of Burchill was absolutely accurate.

"In any case," she was saying, "you don't have to worry about upkeep, all the usual expenditure that property involves. You must have enough of that with all your other places."

"What would you know about expenditure?"

"Enough. We rely on Direct Debits mainly, but we've got a couple of standing orders too, and a joint current account for when we need ready cash, of course. We don't generate enough income to run any high interest savings, but the Bank of Scotland's budget account's quite handy."

The patter silenced Burchill, and Carston had enormous difficulty hiding a smile. Liz's face was still deadpan as she continued. "But then we're not in your league, are we? I mean, you must have all sorts of headaches keeping track of it all. Makes me glad I'm only a parasite. I wouldn't want to have to pay the sort of taxes you do. Must be some job, sorting that lot out."

"You fucking slag," said Burchill.

The dialogue had obviously degenerated quite seriously and, to McNeil's relief, Carston decided that the time had come to take charge. He opted for grave pomposity.

"Now, now, I don't think this is getting us anywhere." He looked at Liz and she saw the smile in his eyes. "Ms. Stanley," he began, deliberately using the joke name to signal to her where his preferences lay, "you've adopted a tone which is rather too provocative. And," he added, swiveling to face Burchill, "you, Mr. Burchill, are permitting yourself to be drawn into indiscretions which, at the end of the day, can only prove counterproductive."

"I'll give you fucking counterproductive," said Burchill, insensitive to Carston's irony. "We'll see what your guvnors think of it all."

"Yes, well I'd prefer to have something concrete to go on before we involve them. I think we've done all we can here for the moment and I suggest that we go and try to get a more precise idea of exactly what's missing from the attic. Mr. Burchill?"

He stood aside, inviting Burchill to leave with him. Burchill was furious. He knew that Liz had got the better of him and that his case for evicting them all hadn't advanced an inch. It was time to call in some of the favors his police connections owed him and put this Carston bastard in his place. He pointed a finger at Liz once more.

"I mean it, you bitch. You're on your way. Make no mistake."

Liz winked and smiled at him, but she was hiding the small chill of fear his words had slid into her. She knew that in any verbal exchanges she would always have his measure, but "on your way" meant more than eviction. He'd sent his muggers before; next time they wouldn't just threaten.

By two o'clock, Carston had made the bed, hoovered everywhere, put two bags of rubbish in the garage, dusted all the surfaces he could see (he thought that actually moving objects to look for dust was masochistic), and conducted a minutely detailed inspection of the whole house. He knew it was mostly a waste of time because Kath was sure to notice something he'd missed the moment she walked through the door, but some rudimentary effort was essential

135

to make the transformation from sty to house. He took a quick shower, then phoned Ross and arranged to meet him in the office at two-thirty. When Ross arrived, it was obvious that Mhairi was still occupying most of his nights. He had racoon circles around his eyes and yawned every five minutes.

"Considered adoption?" asked Carston as Ross flopped into a chair.

Ross put his right hand on the back of his neck and massaged it hard.

"It was nearly four before she went down this morning. I was walkin' up and down with her and thinkin' how in eighteen years we'll probably be buyin' each other pints in some pub."

"I reckon after all this it'll be her round."

"Too bloody right."

Carston smiled and began to brief Ross on the things that had happened since the previous evening. First, he went through his own speculations about why the body had been dumped at Macy's and why the face had been disfigured. Ross listened and, for a change, agreed that they sounded reasonable. He usually preferred something more solid to work with, but for the moment there wasn't anything and anyway he recognized the logic of Carston's arguments.

Carston received this seal of approval with appropriate grace, then gave a detailed account of the visit to the squat and Burchill's reactions. Ross had already come across him on one of his many visits to the station and his opinion matched Carston's own.

"Story is he's got sticky fingers himself," he said.

"Yes," said Carston, "but you try and prove it. I got McNeil to sniff around. There's nothing. Trouble is, he's been away from the country too long and too often for anybody to pin him down. He was six months in Houston and he's only just back from Nigeria."

"Aye. I bet he was screwin' them inside out there."

"Ask the ACC, he's his mate."

"Aye."

"McNeil's supposed to be checking with his lawyer to get an inventory of the stuff that was in the attic."

"This afternoon?"

"Why not? The buggers charge enough. Make 'em earn it." Ross grinned, then yawned again. The infection spread to Carston.

"Your daughter's got a lot to answer for," he said as he stretched and shook himself.

"OK, she owes you a pint, too."

"Right. Now then, what else?"

"What's Spurle up to?"

"Checking out Simpson's mates. And Fraser's been contacting the antiques dealers on that list of yours to see whether they've heard from him at all."

"Long shot."

"If he's doing a runner, he'll need cash."

"If he's doin' a runner, he's guilty."

"Maybe."

"Don't start."

Carston got up and looked out of the window.

"I told you what I thought about it. It's too bloody complicated somehow for Simpson."

"Whenever you get involved in things, they always are."

Carston watched a man crossing the street. He wore black boots and white socks, with red trousers tucked into them. His jacket was also black and made of something that failed to resemble leather.

"Look at this guy," he said.

Ross got up and came to stand beside him. The man had reached the other side and turned to move along the opposite pavement. His black hair was scratched up into stiff short spikes on top and severely cropped at the back and sides. His features were squeezed into a grimace intended to make his eyes seem mean, and his lips drawn upwards in the center to form the archetypal Elvis sneer.

"What about him?" asked Ross.

"Newtonian walk."

"What?"

"That's what I always think when I see guys like that. Newton's third law of motion—equal and opposite reaction." Ross looked at Carston, then back at the man.

"They're goin' to put you away one day," he said.

"No. Look at the way he sways. All the movement's initiated by

137

the points of his shoulders, see? Hunch, dip, hunch, dip. Equal and opposite reactions. Newtonian."

"Are you sure you're a chief inspector?"

"You're young," said Carston. "One day you'll understand."

They both sat down again.

"OK for the briefing tonight, then?" asked Carston.

"Aye. Fine. They'll keep me straight."

"Give us a ring at home, will you? Just to fill me in."

"Aye. What time?"

"Soon as you finish. We should be back by five."

"Aye, OK. Away you go."

Carston nodded, but he didn't get up straight away. "Something else?" asked Ross.

Carston was tapping his forefinger on the desk, obviously lost in some thought or other.

"I was just thinking, you and your logic. I know it usually works but … it's us that make it work."

"What d'you mean?"

"Murderers don't have motives really, do they?"

"Eh?"

"I mean, they just do it. Spur of the moment and that's it. Oh, there's a reason, I know that but you've heard 'em, Jim, you've talked to enough of them. They did it 'cause they were pissed. Or she was nagging. Or the bloke just came along at the wrong time. There's no logic, no measured step-by-step motive. We invent it afterwards. We have to for the fiscal and the jury." He paused. Ross was thinking about what he was saying.

"Murder's just a quick flash of complete bloody nonsense. We're the ones who make it coherent, give it some sort of sense. Christ, in a way, we almost make it normal."

"Not a word I'd ever think of usin' about you," said Ross.

Carston grinned and got up.

"You're right. Thank God Cairnburgh's got you to guide me. I'm off."

"That's true, too," said Ross.

It was a raw day and occasional bunches of clouds suggested that they might be dumping some snow on the Grampian area before too long. Between them, though, huge swathes of powder blue sky poured generous washes of light over the hills, houses, and distilleries of Elgin. Beattie was sitting in a long, beautifully furnished sitting room whose rounded bay window gave onto the magnificent ruins of the thirteenth-century cathedral. She was glad to be out of the wind, but her stroll around the ruins as she'd killed time before her meeting with Colonel Thorpe had set her skin tingling and her blood racing. She was flushed, happy, and ready to do business.

As the colonel topped up his whisky with a little water, she looked again at the room. If its contents were anything to go by, the pieces she'd come to look at would be worth the trip. In one corner there was a Biedermeier satinbirch circular breakfast table with a tip-up top which she knew she could sell for at least fifteen hundred pounds and, set variously around the walls, a mahogany bureau and tallboy, both George III, a line-inlaid mahogany vitrine cabinet, probably Edwardian, and a gorgeous walnut sofa on foliate-headed cabriole legs. Either this man knew his antiques or he'd been lucky in his acquisitions. She'd have to be careful.

He came back to sit in the chair next to hers, put his glass down on the small hardwood chest inset with marble which served as a coffee table, and handed over the box which held the items she'd come to see.

The moment she saw them, she knew that the estimate he'd received (twelve thousand rather than the thirteen she'd quoted to Burchill) wasn't far out. In fact, on a good day and with an eager customer, they might fetch fourteen thousand or more. Along the top of the blue velvet of the display box lay a bracelet set with a graduated row of perhaps forty square cut rubies with a border of pavé set cut diamonds. Below it was a pair of exquisitely worked clips. Each had a central cushion cut ruby surrounded by old cut diamonds in a collet setting. They flashed and burned as she moved the box. It would be a genuine pleasure buying them. She made no attempt to hide her admiration but took care to temper it.

"They look wonderful. I take it there's full authentication—title, provenance?"

Thorpe was old but his mind had lost none of its sharpness. By way of answer, he recited a list which sounded like a plan of attack.

"No provenance but polariscope, dichroscope, spectrascope, thermal probe, refractometer—you name it, they've been poked by it. They're the real thing."

Beattie nodded and smiled.

"May I ask where they came from?"

"You can ask, but it won't do much good. Had 'em for years. Part of a collection the wife's father had in India. Don't think they're Oriental, though. Look European to me. What do you think?"

Beattie held up the bracket and let it turn in the light.

"Yes. French maybe."

Thorpe grunted what might have been agreement and watched the fires twisting in Beattie's fingers.

"What d'you think then?" he asked.

There was obviously going to be little in the way of commercial foreplay in this encounter. Beattie's options were very limited. Since Thorpe had let her in, she'd realized that some of her armory was useless; the old man had long since given up any hormonal enslavement, so wafts of Calèche, pouting, and trills of laughter would all be a total waste of time. Maybe all he understood was the brash military imperative. So be it. She made her own attack.

"Fits all the criteria—beauty, rarity, durability. Very desirable altogether. It'll hold its value. No doubt increase it. Seems like an excellent investment. But then, I'm not the buyer."

It took him by surprise.

"What?"

She put the bracelet back in the box and carried on talking over his question, giving him no time to regroup.

"Client's an idiot. No sense of the intrinsic value of pieces like this. Deals in numbers. You know the type."

She was inviting him to join her.

"Oh yes," he said. "Auction houses are crawling with 'em."

"Yes. Sad really. But then, they're so often the paymasters, aren't they?"

Thorpe nodded his agreement. Again, Beattie left no space for him to speak. "And we're caught in the middle, Colonel Thorpe. We

140

can try to educate them about craftsmanship, finesse, esthetics, the true appreciation of quality—but we might as well take them on a trip round Disney World. I find it very, very depressing."

Thorpe was no fool. Her words had placed him in the ranks of those with impeccable taste, but he didn't really need to be told that; he was confident of his own sense of values. He was becoming slightly wary. Nonetheless, he stayed with her terminology.

"Checkbook connoisseurs."

"In my client's case, not even that."

Thorpe didn't understand.

"Grace and refinement have bypassed him utterly. He even prefers to deal in cash."

The little flick of his head told her that her strategy was spot on. Flawless artistic credentials brought a glow of self-satisfaction, but bundles of tenners which came under no official scrutiny could light real and lasting fires. Whereas a moment before, Thorpe had held the whip hand, the fact that she was in a position to offer a hard cash transaction involving no third party increased her bargaining power by several degrees.

Having dangled the bait, she immediately retreated into abstractions and generalities about the gemstones, their settings, and the development of nineteenth-century cutting techniques. Thorpe was patient with her, but only for a short while. Soon, the promise of the tax-free exchange forced him back to business.

They bandied figures back and forth, Thorpe holding out for twelve thousand and Beattie regretting that she'd been instructed to stay nearer ten. They explored various combinations, juggled percentages and commission charges, looked at top-up possibilities, and gradually crept towards one another's positions. In the end, wooed by the knowledge that he would lose absolutely none of the proceeds to the government, Thorpe agreed in principle to accept eleven thousand. Beattie said that she would put the sum to her client, that she couldn't guarantee his acceptance, but that she was so taken with the beauty of the bracelet and clips that she really would try very hard.

The bargain was eventually sealed to what was obviously their mutual satisfaction with a glass of Highland Park. As the whisky's vapors warmed her tongue and throat, she looked out at the flurries of snow being scattered through the breaches in the cathedral's sandstone walls. The drive back would be tiresome, but the discomforts would be eased many times over by the size of her profit on the day.

Carston found almost every aspect of life baffling. At ten past four, for example, he was standing in the wide concourse of Aberdeen station waiting for Kath's train to arrive and staring at the headlines that had been scribbled on the board advertising the previous day's *Evening Express*. "Aberdeen Mum's Pie Bone Fury," he read on, and the notice beside that, "Aberdeen Surgeon's Tattoo Nightmare." In the end, he supposed, they hid simple enough stories, but the shrieking capital letters implied cataclysmic events. People everywhere wanted life to be as structured, and as dramatic, as the movies. Gore was a prerequisite and he always shuddered when he saw enticements like "Mayhem on the A90 kills five. Pictures." It was the "pictures" that got him.

In the end, the train was only nineteen minutes late—something of a triumph by British Rail standards—and, as he stood watching the bobbing heads of the passengers coming along the platform, he felt an excitement which made him very happy. In all the years that he and Kath had been married, under the familiarities and cosy habits there were still unpredictabilities and passions that kept the relationship fresh. There was also the not completely unconnected fact that a week with no one sharing his bed had sharpened his sexual appetite. It was this thought that, after he'd greeted Kath with a chaste welcoming kiss, made him put his lips to her ear and say, "Want a fuck?"

"No thanks," she said. "I've just had one."

"Where?"

"Lavatory compartment, coach twelve."

"Some lucky bastard," said Carston, taking her case from her.

She did most of the talking as they drove back to Cairnburgh. Carston was having to concentrate very hard on driving. The farther inland they went, the worse the conditions became. The snow was not yet lying very thickly, but what there was had been squelched into that filthy mush that gets thrown up onto the windscreen and seems to turn the glass brown. On several downhill bends Carston felt the back of the car slide away and he was glad when they eventually turned into their own drive. As they were stamping the slush off their shoes on the doormat, Kath looked around the hall.

"Cleaned up, I see."

"Yes," said Carston, looking round guiltily to see what was wrong.

"Well done. I'm very proud of you."

"Thank you."

She reached behind the telephone table and picked up a duster. It must have fallen there during Carston's lunchtime blitz.

"Put that back in the kitchen, will you? I'm going to have a quick shower."

"Jawohl," said Carston, half to himself.

He went through to the kitchen, took a bottle of Asda's Fortant de France from the fridge, and poured himself a glass. As he took a swig, he picked up the cordless phone, pressed memory button number three, and walked through to the living room, listening for someone at the station to answer.

He was put straight through to Ross.

"Just to say I'm back Jim, Anything happening?"

"Not really. They're no all back yet."

"No sign of Simpson, I suppose?"

"No. You were right, though, he's been on to some of the dealers on the list. Fraser and Thom are off seeing them just now."

"So he is looking for funds, then?"

"Looks like it. We checked out Mitchell's alibi for Friday too. He's clear. Like he said, he was at the Red Rum most of the night."

"How about that inventory of the stuff in Burchill's attic?"

"They told McNeil they can't possibly get access until the morning. Some crap about client confidentiality."

"That's balls," said Carston. "Give Burchill a ring. Tell him about it. Get him to ring them and make them give you the list."

"What for?"

"Because I'm a bastard. And I want Burchill to be inconvenienced."

"As long as you don't have to ring him, eh?"

"Do it, sergeant. Now then, where's McNeil?"

"I sent her over to Hilden's. See whether she can get any sense out of him. See whether Simpson's been onto him again."

"OK. When are they all due in?"

"It'll be nearer six than five, I reckon."

"Well, unless there's something you think I should know, you get away home as soon as you've had your chat with Burchill and finished with the team. Briefing me'll keep till the morning."

He rang off and settled back in his chair, wanting deliberately to put Donnelly, Burchill, and all the rest out of his mind. Tonight was for self-indulgence. Kath was home again and his life was back in order. Anchoring himself back into that reality would make him a better thinker in the morning.

Fifteen minutes later, Kath came in, her hair still damp, her face shining from the heat of the shower. She was wearing slippers, her blue toweling dressing gown, and, as far as he could make out, nothing else. He went to the kitchen, poured her a glass of wine, topped up his own, and came back in to sit beside her. They began to talk about nothing in particular, just the pleasure of being together again. His hand went around her back and was soon kneading gently at the flesh of her shoulder and the edge of her right breast. There was no doubt in the mind of either of them what would be happening before they got round to eating. As Carston put down his glass and pushed his face into the hair at the back of her neck, she said, "Jack?"

"What?"

"Have you got a mistress?"

"Yes. She's called Dolores."

"I thought so. I found some long black hairs on the yellow towel."

"That can't be her," said Carston. "She's bald."

They both laughed and then stopped talking altogether.

Seven

"They ought to bring back the treadmills," said Spurle. "That'd soon teach the buggers."

"Treadmills?" said Thom. "What're you on about?"

"Program on cable last night. There's a sheriff in the States thinkin' o' doin' it."

"What?"

"Usin' treadmills, ya bampot. Used to have 'em in all the prisons. Banged 'em up inside the wheels and they spent all day walkin' 'em round. That was the way they pumped up their water."

"You're talkin' crap as usual," said Fraser.

"Ah'm no. And it's no just the Yanks. This guy, the presenter, was talkin' about this minister in Edinburgh, Sydney Smith. He wanted 'em to make life inside borin' as fuck; crap food, hard labor, everythin' uncomf'table as fuck. That's my kind o' minister."

Ross was pinning a list of the day's tasks at the side of the chart opposite the window. He turned to face Spurle. "Aye, and did the program no say why they stopped usin' the treadmills?"

"Nah. Musta bin some Lord Longford prick complainin' about it."

"Wrong. It made the prisoners too fit. They all ended up lookin' like Fraser. Even the skinny ones."

Fraser laughed.

"It's true," said Ross.

"Aye, well, just cut down on their food," said Spurle. "That'd soon bring 'em back down to size."

Ross said nothing. Maybe if they sent Spurle to Damascus sometime he'd see the light. It didn't have to be a blazing shaft of it; a pale glimmer would be better than nothing.

145

The door swung open and Carston stepped in and looked round at them all.

"Morning, everybody," he said through a beaming smile. They chorused an answer and all looked at him with curiosity. Usually, to them, he was predictably ordinary, rarely either losing his temper or being too hearty. The good humor this morning made them all close up to wait and see what was coming. Only Ross suspected that it had something to do with Kath's return, but even he wasn't to know that Carston's well-being was based entirely on the fact that, since six the previous evening and to his own great surprise, he'd had sex with Kath three and a half times. It wasn't a record, but it was comforting to know that he could still do it.

"OK," he said briskly, looking over the notes pinned to the chart, "time to bring me up to date. What about those dealers, Fraser?"

Fraser dug out his notebook and flicked it open. "We only got hold of six o' them, sir. The others werena there."

"And?"

"Aye, Simpson had been phonin' them right enough." Fraser stopped.

"Well?" asked Carston, managing for a change to find Fraser's habit of only ever giving out information in small parcels amusing rather than infuriating. "What did he want? A little chat?"

"Some of them wouldna say, sir. But the rest said he was after more money."

Carston nodded and looked at Ross.

"Aye, sir," said the sergeant. "A runner."

"And how were they supposed to get the money to him?" asked Carston.

"He said he'd be phonin' them again. Sometime today."

"Good. What did you tell them?"

"Let us know the minute they heard from him."

"Good."

"Hilden was one of the ones he called, sir."

It was McNeil. She'd been sitting on the window ledge, looking out at the street as they talked.

"Oh yes," said Carston. "You went round to see him, didn't you? What did he have to say?"

"No much. I was there about quarter to six. He said he got a call around four but the guy hadn't been in touch with him since."

"He's still not admitting it's Simpson?" asked Ross.

"No, sarge."

"How is he?"

"Terrified. Just waitin' for the next attack. He's still shocked from the last one."

"Whose fault's that?" said Ross, still feeling some responsibility for what had happened to Hilden, but also angry with the dealer for bringing the beating on himself by phoning Simpson.

"Ach well …" McNeil let her voice tail off.

"Something else, McNeil?" asked Carston.

"No, sir. Just that he's such a poor wee soul."

Spurle exploded into a scornful laugh. Thom joined him, a beat behind and the laugh half-smothered. Carston looked a warning at them.

"Is that relevant?" Ross asked.

McNeil pushed herself away from the window and sat on the edge of a desk instead.

"Ah don't know. He canna cope, that's all. Ye get the feelin' wi' him that there's disasters waitin' round every corner."

Ross's own feelings at Hilden's weakness had been a mixture of pity and disgust. It was true that he gave off the air of a victim. It was something that Simpson would trade on. Hilden was too easy a touch to miss.

"She's right, sir," he said. "Worth keepin' an eye out for him."

"Who?"

"Hilden. Ah'd bet that Simpson'll be trying to squeeze more out of him."

Carston looked at the lists on the chart.

"We don't have the bodies to cover him all the time."

"Just the occasional check. Just in case."

"Bloody hell," said Spurle. "We canna go babysittin' every poof that—"

"Don't worry, I wouldn't let you near him," said Carston. "Sort it out, will you, Jim?"

"Aye, sir."

147

"Ah can look in," said McNeil. "Ah'm away down to Forbeshill Road to check the stuff in the attic."

"We got the inventory, did we?" asked Carston.

The look Ross gave him was old-fashioned.

"Aye. 'We' did. Ah had an earful from Burchill for the trouble. Accordin' to him, ah'll be joinin' you on the ACC's carpet."

Carston caught his expression, but didn't indulge in any of the frivolous rejoinders that came into his head. He wanted to keep up his sense of urgency, to make sure that the whole team had the same focus on the Donnelly killing. Using the reports and lists that Ross had pinned to the wall chart, he reminded them all of the finding of the body with its mutilations, tied in the visit of Simpson and Mitchell to the squat, and noted the coincidence of the fight at Macy's. He went over Donnelly's record and admitted that there didn't seem to be anything useful there. Finally, he summed up what they had and what their next moves had to be.

"I've got some doubts myself about it, but our best bet at the moment seems to be Simpson. He's disappeared, he's trying to get some cash together, and we know he had a barney with Donnelly on Friday. He's also been running a protection racket on the side and, between you and me, I'm bloody sure he's been working for David Burchill. But if you quote me on that last bit, you'll find your-selves back in uniform before teatime."

He looked over the chart again.

"So, we do everything we can to get hold of Simpson. That means another talk with Mitchell and another tour round his hangouts. Spurle, you can go and see Mitchell. And Fraser, you start with his work. Is he still at Enderby's?"

"Aye, sir," said Fraser.

"Right. Get along there and see what they know. Bellman, you and Thom get back to Simpson's place. Get what more you can out of his wife, then doorstep his neighbors again. McNeil, I suppose you'll be most of the morning at Forbeshill Road?"

"Probably, sir."

"OK. I'll leave you to keep in touch with Hilden. Get him to ring you there if he needs to."

"Aye, sir."

Carston flapped his arms at them.

"OK. Go. And let's get some results."

The incident room emptied quickly and Ross followed Carston through to his office, where they began the coffee ritual again.

"What about us? Where are we going?" asked Ross as he spooned the grounds into the filter paper.

"I don't know about you, but I've got a finance subcommittee meeting, so that'll be me for most of the afternoon," said Carston.

"Superintendent Ridley had some more ideas, has he?"

"I reckon if he has his way, the force'll be cut and cut till there's only him and his filing cabinets left. It's a bloody farce, Jim."

Ross nodded.

"See in the *Gazette* last week? There's four thousand people involved in publishing child pornography, all waiting to be investigated. Guess how many guys we've got in the obscene publications squad dealing with 'em?"

"No many, anyway."

"Seven. That's the whole of the UK. And they reckon the department's over strength, so they're cutting it."

Ross laughed.

"Aye. Sandy was tellin' me about computers. Down in England somewhere, there's one poor bastard of a constable operatin' a single terminal and monitorin' the Internet for porn. He's self-taught too. Talk about a thin blue line."

"You still at your computer?"

"Aye, when I get time."

Ross was an enthusiastic user of software packages, which did everything from organizing his taxes to drawing pictures for his elder daughter. He'd been trying for almost a year to interest Carston in transferring some of their local records onto disks. Carston didn't really need convincing, but the imperatives of budget manipulations meant that there were always other priorities.

"Hard to see how your machine could help us with this one," he said.

"You never know."

"No. It's not ... sort of definite enough. You know what I'm afraid of?"

"What?"

"That's it's just one of those completely accidental, motiveless bloody things. Donnelly's just got in somebody's way and they've stiffed him."

"Bit early to be givin' up."

"Oh, I'm not giving up. Just that … I've got no sort of feel for it. Don't care about Donnelly and can't get excited about any of the people we've talked to about it."

"I thought you were excited by the glass in his face."

"Yeah. It's interesting, but I'm not convinced we're going to find out what the hell it's all about."

"Wait till we bring in Simpson."

"Don't hold your breath, Jim."

They sat waiting for the water to boil.

"Know what I'd enjoy most?" said Carston reflectively. Ross didn't need to answer. "For us to be able to put it down to Burchill."

"You're not serious," said Ross. "You don't think he could've …"

Carston tapped a pencil on the desk in front of him. "Logically, no. He'd never be daft enough to do anything risky himself. But I'm bloody sure he's capable of getting other people to do it for him. And he's got a temper on him."

"Aye. Treats folk like shit, too."

"Yes, so it's not impossible, Jim. I wonder where he was on Friday night."

Ross drew in a breath. "Hard to find out without risking him running to the ACC again."

"Small price to pay if he's in the frame."

"But can you see him and Donnelly together?" Carston got up from his chair and went to the window. "I know. It's just that he gets on my tits so badly. Plays the system, rolls up his trouser leg, all that crap. Without all his bloody money, he'd be a raggedy-arsed welder."

"Raggedy-arsed welder? Have you see how much welders earn?"

"You know what I mean. He's a yob. But he's struck lucky and he thinks he can do what he likes."

"He can."

Carston turned back to Ross, ready to dispute what he'd said.

150

But he knew he was right. The way things were, money always talked. However vulgar Burchill was, however lacking in basic human decency, he'd always be in a position to dictate to them, and his values would always be the ones which prevailed. He nodded his agreement and turned back to the window.

As Burchill leaned towards her to look at the menu she was holding, the bow wave of fragrance that preceded him made Beattie feel sick. It was sweet, heavy, and based on some musk extract that was closer to Bovril than to the aphrodisiac promised by its manufacturers. Its liberal application today had been prompted by her phone call and a suggestion that they should discuss the jewelry over lunch. The fact that she had taken such an initiative was enough to persuade him that commerce might be supplemented by a greater intimacy. They were in L'Estaminet, Cairnburgh's most expensive restaurant. It was on the western edge of town and very close to Burchill's place. Burchill's right hand reached across and pointed to an item on the à la carte menu. It allowed him to rest his forearm lightly on her thigh.

"That's great. I quite often have that," he said, applying a little pressure so that she'd know the contact wasn't accidental.

Beattie resisted the urge to lean away from him.

"Mmm. I'm not a fan of offal," she said, knowing the double entendre would elude him.

"I love it," he said, turning his head to look directly into her eyes. "Can't get enough of it."

The nakedness of the allusion increased her disgust and she mentally added five hundred pounds to the figure she'd quote for the jewels. But she was too cool to betray anything by her expression. She smiled and shifted slightly in her chair so that he was forced to lean back from her again. As he did so, he looked at the curves of her mouth. Her lips were very full and she was well aware of their effect. There was always a sexual component to her dealings with men. At first it had annoyed her, but she'd quickly learned its value and now deployed it to her own advantage whenever it was necessary. Usually, the game was played with much more subtlety and offered subsidiary mental pleasures to her and to whichever male was making the pitch. Burchill, though, had the discretion of a peacock. She'd maintain the smile, which implied mutual understanding, but it would simply be part of the business she was there to transact.

When they'd ordered, she launched straight into her version of the meeting with Thorpe. Burchill listened as she described the jewelry, his face giving nothing away.

"So what's he asking?" he said at last.

Although Thorpe had agreed to eleven thousand, Beattie's intention had been to tell Burchill he wanted eleven and a half. The arm on her thigh and the leer had now pushed that up to twelve.

"Jesus Christ," said Burchill, momentarily dropping the refinement he was affecting. "Bit much for a bangle and earrings, isn't it?"

"Even more when you add my ten percent," she said, rolling the rim of her glass of tonic water along her lower lip and looking steadily at him.

His response was Pavlovian. "We'll talk about what you're getting in a minute."

She smiled again.

"Seriously, though," he went on. "Can't we beat him down a bit?"

"I tried. He's a bit stubborn."

"Are they really worth that much, though?"

"I'd say so."

"He might not know that. How about telling him they're duds?"

"Mr. Burchill …"

"David."

"David. He's no fool."

"No, but in your game, people are being ripped off all the time. Who's to say what's genuine?"

She ignored the unconscious insult.

"Gemstones are all different," she explained. "Their crystal structure … oh, all sorts of things. I could say the diamonds were white sapphires, but a thermal probe would prove me wrong right away."

Burchill found the association of a thermal probe with Beattie very attractive, but she gave him no time to work out an appropriate quip.

"You see, diamond's a much better conductor of heat than any other stones. As for the rubies … Yes, I could try saying they were spinel, but that's got a completely different refractive index. No, I'm afraid that, when you're dealing with things like this, inauthenticity isn't an option." She let the sentence drop away on a tiny bubble of laughter. It sharpened Burchill's eagerness to get beyond business to the other sports he had in mind.

"Twelve grand, then. OK, when d'you want to pick it up?"

Beattie tilted her head to look a question at him.

"The cash. I don't carry it round with me. Well, not quite that much. D'you want to come and get it after lunch?"

Beattie knew exactly what he meant, but she was confident that she could control the way things developed.

"If you like. I told Colonel Thorpe that I'd be in touch sometime this afternoon."

Burchill took out his mobile phone and offered it to her.

"Ring him now."

"I'd rather not. I don't trust those things. Especially not in restaurants."

Her smile flickered and she began to bite gently on her lower lip. He put the phone away.

"You're right. You see too many kids with them, don't you? Talking garbage, just so that people know they've got a mobile. Pathetic, isn't it?"

"Yes. Vulgarity incarnate."

He nodded and looked away.

"So, just before we leave the subject," she said, "let's make sure we're agreeing on numbers."

He turned his head back. She'd stopped nibbling at her lip and was stroking it lightly with her forefinger. The way his eyes were drawn immediately to it increased her scorn for him even further. For Burchill, finesse was a foreign country. She dropped her hand away from her mouth and used the fingers to start counting off points as she made them.

"First, you want the bracelet and the two clips at the asking price of twelve thousand pounds. You want to pay in cash, for which you'll need no receipt. On top of that, there's my commission; ten percent of the gross, that's one thousand two hundred pounds. Will you want a receipt for that?"

He reached out and took the hand with its outstretched fingers. "Isobel," he said. "You know I trust you. Why would I want receipts?" And, with something like delicacy, he kissed the base of her thumb. The pressure was light but his mouth was slightly open. The tip of his tongue slipped over her skin and she wanted to pull her hand away and leave. But this invasive, flesh-crawling gesture was putting the seal on an arrangement that would bring her a profit of two thousand two hundred pounds. For that, she could tolerate the slug trails he was leaving on her hand.

McNeil was sipping warm, weak instant coffee in the squat and trying to draw some coherent sentences out of Fran. She felt like Mother Theresa. Before coming to Forbeshill Road, she'd spent twenty minutes in Hilden's shop listening to him talking about antiques. He was a wreck. There'd been no sign of Simpson but Hilden had woken up every hour or so during the night, thinking he'd heard a noise. McNeil had called on all her counseling skills to ease out some of his worries, suggesting that Simpson was probably miles away and reassuring Hilden that his protection was a high priority for herself and her colleagues. His own response to that had been something like a nervous snicker and she'd feigned an interest in the trash lying about the shop just to get his mind onto other things.

With Fran, it was even less easy. There seemed to be no subject which connected to her, and McNeil had had to resort to speaking about herself in order to establish some sort of solidarity. But Fran showed no interest in sisterhood and met every advance with silence, a curl of the lip, or a direct negative. McNeil had learned to be hard in her dealings with Spurle and the others, but it hadn't clouded her basic sensitivity to people's moods and concerns. Her natural reservations about squatters increased her wariness but left her empathies intact. Liz, for example, had generated a clear pulse; its intention and effect had been antagonistic, but at least they'd interacted. From Fran, she felt only a hollow, a deep pit into which her words were falling as if unheard. And the experience concerned her; in simple terms, there seemed to be no one at home.

McNeil was telling her why she'd joined the force. The true reason was an intense, stubborn determination not to accept the second-class status of her sex. She'd read about a female assistant chief constable who'd had to take early retirement because she'd rocked the boat. Her promotion had been blocked time and time again and preference had been given to demonstrably less able candidates whose only qualification seemed to be the fact that they had a penis. As she read, McNeil felt an increasing need to test herself in the same sort of context. She wanted the fight, needed to impose herself, and talking about it would achieve nothing. Action was the only way.

She was too sensitive to use the terminology of challenge and struggle with Fran, though, and opted for a version which was equally true but more discreetly packaged.

"Not enough women in charge, that's what I reckoned. Thatcher was in Number Ten but, well … she's not even a human being, never mind a woman, eh?"

Fran's eyes stayed on the fingers which were picking at her trainers.

"Ah mean, there's some of the guys back at the station who're fine, but, ah don't know, wi' guys, there's aye somethin' lackin' somehow. They canna seem to get theirselves out the road. An' for so much o' the stuff we do, ye just need to listen. Some o' the guys are no so good at that."

She noticed that the fingers were clenching tightly at the lace on the left shoe and that there'd been a little shake of the head.

"What do you reckon?"

Fran shook her head again and gave a little shrug. McNeil waited. Maybe she'd done enough to get Fran to start contributing. The silence spread. McNeil was afraid she'd lose some of the ground she'd gained. She tried a direction she knew might be risky.

"The guys here seem OK, mind."

She was relieved when Fran immediately gave a little nod. Despite appearances, there might have been things going on in the house which were contributing to whatever Fran's problems were.

"They're OK."

"We've got to be grateful for small mercies, eh?" said McNeil. But the lightness of her tone and the encouragement it was supposed to convey froze as Fran's pale blue eyes lifted to look directly at her.

"Look, I know fine what you're tryin' to do. And it's good of you to try. But you're wastin' your time."

Her voice was gentle and the words she spoke were considered and sincere.

"You sure?" asked McNeil, her own voice dropping lower to match Fran's.

"You're tryin' to cheer me up. Will's been tryin' to do that for years. Why d'you think you're goin' to manage it in a couple o' minutes?"

"Ah don't. But ah've got to try, haven't ah?"

Fran shook her head. "No. Look, I've nothin' against you, but I'd rather ye went away."

"But if ye could just ..."

"No."

It was almost a shout. The eyes had tears in them now but they still looked steadily at McNeil. The person behind them seemed miles away. When she spoke again, the control was back.

"Christ, look, when it's priests and Jehovah's bloody Witnesses tellin' me how lucky I am, it's different. Those stupid buggers don't know any better. But you're a bloody policewoman. You've seen it all, for God's sake. Must have. It's everywhere. Never stops. How the hell can you tell me to cheer up?"

"Aye. Ye're right. It's no easy. But Fran, ye canna let them win."

"See? You don't really understand at all. It's no winnin'. It's just there. It's no a game."

"Ah know it's no, but ..."

"I was ten years old when my uncle Geoff started shaggin' me."

The words were spoken with no greater emphasis than any of the others had been. They expressed no self-pity and although the intention had obviously been to shock, the information was presented as a simple, self-sufficient fact. McNeil nodded and lifted her hand to her forehead, as if to focus the thoughts that had just been triggered in her brain.

"He called me cute kiddie names while he was doin' it. My dad didn't; he just shagged me."

156

McNeil had been here before, feeling the ground dissolve underneath her, having a sense of herself shrinking to a tiny flailing scream in a huge emptiness. She was beyond anger, relegated to a helplessness in which she could reach out with no hope of touching anything.

"Aye, you're right in a way," she said at last. "Ah have seen lots, but there's always more to come. Ah'm sorry."

Strangely, the tears had not yet overflowed. Fran's eyes seemed brimming with them and yet they stayed sparkling along her lower lashes. They made the half-smile she gave McNeil seem even more desolate.

"Crap at my job, aren't ah?" said McNeil.

Fran shook her head. "You're no so bad. But what can you do?"

"Just what ah can," said McNeil. The contact had been made in sorrow, but it had been made. She wanted to transform it into something more positive. She picked up a fat envelope which she'd brought with her. "F'r instance, the real reason ah'm here's to look at the stuff in the attic. Got to check it off with these lists. Want to give us a hand?"

"Therapy, eh?" said Fran.

McNeil tapped her fingers on the envelope and thought for a moment.

"Aye," she said. "But it'll make mah job easier too."

The half-smile had gone but Fran got up and said, "OK. Let's go."

As they went up the stairs and into the attic, McNeil kept up her patter, concentrating on the good things that happened in the course of her work, stressing the fascination of actual detection. Fran didn't answer much but she was obviously listening and McNeil knew that it was important to keep the channel open. When they actually started on the pile of Burchill's goodies, they quickly got into a rhythm which gave their contact a new impetus. McNeil hauled down boxes, opened them, and identified what she thought their contents were as Fran checked them off against the lawyer's lists. They even managed to laugh once or twice as their mutual ignorance of some of the objects made it difficult to match them with any of the descriptions.

It was during one of these interludes that McNeil saw something which caused a sudden rush of excitement. She was standing beside

Fran, trying to find a sketch of the design on the lid of the small enamel box she was holding. Fran was flicking through pages, stopping at every photograph and diagram. One particularly flimsy page was difficult to turn, but when it eventually fell into place, McNeil knew at once that she'd seen it before. It was a pencil drawing of two aspects of a crystal decanter. On the left-hand side of the sheet, there was its full outline and, above it and to the right, a detail of the pattern which had been cut into it. She put her hand out to stop Fran turning over any more pages.

"That's not it," said Fran.

"Ah know," said McNeil, "but … ah just wanted to look. Bonny, i'n't it?"

Fran looked at the drawing, then at her. "If that's what you like," she said.

There was a hint of scorn in her voice and, despite the importance of what she thought she'd just discovered, McNeil didn't want to jeopardize the relationship that was beginning to form.

"Aye, ye're right," she said. "Out o' mah league."

But, as Fran began to search once again, McNeil made a mental note of the decanter's reference number and looked forward to the revelation it would allow her to produce at the evening's briefing. Serendipity normally had no place in the grinding processes of her routines but when it did arrive, its effects were electric.

Carston was wondering whether it would be worth being a blackbird. He was sitting in a meeting listening to Ridley enthusing about a system for balancing operational expenditure with below the line fiscal exemptions targeted to encompass local variables. The bird was in the bleak branches of a tree outside fluffing at its feathers. OK, it was cold and unlikely to live a very long life, but it also never had to listen to garbage. Carston's musings extended into more abstract speculations about whether a short life mattered if it was lived in total freedom. But he did enjoy life and, in the end, he reckoned he'd opt for a longer life span. After all, only some of it had to be spent in the company of Ridleys and there was also the thought that the gifts of flight and song were somewhat attenuated by having to belong to a species known as *turdus*.

Carston looked at the droning Ridley and thought how much more suited to such a classification he was than the beautiful creature in the tree outside. His nose was a different color from the rest of his face, but not in the usual way. The dark, bulbous excrescences built on booze and other indulgences were at beast a sign of commitment, albeit to self-destruction. Ridley's nose was a small, pale hook shoved between florid cheeks. It looked powdered. And it seemed to be pointing at Carston. And there was a silence in the room. And Carston was suddenly aware that he was expected to answer whatever question had just been put.

"I'm not sure," he said. The others waited for more. He took his usual escape route—the bullshit alternative.

"I mean, I've always thought that scheduling deficits to coincide with predetermined quota alleviations was a sine qua non of creative accountancy. Aggregated fluctuations across departmental parameters, profitability scans in non-operational indices, multi-dimensional resource allocations, things like that."

Most of the assembled departmental heads knew that he was taking the piss, but none of them could ever prove it. And none of them was prepared to challenge him in case what he was saying actually made sense. As on previous occasions when he'd had to resort to the technique, their fear of their own inadequacies kept them quiet. All of them had suffered under the latest round of cuts and so they were glad that the onus of replying fell on Ridley. Carston leaned forward onto his elbows and looked along the table to the pale-nosed chairperson.

"What do you think?"

Ridley's bullshit was far less practiced than Carston's and it showed.

"Well … it depends. I mean, you … you may be right. You may have a point, but the point isn't that, is it? It's … It's what I was saying."

"Ah," said Carston, sitting back again and helping Ridley off the hook.

"No, there's only one way to approach the redefinition of resources …," said Ridley, and he was back on track again, shoveling percentages into heaps and sculpting the heaps into tight geometric

159

shapes. The bird had gone and the brief satisfaction Carston had felt from shafting Ridley quickly dissipated as he had to go on enduring the pointlessness of the meeting and wasting time which would be more profitably spent on grappling with the complexities of what had happened to Donnelly.

Seventeen Inverdee Crescent was a detached Edwardian villa with lots of garden around it and screens of cypress to shield it from passersby and neighbors alike. It was a solid but elegant construction of Peterhead granite with a price tag that, despite recessions, got relentlessly bigger every year. Behind this external grandeur, Beattie wasn't surprised to discover an interior dictated by a taste which she'd identify as eclectic or nonexistent, depending on how diplomatic she needed to be. Electronics predominated. Lights had dimmers in place of switches, the CD player slid out of the wall, the cocktail cabinet rose from its teak enclosure in a pulsing of lights like some old-style theater organ. The few objects of value and/or interest that Burchill had chosen to leave around the place as decorations were diminished by the inappropriateness of their context. The prime example was a late George III ash and crossbanded bureau. It was a beautiful piece and might fetch two and a half or three thousand at auction, but Burchill obviously saw it as a handy display cabinet for the plastic models of drilling bits and downhole assemblies, which illustrated the principles of the tool which had made him rich.

Burchill was at the dazzling cocktail cabinet, pouring her a vodka she'd already refused. He'd had a lot to drink over lunch but seemed unaffected by it. His good mood centered on the acquisition of the jewels or, more importantly, the fact that he'd managed to slide another few thousand pounds out of his ledgers and away from the Inland Revenue. After the first hand-kissing incident, he'd retreated, at least physically, into more discreet postures and although she'd had to endure his limping innuendos, she'd managed to hold her smile and exercise the light control the situation demanded.

"I think I should call Colonel Thorpe, don't you?" she said.

Burchill waved a hand at an ornament on the bureau beside the plastic models. It was a golf trolley carrying a bag with a full set of clubs.

"Help yourself," he said.

Beattie walked across and found that the ornament was, in fact, a telephone. The bag and clubs were the handset and the trolley the receiver. The dialing buttons were let into the heads of the clubs, ostensibly identifying the irons. It was one of those examples of taste that are so bad that they sometimes have a certain attraction. This one didn't.

"Cute," she said as she began dialing.

Burchill brought the drink to her as she was suggesting to Thorpe that she could drive up to Elgin that afternoon. He motioned for her to cover the mouthpiece.

"I'll drive you," he said.

She shook her head. "Not a good idea. Best for you to remain anonymous in this sort of deal."

He didn't know why that should be, but she was calling the shots, so he handed her the drink and took his whisky to the white leather sofa in the bay window. She finished the call and went to sit in a button-back tub chair which had been recovered with material printed with a Charles Rennie Mackintosh design.

"I ought to get going right away," she said. "You know what the roads are like till you get to Keith and Fochabers."

"Relax, Isobel. I told you, if there's a problem I'll drive you myself." He hurried on before she could protest again. "I could just drop you there and keep well out of sight. What do you think?"

"I appreciate it, but it's not worth taking the chance. I really ought to do it myself."

He grinned. "You're a hard woman, Isobel."

She smiled back. She had nothing left to say to him; lunch had exhausted all her polite inquiries about his work, the antiques he'd collected, his imminent tenure of the captaincy of the golf club and his plans to move back south. Into everything they'd spoken about, he'd dropped repeated allusions to what he saw as the developing nature of their relationship. Beattie had sidestepped all of them and her patience was at its limits. Burchill wasn't entirely insensitive; he could feel the change in her, but now that he'd

161

managed to get her back to his place, the opportunity mustn't be wasted.

"Oh," he said, seeming suddenly to remember something. "I meant to ask you. Somebody was telling me about a … what was it? … a bee and sheep or something like that?"

Beattie was immediately alert but anxious not to show it.

"Goat and bee, probably."

"Yes, that's it. What do you know about them?"

"Well, if it's what I think, it's a cream jug, porcelain. Eighteenth-century. Why?"

"There's this guy thinks he can get his hands on one. I wondered whether it was worth it."

He'd done his research well. Knowing her weakness for Chelsea ware, he'd been putting out feelers for pieces he might get which would impress her. He'd even toyed with the idea of offering her one for services rendered. The trouble there was that no services of the sort he had in mind had yet been rendered. Needless to say, there was no goat and bee jug, but he'd read about how desirable they were and memorized a few specifics.

"It's only just over four inches high but he wants ten grand for it. Bit small for ten grand. What do you think?"

Beattie knew that, depending on its condition, it could be worth even more than that. She deliberately switched off all signs of interest and adopted a casual tone.

"Depends. What else did he say about it?"

"Don't remember really. I think he said the date was 1745. It's got blue and red things on it. He reckoned it was OK." For a jug like the one he was describing, "OK" was an Atlantean understatement. Burchill knew it. So did Beattie. And she wanted at least to see it, hold it, even outbid Burchill for it if she had to.

She took a sip of vodka, then gave a little shake of her head.

"Don't know really. It could be alright. I'd need to see it."

"I could try to arrange that," said Burchill, putting his feet up onto a tapestry-covered stool. "What sort of things would you be looking for?"

Since she was for the moment imprisoned with him, Beattie was glad to take refuge in talking about the objects she prized more than any others. She spoke of the marks which identified the four distinct Chelsea ware periods—the triangle, then the raised anchor, followed by the red, and finally the gold anchor. Her gestures became more expansive as she described the grayish opaque book of pieces from the raised anchor period, caused by the introduction of tin into the glaze. Articles carrying a red anchor also excited her, but she would never rely solely on the mark to authenticate a piece because so many other English porcelains used it. And while the extravagant decorations of the gold anchor period had gone out of fashion a bit, they were still exquisitely made and worth an investment. But, of course, she warned, the anchor must be less than a quarter of an inch high. A large anchor was one of the signs that identified the nineteenth-century copies made in France by Emile Samson.

Burchill watched her breasts rise and fall as she spoke and as her passion for the subject made her more animated. Thanks to his own inquiries, he knew the basics of what she was saying, but it held no interest for him beyond the access it gave him to her excitements. At appropriate moments, he feigned curiosity and asked questions that set up further digressions into hard and soft pastes, Coalport and Minton reproductions, and the finesse of recognition. He refilled his glass several times and was annoyed when she consistently refused his efforts to do the same to hers. It was when he stood over her for the fifth time, angling the bottle of vodka towards her glass, that she drew back far enough from her beloved porcelain to recognize that she'd been talking to herself for some time. Immediately, she put down her glass and stood up. To her relief, Burchill stepped away and took the bottle back to the cocktail cabinet.

"God, look at the time," she said. "I've got to be on my way. It'll be dark before I get there."

The remark was foolish; it was nearly three o'clock and the daylight had already almost gone. The sensors in the framework of the window had been continually relaying signals to the central console, causing it to adjust the interior lights to compensate for the gloom outside. She hadn't noticed the changes.

"What do you think, though?" asked Burchill. "Should I get this goat and bee or what?"

"Oh yes. It's certainly worth a look. I'd be happy to authenticate it for you if you wanted me to. But now I really must get going."

"OK," said Burchill, to her surprise and relief. He looked at her, raised his glass and smiled. She waited, unsure what to do.

"What is it?" he asked at last.

"Well, the money. For Colonel Thorpe."

He slapped his brow.

"Ah, of course. Forgot all about it. Hang on."

He put down his glass and went out. Beattie was angry with herself for letting her control slip. She'd almost talked her way into becoming a sort of confidante of his in the matter of the goat and bee jug and she'd been talking as if they were equals. Now she was faced with a four-hour round trip on dark, slippery roads through the Cairngorms. The only advantage of the delay in setting off was the fact that Burchill had obviously had far too much to drink to be capable of driving. She guessed that he'd probably make the offer again, but it was out of the question.

She was looking out of the window at the gray shapes of two paper birches when he came back in with a linen holdall. He held it out and she went to take it from him.

"Twelve thousand pounds," he said.

It was absurd. Like a scene from some low-budget crime movie.

"Right," she said and turned to move to the door.

"Is that all?" he asked.

When she turned back, he was holding a fat envelope towards her. He angled his head and raised his eyebrows, seeming to inquire whether she wasn't interested in what it was.

"Another twelve hundred," he said. "All for you."

She gave a nervous laugh and held out her left hand. He moved the envelope slightly to one side and took her outstretched hand. Once again, he bent so that his lips were pressed against her palm. His grip on her wrist was firm.

"I've enjoyed this afternoon," he said, pulling her towards him.

She tried to free her hand.

"Oh, come on, Isobel," he said. "What's the problem? We both know what's what, don't we?"

"No, we don't," she said, trying to impose herself by a puzzled smile and a show of surprise, giving him the option of withdrawing without losing face. "Look, David, I've got to get going. In this weather, it's ..."

Burchill was committed. There was no thought of losing face or compromising future contacts. The whisky combined with her proximity to uncover one of those frequent hungers which were so fundamental to his way of being. It had grown as he sat watching her speak, seeing her eyes sparkle and her lips shine. He couldn't see beyond the fact that this woman had come voluntarily to his house, that she'd laughed at his jokes over lunch, and that she was a partner in something illegal. He'd seen her in action before; she was hard, she knew the score, and she knew bloody well that he wasn't handing out twelve hundred quid just to say thank you for a couple of bits of jewelry.

She'd dropped the holdall and was pushing at him with her free hand. It was still restrained, there was no panic, no violence; she was simply trying to get free. He threw the envelope aside and grabbed her. Both his arms were now around her back and his cheek was hard against hers.

"Isobel, for Christ's sake. What's the matter? There's no need for this. Just relax. There's nothing to be afraid of."

"I'm not afraid. I just want to go. I want to get to Elgin. I ..."

He stopped her by jamming his mouth against hers. Their teeth ground together and his tongue dug at her stretched lips. She moved her head aside, but he brought one of his arms up and held the back of her neck with it to force her face back towards him.

"Forget about fucking Elgin," he said "You're here now. So just fucking relax."

She wanted to cry. Suddenly, overwhelmingly, she knew what was coming and that there was nothing she could do about it. He was strong, hard and he'd stopped pretending. His arm was bending her neck so much that she was afraid he'd break it and his grip around her back made it difficult to breathe. Even if she could scream, no one would hear her. She'd let herself wander into this nightmare like some trusting virgin and she was about to be raped. Burchill's mouth was sucking and tearing at her face. He was saying nothing now and his attentions were savage. He'd quickly gone beyond supplications and was capable of doing her unimaginable harm. All the books said that the best technique was submission; it didn't stop them but it could lessen the hurt. She wasn't aware of the tears running down her cheeks as, the next time his mouth came up against hers, she opened her lips and pushed her tongue hard into it, licking up against his palate, tasting the sourness of his whisky. His breath came rushing nauseatingly out into her as he sighed his satisfaction at her response. His grip slackened and his hands came round to clutch at her breasts. She pulled away but was immediately grabbed again and forced down to the carpet. He flung her onto her back and kneeled over her, his legs pinning her arms at her sides.

"Don't worry, Isobel. You'll like it," he said as he deliberately tore the buttons from her blouse one by one. Again, she was wearing no bra and he looked at her breasts as he reached behind him with his right hand and kneaded hard into her groin.

Her tears excited him even more. His left hand was opening the zip on his trousers and his eyes now were on her bruised lips. The need to force himself between them beat in his head. As he hoisted himself up and pulled her face into his crotch, she began to gag, her abdomen convulsing and the muscles of her throat going into spasm to reject the thing that was choking her, bruising her, tearing the edges of her mouth. Her body heaved against the assault, but Burchill's fury was stronger. It was a kaleidoscope of pain and she tried to think herself away from it, project forward to a time when it would be over. But she was given no freedom to influence what was happening. After he'd finished, temporarily, with her mouth, he turned her onto her stomach and new fires were set raging in her body as he probed and plunged at her anus. Wave upon intricate wave of torment surged up from the base of her spine. And he was swearing at her, calling her "bitch," "whore," "fucking slag" with each thrust, his excitement twisted higher by the blood which was staining her back and running into the fibers of the carpet.

By the time he turned her over once more and concentrated on her mouth again, the pain was just part of the maelstrom in her mind. She was aware now of the time passing and of her whole body as a wound. Again and again, she gagged as he scoured at the inside of her mouth, deepening the cuts, bruising more of the delicate tissues of her throat, and she tried to detach herself from the agony. When he eventually entered her vagina, it was almost a relief. He was still violent, angry in his heaving, but the worst of his excesses were over. As he eventually ejaculated, he gave a loud gasp, which was near to a shout, and pulled at her hair so hard that some of it came away, tearing out small pieces of scalp. After a few moments panting, he pushed himself up on his arms and looked at her. Her face was ravaged, stained with tears and blood, but she was no longer crying. She looked back at him and was appalled when he smiled at her. Then he rolled to the side, lifted his forearm across his eyes, and lay on his back on the carpet, breathing deeply.

Beattie got up, adjusted her clothes, and fetched her coat from the hall. She put it on, picked up the holdall, and the envelope and, still not having looked at Burchill, went out to her car. As she opened the front door, she heard him laughing. But it didn't matter. She drove home to Victoria Street, letting the tears flow freely but silently. Once inside her flat, she put Burchill's money in her safe, made a phone call and sat on a kitchen chair, waiting.

Eight

On Tuesday morning, McNeil was late. The previous afternoon, Carston had been surprised when she hadn't arrived for the usual briefing and concerned that there was no word from her by the time he went home. His curiosity was piqued further when she'd phoned him there halfway through the nine o'clock news. First she'd apologized and reassured him that everything was fine, then asked if she could have his authority to get some backup resources from their labs. She sounded weary and Carston didn't want to put any pressure on her by asking what she was up to. He knew that she could be trusted. He'd given the permission she was after, then been reassured by her that he'd be pleased with what she had to offer.

When she came in, she was still breathless from having hurried and clearly in a somber mood. She said a brief "sorry, sir" but didn't elaborate on what had kept her; of all the team, she was the most circumspect about both her work and her private life. Spurle tutted loudly as she threw her coat over the back of a chair, but the quick look she flashed at him penetrated even his insensitivity. She'd spent a lot of the previous day empathizing. It had been long and fraught. In the end, other's people's miseries got to you and if Spurle stepped a millimeter out of line, she'd welcome the chance to release some of the energy that had built inside her.

Before she'd come they'd been reviewing the information on the wall chart while they waited for a promised fax from the forensic lab in Aberdeen. The chart had been tidied and rationalized. Ross, needing to stay in the incident room all of Monday to coordinate things if anything cropped up, had spent the afternoon establishing a chronology of events and correlating the movements of everyone concerned. There was a series of columns. The vertical axis began at Friday and ended at Monday. Each day was further segmented into four, marked morning, afternoon, evening, and night. The other axis was for people. Simpson, Mitchell, and the five squatters had a column each. The final column was for the antiques dealers who'd been contacted by Simpson. They were there not because any of them were suspects, but because they might be useful in helping to pin down Simpson's movements. When Carston had first seen the chart, he'd mouthed yet another little silent prayer of thanks for his sergeant. A glance at the display was enough to tell him who was where at any time, who they were with, which alibis matched, and where there were gaps which might be significant.

"Can I add something, sir?" asked McNeil.

"Go ahead," said Carston.

She took a photocopy of a document from a folder she was carrying, went to the chart, and pinned the piece of paper beside the photograph of the wound which had killed Floyd. She took a pace back and turned to look at the rest of them. They all peered at the new piece of evidence and Carston moved closer to the chart to examine it. It didn't take long.

"Brilliant, McNeil," he said. "Where'd you get it?"

"That inventory of Burchill's stuff. That's the design on a decanter he had. Part of a set from Edinburgh Crystal. No sign of any of it in the attic."

Although the markings around the wound were relatively short, there was little doubt that the two patterns matched. The flutes and swags of the cut glass curbed inwards to meet at the edges of the decanter; the dark line in Floyd's scalp and the hard little tributaries that ran into it at regular intervals mimicked them exactly. It left none of them in any doubt that they'd identified the murder weapon.

"Magic, Julie," said Fraser, and his expression showed that he meant it. Murmurs from all the others, including Spurle, indicated that, for the time being at least, she was one of them.

"Ah'm no sure how much it helps, though," she said. "Ah mean, what's Simpson doin' batterin' folk around the head with crystal decanters? No his style."

"He'd use whatever was nearest. Plenty o' stuff like that at

Enderby's. And for him, doesna matter if it's a baseball bat or a chandelier, as long as it hurts," said Fraser.

Carston knew that he was right, but McNeil's discovery had opened up an interesting new area. Their search for the location where Donnelly had actually been killed could be narrowed down because there were only certain places you'd expect to find decanters. Enderby's, the auctioneers where Simpson worked part-time as a gopher, was one of them. On top of that, this particular decanter had belonged to Burchill. It was a connection that gave him a small nudge of pleasure.

"Explains why forensics found all the glass on him," said Ross.

Carston's thinking had been going the same way.

"Might explain the glass stuck in his face, too," he said.

They all looked at him, not sure of the connection he was making. He spoke the thoughts as they came to him. "If you've killed somebody with a decanter and there's glass everywhere, there's no way of getting rid of all the bits, is there? Trouble is, if you're thinking clearly, you'll know that sort of glass'll be easy for us to identify. So what do you do?"

Nobody offered to answer.

"You sprinkle a bit more over him, a different type, cover him with so many bits of glass, the stuff from the decanter'll get lost among it. And you stick the broken end in his face so that we think that's what you've killed him with. And it looks like a bar fight that went too far."

Ross was nodding his agreement.

"The trouble is," Carston went on, "that sounds too clever by a long way for Bazza Simpson."

"No really," said Ross. "Donnelly was dead for a while before he got the glass in his face. It doesn't take a mastermind to know we'll find that out. If it's tryin' to fool us, it's no a very good effort."

"Maybe not, but somebody's tried. And our Baz hasn't bothered to cover his tracks in the past."

"Aye, but he's no killed nobody neither," said Fraser. "Not that we know about."

"Right," said Carston. "I reckon we've waited for him long enough. You're sure nobody you talked to yesterday knew anything?"

He looked round at them. They all shook their heads.

"OK, then. Like we said, looks as if he's done a runner. Jim, put out a general call. Send his photo round. Get onto the media." He took the photocopy of the decanter design off the wall and turned to McNeil.

"This was part of a set, you said?"

"Aye, sir."

He handed it to her. "Right. Look out the patterns for the glasses that go with it. Get onto Edinburgh Crystal, fax them a copy to see whether it's a common design. The rest of you, there's no point all of us sitting here waiting for forensics. Get copies of those patterns and get round anywhere that might sell this sort of thing. See if they've seen it or heard anything."

They all started getting ready to leave. "And don't forget we're looking for Simpson, so keep your eyes open and keep on asking questions about him."

Ross followed Carston into his office. On the desk, there was an envelope marked "DCI Carston. Private." Carston opened it and said, "Shit!" Ross waited to be enlightened.

"We've got an appointment upstairs. As soon as we've finished the briefing, it says. Beresford."

Donald Beresford was the Assistant Chief Constable of the West Grampian force.

"So Burchill meant it."

"Seems like it. I don't suppose it's a social call. Let's have some stimulants first."

Ross switched on the machine to warm up the coffee.

"Nice bit of work by McNeil," he said.

"Yes. She's a bloody good copper. It's a shame we'll be losing her."

"That definite, is it?"

"Well, no, not definite, but you know the policy nowadays—once she makes sergeant, she'll move back into uniform."

"Aye. I can see why they do it, but it's a bit of a waste."

Carston nodded. Moving individuals between branches made for lots of flexibility and stopped them getting stale, but it didn't take account of the experience that was being lost when you made a detective sergeant into an inspector in Human Resources, then a chief inspector in the Traffic Division or whatever. It was one of the reasons that he'd curbed his own desire for promotion. Apart from the fact that he'd be moving into the hierarchy so loved and manipulated by Ridley and others, he wanted to stay in the CID and indulge his passion for speculation. He was also convinced that he'd be more use to the citizens of Cairnburgh doing his present job than becoming a facilitator or whatever the current term for "bloody waste of time" was.

"So," he said, "what about this decanter? Where do we start?"

"The places you've just sent the team to see—antique shops, glass showrooms ..."

"Auction rooms."

"Right."

"Have we checked Enderby's?"

"Not the place, no. It was shut at the weekend. Fraser spoke to the boss yesterday but there was no sign of Simpson."

"It's worth us having a proper look, though."

"Aye, it's auction day today. There'll be a sale this mornin'. Might be worth gettin' along there. There'll be some dealers there."

"Right. Good idea. As soon as we're finished with the head-master, you can nip along and see what's what."

"What about Burchill? We going to talk to him?"

"What, because it was his decanter?"

"Aye."

"Be nice, wouldn't it? Put him on the spot. See how he wriggles."

"Is it likely, though?"

"What d'you mean?"

"Well, he's speakin' about pressin' charges against yon squatters. If he's involved with Donnelly's murder, he's no goin' to be goin' out o' his way to be anywhere near us, is he?"

Carston thought about this.

"He's devious enough to do that, Jim. Could be a double bluff, too. Deflecting attention, forcing us to connect him with things other than the killing."

"Aye, and he's no got a very high opinion of us in any case."

"You can say that again."

Ross was silent for a moment, then said, "It's a wee bit of a coincidence, though. That decanter belongin' to him."

Carston nodded, then ran his right hand through his hair before clasping both hands behind his neck. "I wonder," he said. "Just our luck for it to be nothing at all. Donnelly was probably nicking it. He had it with him when he met whoever killed him. Maybe they had a row. The decanter was just handy, that's all. Burchill's only involved because Donnelly was squatting in the place where he kept some of his antiques."

"So Donnelly was tryin' to fence the stuff?"

"Could be. No use to him otherwise, is it?"

Ross shook his head and began pouring the coffee.

"That's another thing that's against it being Simpson," said Carston.

"Why?"

"Well, if he's had a set-to with Donnelly in the afternoon, they're hardly going to be doing business together a couple of hours later."

"Maybe Donnelly was on his way somewhere and just came across him."

Carston sat forward again and took the mug Ross was handing to him.

"Or Burchill. You're right. Could be this, maybe that. The decanter's a find, but I wish they'd hurry up with that bloody forensic report."

His complaint was unreasonable. The murder was only three days old and yet he'd been promised the report already. Normally, it took weeks for a job to be processed through the system; this one had been given an unheard-of impetus by the efforts of Brian McIntosh. It was just that things had happened so fast at the weekend that the lull on Monday gave the impression that they'd come to a full stop. He stood up and carried his coffee through to the incident room. Ross went with him. McNeil was the only one left there. She was speaking on the telephone. Carston went to the chart and ran his finger across the Friday evening slot.

"So, he's killed between nine and twelve. Everybody we've talked to is more or less covered for then. Fran and Will were at the club, though, and they're alibi-ing each other. The only gaps are for Simpson."

McNeil had finished her call and was making a note in her book. "That wee girl, Fran. She's no right, sir," she said.

"In what way?"

"Just depressed. She's had enough. Ah think we should keep an eye on her."

Carston shook his head. He liked McNeil's sensitivity but he had no slack to give for social work. "She's still part of the investigation," he said, "but we can't give her any special treatment."

"Aye, ah know. Ah'll do what ah can."

Carston nodded, then turned back to the chart, genuinely sorry that he couldn't offer her any reassurance. He dropped his hand to the Friday night slot. "He got dumped at Macy's between four and five-thirty. Nobody's really covered for then. All the squatters reckon they were asleep, Benny Mitchell had left the Red Rum but he was out of his skull. And again, where was Simpson?" His eyes moved over the chart, matching individuals with one another, stretching time scales to see whether that made any difference. It was difficult to see past the blanks in the column under Simpson's name. He picked up a black marker pen and slowly drew a line down the far right-hand side of the chart, creating another column.

"What's that for?" asked Ross.

"Whoever did it?"

"Going to put a name to him, then?"

Carston was about to answer with a version of "innocent until proved guilty" but suddenly stopped and thought for a moment before obliging Ross by writing "Burchill" at the top of the column.

"Very funny," said Ross.

Carston had become brisk again. "Jim, I reckon he deserves a place up on our wall. Come on. Let's get the crap over with."

He put his half-drunk coffee on a desk and left the room. Ross drained all of his, then hurried after Carston, catching him in the corridor which led to Beresford's office.

They'd been with him for several minutes before he eventually got round to the business they knew was on his mind. His embarrassment was obvious. He knew they were both good officers and he didn't like having to speak to them simply because Burchill had put in a complaint. Nonetheless, a brother had asked for his protection and he wasn't in a position to refuse it. He brought up the subject apologetically, conversationally, making a tacit plea for their cooperation in smoothing the path he had to follow. Ross remained silent, but Carston had no intention of ceding anything to Burchill's abuse of his supposed privileges. First, though, he disarmed the ACC.

"Well, Mr. Burchill's certainly had a lot to put up with from these quarters," he said, "and I'd hate to think that we've been making things worse for him."

"Oh, I don't think it's all that bad. It's just that he's not convinced we're following the right lines of inquiry."

"Had much experience of detective work, has he, sir?" asked Carston, with a smile intended to persuade Beresford that he was simply joking and helping to keep the interview relaxed. Instead, Beresford felt threatened.

"It's no joke, Jack," he snapped. "The man's got a helluva lot of influence. He could do us a lot of damage. Make things very difficult for the police committee."

"He's making things difficult for me already," said Carston.

"Well, lay off, then. Concentrate on getting rid of those squatters."

"We're in the middle of a murder inquiry, sir. Getting rid of squatters is a long way down my list of priorities."

"Well, shift it up, then," said Beresford menacingly. "And keep away from Burchill."

The interview had progressed very quickly to flashpoint. Carston was having difficulty preventing his anger from showing.

"Can't do that, sir, I'm afraid," he said.

"Well, you'd better."

"Out of the question," replied Carston with a determination that alarmed Ross.

"What?" said Beresford, his pinched little face red with his own suppressed anger.

"We've just found out that the murder weapon belonged to him."

It was nicely timed. Beresford had no counter to it and the initiative was with Carston.

"What do you mean?" was all Beresford could manage.

"The murder weapon, sir. It belonged to Mr. Burchill," said Carston, deliberately adding no further explanation. Beresford's embarrassment at the whole interview was further compounded.

"You mean he's a suspect?" he asked.

"I haven't ruled anything out," said Carston. "But this weapon thing … it means I'm going to have to talk to him again, find out what his movements have been this weekend. It's central to the inquiry now, if only for elimination purposes."

It sounded reasonable. Ross knew better, but Beresford found himself having to shift his responsibilities as a police officer above the favors he owed Burchill. He sat in his chair, obviously thinking about what Carston had said.

"For Christ's sake, Jack," he said at last, "try to be a bit diplomatic about it. I mean, with people like that there are ways and ways."

The whole conversation had turned out to be more uncomfortable for him than it had been for the others. He tried to shrug it off by asking about the investigation and how it was progressing. Carston answered him honestly enough but, whenever a chance arose to imply that Burchill had somehow obstructed progress, he took it. Ross, a devotee of the quiet-life approach where his superiors were concerned, wished that Carston would just make the necessary small talk so that they could leave with everyone feeling secure. But Carston had been subjected too often to the imposition of unearned privileges and the stifling effects of the old-boy network to make any concessions. By the time they left, Beresford had made a mental note to put whatever obstacles he could in the way of Carston's promotion but had had to accept that he'd be getting more phone calls from Burchill and that, for the moment, he'd be helpless to be of any service to him.

In the corridor outside, Ross stopped, took a deep breath and said, "Ye're as thrawn as my wee Mhairi. Ye want a bloody good hidin'." He walked on, stopped at the top of the stairs and turned back to Carston. "Sir."

Enderby's was definitely not Sotheby's or Christie's. The lots arranged around the big saleroom were mostly junk. Some of the

176

furniture looked interesting and there were two watercolors that might fetch a decent price, but the smaller objects spread over the long table at the front were things that had been cleared out of attics and garages and grouped together by the boxful. Picture frames were stacked with old family photographs, candlesticks with jugs and bottles. One tray carried nothing but buttons. There were books, embroidered tablecloths, clocks and plates, old golf clubs, seven television sets and three vacuum cleaners, walking sticks, and fire irons. It was hard to believe that anyone had ever been proud to own any of it, but it must all have belonged to someone. From the intimacy of an interior it had been ejected into this public squalor alongside other pieces whose values and associations had been lost. The men and women looking out of the photographs saw only strangers.

And the strangers were sitting in rows on chairs and sofas that would eventually be sold with the rest of the things in the room. Those who'd been too late to get a seat were standing around the sides of the room, leaning against desks, tables, and wardrobes, or crowded at the back in front of the columns formed by a dozen or so rolled up carpets. The people seemed as variegated as the lots that were on offer. There were a few dealers, most of them wearing caps, one of which claimed that its owner was an admiral in the US Navy. In the seats were some people who were not there to buy but came every week because it was warm and vaguely entertaining. The voices of some of the bidders as they called out their paddle numbers when they'd been successful were posh enough to suggest that they too were there for the entertainment and simply doing a bit of bidding as a hobby. Among those standing were several young people, some of them couples, whose selective bidding indicated that they were serious about what they were doing. Maybe they were trying to get a foothold in the antiques game. Or maybe they were just desperate.

The auctioneer, a man in his forties with gray hair and a wispy gray beard stained with food, droned drearily through the lots, reluctant to put much enthusiasm into his efforts, knowing the limits of those he was dealing with. They had sales every other week and the same people came to them time after time. Each trayful of garbage went for around twenty or thirty pounds and, in this first part of the sale, the only excitement was caused by two very determined people who were interested in the same lot, a round white clock with an advert for Eno's Fruit Salts on it. Bidding started at twenty-five pounds but went to what everyone else knew was the ridiculous figure of one hundred and twenty before one of the bidders shook her head and the other pretended to look pleased that he'd spent so much.

After a short break around eleven o'clock, the auctioneer moved to the furniture. The main entertainment was over and there were now fewer people in the room. Those remaining were dealers and a few private individuals who had picked out a table or some other piece they hoped to get cheaply. They all knew more or less what they wanted and how much they were prepared to pay for it. The sale was much faster and, one by one, the chairs, chests, tables, and sideboards were sold and stacked at the other end of the room. The auctioneer moved along with the group of bidders around him. It was when they got to the third carpet that things went wrong.

The first two had been toppled to the ground and unrolled to show their patterns and colors. They'd both been bought by the same individual, the man with the admiral's baseball cap. As the third carpet was pulled upright, everyone knew at once that it was different. The two assistants doing the job had difficulty in getting it vertical and, as soon as they did, it fell forward out of their grasp and landed with a loud thump. It had looked quite funny but no one laughed. Sticking out of the bottom of the carpet was a foot. It was wearing a blue sock and a dirty white Nike trainer and it was very, very still.

Ross was on the point of leaving for Enderby's when the call came through. Carston picked up the phone and, a few seconds into his conversation, signaled to Ross to wait. When he finally put down the receiver, he was silent for a moment before saying, "Well, Jim, what do you know—I'm going to have to come with you."

With Carston's team so heavily involved in the Donnelly murder, the investigation of the body discovered at Enderby's should have been given to one of the other DCIs, but the fact that Carston's prime suspect worked there made it seem possible that inquiries might overlap. Carston had been assigned to the case and left to decide whether there appeared to be any links and what extra resources he'd need.

He and Ross left McNeil in charge in the incident room with instructions to try to chase up the fax they were waiting for. From Edinburgh Crystal she'd learned that the pattern on the decanter was one they'd used since the nineteenth century. That meant that there were hundreds of them. It was a popular style and tracing an individual set was impossible. Carston told her to tell Spurle and Thom to take over Fraser and Bellman's patch as well as their own, and to get Fraser and Bellman down to the auction rooms to start taking statements from the witnesses. He also took some pleasure in phoning Beresford and asking for more men. Astonishingly, Beresford told him that he'd have to apply directly to Superintendent Ridley, who'd taken over "human resource allocation." It was a task Carston put off until later.

"What the hell's going on?" he muttered as they pulled in alongside the other police cars which were sealing off the road outside Enderby's.

"What d'you mean?"

"Two bodies in five days. It's like bloody Chicago."

They went straight through to the main room, where the crime scene team were already part way through their painstaking procedures. They'd taken fibers and other samples from the carpet and gradually unrolled it to reveal the rest of the body. Two of the auctioneer's white-faced assistants agreed that, from the clothes, it looked like Barry Simpson, but there was no way of confirming that just yet. When the team had unwrapped the three large pieces of sacking from his head, they'd found that there was no face left. The scalp and hair seemed intact, but from halfway down the forehead to the top of the torso there was only a pulp. Twists of flesh were caught with splinters of bone, the jaw and teeth were shattered, a small lump of gray paste was all that was left of the right eyeball, and the left one had disappeared completely. Carston never got used to this. He loathed seeing human beings reduced to lumps of matter. He felt an overwhelming sadness at the obscenity of wounds which opened up the fragile interior tissues and gave even the most casual glance access to breaches not only in the body but somehow also into what had been the person. Violent death not only took everything away, it reached back into the victim's life and shredded whatever decency it may have had.

Brian McIntosh was on his knees, studying the tangle of meat and talking into his dictaphone. He looked up and heaved himself to his feet as Carston stopped beside him.

"Epidemic, isn't it?" he said.

"Morning, Brian," said Carston. "What've you got?"

"Just what you see so far. Doesn't seem to be anything else, just four or five wallops across the face with that."

Carston looked round at where he was pointing. The team had set up one of the auctioneer's trestle tables to lay out the pieces of evidence they'd picked up and dropped into plastic envelopes. One of the items was a baseball bat.

"I don't think he knew what hit him," McIntosh added, scratching at his beard. "I reckon he was lying on his back … on this carpet by the look of the stains there." Again, his hand sketched a gesture to follow the spread of the bloodstains which had exploded in rays and splashes out from the broken head. The body had obviously shifted its position when it was wrapped in the carpet, but the place where the head had been when the bat had done its damage was obvious. The majority of the stains projected from the right-hand side, but there were some shorter ones to the left.

"The first hit knocked him unconscious, maybe even killed him. There's no sign of him trying to defend himself."

"Too early to give me a time?" asked Carston.

The scratching became a stroking, a rearranging of the hairs under his chin.

"Secondary laxity's not set in yet, and there's no putrefaction to speak of. Usual reduction of adenosine triphosphate …" He stopped, waiting for the protest he'd hoped to provoke.

"Stop taking the piss," said Carston.

McIntosh shook his head sadly. "If only you'd get an education. What I'm saying is that rigor's still there. It generally takes about thirty-six hours to wear off but with this cold weather it'll probably be longer. So I'd say … what? … day and a half, two days?"

"So, sometime Sunday night? Early Monday morning maybe?"

McIntosh nodded. "That'd be about it."

Carston put a hand on his shoulder. "Thanks, Brian. D'you think you could do the business with Aberdeen again? They must have worked treble time to get the Donnelly stuff for us. It's coming in today. What d'you reckon for this one?"

McIntosh smiled. "I'll see what I can do."

Carston patted his shoulder and moved with Ross over to the rows of plastic bags on the table as McIntosh kneeled to his work once again. Carston bent over to look more closely at the baseball bat. It was heavily stained with dried blood and there were little nausea-inducing lumps still sticking to it.

"I'd say that's Simpson's. Look, 'HomeRun.'"

Ross looked and nodded.

"S'pose it is him, then. Don't fancy askin' his wife to identify him."

"No. Dental records are out, too. But his hands are OK, we'll get his prints."

He looked through some of the other items lying there. One of them made him whistle. It was a large brown envelope which was gaping open because of the bulk of its contents. It was full of bank-notes, mostly tenners from what Carston could see.

"Whoever he was, he wasn't poor."

Ross had picked up two of the other plastic envelopes. A label identified their contents as being from the back pocket of the victim's trousers.

"Interesting," he said, holding it out for Carston to take.

Carston looked at the pieces of paper in the envelopes. On one he read, "Raised anchor—52. Red anchor—56. Gold anchor—56–69." The other was equally enigmatic. It was torn from a notebook and had the name "JASON D" printed at the top with a row of numbers underneath it.

"What d'you reckon?" asked Carston. "A clue?"

Ross shrugged. "Only Jason D I've heard of is Jason Donovan."

"So, you reckon Bazza was a fan? And what are the numbers for?"

181

Ross took the envelopes back from him, looked at them again, shook his head, and put them back on the table. "Pass," he said.

"And what's all the stuff about anchors?"

Ross shook his head again. "I don't know, but it's just the sort of thing you like to play with, isn't it?"

"Yes," said Carston emphatically.

The other items seemed innocuous: cigarettes, matches, a handkerchief that could have doubled as a floorcloth, two short biros with "Ladbrokes" printed on them, and a few coins. Carston turned away and looked at the people in the room. They were all busy and yet moving very slowly as they inched their meticulous way over the floor and furnishings looking for things unknown. If the lump on the floor was Simpson, it posed all sorts of questions. It was still possible that he'd killed Donnelly but a bit of a puzzle as to why he should then be a victim himself just a couple of days later. And if he wasn't responsible for the first murder, they'd have to retrace their steps with Donnelly as well as beginning a fresh investigation on Simpson. It looked very much like the call to Ridley couldn't be postponed for long. He left Ross to keep track of what was going on in the saleroom while he went upstairs to the offices. Fraser and Bellman were in one. They'd arrived just after Carston and were working their way through the thirty-four people who'd been in the room when the body had fallen out of the carpet. They were listening patiently, asking simple questions, and writing out statements in longhand. It was a job that had to be done but which so far had added nothing to what was already known.

The auctioneer, William Enderby, was in the front office. It was a dreary place, a cliché needing only a seedy, unsuccessful private eye to complete it. Enderby was trying to concentrate on a pile of letters on the desk. He was glad to see Carston because the irruption of a corpse into a routine he'd been following for twenty-odd years had dislocated his perceptions. He needed to understand what was going on, needed help to find out where he was supposed to belong among all of this. Carston was aware of his disorientation and tried to make the interview seem more like a chat. He left his notebook in his pocket and listened as Enderby tumbled his words out, eager to distance himself and his business from the event. In

182

spite of himself, Carston found his eyes drawn back to the stains in his beard again and again. Enderby was a long way from the auctioneers one saw occasionally on the television news as they took telephone bids from Tokyo for another Van Gogh. He belonged to this office.

When Carston asked him about the notes they'd found in the pockets of the murdered man, however, the image of failure disappeared momentarily as the expert surfaced.

"Chelsea ware," he said with hardly any hesitation. "The numbers are years. What were they?"

"Sorry, I can't remember. I didn't make a note of it."

"I'm sure that'll be it. Raised anchor's the early period, red one's later, and the gold one's probably … oh, seventeensixtyish."

"Why would someone have a note of that, though?"

Enderby blew out a little disclaiming snort. "No idea. The only thing I can think is that, if it's Simpson, somebody asked him to look out for it. Customers often leave bids with the men, ask them to keep an eye open for particular things they're interested in." He paused, then added quickly, "But he'd never get that sort of thing here."

"Oh?"

"No. Not anymore. Might have in the old days. When we still got house clearances."

"Doesn't that happen any more?"

"Not if there's anything worth having. We only get the leftovers. When the big places come up, the dealers are in there right away, buying up the best pieces privately."

"Don't you get dealers here, then?"

"Not the big ones. This is just bits and pieces."

Carston nodded his interest. "The Antiques Road Show" gave the impression of a genteel club where people gathered to indulge their interest in various forms of aesthetics. It was a shame (but no surprise) to find that, like most others, the business was driven by greed and competition.

"The carpets," said Carston. "Where were they from?"

Enderby had been beginning to relax. His mood changed again, the memory of the body returning.

"That was a house clearance. Up near Forres. We fetched them in the van last …" —he flipped open a diary on the desk to check his information— "… Wednesday. Then they would have been stored in the basement for a couple of days till the men brought them upstairs after we closed on Friday."

"Where would they have put them then?"

"Stacked them in the saleroom. Where you saw them."

"And they haven't been moved since?"

Enderby shook his head. Carston paused for a moment to take stock of the information. If the carpets were in place on Monday morning, it meant that the killing must have happened on Sunday night.

"Was anyone in at the weekend?" he asked.

Enderby shook his head again. Carston realized he was staring at the stains in the beard again, and hastily averted his eyes.

"Who's got keys to the place?"

"Me, my partners, Jean, that's my secretary, and Dougie Craig, the foreman."

"Simpson didn't have one?"

"No."

"So how did he get in? Have you checked to see whether there was any break-in?"

"Why should I? Nothing's been stolen. We'd have noticed something yesterday."

"How many entrances are there?"

"Just the two. But we never use the back door. Always the front, even when we're unloading."

Enderby's tone was defensive. It was slowly dawning on him that the very fact of being the owner of the premises where someone had been murdered meant an inevitable involvement, however much he might wish to distance himself from it all. The suggestion, however faint, that he'd been somehow remiss in not safeguarding the place made him feel guilty. Carston changed the subject and asked about Simpson. He obviously wasn't a particular favorite of Enderby's, and the firm had only been using him part-time. He had a tendency to lose his temper and kick out at whatever happened to be near when he did. Twice that had meant splintered pieces of

184

furniture. His wages had been docked the appropriate amount, but no one had had the courage to discipline him in any other way. Enderby even admitted that he'd wanted to get rid of him on several occasions but had been afraid of both his immediate reaction to a dismissal and the subsequent vengeance he was bound to take.

"You say he was part-time," said Carston. "Any idea what other jobs he had?"

Enderby looked down at his desk, seeming to consider the question. "No, not really."

"Not really? Can you be more precise?"

Enderby shook his head, this time more slowly.

"I don't know. He was supposed to be a … collector. But that had nothing to do with his work here."

"A collector? What, antiques?"

Enderby smiled. His beard sparkled. "No. Money, debts, things like that. But I don't know anything about it. It's just what people said."

"D'you know who he did this collecting for?"

Again the shake of the head. "No idea. None at all."

Carston changed tack for a second time.

"If you don't mind, I'd like your permission to look at your books."

Enderby felt he was being attacked from a different quarter. Carston did his best to reassure him. "It's just to get a list of what you might call your regulars, people who came into contact with Mr. Simpson. I mean, we don't know that it's him yet, but if it is … well, we need all the help we can get."

Enderby wasn't completely reassured. Carston hurried on.

"Also, it might be useful to know what sort of things you've been buying and selling, whether any of them were of particular interest to him, whether he bid for anybody in particular, that sort of thing."

Reluctantly, Enderby agreed to look out the things he wanted. Carston stood up, thought about offering to shake hands with the man, but decided on balance to keep his hand in his pocket. The condition of that beard suggested that hygiene wasn't one of Enderby's priorities.

"Right. I'll get one of my chaps to come in and fetch them. And maybe get a written statement from you if that's all right?"

Enderby nodded miserably. Carston felt sorry for him, not because of the distress this inquiry was causing but because he was trapped in what looked like a narrow, gray life in a world where treasures and pleasures were always just beyond his horizon. Carston's job seemed to bring him into contact with lots of similar individuals and he always felt helpless before their inadequacy. "Mind you," he thought to himself as he went back downstairs, "it wouldn't hurt him to wash his bloody beard once in a while."

He caught Ross in mid-yawn. He was superfluous in the sale-room, so the two of them went to look at the back door. It was closed but the Yale lock on it was broken and the bracket holding the single bolt just below it had been knocked out of the wood.

"I'm not surprised," said Carston. "This was Simpson's work. I bet he's been in here all weekend."

"Do you think this is where he phoned the dealers from?"

"Probably. Get onto BT. Find out what calls have been made."

"Right." Ross bent to look more closely at the lock. "Amateur job, isn't it?"

"Yes. He just shoved it in."

"Why, though?"

"Good question. He must've known we were after him. But what for? Was it him who killed Donnelly?"

Ross shrugged and looked round at the dirty passageway. "Not necessarily. Could be just the GBH on Hilden. With his record, he'd be in enough trouble if we got him for that. Maybe he just wanted to keep out of sight until things cooled down."

Carston gave a small nod, looked at the door again, and turned to go back to the saleroom. There, he asked the sergeant in charge of the team to make sure they searched the passageway to the back door and checked the door itself with the same sort of attention they were giving to the room.

McIntosh had left but the body was still there with the jagged halo of bloodstains slightly above it. Carston was pretty sure it was Simpson and, as with Donnelly, he couldn't avoid a small satisfaction at feeling that justice had been done, that the code by which Simpson had lived had been applied to bring about his death. This association kept the two murders together in his mind. His eyes moved slowly over the details of the body and the carpet on which it was lying and which had been used as its shroud. As McIntosh had said, the deed had been very localized. There'd been no struggles, no traumas other than the crushing of the skull. The floor and the rest of the room were untouched by the event. There was little doubt that Simpson had been lying there, probably asleep, certainly unaware of the presence of anyone else, and his attacker had simply picked up his bat and swung it down into his face. They'd just seen how the killer had got in (unless, of course, he was one of the ones who had a key), but the question was, who'd know that Simpson would be there? Carston recognized the feeling of anticipation that had built in him since he'd arrived at Enderby's. The most difficult cases were those which happened in the open, in the middle of a field or something. There, you had no idea where to start. But any interior gave immediate lines of inquiry. Who owned it? Who else had access? Why was the victim there? There were direct, specific questions with unequivocal answers. In this case, the possible culprits weren't immediately obvious, but the application of some intuitive thinking tempered with cold logic ought to produce a few names in a fairly short time. It was a problem calling precisely on the contrasting skills he and Ross had to offer.

They started on it as soon as they were in the car.

"What d'you reckon then, Jim?"

Ross checked the rearview mirror and pulled out before he answered.

"One of the ones with a key. Or somebody who knew the back door would be open."

"Maybe not. Could have gone there with the intention of breaking in but found there was no need to."

"In any case, they went knowing he was there."

"So who'd know that?"

"Benny Mitchell."

"Mmm. Don't fancy him for it somehow."

Ross swung the car right at the lights into Glasgow Road. "Those calls he made—to the dealers," he said as he tucked in behind a Fiat Uno. "It'd be useful for us if he'd done that from Enderby's."

Carston thought for a moment, then agreed.

187

"Yeah. Even if he didn't tell them where he was, they'd know by checking where the call had come from."

"Right. So that's a nice wee shortlist for a start."

Carston was nodding. "Yes, and with him at them for protection money, none of them are going to be pals of his."

They stopped at a crossing. An old lady was hovering suicidally at the curbside, unsure whether to risk the first step, even though the lights were in her favor. Ross smiled at her and gestured that she could cross. She was still undecided, but suddenly made up her mind, stepped into the road, and began scurrying to the other side, obviously distrustful of the machines around her.

"It'd be too good to be true, wouldn't it?" said Ross when she finally reached the haven of the opposite pavement.

"What?"

"Motive, opportunity, and identification; all because of a phone call."

Carston thought about it. "It'd fit with what's been going on so far."

Ross glanced at him, waiting for his explanation. "It's all slotting together nice and conveniently. Burchill sends Simpson round to the squat. He threatens Donnelly. Donnelly's killed with a decanter belonging to Burchill. It's too pat, too neat."

Ross's reply combined exasperation and disbelief. "Hang on. It's no that tidy. There's still bloody great holes in it all. And anyway, who did Simpson?"

Carston was already nodding. "I'm not saying any of it convinces me. And I'm not complaining about the links either; I just think there's something else, something we're not getting."

"Like what?"

"If I knew, I'd say. There's no … people in among it all."

Ross yawned. He recognized the tone. Carston was thinking aloud again. His voice was always quiet and soft (the sort of "poovy English voice" you heard in toilet paper ads on telly, according to Spurle), but it slowed and dropped even lower whenever he shifted across into speculation. There was no real need to reply.

"What I can't work out, though, is what's triggering it," Carston continued. "Clubbing somebody's face into a pulp, digging up somebody else's with a glass; that's not just punch-up violence, it's passion. Personal. Off the scale. But all we're talking about is protection money, repossessing a house, fencing antiques. In Cairnburgh, for God's sake. It's all too small."

He was silent again. Ross was quiet too. He knew that it would be very easy to point out the flaws in what Carston was saying. However extreme the violence, nowadays its extent meant nothing. Heads were kicked, kidneys ruptured, stomachs stabbed, all as part of a night out. But in a way, Carston was right. When a perpetrator was lifted out of the herd whose stampeding he'd shared, there was usually something about him that prevented him being classified as a mere thug. Ross had little time for the social workers' bleatings about deprived childhoods or sociopolitical alienation, but he did acknowledge that motives and impulses were rarely one-dimensional. The difference between him and his boss was that he preferred to make his case before issues of personality began to cloud it.

He changed down and felt the rear of the car slide a little as he turned up into Durnford Street.

"I bet we've already talked to him," said Carston suddenly.

"Who?"

"The bloke who did it."

"Or the woman?" said Ross, not with any individual in mind but simply to sidetrack the speculation.

"Maybe," said Carston. "He, she, I don't know. But I'd be surprised if any new direction opened up." He looked out at the Christmas shoppers heavily bundled against the wind. "It'd be a helluva coincidence if this was all to do with something else. No, whatever's going on, we've already talked about it. We just need to know what it is."

Nine

The drive back took them past so many groups of people staggering under parcels and packages that Carston felt unreasonably irritable when they got to the station. Everything about Christmas prompted a subliminal "Bah, humbug!" from him. It wasn't that he was mean—his presents for Kath were sometimes embarrassingly expensive—but the sight of people being drawn into the swelling of expectation, the accelerating excitement as they all hurried towards a fulfillment that never happened, made him angry that lives were normally so flat that they needed such tinsel hopes. Christmas was a yearly reminder, which came more and more rapidly, that time was passing and that previous dissatisfactions hadn't gone away. The eager climb through the cheap bonhomie of early December led only to the drop into the hollow of the festival itself, evenings of trumpeted but tedious television, family rows, and lonely suicides. And in Scotland, it dragged on into Hogmanay, when the antagonisms of the rest of the year were shelved for the time it took to swap nips of whisky. It wasn't until mid-January that tongues began to lose their fur, stomachs settled back into the routine of accepting substances that weren't several percent proof, and the comforting norms of hatred and mistrust were re-established.

As he got out of the car in the station car park, he muttered a "Merry bloody Christmas" to a man and a woman who were walking along the pavement struggling to control carrier bags which the wind was trying to drag from them. Ross heard him and, knowing the impulse that prompted the words, smiled and called across, "Thank you, sir. You too." Carston flicked a V-sign at him, chuckled, and followed him into the station.

Sandy Dwyer was being patient with an old couple who were arm in arm and standing so closely together that they were like a single body.

"We tellt the wee boy ye sent roon, but he wisna interested like," the man was saying.

The woman nodded hard.

"But we've got his report here," said Dwyer. It was the fifth time he'd told them.

"Aye." (It was the woman's turn.) "But yon loon wisna carin', ken?"

"Aye, he was," said Sandy. He lifted a notebook for them to see for the fourth time. "He wrote it all down here, look. I told ye before."

"Ah ken, ah ken," the woman went on, "but that's nae it, see? That's nae fit we're spikkin' aboot. It's yon PC. He wisna listenin'."

Dwyer seemed relieved to see them arrive. He asked the old couple to excuse him a minute, then reached under the desk for a piece of paper, which he handed to Carston.

"Phone call from DS Paskett in Aberdeen. Wants you to call him back as soon as you can."

Carston took the piece of paper and grinned at Dwyer as the old woman started explaining her problem all over again. As he and Ross went through the door and up the stairs, all the desk sergeant could manage was a grim shake of his head.

The incident room was empty. They'd left Fraser and Bellman at Enderby's and Spurle and Thom were having to cover twice the number of premises selling glassware and so wouldn't be back until late. Carston had no idea where McNeil had gone but, with so many things to do, it obviously made no sense for her just to sit waiting for orders. It reminded him that he couldn't put off the request for extra resources any longer. He went through to his office and, as Ross started making the coffee, he took off his coat, hung it behind the door, and punched Ridley's extension number on his phone. His call was answered after only one ring.

"Yes?" said Ridley, efficiently.

"Who's that?" asked Carston, unnecessarily.

"Superintendent Ridley," came the reply, the efficiency now coated with irritation.

191

"Carston here. Requisition request. Double murder investigation. Resources extension imperative."

"What?"

"Two bodies dead, about half a dozen living ones trying to cover all the options. Numerically untenable. Equation doesn't gell."

"Equations don't gell, Carston. Stop talking rubbish."

"Right you are. It's just that I was in the ACC's office earlier today. He was anxious for me to expedite the investigation. I'll process my human resources requisition directly through him, shall I?"

"No." The response was instantaneous. It was followed by a short pause as Ridley tried to assess his options. "You'll have to put it down on paper. I'll see whether we can re-route …"

"No time," said Carston. "I'll talk to Beresford." And he rang off before Ridley's next excuse formed. Immediately, he consulted the piece of paper he'd put on his desk, punched out the number of Grampian Police headquarters in Aberdeen, and asked for Dennis Paskett's extension.

"Dennis?" he said, when he got through. "Jack Carston."

"Ah yes, Jack. Thanks for callin' back. I'm lookin' for a spot of help."

"Well, we're up to our eyeballs but I'll do what I can."

"We've had a complaint from a Mrs. …" There was a pause while he riffled through some papers. "… McGee. About her daughter. Seems she was assaulted Friday night."

Carston was intrigued. Why should Cairnburgh be involved with one of Grampian's cases? The answers came right away.

"She lives here in Aberdeen but she was staying with a friend in your neck o' the woods. The two o' them went out clubbin' in town there. Met this guy and he took 'em to a hotel and roughed 'em up a bit. The lassie said nothin' but her ma saw the marks on her and dragged her in to us."

"Oh shit, I hate that sort of stuff," said Carston, his disgust at the crime managing to push aside the thought that he didn't have the resources to devote to yet another avenue of inquiry.

"Aye, me too," said Paskett.

"OK. Like I said, we're a bit pushed, but what d'you need done?"

"Well, if you could talk to the other girl first and then maybe go and see him."

"Who?"

"The guy. It won't be easy, Jack. He's got a bit of a reputation for making trouble. Name of Burchill."

Carston felt an immediate rush of adrenaline.

"Burchill?"

Ross turned quickly to look at Carston.

"Aye. You come across him, have you?" asked Paskett.

"He's right in the middle of the shit we're dealing with now. It'll be a pleasure to get the bugger. What have you got on him?"

"Not a lot. The lassie says her friend knew him. Seems she's been out with him before. She warned her he'd be rough but reckoned he paid well."

"So they're prostitutes, are they?"

"No. Just lassies, Jack. Putting a bit by for the future if you like."

Carston shook his head.

"OK, Dennis," he said. "Put together everything you've got and fax it to me right away. I'll get on with it myself. Like I said, it ties in with our stuff anyway."

"Thanks, Jack. I appreciate it."

"No bother, Dennis. I owe you plenty."

He put the phone down, swung round in his chair, and, to Ross's amazement, punched both fists forward and shouted, "Yes, you bastard!'

"What? What?" said Ross, impatiently.

In two sentences, Carston laid before him the treasure he'd just been given. Ross's smile showed that he shared his chief's reaction. The trouble was, he didn't believe in luck.

"Too good to be true," he said.

"Wait till we get the fax," said Carston. "Dennis wouldn't've asked unless he thought there was something worth following up."

"Aye, but what? One mother's word, a couple o' lassies who've accepted money from him. That's no goin' to bother him. He'll have his brief on it like a flash."

Carston was nodding. "Yes, and all his mates at the Conservative Club, no doubt. Still, it's more than we had before."

"You did say Friday night, didn't you?"

"Yes," said Carston. "I picked that up too. Could get him off the hook for Donnelly. Let's wait till we get the stuff from Dennis, though."

As he reached for a pad, he noticed for the first time a roll of fax paper at the side of his desk. He pulled the top free and saw that it was the forensic report from Aberdeen on Donnelly. McNeil must have brought it through before she left.

"Gets better and better," he said.

Ross looked up.

"Donnelly's forensic report."

"Ah, good."

While Ross finished making and pouring the coffee, Carston began to scan through the flimsy roll of paper. There were only a few paragraphs. Not surprisingly, given the place where Donnelly was found, there were all sorts of fibers, compounds, and debris on him. The opening paragraphs of the report made it clear that the significance of any specific elements would be compromised by the proliferation of traces of just about everything that had ever been thrown into Macy's dustbins. But then, having carefully covered their tracks in good academic evasions, the lab's scientists had identified one or two things that might be useful to their investigation.

"What's silica?" Carston asked as Ross brought the two coffees round and stood behind him to read the report over his shoulder.

"Sand," said Ross. "Why?"

Carston pointed at two columns of figures. In one, under the heading "Silica" was the figure seventy percent, in the other fifty percent.

Ross pointed to the column containing the lower figure.

"That's lead crystal. The other one's just ordinary glass."

"Yeah, so they say. Shows we were right about that then. There's plenty of the ordinary stuff but lots of the crystal too. Most of it over his shoulders and down the back of his jacket. So it could well have been some sort of cover-up effort."

Ross nodded. He was still reading.

"What technique did they use? Oh aye, differential thermal analysis. The bits must've been too small for emission spectrography."

Carston lowered the fax to the desk and turned to look at him.

"D'you know it's vulgar displaying knowledge like that?"

Ross straightened up and went round to the other side of the desk to sit on a chair. "Just tryin' to broaden your mind," he said.

Carston shook his head sadly and went back to the report. There were more figures, tables, and analyses, but the only other thing which struck him as being of immediate interest was the final paragraph.

"D'you know you've probably got specks of paint in your pockets or your turnups?" he said.

"Wouldn't be surprised."

"According to this, sixty-three percent of people do."

"Fascinating."

"They found some on Donnelly's trousers."

"So?"

"Reckon it might be useful. It's little chips and flakes and there are several layers to them. Easier to match when they're like that."

"Aye. There's two and a half thousand possible combinations," said Ross carelessly.

Carston looked up. "What?"

"Aye. With all the shades of topcoat, primer, undercoat—some forensic guy worked it out. Two and a half thousand."

Carston smiled, then matched Ross's tone as he added, consulting the scroll, "Yes, but this is even better than that. The pigment in the yellow layer here's lead chromate—inorganic compound. Means it's older stuff. Modern paints use titanium dioxide with organic dyes for pigmentation."

Ross was unfazed. "What did they use, thin layer chromatography, spectrographic analysis, or X-ray diffraction?" he asked, with apparent seriousness.

"Piss off," said Carston.

He dropped the scroll onto his desk. Ross reached across, picked it up, and started looking through it.

"It's not bad, is it?" he said.

Carston nodded his agreement as Ross went on. "The glass. And especially this paint. They didn't find any of it under the steps at Macy's ... well, only a couple of flakes, and they probably came off Donnelly. And if it's not modern, it narrows the field for us."

Carston blew onto his coffee to cool it, took a tentative sip, and put the mug down again.

"Antiques again, isn't it?"

"Well, not necessarily. I mean, think how many folk in Cairnburgh haven't painted their houses since they moved in."

He was right. Apart from the incomers, most of whom had been drawn there by the oil and who'd brought with them the tones and manners of the seventies and eighties, house-owners tended to favor the dark browns that had been good enough for their parents. Even when they did redecorate, they tended to leave the solid binding layers of the previous generation intact and simply skim a fresh color over the top of them. No, it was no surprise to find that flakes of paint picked up in this part of the world were best looked at by archeologists.

Ross read on and picked up on several of the findings. They talked through them, but decided in the end that the report was useful but didn't push the investigation much farther forward. Ross was cutting it into separate sheets for filing when the telephone went. He made to get up, but Carston waved him back down into his seat and picked the receiver up himself.

"Carston."

"This is very inconvenient and it's going to play hell with the rotas for December and January."

Carston mouthed "Ridley" to Ross.

"Super," he said, managing to make it sound both like an acknowledgment of Ridley's rank and a comment on his information. Ridley didn't notice. He was launched.

"I can't do anything before next Monday but …"

"Monday? I need them now."

Carston was wasting his breath. Ridley had gone on speaking over the interruption.

"… I've re-resourced the patrols in B section and decentralized them into segregated groups of three with an overlap on the shift change. It means twenty-eight percent of them have to double up their crossover shift and God knows what impact that'll ultimately have on overtime."

"I see," said Carston, who didn't.

"It gives you a nominal pool of twelve uniformed constables with the option of two sergeants with effect from Monday next."

"A nominal pool."

"The names are in the system. You'll get a print-out by seventeen hundred."

"I can't tell you how grateful I am that you went to so much trouble. It's very much—"

Halfway through his reply, the line went dead.

"We've got a nominal pool," Carston told Ross. "Makes you glad to be alive, doesn't it?"

Later, at the briefing, the squad was equally unimpressed by the thought that, with a double investigation on their hands, they were getting very little help and that it wouldn't be arriving until after they'd done all the tramping around that early questioning always entailed. Carston cheered them up a little by telling them about the development with Burchill, but warned them against getting their hopes too high about it. In fact, they were all glad to hear that he was going to be dealing with that himself; they could already foresee more overtime than they wanted piling up.

"We've had a call from the scene of crime boys," said Ross. "There's no need to bother Simpson's wife for identification. They checked the prints and it's him alright."

"Good," said Spurle. "Bastard got what he deserved."

McNeil looked at him before saying, "We should at least tell his wife that he's dead."

Carston had already decided to do that himself, but McNeil went on. "I'll do it, if you like."

"Right," said Carston, pretending it was simply a delegation of duty but genuinely grateful to duck the chore. McNeil made a note in her book.

"So, what did you get at Enderby's?" asked Ross.

"No very much," said Fraser. "None o' them had much to say. 'Dinna ken nothin', havena seen nothin', nothin' to do wi' me.' The same story from everybody."

"Same wi' they china shops," said Spurle. "They all kent the pattern but they sell so many, there's nothin' special they can remember about any o' them."

Bellman and Thom were nodding their agreement and Carston

sensed the weariness in them all. Whereas the forensic evidence had been building nicely and allowing plenty of room for theories, the foot-slogging stuff the team had been doing had produced very little. And it didn't really surprise him. The more they looked inside the world of antiques and auctions, the more evident the little rivalries and secrecies became. When a large part of the job consisted of hiding truths until they could be made to yield their greatest profits and forcing competitors to spend more than they wanted to, it was natural that openness and cooperation should be in short supply. His impulse was somehow to offer the team some time off, but it was impossible. He forced a cold efficiency into his tone.

"Right. Spurle, Thom. Before you leave tonight, ring Enderby's. Chase up those books we've asked for. Fetch 'em on your way home or tomorrow morning. We can start looking through them first thing. Fraser, you and Bellman, get onto BT again, get the list of calls made from Enderby's over the weekend and see who's there. It'd be handy if you could get all that done before tomorrow's meeting. So get onto that now. McNeil, after you've been to see Mrs. Simpson, see if you can find Mitchell. He hasn't seen you yet. Maybe a female angle can get something else out of him. See if Sergeant Dwyer'll let you have that probationer to go with you. What's her name?"

"Ellis," said Ross.

"Right. Good experience for her. Might disorient him a bit. I've no idea what you'll get but do what you can. Anything'll be more than we've got so far."

"Right, sir," said McNeil. "Is that it?"

Carston looked up to see whether there was any irony intended, but there was no sign of the lopsided smile that usually accompanied her jousting with Spurle. In fact, her face looked tired and pale.

"Is everything OK?" he asked.

"Fine, sir," she said, and the corner of her lip slanted up into the familiar grin. He knew that she was forcing it but for the moment, he didn't have time to find out why.

There were parallel smears of blood along the wall and more had dripped onto the floor beside the sofa and into its green floral pattern. In terms of quantity, it didn't amount to much but, for everyone in the squat except Fran, its significance was enormous. It had come from Jez's nose and mouth. Will had punched him twice in the face and, as Jez ducked and put up his hands to press them against the bleeding, he'd hit him once more in the stomach. As he fell back, his fingers spread the stains on the wall and the blood flowed freely down his front. He was now upstairs in the bathroom, trying to repair his face, and Will had stamped out of the house into the cold and dark. Liz was at the window, staring at the blackness, and Dawn was in the kitchen, filling a bucket with hot water. Fran was in her bedroom, the room she shared with Will. She was sitting on a cane chair beside the bed, using a wooden toothpick to pick at her nails. They were clean, but she continued to slide the sharp end under and along each one, mindlessly looking for a spotlessness she could never achieve.

Nothing like this had ever happened before. There'd been differences, arguments, lost tempers, but never this sort of directed, personalized violence. And yet, in a way, they'd all felt it coming. There'd been a tension in the place ever since Floyd's murder, and the external pressures, which they usually met with a unified resistance, had begun to seem irresistible. They began to blame one another for the irritations they felt and, over all that, all the time, they had the inescapable spectacle of Fran's progressive degeneration. This week, she'd rarely spoken. At first, she'd gone to her room and pretended to read but, since lunchtime on Monday, she'd dropped even that facade and sat silent and alone on the cane chair or on the bed, picking at her fingernails or clutching her knees to her chest. Her stillness was frightening. It was as if Fran had gone away, leaving a replica to fill her space.

Tonight's episode had started with two creases in Dawn's white cotton blouse. She'd been shopping that afternoon and got back later than usual. Jez had spent the time she was away wondering why she'd insisted on going alone. He often went with her, even though he hated the whole business, and today's refusal had been enough to start his mind working on its usual inventions. When she eventually came in, she was carrying only a small bag of food things, which she could have picked up in a fraction of the time she'd been away. Jez said nothing but his imaginings suddenly hardened into certainty. He looked at her as she took bread and vegetables out of the bag and put them in a cupboard. She looked flushed and guilty, moving quickly and deliberately, keeping her back to him to avoid meeting his gaze. And her blouse was heavily creased. It wasn't the normal creasing it would get from her just sitting down and leaning back into a chair; it was more than that. There were two almost parallel folds, which could easily have been made by someone pulling the blouse up and then by Dawn lying back against the creases. And being pushed against them again and again.

"Fucking whore," said Jez.

Dawn turned her head. One look at his expression was enough to tell her what to expect. He was off in his fantasy world, chasing the torments he hated so much. She had no idea what particular demon was responsible this time, but she'd come to care less and less about his ravings and was angry that he still tried to treat her as a possession. She said nothing. For Jez, her silence was a confession of guilt. If there was no denial, it meant that he was right. She'd been fucking somebody else again. He was sucked down into a helpless fury, hating the person who was hurting him so much and simultaneously being gnawed at by the thought of other hands and lips exploring her. Once again, he retreated into his pain, out of reach, and replayed in his mind the images of the afternoon she must have spent.

Normally, Dawn let a little time elapse and then started to coax him out of his nightmares with the comforts only she had to offer, but recent events had eroded her patience. The place and its people were becoming intolerable. So, this time, she left him in his self-created void, from which his silence spread relentlessly. Liz tried once or twice to talk about things which had previously brought them together, but it was too late. There was no response from Jez and Dawn's own anger was making her feign a lightness and carelessness she didn't feel. Will's concerns, as ever, were with Fran. They all gave up and waited for whatever would defuse the menace that seemed to have gathered. The time passed and Jez's sullen resentment continued to ooze out over all of them.

After almost two hours of it, Dawn had had enough. They were all in the front room, doing various things either to pretend the gloom wasn't there or to step aside from it. Jez was hunched in a chair, his forefinger stroking a light pattern on his thigh, his eyes lowered, and his mouth moving slowly as he bit gently at the inside of his lips. His whole body expressed the notion that he'd been somehow abused, betrayed, and yet it was his fragile ego that was looming over their whole evening, coloring it with the drabness of his insecurity. He wasn't the victim; they were.

"It's over, Jez. I want the others to hear it, too."

She eased her anger aside and left only flat unconcern in her tone.

"Don't make it worse, Dawn," said Liz.

"Can't get any worse," said Dawn. "I don't belong to anybody. I'm not some gadget that Jez has got hold of to relieve him now and again."

Jez's eyes lifted to look at her.

"It's true," she went on. "I've had enough. Of you, this, all of it. I'm going. And you're not coming with me."

"Bitch," said Jez, the control he was trying to maintain already wavering.

Dawn's anger, too, pushed back up into her. "And I'm sick of being called bloody names because of your stupid bloody hang-ups."

"It's because they fit you, you slag," Jez shouted.

"Oh for Christ's sake …" Liz began, but Jez's fury had been released.

"You'll fuck anything that moves, you bloody whore."

"Yes," said Dawn, standing up and walking to lean over him in his chair. "Anything that moves. On my back, legs in the air. Mouth, arse, fanny, wherever they want it. But not you, kid. Not fucking you."

And he slapped her. For the first time, in all their hot, screaming rows, he slapped her across the face.

Will had said little so far, but the pistol crack of Jez's hand on Dawn's cheek snapped into him too. He jumped up, pulled Jez to his feet, punched him in the face twice, and then in the stomach.

As Jez fell, there was silence again, now given texture by the sounds of Jez sniffing and sucking back the blood and the louder noise of Will's own sobbing.

The urgency of the rhythm which Carston had established the previous evening continued on the Wednesday morning. As he looked through the glass panel in the door to the incident room, he saw that everyone except Fraser was bent over pieces of paper taking notes or comparing different entries. Fraser was holding up a small box and saying, "Complete tool kit." One by one, he folded instruments out of it. "Five wrenches, three screwdrivers, a scratch awl. High carbon tempered stainless steel, all of them. Less than fifteen quid."

Carston had never been to Fraser's house but imagined it whirring with gadgets and choked with special offers. He pushed open the door and went in.

"*Votre attention, s'il vous plaît,*" he said.

Fraser grinned hugely and said, "*Avec beaucoup de plaisir, monsieur. Comment allez-vous?*"

"Never mind that. There's work to be done."

Smugly, Fraser put the box back in his pocket and lifted a blue folder from his desk.

"All ready, sir."

The previous evening, he'd got the list of calls Simpson had made on the Sunday. There were eleven names on it. Carston nodded his appreciation and turned to Spurle.

"How about you, Spurle?"

In answer, Spurle put two small ledgers on top of the one he was studying.

"Everything since the beginnin' of September," he said. "Sales, customers, prices, the lot." He added a fourth thin volume. "And this is the year's accounts."

"Excellent."

"Aye. He didna have them ready last night, so ah got him up this mornin'."

This curt report of how he'd got hold of the books hid the fact that Enderby had been frightened out of his skin by the threats

Spurle had made on Tuesday evening when they weren't immediately to hand. He'd slept very little, spending most of the night collating the information Spurle had demanded and presenting it in the tidiest possible format in order to preempt any further intimidation. It was as well that he went to such trouble because Spurle had rung his doorbell at six-forty that morning.

"Anything interesting?" asked Carston.

"Hard to say. Just names and fancy prices fer crap as far as ah can see."

"Any sign of Simpson's name?"

"Aye, sir. Now and again, when he's bid fer some punter who wasna there fer a sale."

"Good. Get those on a separate list."

Spurle shuffled the papers on his desk and held up an A4 sheet with some notes scribbled on it.

"Ah've already started."

"Bloody hell! You after promotion or something?"

"Just doin' the job," said Spurle quietly, wrongly assuming that he was being patronized.

"All part o' the service, sir," said Fraser.

"OK. Have you put the lists together at all? The phone calls and the list of clients?"

"We're on that now, sir," said Bellman.

He and Thom were at the window, with several sheets of paper spread out over the broad sill. They were sorting them into piles. Carston turned to Ross. "Is there some bonus scheme I haven't heard about?" he asked.

Ross shrugged his shoulders.

"Maybe they've been speaking to Superintendent Ridley," he said. As he spoke, his words were distorted by a yawn. This time, it wasn't Mhairi's fault but McNeil's. She was leaning over her desk, her head pushed forward, her mouth wide open in an enormous yawn which had started before Ross's and was still going when his was over.

"Tired, McNeil?" said Carston, himself feeling the contagion but contracting the muscles of his throat to resist it.

McNeil nodded. "A wee bit, sir. Ah'm fine, though."

"What happened with Mrs. Simpson?"

"No problem. She pretended to cry but it was just for show. Ah reckon she's glad to be rid o' him. Ah don't think he was over-gentle wi' her. And there's nae kids."

Carston nodded. "What about Mitchell?"

"Waste o' time. Ah don't think he knows anything about it. Ah checked the statements he made before. He just repeated all the same stuff. And he's no bright enough to be hidin' anything."

"OK. Well, I'm sorry to have interrupted your efficiency drive. Spurle, you stick with what you're doing there. Let me have it when you've got it all sorted. The rest of you, when you've finished that stuff, get the list of customers and go and see them. We've already talked to most of them, but that was before Simpson turned up. And there may be others we've missed. Find out what contacts they had with Simpson. And find out where they were on Sunday from about six onwards." He turned to go back to his office but paused at the door. "I'm sorry. I know you've been putting in a helluva lot of legwork. But we need to move on this. When we get the extra bodies, I'll try to get you some time off. Meantime, well …"

He didn't know what else to say and so he went out, hoping they sensed how much he appreciated their efforts. Ross followed him and shut the door.

"Fat fuckin' chance o' that," said Spurle.

In Carston's office, Carston and Ross said nothing at first. Just as the team were overstretched by the sheer numbers of people they had to visit, so Carston felt that there were too many fuddled layers to the whole business. They'd failed to make any decent connections, the two victims were the sort of individuals who might have been wished dead by hundreds of people, and, apart from the intriguing mosaic of forensic anomalies, there were no aspects to the case which invited them even to indulge in vague speculation. And there was always the possibility that there was no connection whatsoever between the two deaths. Carston was slightly annoyed with himself for having been unable to get an angle on it all. And there was still no fax from Aberdeen about the complaint against Burchill. He decided to ring Paskett at lunchtime if they hadn't heard by then.

"Where do we go, Jim?" he said at last.

"Round to Burchill's place?"

Carston shook his head. "We're waiting on Dennis's fax. Can't go before we've seen that."

Ross frowned. "Takin' his time, isn't he?"

"Yes. If we've heard nothing by lunchtime, I'll give him a ring."

Ross got up, took a file from a shelf, and started looking through it. "At least Jason Donovan's off the hook, though."

Carston looked at him.

"What d'you mean?"

"Did you no see yon ledgers Spurle brought back?"

"I had a quick look. Why?"

"See how the monthly totals were entered?"

Carston was baffled. His forte was seeing shapes in the cotton wool of motives and the fogs of people's psyches; things like numerical patterns were Ross's province.

"They were totals, numbers. What was so special?" Ross had found what he was looking for. He handed Carston a slip of paper. It was a copy of one of the notes found in Simpson's pocket.

"Did you no see? Every month, there was just the initial. J, F, M, A down the page."

Carston looked at the bit of paper as Ross continued. "Simpson's thing's the same. Look at the numbers. One under each letter. Same system. It doesna say Jason D at all. There's no real gap before the D. We read it that way because we expected there to be. That's just Bazza's half-yearly accounts; July August September October November December."

Carston laughed. "Mundane, Jim, but spot on. Pity, I fancied a trip to Australia to extradite him."

"I bet that's what Simpson's been collecting from his clients," said Ross.

"Yes, that's what the envelope of money was about." Carston did a quick calculation. "He was making a bob or two at it, wasn't he?"

"Aye. Nice wee sideline. Plenty of motive to get rid o' him, too. If he's collecting that sort o' money from you every month."

"Yes. Tell you what, let's get those lists in here. We'll sift through them. Spurle might miss something. He can go with the others."

"Wish the buggers'd get up to date," said Ross as he made his way to the door. "If they'd got computerized records, it'd take half the time."

They spent the rest of the morning with books, files, and lists spread across both desks, matching references, creating subdivisions, and whittling the mass of figures and names down to a few relevant pages. Carston was happy for Ross to direct the whole operation and kept getting sidetracked into looking at a specific ledger entry and trying to recreate the circumstances of which it was the only remaining sign. There were small and large sales, bidding records, private arrangements, strange reserve prices that couldn't possibly be legitimate, and other entries that made no sense to him whatsoever. He was sure that the main purpose of the entries was to give form and respectability to some very dubious undertakings. The Enderby ledgers offered a selective, structured narrative of highly complex and, no doubt, very grubby events.

By eleven o'clock, they'd reduced the mountain to just three lists. The first was the one which Spurle had started. On it were the names of sixteen people who had had some special dealings with Simpson in connection with his work at the auctions. Most of them were also on the second list, which was much larger. It identified every client who had had any sort of transaction with Enderby's, either as buyer or seller, in the past three months. The third list was Fraser's note of the people Simpson had phoned from work at the weekend. Ross tapped one of them.

"Hilden. He's on all the lists," he said.

"Yes, we knew he'd been called. He told McNeil, remember?" He ran his finger across the sheets of paper. "It's not just him, though. Look, 'Irvine,' 'Irvine,' 'Irvine,' 'Beattie,' 'Anderson,' 'McStay'—they're nearly all on all three."

"Aye, I suppose it's no great surprise."

"No. Simpson came across them all at work. Didn't need to go looking for business elsewhere. Too lazy for that."

"Or too thick."

"Yes. More likely." He pointed to two more names on the phone list. "It makes these two a bit more interesting."

"Why?"

"They're not on the other lists. So what have they got that makes them worth a detour?"

Ross jotted the two names down on a yellow Post-it slip.

"I'll get Sandy to call the lads. Get one of them to check on these two."

Carston nodded.

"I suppose you spotted our mate here, too?" he said. Ross grinned. There was no need for him to look at the piece of paper to see who Carston was talking about.

"Burchill? Aye."

The name appeared twice, once on the phone list and once as a client with a special connection with Simpson.

"Why d'you suppose he was phoning him?" asked Carston.

"Not for protection money, that's for sure."

"Must have been after something, though. Wages maybe? If he's short of funds …" There was a tap on the door and a constable came in with a single sheet of fax paper.

"You wanted this as soon as it arrived, sir. Fax from DS Paskett in Aberdeen."

"Ah yes, thanks."

He read quickly through the notes and was disappointed to find that there wasn't much more than Paskett had already told him. There were the girls' names, the name of the hotel, and some times.

"That's interesting," he said, still intent on his reading.

"What?"

"The girls were with him from about ten and got home about twenty past two. So he could still have killed Donnelly before he met them and gone back and dumped him later. That would explain why the body was just left lying for a while."

"That's a big jump, sir," said Ross, who was as keen to see Burchill inside as his boss but less ready to make assumptions before he had some tangible basis for them.

"Yes, I know. But I'd sort of got it into my head that the girls would be an alibi. I'm just glad they're not."

"The fiscal may want a wee bit more than that."

Carston looked at him and shook his head. "God, what a bloody killjoy you are."

Ross grinned. "Thank you, sir."

Carston handed the fax across to him. "Get the number for this girl. Let's give her a ring. See if she's available for a chat. We'll take McNeil with us."

Ross lifted a telephone directory down from its shelf, looked up the number, and dialed. When he heard the ringing tone, he handed the receiver over to Carston. He didn't have long to wait. It was answered by a young woman.

"Hullo."

Carston pulled the fax towards him and checked the name on it.

"Hullo. This is Detective Chief Inspector Carston, West Grampian police. Is it possible to speak to Anna Robertson, please?"

There was the usual hesitation. Did everybody have something to hide?"

"What about?"

"Is she there?"

"Yes. Speaking."

Carston gave Ross the thumbs up sign.

"Ah good, Ms. Robertson. Would you mind if we came round to see you?"

"What for?"

"I'd rather not speak about it over the phone."

"But what's it about?"

It didn't sound promising. Her tone was stubborn, not far from aggressive.

"Last Friday night."

The silence left no doubt that his words had had an effect.

"What about it?" she said at last.

"I'd really rather ..."

"What's it about?"

The gentle approach wasn't going to work.

"Where were you from about ten o'clock?"

Again there was a pause. He heard another female voice in the background before the woman said, "Here."

"Where?"

"Here. At home. Watching telly."

Carston didn't know how he knew, but he was sure that she was

208

lying. It wasn't just that her response contradicted what the McGee girl had said. Anna's answer had been too definite, she'd taken no time to consider it.

"On your own?"

"No. With my ma."

Carston heard muffled sounds as the receiver was covered and she spoke with someone else.

"Is your mother there?" he asked.

By way of answer, a different voice came on the line.

"What's all this about? This is Anna's mother."

"Mrs. Robertson. It would be much better if we could come round and …"

"What for? What's it about?"

She sounded as edgy as her daughter. Carston wondered what the hell they had to hide.

"We just wanted to ask her about Friday night."

"She was here with me. All night. We were watching television."

"I see." Carston was going to get nothing at all out of them. "Well, that's that then. If you don't mind, though, what I'll do is … I'll just send one of our WPCs around to confirm it. Would that be alright?"

"What for? There's nothing to …"

"Would that be alright?"

"I suppose so. But if …"

"Thank you very much for your cooperation, Mrs. Robertson. I'll get on to that right away. Goodbye."

He put the phone down hard.

"They're lying," he said. "Reckons she was with her mother. Watching telly all night, according to them. I don't believe a word of it."

Normally, he would just have been puzzled, maybe irritated by the incongruity of their response, but the fact that it might let Burchill slip away from them made him angry.

"Get McNeil round there right away, Jim. Fill her in on what it's about. See if she can't use her counseling techniques on them." He reached for the phone. "We'll go round to see Burchill. I don't care if he's got the all-clear from them; the bastard's still not got it from me."

Ross pointed at the ceiling, reminding his boss of Beresford's presence upstairs.

"Careful," he said.

"I'll be all sweetness and light," said Carston as he checked his notebook and dialed Burchill's number.

Burchill had miscalculated again. It seemed to be happening more and more frequently and could soon start showing up in the company's figures. That morning he'd had a meeting with representatives of Conoco, who were thinking of using his Burchdrill to explore the new blocks they'd been awarded in the latest round of bidding. He knew that there was still no real competition because other suppliers hadn't yet been able to combine directional drilling and permeability analysis in the one tool. The Conoco guys knew it too and, for all their size, Burchill reckoned that they needed him as much as he needed them. Unfortunately, he'd expressed that opinion as part of his presentation and created a wariness in the others which tightened their negotiating stance. So when he'd refused to consider a partnering alternative to the normal subcontracting arrangement, the meeting had stalled and the reps had left with smiles and handshakes but also with a clear indication that they wouldn't be getting in touch again unless he was prepared to rethink his position.

The bitterness of losing such a big contract was still burning in him when his secretary phoned through the news that the police were coming to the office to speak to him. He swore and banged the button to disconnect her. He wasn't really surprised. He'd been expecting them. But he knew they didn't have anything. He'd just need to say as little as possible.

Carston and Ross arrived at two-thirty. He made them wait in reception for almost fifteen minutes before he told his secretary to bring them through. Carston's huge smile and extended hand as he came into the office implied that the wait had gone completely unnoticed.

"Mr. Burchill. So good of you to give up your time," he beamed.

Burchill ignored the outstretched hand and pointed at two chairs. Carston's smile broadened and he sat down and looked around the office. It was very flash; two stainless steel sculptures, a giant plastic model of the Burchdrill, and four white, foam-filled bucket chairs. Behind his walnut desk, Burchill looked very much the part in the outfit he'd selected for the Conoco meeting. The black jacket of his Karl Lagerfeld suit was on a hanger behind the door so they got the full effect of his cream silk shirt, the thin, gold Patek Philippe watch peeping from under the cuff, and the dusty claret tie by Pierre Cardin.

"Business looks good," said Carston, seemingly glad that fate was being so kind to Burchill.

But Burchill didn't trust Carston an inch.

"Cut it, Carston. What's the problem?"

"Problem?" echoed Carston, his eyes wide with apparent incomprehension.

Ross had been afraid that the enforced wait would provoke Carston's more childish impulses and didn't want Beresford to get any more ammunition against them.

"We wanted to ask you a couple of questions about one or two things in connection with our investigation, sir," he said.

"What investigation?"

The question surprised both his visitors. He knew all about Donnelly. Maybe he'd heard about Simpson, too. Or maybe he'd been expecting fallout from his evening with the two girls. Carston opted for an oblique approach. He took out a copy of the pattern McNeil had found in the lawyer's inventory and handed it across the desk.

"D'you recognize this?"

Burchill shook his head and handed the paper back immediately. What were they up to?

"Well, it's the pattern on a set of Edinburgh Crystal which came from your premises in Forbeshill Road."

"What d'you mean, 'came from'? Got nicked from, you mean."

"Floyd Donnelly was killed with the decanter from it," said Carston, dropping his smile and the previous lightness of tone. "We'll be checking prints on it for elimination purposes."

It amounted to an accusation. In their previous contacts, they'd given Burchill no reason to think that he was under any suspicion where Donnelly was concerned, but Carston's words carried an unmistakable edge. What sort of game was he playing?

Ross was as confused and wary as Burchill. There were no prints. There wasn't even any of the decanter left. Carston was out on one of his limbs.

"We wondered if you could tell us where the set came from?" Burchill was totally disoriented.

"I don't know. It came with the house. There was all sorts of crap there. I bought the lot. Never used it. You'll need to …"

Carston's next question cut across his words.

"And how about your connections with Barry Simpson? What can you tell us about them?"

Different sorts of warning lights began to flash for Burchill.

"What do you mean?"

"Barry Simpson. He did a few … jobs for you, didn't he?"

Burchill didn't like this at all.

"What d'you mean?" he repeated.

Carston frowned and in turn repeated, very slowly, separating the words and articulating with exaggerated care, "Barry Simpson did a few jobs for you, didn't he?"

"What's going on?" asked Burchill.

"Mr. Burchill. Did he or didn't he?"

"OK, yes. Now and then."

"What sort of jobs?" asked Ross.

"Various."

"Like?" asked Carston.

"I asked him to look out for stuff at the auctions where he worked."

"Is that all?"

Burchill hesitated, then said, "What else would I need him for? If he's been saying …" He ended the threat with a shake of his head.

"What sort of things were you interested in?" asked Ross.

"All sorts."

"Ceramics?"

"What?"

"Ceramics? Pottery? Stuff like that?"

"Yes, sometimes. Last time it was stuff called Chelsea ware."

"With the anchor trademarks."

"Yeah. How d'you know that?"

"Mr. Simpson wrote it down."

Burchill laughed. "No, I don't think so. He wouldn't have done that …" He stopped when he realized what he was saying.

"Why's that?" asked Carston.

"What?"

"Why wouldn't he have done that?"

Burchill was thinking hard. "The competition …" he began, but the telephone's ring saved him. He grabbed the receiver, listened, then held it towards Carston. Carston took it and said "Yes?"

"It's DC Fraser, sir. Sorry to bother you, but when ah heard you was wi' Mr. Burchill, ah thought you'd like to hear what's came up."

"Go on."

"Those two names ye gave us, the ones Simpson phoned who werena on the other lists."

"Yes, well?"

"Mr. Burchill's their landlord. He owns both the shops." Carston turned away from Burchill to conceal any reactions.

"I see. That's confirmed, is it?"

"Aye, sir. Ah've been there spikkin' to them masel'."

"OK, Fraser. Thanks. You were right to let me know."

He waited to hear the click as Fraser rang off, then handed the receiver back to Burchill.

"Sorry about that, sir," he said. "Now then, have you had any phone calls from Mr. Simpson recently?"

"No."

"Are you sure?"

"Course I am."

"How about Sunday night?"

Burchill couldn't work out what it was all about. He wondered what they'd got that gave them the confidence to be so upfront with their questions.

"Sunday night? I don't know. I might have."

"I thought you were sure you hadn't heard from him," said Ross.

"I don't know, do I? He might have called. I don't log every fucking call I get."

"No, but BT and Mercury do. And all the cellnets and things, don't they?"

Again, Carston was implying that they had more than they did. It was a risky strategy.

"This call. It wouldn't have been anything to do with rent collecting perhaps?" he added, all innocence.

Burchill snapped. "What the fuck is this? Are you accusing me of something?"

"Certainly not, sir. If we were we'd have cautioned you and … oh, there are all sorts of formalities."

"Well, it feels like a bloody inquisition to me."

"Guilty conscience, sir," said Carston with a smile, suddenly adding, "Where were you on Friday, by the way?"

The shadow which crossed Burchill's face made Carston even more sure that Anna Robertson and her mum were lying.

"Why?" asked Burchill.

"The Mount Atholl Hotel, wasn't it?" said Carston, ignoring his question.

The constant shifting of his point of attack was making Burchill flounder. He felt accusations all around him and wasn't sure which ones he should be dealing with. He'd already forgotten the sex with the two girls, so why were the filth bringing that up? Had the bitches said anything? Carston gave him no time to recover.

"How about Sunday?" he asked.

"Sunday? Why?"

"We're checking the whereabouts of all Mr. Simpson's connections."

Burchill was shaking his head and rubbing his thumb along the fingers of his right hand.

"Sunday, Mr. Burchill?"

"I was at home. All day. I went out later on. For a drink."

"What time would that be?"

Burchill had had enough. He didn't know where he was and they suddenly seemed to know an awful lot about his business. He stood up and went to open the office door.

"OK, that's it. This is harassment. I want you out of here. And next time you want to talk to me, I want my lawyer here to listen."

The two policemen looked at each other before standing up.

"Well, that's within your rights, sir," said Carston, genuinely taken aback. "I find it a bit surprising. This is just an inquiry. I thought it would be better here than down at the station."

Burchill's impulse was to trade insults with him, but he suspected he might be in deep shit and he managed to say nothing as he waited beside the open door.

Carston and Ross had no option but to leave. At the door, Carston paused.

"I think we're going to have to talk to you again, sir," he said, his tone restrained and very serious.

"Fuck off, you slimy bastard," said Burchill.

Carston waited until they were in the car before speaking. He slammed the passenger door. "Guilty," he said.

Ross had made no move even to put the key in the ignition.

"Well, there's certainly something goin' on. First he pretends he's forgotten what we're investigating, then he gets shifty, then he kicks us out and he's shoutin' about lawyers. Mind you, you took some chances."

"Not really, Jim. He's been up to something all right. That was obvious. And it's not just with the two girls in the Mount Atholl. I want him in. I want to put the bugger on the spot."

"He'll have his brief next time, I bet."

"Guaranteed. Still, might make it more interesting. First thing we do when we get back is send somebody round his neighbors. Find out what time he came home on Friday. I want this bastard."

They drove off, picking over the conversation they'd had, probing Burchill's responses, and agreeing that he was definitely trying to hide something and that, with any luck, it might well be connected with Donnelly or Simpson. In Carston, their talk produced a familiar little excitement. There were things other than facts, materials, objects to be dealt with. He was back among the eccentricities of temperaments, comfortable in the space and freedom they offered.

McNeil was already there when they got back. She'd got absolutely nothing from either of the Robertson women. She had the same feeling as Carston that they were hiding something or other but neither of them was going to give. Carston thanked her and phoned Paskett to bring him up to date.

"I'm no surprised," said Paskett. "We've had dealin's wi' him before. They're all frightened of him. The lassie that came up here wasnae really willin' to say nothin'. It was her ma made her. If she ever had to be a witness, she'd be a liability."

"Well, don't worry, Dennis. I'm not giving up. I'll let you know how it goes."

He rang off and sat back in his chair, deciding which direction to take. For himself, a spell of quiet reflection was in order. With the new information about Burchill, he wanted to look again through everything they had. Now, it had a focus. But he also needed a bit more substance. Burchill's tendency to socialize with senior officers meant that they had plenty of photographs of him on file. He sent Ross to get one to take to the Mount Atholl Hotel to find out a bit more about what had gone on there on Friday.

Bellman and Thom came in as Ross was leaving and Carston sent them straight out again to Inverdee Crescent to ask about Burchill and Friday night. Then, left alone in the office, he made himself go over the lists and ledgers again. He put his feet up on the desk and started rearranging the facts in a broader, more imaginative context. He tried out various scenarios involving Burchill, Simpson, and Donnelly. In most of them, Burchill was calling the tunes, manipulating people and money, but always staying so well clear of events that linking him with them was impossible. When he tried leaving Burchill out of the equation, he was just left with two low-life corpses, which could simply have been thrown up by a normal weekend's carousing.

When Ross got back just after five, his news was enough to bring Burchill right back into contention.

"Bingo," he said, as he threw the photo on the desk. "Barman in the Loch Dornie lounge says he was there wi' two lassies from just after ten. Used one o' their rooms and left around two o'clock."

"With the girls?"

"No. Got a taxi for them."

"Did you get descriptions of the girls?"

"Better than that. One of them was Anna Robertson. She's been there with him before."

Carston's smile was enormous. "Christ, what a great detective you are, Jim."

"I ken."

"We'll have the bastard in first thing in the morning."

"You got any other angles then?"

"On Burchill? Maybe. Let's see what he gives us himself, though. If we're lucky, we'll be able to charge him with the assault in the hotel, then follow through to Donnelly."

"Aye, and wee pigs will fly past the window."

They cleared up their desks and were both in good spirits when they left for home, excited at the prospect of tying Burchill into the intrigue which had already caught Donnelly and Simpson.

Carston took his preoccupations home with him and tried talking them over with Kath. She'd been back only three days and yet the uneasiness of living on his own was a distant memory. All their old habits had slipped back into place as if she'd never been away. She was used to acting as a sort of testing ground for his ideas and often threw in a perspective he hadn't considered, sometimes redirecting him into more productive musings. Tonight, though, as they talked, her reactions and suggestions, colored perhaps by his descriptions of Burchill's antics, only managed to echo his own.

At last, he decided he'd had enough of work and that they'd spent enough time wandering round in the same circles. He leaned forward, kissed her on the cheek, and filled their glasses with the last of the Cahors, a 1990 Couaillac which she'd found in some catalog.

"I've been to Enderby's a few times, you know," she said, swirling the wine around in her glass.

"Oh? What for?"

"Just nosy, really. Now and again they get some old cameras in, too. I remember one I just missed. A Kodak. Turn-of-the-century taper bellows. Compound shutter. It was gorgeous. Bloke paid seventy-odd pounds for it."

"I'm glad you missed it."

"Miser."

He put the empty bottle on the coffee table and leaned back again.

"What d'you make of them?"

"Who?"

"The ones who go to the sales. The dealers, that lot."

"They're not really dealers. Not big-time anyway. Most of them are just pottering about."

"Yeah. That's the impression I get. Sad sort of place really."

"I wouldn't say that. They like it among all that dust and rubbish, sifting through all those broken bits and pieces. They're just … ordinary."

For a moment, Carston was very still. Kath's words had suddenly created a little itch of curiosity in him. The picture of Simpson lying faceless on the carpet came into his mind.

"They're the ones to watch," he said.

Ten

Mhairi had finally fallen asleep just before four. Ross had put her down, looked briefly at the tiny, innocent body that was contriving to undermine his whole routine, and gone to bed. But he was awake again at six, his mind racing. He gave up the idea of grabbing another hour, slipped downstairs, shivered through a bowl of muesli, and was at the station by seven-thirty. He was surprised to find Carston already there and glad to be able to pour a mug of freshly made coffee.

Carston was going through Enderby's accounts again.

"Looking for something special?" asked Ross.

Carston didn't answer. Instead, he pushed away the book in front of him, leaned back in his chair, and rubbed his eyes. Then he reached for a notebook and flipped it open.

"When you first went to see Hilden, you said the place was filthy."

"Well, maybe not filthy. Untidy. Dusty."

"Right. But he'd cleaned it up the next time."

Ross thought for a moment.

"Aye. Just the passageway. The stuff Simpson had smashed up."

"Nothing else? Not the shop?"

"No."

"So he was beaten up in the passageway, too."

"Aye."

Carston paused a moment.

"Why did he clean it up, Jim?"

"Just to make room. To get in and out."

"But he could have done that by just chucking the stuff aside. Why clean it?"

Ross shook his head.

"Seems a natural thing to do to me. What's this all about? Why the sudden interest in Hilden?"

Carston got up to refill his coffee cup. His reflection in the blackness of the window was patterned by the threads of frost which had crept over it through the night.

"Last night, I was thinking about how Burchill's name's turned up everywhere. It's one of the things we've got on him. A reason for calling him in. The trouble is that I want him to be guilty. It'll make my Christmas to charge that bugger with something serious."

"Aye, well, he's up to somethin'. The way he was yesterday ..."

"Yes. And guess what time he got home on Friday, or rather, Saturday morning?"

Ross waited.

"Just past four-thirty. One of his neighbors is a GP. He was just back from a call."

"Great," said Ross, genuinely pleased.

"Yes. So he's not covered from nine to ten—that's part of the window Brian McIntosh gave us—or from two to four-thirty, which is when the body could've been dumped."

"Gives us a bit of leverage."

"Yep. I've already phoned. He'll be here at half past."

Ross was slightly anxious.

"Have we got enough?"

"What, to charge him? No. Not yet. But there's the woman's complaint and so much circumstantial stuff, so many links with Simpson. And I've got a few ideas."

Ross was immediately wary. "Like?"

Carston tapped the side of his nose. It wasn't a reassuring gesture as far as Ross was concerned.

"And where's Hilden supposed to fit in?" he asked.

Carston waved a hand over the papers on his desk.

"Looking through this stuff. It started me thinking about him. Something Kath said last night, too." He stopped and tapped his lower lip with the knuckle of his forefinger, obviously reflecting on something. "The trouble is, he's such a pathetic little prat."

Ross frowned. He didn't see the connections Carston was trying to make.

"We've been big game hunting, Jim, haven't we? Burchill's got his finger in all these pies, dodgy dealings everywhere. He's not just an oilman; he's into antiques, property, the Masons. There's this sort of web stretching out from him."

Ross sighed, prepared for an excursion into the sort of flimsy fancies he loathed.

"It's true," insisted Carston. "At least, it is for me. And it's made me think too big all the time. Conspiracies, big money motives, that sort of thing. I've been putting these individuals into boxes, fitting them into a bigger scheme. But none of it's big time, is it?" He waved a hand over the ledgers and papers on the desk. "Look at this lot. It's pennies. It's lots of little ... nobodies. Donnelly, Hilden, Enderby, a bunch of squatters, small-time thugs like Simpson and Mitchell."

"Aye, well they're all still in the frame. I'm no ignorin' any o' them."

"No, neither am I. But I was getting too wrapped up in forensics. The bits of glass, the flakes of paint, they were so bloody inviting."

"Oh come on ..."

"No, I mean it. I realized just last night. We've been stuck with lists and proofs and patterns. We've stopped thinking about people. Donnelly, Simpson—they were both battered. It's not a cold, corporate killing. Like I said before, it's passion."

Ross couldn't help snorting his impatience. "Passion! And you're askin' about Hilden! He's as passionate as an Arbroath smokie."

"He's also scared shitless."

Ross's head was shaking but as Carston continued to talk through the things he'd been mulling over since they'd left Burchill's, his frustration decreased. Fundamentally, there was no real disagreement. They'd both been appalled on far too many occasions by the extremes of which people were capable. Mutilations worthy of the most imaginative special effects experts were perpetrated by harmless-looking men and women. Ordinary people were capable of extraordinary things. What Carston was trying to do was bring the investigation back down to that basic level and clear out his own misconceptions. The temptation to angle everything towards incriminating Burchill might well have the reverse effect and lead to oversights that gave him escape routes. By starting from scratch, he could look at everything, including Burchill, from a fresh perspective. He'd set aside most of the previous notes he'd made and the pages he was now flipping through had been freshly filled in the early hours.

"You see, you could hardly get smaller fry than Hilden. I was looking at how much he's made from things he's put into Enderby's sales. It's not even peanuts, Jim."

"So he's poor."

"Yes. But he's got rent to pay. And …" Carston stopped, forcing Ross to look at him to see why. He slowly lifted his notebook and tapped his finger against an entry. It was too far away for Ross to read.

"And?" said Ross, irritated.

"Who d'you think his landlord is?"

Ross knew immediately. "Burchill."

"Bingo." Carston shut his notebook. "So Simpson's a collector for Burchill. He also had his own little protection business on the side, which Burchill may or may not be part of, and on both accounts, he's hassling Hilden, who's flat broke. Bloody good motive, isn't it?"

Ross nodded his agreement, but the image of Hilden scraping flying strands of hair down over his dome came back to him. He couldn't believe Carston was suspecting him of something.

"Surely, you're no sayin' you think he … I mean, there's nothin' to him. He couldna even lift a bloody baseball bat, never mind hit somebody with it."

"Jim. Simpson was asleep."

Ross pointed to the chart on the notice board. "OK, but what links Hilden with Donnelly? And even if there is somethin', he's got an alibi. Friday night, Simpson was beatin' the shit out o' him. I saw the condition he was in. There was no way he could have killed anybody then. Even a couple o' nights later, when Simpson got it, I reckon he'd have been hard-pushed."

Carston was already nodding. They were all arguments he'd already thought of.

"I know, Jim. I'm just playing with ideas, though. Just looking at the angles."

He went over to the chart and studied it for a while before turning back to Ross.

"Look at it another way," he said. "Who's the only person who could confirm his alibi?"

Ross looked at him and smiled.

"OK, OK, Simpson. But this is a gag, right? I mean …" He looked at his watch. "Burchill's goin' to be here any minute."

"I know. He's the main man. We can use Hilden and his other tenants to get to him."

Ross couldn't see where Carston was going with this at all. He took refuge in looking through the papers that had been left on his desk for him. Almost at once, the phone beside him rang. He picked it up and listened, nodding.

"Burchill," he said to Carston. "He's here."

Carston got up. "Send him to interview room one. We'll give him the works."

"He's expectin' that," said Ross, the phone still cradled on his shoulder.

"What d'you mean?"

"Palisser's with him."

Carston nodded grimly. Palisser was a lawyer whose greatest pleasure in life seemed to be to humiliate Cairnburgh's finest. He was no crook, but his manipulation of the law on behalf of clients had broken many apparently watertight cases and redefined the careers of several policemen. The only comfort Carston could take from his presence today was that it probably meant that Burchill was guilty and needed all the help he could get. It might make the interview interesting, but it certainly wouldn't make it any easier.

"OK," said Carston. "I'll go down and get started. Before you come, though, get on to Dennis Paskett and see if the girl up there's willing to pick him out of an identity parade. If she is, let's get one fixed for later this morning. It'll give us a bit more time with him. And the team'll be here soon, so you might as well brief them before you come down."

Ross nodded and began speaking into the phone again as Carston took a very deep breath and went out and down the stairs.

When the team got in, Ross's briefing was a short one. Their inquiries the previous day had produced nothing new. Every one of the dealers they'd spoken to so far had an alibi for the Sunday night and they all continued to deny any knowledge of anything. In a way, with Burchill being interviewed, their efforts seemed almost irrelevant. They needed to be directed more specifically at the areas in which Carston thought he was involved, but jumping the gun, especially with Palisser around, could destroy everything. There was no option but to continue the grind through the client list. Fraser said that it was a "dommage," making the word rhyme with "homage" and Spurle's sullenness was more eloquent than a sermon, but they dragged off into another freezing morning of enforced politeness.

The atmosphere in interview room one was icy. Carston had decided to record everything. "For your protection and ours," he'd said pointedly, directing his remark at Palisser. He sat opposite the lawyer and Burchill at a small table. A uniformed constable stood by the door.

Burchill had dressed with his usual care, choosing a black Paul Smith jacket in cashmere and a dark green Kenzo shirt. They reeked of stale cigarette smoke but they were very classy. Both were beautifully cut and separated him not only from Carston, in his best Marks & Spencer suit, but even from Palisser, whose outfit was from Austin Reed. There was no doubting where the power lay. Since the beginning of the interview, he'd made it clear that he'd come under sufferance and that, when it was all over, it would be his turn to attack. Palisser had frequently had to put a hand on his arm to urge him to control himself and make sure he said nothing Carston might be able to use.

Carston had tried to stay with generalities to begin with. He wanted to keep the main accusations in reserve, reckoning that they'd have more chance of success if he'd managed to frustrate Burchill a little and edge him into the wrong defensive strategy. It would also help to have Ross there to pick up on anything he might miss. The problem was that Palisser had obviously briefed Burchill quite thoroughly and had his own idea of what the shape of the interview should be.

"You must appreciate the difficulties we're having, though,"

Carston was saying to Burchill. "Two murders, one of them perpetrated with property belonging to you, the victim of the other an associate of yours …"

"Associate! Barry fucking Simpson!" Burchill felt insulted. Once again, Palisser's hand reached across to him.

"… an associate of yours," Carston went on patiently, "with notes relating to dealings with you in his pocket. He also phoned you the night he was killed."

"Would you care to make your point, Chief Inspector?" said Palisser, his voice quiet, polite, cultured.

"Well, we'd rather like your client's help in eliminating him from our inquiries."

"Easy," said Burchill. "I had nothing to do with any of it. Is that it? Can I go?"

Carston smiled. "Ah, if only it were that simple. But there are other issues."

"Like?"

"Well, rent collecting, for instance."

Carston waited. Neither of the others took the bait. That in itself told him that Burchill knew what was coming and was defensive.

"One or two of your premises, antique shops especially. Simpson acted as a rent collector for you, didn't he?"

"Who said so?"

Carston consulted his notebook.

"Three of your tenants. Oh, and Simpson's assistant, Benny Mitchell, another of your associates."

"Fuck off, Carston," said Burchill, angry at the use of the word "associate" again.

Palisser dived in to retrieve the situation.

"Chief Inspector. We've been here for almost ten minutes and so far you've given no clear idea of why my client's been called in. I think I'm going to have to insist that you say exactly what's on your mind."

"Yeah, put up or fucking shut up," said Burchill.

"Very well. What I want to know most of all is where you were on Friday evening."

"Why?" said Burchill.

"To eliminate you from our inquiries," said Carston, managing to hold his smile.

"And exactly what is the subject of those inquiries?" asked Palisser.

"Oh, there's more than one. There's the murder, of course, and a couple of assaults."

Burchill said nothing. It was another good sign. Carston pressed on.

"Another tenant of yours. A Mr. Hilden. Antiques shop in …"

"What the fuck's that got to do with me?"

"Ssh. Let's hear the chief inspector out," said Palisser.

"I haven't been near that place in months."

Carston looked surprised. "Did I say it happened at the shop?"

Palisser was trying to keep his own annoyance with Burchill in check.

"You were saying, Chief Inspector, a murder and two assaults. How, specifically, can we help you?"

"I'd like to know where your client was when they happened. Friday night first."

Palisser looked at Burchill. Burchill picked at a fingernail on his left hand.

"Well, Mr. Burchill?"

"I went out for a drink."

"What time?"

"I don't know. Eight, nine."

"Where'd you go?"

"Don't remember. Might have been the golf club."

"Alone, were you?"

"Yes."

"I see. Having a drink on your own at the golf club."

"Far as I remember, yeah." He suddenly seemed to recall something. "Oh, I called in at the Atholl, too."

Carston nodded as if that had cleared up a little difficulty he was having.

"Yes, the Mount Atholl. I asked you about that yesterday. Didn't I?"

"Did you?"

226

"And you were alone there, too."

"Yes."

"You didn't see Anna Robertson? Or Penny McGee?"

Carston had dropped the names quietly, hoping for an effect. He was disappointed. Burchill looked straight at him.

"Never heard of them," he said, and Carston felt a twist of alarm as he saw a smile on his lips.

"You didn't book a room, then?"

"I don't need to. My company's got an arrangement there."

"I'll rephrase it. You didn't avail yourself of a room?"

"Nope."

This was wrong. He was too confident.

"Well now, that's strange, because the barman says you did."

The smile dropped away for a moment.

"He's a lying bastard, then."

"And what time did you leave?"

"No idea. I was rat-arsed."

Palisser let nothing register on his face, but Carston would have bet a lot that he wasn't relishing this.

"Oh dear. You didn't drive, I hope."

"Nope. Taxi."

Carston allowed himself to look puzzled.

"Well, you see, this gives me some problems, because the barman says you were there, with the two girls, that they left in a taxi around two and that you'd arrived in your car but that the car wasn't there when he closed the place up, so he assumed you'd driven home."

"I told you what I think of that prick."

"And then there's your neighbor, Dr. King, who actually saw you driving."

"Where?"

"Up into your driveway. About half past four."

Burchill's lips tightened and he shook his head. But he had nothing to say. Palisser stepped in again.

"But I don't see why you're trying to tie any of this in with these murders and assaults."

Carston let his impatience with the interruption get to him. When he spoke, his voice was harder than he intended.

"Because your client's version of events differs significantly from those of four other independent witnesses, because he won't tell us where he was when Floyd Donnelly was murdered or when the body was dumped, and because one of the assaults was committed on the two girls in the hotel room where the barman says he took them."

"And which my client categorically denies." Palisser's words were quiet, reasonable, and, consequently, all the more irritating. Carston was saved from an intemperate reply by a knock on the door signaling Ross's arrival.

"A quick word, sir," he said from the doorway.

Carston got up, turned off the recorder, and went out. He shut the door behind him and sucked in a deep breath through clenched teeth. "That bastard," he said. "I've got to have him, Jim. It's getting personal now."

Ross looked along the corridor at a uniformed constable armed with a polystyrene cup and a bacon roll.

"No chance, sir," he said in a whisper.

"What?"

"Mrs. McGee, the woman in Aberdeen. She's withdrawn her complaint."

"What?"

"She phoned DS Paskett last night. Says her daughter was lying. She's saying she wasn't here on Friday at all. Stayed at her boyfriend's place in Aberdeen. They had a fight. Those marks on her, they're from him." The constable disappeared into an office. "Anyway, that's what she's saying now," Ross finished lamely.

Without that direct complaint, they had nothing. All the indicators implicated Burchill; the way he'd reacted all the time had convinced Carston that he was involved, but until suspicions hardened into accusations they were going to have to let him go.

"He's got to her, Jim."

Ross nodded. "That's what I thought."

"Threatened her. Offered her cash. Both maybe."

"Aye. Just like the other lassie and her mother."

"And he'll be at the barman before we can do anything about it. Next time we talk to him. He won't remember a thing either.

Or he'll say he made a mistake." Carston turned and hit the wall hard with the side of his clenched fist. "Bastard!' he said. "There's nothing left. All we've got's the doctor seeing him drive back at four-thirty."

He gave a deep sigh and forced himself to push his anger and annoyance back down.

"Right. If we haven't got the complaint to fall back on, we're in trouble if we keep him here."

"And he'll be all the more prepared when we bring him in again."

"Yes, you're right, Jim. OK, away you go. I'll be with you in a minute."

Inside the room, Carston flicked his head at the constable to tell him to leave, then turned to Burchill and Palisser with his face composed into the best smile he could manage.

"Well, gentlemen," he said. "Thank you very much for your time. We'll be in touch."

They were as surprised as he'd hoped they'd be.

"That's it?" asked Burchill. "That's all?"

Carston simply widened his smile.

"Come on, you bastard, what's the score?" said Burchill, getting to his feet.

Palisser restrained him yet again.

"Chief Inspector, this is all very regrettable. You seem to have been wasting my time and that of my client. I think we deserve some sort of explanation."

"Of what? You've very kindly come in, helped us with our inquiries, and now I'm simply thanking you."

Palisser was still seated. "I see," he said before rising slowly. He seemed to consider something before speaking again.

"You know very well," he said, "that being summoned to a police station often compromises one in the eyes of others. Implicit in the process is something akin to defamation of character."

"Not at all, Mr. Palisser," replied Carston, his steady smile hiding the fact that he was uncomfortably aware that Palisser was right. The lawyer pressed on.

"It seems clear to me that we were brought here on something like a whim of yours and there are lots of questions which need to

229

be answered, simply to protect innocent members of the public from misplaced or misapplied police procedures."

Carston had nothing to say but his discomfort didn't have time to register because Burchill had had enough of Palisser's measured tones.

"Yeah," he said, his finger wagging uncomfortably near to Carston's face. "You're in deep shit, Carston, make no mistake. False accusations, wasting my time. You'd better get yourself a lawyer 'cause this is going to be official. I'm going to bust you, you fucking cunt."

"I'll see you out," said Carston.

"Fuck you. We'll see ourselves out. And you'd better start clearing your fucking desk. You're finished here."

He slammed out of the room, followed by Palisser, who at least had the grace to glance at Carston with what might have been a sympathetic apology before he disappeared.

The whole thing had been disastrous and Carston knew that the threat was very real. Without the complaint against Burchill, there really wasn't enough solid evidence to bring him in, even for a harmless interview. Also, he'd allowed himself to drop hints and accusations into their exchanges which Palisser would no doubt have filed away for future reference. But worse than all that was the thought that, once again, Burchill was being let off the hook. He was free and able to buy and bully his way into whatever took his fancy, using and discarding other people as the mood took him. When people like him kept on succeeding, the only response was despair.

Back in his office, he sat in silence. A morning which had held such promise had thickened and soured. The information he'd marshaled to open up Burchill's smugness was useless and he knew that before long, he'd be having to waste energy on defending himself against official complaints. Ross sensed his mood and, although he'd advised caution in their treatment of Burchill, he felt no satisfaction at having been proved right.

"It'll have to be Plan B then, eh?" he said at last.

Carston looked up.

"The masked avenger," Ross went on. "The bald, one-man epidemic."

"What the hell are you talking about, Jim?"

"Hilden. I thought you wanted to see him."

Carston forced a little laugh; there wasn't much humor in it.

"That was an hour ago, when I was young and optimistic," he said.

"So you didn't mean it?"

"Of course I did." Carston's tone was slightly impatient. He recognized it and stopped. Ross was obviously trying to lift the mood. And he was right; the Burchill business was just a hiccup. There were still legitimate questions to be asked, and the train of thought that had led to Hilden was still potentially interesting. He sighed deeply, tapped twice on the desk, then roused himself.

"Right. Back to work," he said briskly. "Come on, you can introduce me."

When they got to Nostalgia, Hilden wasn't keen to let the police into his shop yet again but didn't know how to refuse them. Once inside, Carston saw right away what had prompted both Ross and McNeil to feel sorry for him. He looked uncomfortable, threatened. He stood among the piles of other people's cast-offs, his head lowered, ready for yet another hostile invasion of his sad privacy. As they talked with him about relatively inconsequential things, he was as closed and secretive as all the other dealers seemed to be.

It was Ross who made the first small piece of progress with him.

"Did you think any more about those photos I showed you?" he asked. "The two men."

Hilden nodded, his eyes still on objects at floor level.

"Yes. I ... er ... It was them."

"Both of them?"

Hilden nodded again.

"I thought I recognized them right away. But I was afraid to ... I'm sorry." His hand went to his head, this time not to chase hairs but to touch the dressings on his wounds. "I wasn't thinking straight."

Ross made sympathetic noises. With the prints on the sword, the extra I.D. simply confirmed what they could already prove. The important thing was that Hilden was beginning to make contact with them. Both Ross and Carston were careful to nurture the trust, but when they began to ask about his landlord, his eyes started once again to flick nervously from them to the objects stacked around them. The thought of Burchill clearly disturbed him. Carston decided it was worth pressing.

"Have you had any problems with him?"

"What sort of problems?"

Carston shrugged. "I don't know. Any sort."

"No."

The answer was too quick.

"He's a bit of a tyrant, I hear, especially where money's concerned. Is that right?"

"I wouldn't know."

"You make sure you're never in arrears then, do you?"

This time there was hesitation. "I try to."

"I see."

"What? What do you see?"

The sharpness of the question surprised both Carston and Ross. Hilden seemed suddenly to have got angry. Carston's remark had touched a nerve and Hilden resented it.

"Mr. Burchill's got no complaints against me," he went on. "Ask him."

"We have," said Carston.

Hilden's anger disappeared with equal suddenness. His eyes flicked to Carston, then away again.

"What did he say?"

Carston had to improvise. "Well, that on the whole there are no difficulties. But just once in a while …" He let the implication drag on. Hilden's eyes dropped to look again at the bare boards between his feet.

"I paid him," he said, to Carston's relief. "He got his rent." He paused. At last he added, "It's not easy. Especially the way things are."

Carston noted the present tense. He guessed that Hilden was still having rent troubles. It would be useful if he were. Might add a bit more weight to his motives. And yet, even as the thought formed, it was accompanied by another little swell of pity; Hilden really was a tragic figure. His life was obviously a sequence of defeats, of slow days among discarded effects. His bandages had been replaced by bits of sticking plaster whose edges were already black and curling away. The redness of his anger had gone, leaving his usual dusty yellow pallor; his left hand was scraping incessantly at the long strings of his greasy hair and patting them against his scalp. Whatever secrets his past concealed, distant or recent, it was unlikely that his future would produce anything very reassuring.

"Has Mr. Burchill been threatening you at all?" asked Carston, dropping all accusation from his voice.

Hilden said nothing, then shook his head.

"Did he send people round?"

Nothing.

"We can stop him doing it, you know."

There was still no response.

"But we can't do anything unless you tell us about it," Carston went on.

Hilden mumbled something into his chest.

"I'm sorry?" said Carston.

Hilden's head came slowly up and, for a change, his gaze was steady as he repeated, "That's what started it in the first place. Telling you."

"But that was Barry Simpson. He's dead."

Hilden's eyes flicked away again and he was silent for a moment.

"You think he's the only one there is?" he said at last.

Carston was annoyed with himself. Hilden was right; it wasn't just Simpson. For all his weakness, Hilden did have one irritating talent; his passive victim's air made others feel guilty. Faced with someone whose life seemed such a comprehensive failure, it was difficult to be accusatory. As Carston changed tack to ask him where he was on Sunday evening, it seemed like some sort of violation but it had to be done. His answer was utterly predictable.

"I was here."

"Was anyone else …?" There was no need to finish the question; his head was already shaking.

Already depressed by the encounter with Burchill, Carston felt his irritation growing to a degree which threatened to interfere with his judgment. It wasn't that he lacked sympathy; quite the reverse, his natural impulse to reassure the man was getting in the way. It was Ross who supplied the necessary diversion.

"We were wondering if you'd be willing to help us out, sir," he said.

Hilden looked at him.

"Simpson's assault on you last Friday …"

Hilden waited.

"You see, we need to know where he'd been in the couple of days before he was killed. We know he was here, but what we need to do is find out what sort of traces he got on his clothing from you or your shop."

"What for?" asked Hilden.

"Well, he obviously picked up bits and pieces everywhere he went and if we can eliminate any of the ones we know about, it'll mean we can concentrate on the rest."

Carston was impressed. Here was Ross arranging to get samples which might incriminate Hilden and yet selling it as a way of excluding him from their inquiries. Perhaps understandably, Hilden was suspicious.

"I'm not sure about that. Is it normal procedure?"

"Absolutely," said Carston. "It's called exclusory as opposed to confirmatory evidence."

Hilden thought about it for a while.

"What will it involve?"

"Hardly anything," said Carston, taking over Ross's suggestion. "We'll just get a couple of samples of dust and things from the hallway and …"

"No."

The refusal was surprisingly quick.

"Why not?"

Hilden's head was shaking again. The victim was back.

"It doesn't sound right. You're looking for something."

"Yes. We told you. Things we've already got." Carston decided to push his luck. "Things that may link you with Simpson. If we can find out what they are, we can set them aside."

It was a persuasive argument but Hilden continued to be stubborn. In the end, it was only when Carston reassured him that he'd be present when the samples were taken and could object to anything he wasn't happy with that he agreed, albeit with much reluctance. It was a victory which Carston didn't want to jeopardize and so he immediately stood up and apologized for taking up so much of Hilden's time.

The three of them went into the passageway and Carston looked briefly over it.

"We'll leave it to you then, sir. All we need is something from somewhere he was at the time of the assault. I'll send a couple of men round right away and then we'll be out of your hair."

As Hilden's left hand lifted instinctively towards his head, Carston blushed at the inappropriateness of his remark and bustled out of the shop. Ross followed close behind, a grin tugging at the corners of his mouth. As he drove away, they both allowed themselves to break into laughter.

"I know, I know," said Carston, adding, in a less amused tone, "What a sad little bugger."

Sleet began to stain the windscreen. Ross switched on the wipers.

"By the way. Congratulations," said Carston.

"What for?"

"Low cunning, consummate hypocrisy, whatever you want to call it."

"Just doin' my job."

Carston grinned, then thought about the next step.

"I think you should go back with the guys when they get the samples. Play along with him, keep him sweet. But see what you can get in the way of scrapings. He's already had a bloody good clean up, but see what's down between the boards, in the cracks."

"He'll be watching us."

"Yes, I know, but a few of your lies'll sort that out. I'll phone George Reid in Aberdeen. Pretend I'm calling in a favor. See if he can do a special job on the stuff for me right away."

It was nearly eleven o'clock and yet, with the clouds piled thickly overhead, daylight hadn't managed to establish itself. Christmas lights swung in the wind and looked very bright against the grayness of the air. The traffic crawled more slowly as the sleet thickened. Carston turned to look at a thin, red-haired youth who was wearing only jeans and a T-shirt. The message on the shirt was "I'm Horny!" Carston didn't believe it, not in this weather. He looked over the other shoppers, but none of them registered with him. His mind was still on Hilden. The new direction they'd taken that morning had shown almost immediate results. Burchill was a disaster, but with Hilden they seemed to have broken out of the closed repetitions of the past couple of days. It might still all prove illusory, but his appetite had been rekindled.

"You know," he said, "I'd like to get that stuff up to George today if I can. How're you fixed?"

"No bother. I'll go. Jean wanted a trip anyway. Christmas shopping. I'll drop her in town. Thursday's late shopping day."

Carston laughed to himself.

"You know everything, Sergeant," he said.

Isobel Beattie was at the window of her flat. On the sill before her were two small jugs. Her fingers traced over the soft, cream-colored glaze of one of them as she looked out at the saturated air. She wore no makeup and the lips whose power she'd used so frequently were tight and drawn. The weather didn't worry her; she had no intention of going out. It was just another wall between herself and other people.

On Tuesday, still gripped by the hard fury that had filled her the moment she left Burchill's, she'd driven up to Elgin and bought the jewels from Colonel Thorpe. She was so full of hatred—for herself and others—that she'd taken a bitter delight in knocking the price down by another five hundred. She didn't need the extra profit, but it gave her a savage pleasure to exact a tiny revenge, even if its focus wasn't clear. She'd wrapped the jewels in plain brown paper and had the package delivered by courier to the offices of Burchdrill. Burchill must know that what had happened between them was rape and he'd surely be expecting her to report it. Sending him the jewels would make him think that it was business as usual, that he was safe.

It wasn't until the evening that the effort of control the whole process had needed began to show. The following morning, she'd tried to shake herself into action and she'd gone down and opened the shop. But after only an hour, she'd found herself shouting at a client in a fit of unprovoked temper and shaking so hard that she was unable to handle any items for fear of breaking them. Without any attempt at explanation, she'd asked the client to leave and closed the shop. It had stayed that way ever since. There were so many messages on her answering machine that the tape was full but she felt less and less able to deal with them. She'd set things in motion the night of the rape. It had taken lots of courage, but she felt in her heart she'd made the right decision. All she could do was wait for them to exact the retribution she was owed. She turned and went to take a shower. It was the third that day.

George Reid had made it clear to Carston that he was doing him a favor way beyond anything he owed him but promised nonetheless to give the Hilden samples priority. When Ross delivered them, he told him they'd be ready on the Saturday morning. As a bonus, he offered the news that the full report on Simpson would be ready then, too, but that still meant that the rest of Thursday and all of Friday would be like a gap in a continuum. After the buzz he'd got from the meeting with Hilden, it seemed to Carston that the investigation had suddenly stopped. He hated just waiting. On top of that, Palisser had filed an official complaint on behalf of Burchill, and Carston had received formal notification that he'd have to answer the allegations. The case would be handled initially by Beresford, so the omens weren't good.

To fill the time usefully and to collate the items he'd need for his defense, he looked once again through all the case notes they'd accumulated, concentrating on those which had nothing to do with antiques or dealers. Nothing new emerged, but he did notice one or two inconsistencies which he should have spotted before but which his preconceptions had obviously hidden at the time. The only real advance in their knowledge came with the news that the fingerprints found on the baseball bat and the lock of the back door of Enderby's belonged to Simpson. There were no traces of any others.

Exactly one week had passed since Floyd's death. The date was marked at Macy's by even bigger Friday night crowds than usual. The club had remained closed the rest of the previous weekend because of the investigation and so its clientele had been starved of their sole source of exoticism in Cairnburgh. The added notoriety of having had a body shoved under its front steps meant that Neil, Frank, Mark, and Big Tam were very busy. Those they wouldn't let in, or who had to wait until there was more space, were content to stand shivering beside the steps. The chill came partly from December and partly from the delicious proximity of the residues of violent death.

The same evening, Anna Robertson and Penny McGee were once again with Burchill at the Mount Atholl Hotel. He'd sought them out and made it clear that all was forgiven. It was going to cost him, but he reasoned that what he was buying was freedom from Carston's attentions. Despite McGee's misgivings, he'd persuaded the two girls that another couple of hours with him would be worthwhile. Sure enough, when they left in the early hours of Saturday, they were each four hundred pounds richer. Somehow, this time, they'd managed to smile through the pain. It was better than being jobless and broke. Just.

On Saturday morning, Carston and Ross started their trip to Aberdeen in darkness but by the time they reached Queen's Road, the sun had come up into a sky empty of clouds. The transformation was total; from the soggy grays of the week to a hard, shining clarity. The shadows were sharp and, although the air temperature was still below freezing, the day looked inviting. Ross was particularly appreciative because, for the first time in a month, he'd slept right through the night. In fact, he had started into wakefulness at six-forty, suddenly terrified that something had happened to Mhairi. She'd gone to sleep between ten and eleven and they'd heard nothing from her since. He hurried to the nursery and found her still soundly asleep, fluffy little snores coming from her tiny lips. He wondered whether the long drive in the car to Aberdeen on Thursday afternoon had anything to do with it and was ready to make it a daily trip if this was the effect it had.

In the Nelson Street labs, George Reid took them through to his office, handed over the full forensic report on Simpson, and left them with it while he got back to working on the samples from

Hilden's shop. It was the usual, thorough, detailed analysis obscured behind technical terminology and lists of curious substances. Together, Ross and Carston read it over in silence, Ross constantly making notes on a piece of scrap paper he'd taken from a pad on the desk.

Carston finished first and sat back as Ross continued to study it. When he eventually put his pen down, Carston said, "Well?"

"Interesting."

"Very interesting? Or just interesting?"

"Very."

"For example?"

"Well, Simpson didn't kill Donnelly, did he?"

"Why not?" asked Carston, knowing the answer already.

"The lead crystal glass. Just a few bits round the bottoms of his trouser legs. If he'd hit Donnelly, he'd have the stuff all over him."

"So why's there any there at all?"

"He's had some sort of contact with Donnelly after he was killed. Helped to shift him, perhaps."

"I doubt that. If he'd picked him up, there'd be more of it. He's just brushed against the body. Maybe not even that. Maybe he's just been to the place where Donnelly was killed."

Ross was nodding as he looked at his notes again.

"There's more of that paint, too," he said.

"Is it the same stuff?"

"Think so. Lead chromate. Not as much as they found on Donnelly, but enough."

Carston stood up and stretched.

"So, they've both been in the same place. Could be that squat. We know the two of them were there last Friday afternoon."

"Aye, but that glass on his trousers … Wherever it was, Simpson was definitely there after Donnelly was killed."

Those were the features of the report that had obviously struck both of them most forcibly. They went over the rest of the findings—the carpet fibers, wood splinters, and other traces that had probably all been picked up in the course of his last weekend at Enderby's—but nothing else seemed to indicate any links between the two bodies. The two deaths were connected, but there was little doubt that Simpson had had nothing to do with Donnelly's. The tie-up was elsewhere. Already, their trip had proved valuable. Its value rocketed when Reid eventually brought through his notes on Hilden's shop. He was whistling "Flower of Scotland" and seemed quite pleased with himself.

"Right, Jack," he said. "This is supposed to be a favor, yes?"

"Yes," said Carston.

"Well, I think you owe me several."

"Why's that?"

"Depends what you're looking for in this lot."

"Whatever we can get."

"How about two sorts of blood for a start?"

Ross whistled. Carston pointed a finger at Reid. "George, whatever you want, it's yours. I'll even have your baby. Tell me more."

Reid put his handwritten notes on the desk between them. They were hard to decipher.

"I'm glad it was only a small sample," he said. "There was all sorts of stuff, even in that little bit you brought up."

He took them through the main findings. The two samples of dried blood had been scraped from between the floorboards.

"Have you got a DNA profile on them?" asked Carston. Reid shuffled the notes and pulled out the familiar sets of bars. Carston took them and then pulled the report on Simpson towards him. In it, he found the DNA markers for the profile of Simpson's blood. He held them up for Reid.

"Any match, George?" he asked.

Reid looked hard at the three sets of markings, then began to shake his head.

"Nope. Sorry, Jack. These two are different."

"That's OK," said Carston. "Can't expect miracles. Can you do me a favor, though?"

"Another one?"

"Have you got a duplicate of the report you did for us on that guy Donnelly?"

Reid went to a filing cabinet and took out a folder.

"Only put this away yesterday. What're you after, the DNA?"

"Yes."

Reid riffled the edges of the paper in the folder and stopped at a stiffer piece of card. He took it out and held it beside the sample from Hilden's shop. His head began to nod and he leaned closer.

"Spot on, Jack." He pointed to one of the charts. "This one's Donnelly."

"Yes," said Carston, almost leaping out of his chair.

Ross shared his excitement but immediately began to check his own enthusiasm. They now knew that Donnelly had been at Hilden's. Of course, the blood didn't necessarily mean he'd been killed there; he could have had a nosebleed or even tripped and fallen over some of Hilden's clutter. And there was always the consideration that blood group evidence could only be used legally to prove innocence and not guilt. Nevertheless, it was a huge, and for him unexpected, leap forward.

He held up his own notes for Reid to look at.

"Did you find any of this in the stuff I brought up?" he asked, pointing to a jotting halfway down the page.

"Bags of it," said Reid immediately. "One of the main ingredients."

Ross's satisfaction began to grow again.

"The paint, sir," he said. "Looks like we're there."

"We're a bloody long way down the road, anyway. Thanks to you, George."

Carston knew that, although they'd established the presence of both Donnelly and Simpson at Hilden's shop, nothing they'd discovered yet incriminated Hilden. But his alibi—that he'd been beaten up by Simpson and spent a painful night at home before going to the hospital—had always seemed strange. Eventually, they'd have got round to checking it, but they'd all been too busy with the double investigation and Burchill's probable involvement had been so tempting. All the same, Carston was mentally kicking himself. He used Reid's phone to dial the Laidlaw Memorial Hospital in Cairnburgh, identified himself to the duty sister in Accident and Emergency, and got her to look out Hilden's records. She didn't feel able to answer his questions herself and fetched the consultant. After a fascinating few minutes of discussion, Carston thanked the man, disconnected the call, then immediately phoned the station in Cairnburgh. He arranged for Hilden to be brought in for questioning but, since they'd only be able to detain him for six hours, he didn't want him at the station until he and Ross got back. He looked at his watch, reckoned that, on a Saturday, they'd need a bit longer to get home, and said they'd be there at three. Less than fifteen minutes later, having made extravagant promises to Reid to repay him for giving them such clear leads to follow, they were well out of Aberdeen and driving west into the glare of the already dropping sun.

Carston had been talking most of the time, setting out the strategy they'd use when they talked to Hilden and marveling that the man had been under their noses all the time, telling them the flimsiest stories and yet managing to seem just part of the background. He was sure that Hilden had been around when Donnelly was murdered. The details of his alibi were bizarre.

"According to the consultant, he was beaten up early on Saturday morning, not long before he went to casualty. He was still bleeding. If it'd happened on Friday night, there'd have been clotting, more bruising would have developed, stuff like that."

"So he's covering up."

"Looks like it."

"Explains a few things, doesn't it?"

"Yes. Makes us look bloody fools, too. We should have looked a bit more closely. I mean, saying he waited all night after Simpson had beaten the shit out of him—not very likely, is it?"

"Aye, and phoning Simpson in the first place, virtually inviting him to give him a kicking—it was all to get an alibi."

"Crap alibi, too. Dead easy to crack. Surely he must've known we'd ask the doctors about it at some stage? All he does is draw attention to himself. Christ, Jim, he'd have been better off just going to bed and saying nothing."

"Aye, but … It's still no right, is it?"

Carston's head was shaking. "I can't make any sense of it. You see, another thing the doctor said—some of the thumps he got were older ones."

"What d'you mean, older?"

"Three bruises and cuts on his left forearm and two on his

242

thighs. He reckoned they'd been done several hours before the rest."

"What?"

"Yes. Like you said, Jim. It's not right."

They drove on, each trying to find the key to the enigma into which Hilden had so suddenly grown. His fabrications seemed intricate, baffling, and yet they were basically inept and very easy to demolish. But what were they for? Ross was annoyed with himself for letting his judgment be clouded by the pity he'd felt for the man, but Carston felt a perverse sort of pleasure that their search had led them not to the grand intrigue he'd been assuming as he considered Burchill's empires, but to a ramshackle structure, flung together from the whims of a single, feeble individual. He was pleased, too, that the forensic findings still didn't offer a simple proof but needed some intuitive probing to deliver a result.

They arrived with more than fifteen minutes to spare and had time to set up the interview room the way that suited them. They read and talked over the old information and added their new findings to it. There were plenty of discrepancies for Hilden to explain.

He was brought in just after three. If his appearance had provoked pity before, his present condition merited an entire charity. There was the same pallor, the same pinched face under the white dome with its stripes of hair and patches of sticking plaster, but he seemed to have shrunk even further in stature. As he sat in the chair Ross held out for him, he sank down, brought his feet together and back, lowered his head, and folded his left arm over his right in his lap. He was defeat incarnate. Even with what they knew and suspected of him, Carston and Ross both felt embarrassed by his weakness and uncomfortable about the accusation they would be making. Carston explained that he wasn't under arrest and that, if he wanted them to, they would tell a solicitor and one other person that he was being detained. Hilden listened, considered the information, then shook his head, which he'd kept lowered throughout. Carston then added that they had the right to search him, but that they weren't going to, and that they simply wanted to ask him some questions.

"You needn't answer them," he went on. "The only thing you

have to tell us is your name and address. That's the law. D'you understand?"

Hilden thought again and nodded.

They began gently, avoiding the incriminating evidence they'd brought back from Aberdeen with them. Ross took the lead at first as he went over some of the statements Hilden had made to him during their first meetings. Hilden said very little, usually confining himself to little nods or shakes of the head, which Ross had to get him to articulate as yes or no for the benefit of the tape recorder. All the time, it was as if he were waiting for them to say something, tolerating the rerun of old conversations but anticipating something more searching. It was when Carston came to their most recent visit to his shop that Hilden himself took the initiative.

"I knew I was in trouble when you asked to take those samples," he said, his words muffled by the fact that his head was still lowered onto his chest. The two policemen were immediately alert.

"What do you mean, trouble?" asked Ross.

"Saying it was to eliminate me. It wasn't, was it?"

This was dangerous.

"We needed to know Mr. Simpson's movements," said Carston, knowing how lame it was as a reply.

Hilden nodded. "I half believed you. I wanted to, you see? But you were always going to catch me. You were bound to."

This was astonishing. Suddenly, with no pressure or sleight of hand, they were getting what sounded like a confession. For a moment, neither knew what to ask, in case they redirected Hilden's thoughts the wrong way. But what he'd admitted seemed to lift his spirits a little. For the first time since he'd arrived, he lifted his left hand across his head in the familiar gesture and raised himself slightly in the chair. Fortunately for Carston and Ross, who didn't yet know what he was confessing to, he started to talk again.

"My shop's near where he lived. That's why it ..." He paused, looked up and went on, "I never made much out of it, you know."

This was getting worse. What the hell was he talking about? Carston had to get it all focused.

"I know," he lied. "Maybe it'd be best if you just told us about it. From ... well, whenever you think it started."

"That's easy," said Hilden. "He came with some silverware."

"That's Mr. Donnelly?" said Carston, praying that his guess was right.

Hilden nodded. "Yes. Said he'd found it in an attic. Never tried to pretend. Told me it was stolen."

"Why did he come to you?"

Hilden hesitated. His eyes flicked up to look at Carston, then dropped away again.

"I suppose mine was the first shop he came to."

"And he wanted you to sell it for him?"

"He wanted me to buy it. He just wanted cash right away. It was the same every time."

"So you bought it, then sold it on?"

After a slight pause, Hilden nodded, the confession to being a receiver of stolen goods immaterial in the context of his main crime.

"How long did this go on?" asked Ross.

"Started about five or six weeks ago and he came in every two or three days. I can show you exactly when in my books."

As he described his dealings with Donnelly, he continued to surprise them. He was meticulous in his self-condemnation, offering them proofs, dates, times, digging a deeper and deeper hole for himself with every word he spoke. Carston suspected he was ridding himself of guilt. But the police couldn't give him absolution for the sins he had committed.

That Friday, Donnelly had spent the evening in the pub and come to the shop at chucking-out time. He was very drunk. There was dried blood on his face from a cut on the side of his head; more of it stained his jacket. He was angry, hyper, and the alcohol made him seem very dangerous to Hilden. He had a set of crystal glasses and a decanter and he wanted a hundred pounds for them.

"Didn't just want it, *demanded* it," said Hilden. "I told him, I didn't have it. It was true. And anyway, it wasn't worth that much." He stopped for a moment, sidetracked by the thought of past transactions, then continued. "He didn't believe me. Shouted. Swore. Eff and cee and things like that. And he picked up that sword I gave you. It was in a hat stand there. One of the nicest things I had. Got it from Inverness one time. Seventeenth-century. And he just swung

245

it round and hit me. There." He lifted his left arm and touched a point a couple of inches above the wrist. "I was really scared. He was wild. He'd never been like that before. Said he'd kill me. Called me names. Hit me again. But that time he dropped the sword and he had to pick it up. I hit him as he was bending over. With the decanter. I was still holding it. It broke. Pity."

The only change in his voice came in the last few words. His tone softened; the loss of the decanter affected him more than the damage to Donnelly.

"Then what?" prompted Carston.

"Well, he was dead. Not right away, his pulse kept going for a little while. Then it stopped and he was dead. His blood was on the floor. I didn't know what to do."

"So what did you decide?" asked Carston after a little wait.

"I didn't. Not at first. Just left him lying on his face and had a cup of tea. It's good for shock. Then I heard the sirens. Thought you were coming for me. But they went on. Into town."

Carston looked at Ross. Hilden noticed and explained. "There was a fight there. I had the radio on. The local news. Northsound. That's where I got the idea."

His elliptical style was driving Carston crazy. He longed for an extended, coherent sentence in which he wouldn't have to fill in connections.

"I'm sorry," he said. "What idea?"

Hilden's face still showed nothing. "The idea of taking him to Macy's. Make it look like he'd been in the fight. That's why I put the glass in his face. I didn't want to get anyone blamed, just to get him away from here. Make him part of the fight."

"How did you take him into town?" asked Ross.

"In the car. It's old but there's plenty of room. You'll probably find more blood in the boot."

Carston was desperate for a cup of coffee and time to think, but Hilden ground quietly on.

"It was quite late when I got back. There was lots of blood in the passage. I cleaned it up—well, tried to. Got most of it done but there were still odd marks so I decided to cover them up."

"With what?"

"Well, more blood really. Nothing else would do, would it?" Neither Carston nor Ross had ever conducted such a bizarre interview. In the same, calm way, Hilden went on to describe the extraordinary sequence of events he'd then initiated to cover the signs of the murder and provide himself with an alibi. The blood he'd used to cover Donnelly's was his own.

He'd taken the sword and hit himself on the legs and the arm, drawing blood and rubbing it onto the floorboards. But there didn't seem to be enough. So he'd decided "with some reluctance" that the only way was to get beaten up. By calling Simpson, he made sure that he'd have an excuse for bloodstains on his floor and also an alibi. He just hoped, as he said, "that it wouldn't hurt too much."

"I phoned him. It was ... oh, sometime on Saturday morning. Before the shop opened. Quite early. I knew he'd probably still be in bed. But I had to call him when there were no customers around. I didn't want people seeing him here."

"What made you think he'd come round?" asked Ross.

Immersed in the details of his plotting, Hilden seemed almost eager to explain it to them.

"Well, I couldn't be sure, so I said I'd been thinking about it and that I was going to phone you. I thought he'd probably come round to try to stop me."

"And he did."

"Yes. But when he arrived, I said I'd already told you. He lost his temper. The sword was there. He picked it up and ..."

He stopped and Carston saw the tears glistening in his eyes.

"There was plenty of blood then."

The whole thing was ludicrous. Not a single aspect of the planning had any chance of success. Hilden had thought that the self-inflicted bruises would make it more difficult for the doctors to put a time on the assault, that his blood would obliterate traces of Donnelly's, and that a glass pushed into an already dead face would send the police galloping after nonexistent street-fighters. The only value it had for Hilden was that its ineptitude suggested that the crime itself couldn't have been premeditated.

When he'd finished and he'd answered the many questions that his story had thrown up, he still sat in quiet bewilderment. They charged him, told him they'd be sending their report to the procurator fiscal, then arranged for a car to take him home. There was no need to warn him to be ready to appear when summoned; his attitude towards them was that of a child. He'd told them everything, put himself entirely in their hands and at their mercy; now it was up to them.

The car carrying him pulled away into the darkness. Despite the cold, Carston and Ross stood and continued to look along the street even after it had disappeared, subdued and saddened by the experience they'd just had. It had obeyed none of the rules, made a nonsense of the street-bashing the team had been doing, laid before them an unmitigated confession of guilt—and yet it had all been delivered by an innocent.

As they walked back in to try to make sense of it all, Carston was dissatisfied. He said nothing to Ross, but, despite the comprehensiveness of what Hilden had said, he felt there was something missing. The amateurishness of the crime and the attempts at covering it were unsurprising and fitted the individual who claimed them. But he couldn't see Hilden bundling Donnelly's body into a car, lifting it across a pavement, pushing it under those steps. The man just wasn't big or strong enough to do it. And he didn't have the nous. There must have been somebody else involved. His hesitation when they'd asked him whether he wanted to contact anyone, the halting, unconvincing nature of some parts of his narrative, convinced Carston that, for all its incredible detail, the story wasn't yet complete.

And, of course, there was still Simpson.

Eleven

It had been a very full week but the normal Sunday indulgence of trawling through the papers held no appeal for Carston. Once again, he'd slept badly, his thoughts returning again and again to Hilden's confession and the petty but irritating anomalies he'd seen in some of the case notes. Kath saw the symptoms and, annoyed that her own reading pleasure was being interrupted by the savage rustlings he was making, suggested that their marriage could only be saved if he left immediately for work. Carston kissed her, then, gratefully, set off through the empty streets to the station.

He'd noted the various things that had bothered him as he'd re-read things on Thursday and Friday. He'd found one of them in statements Spurle had taken at the squat and others in his own notes of his visit there with Burchill. In the quiet of his office, he looked at them again. Some of them seemed, in retrospect, a bit contrived, an attempt to build a theory out of nothing. But there were others which weren't so easily dismissed. The squatters had all claimed that Donnelly was the only one of them who'd gone into the attic and yet, here in his own notes, he read, "What the hell would we want up there? Can you see us flying kites?" When Carston had been up there with Burchill, the kite had been out of sight behind a stack of newspapers. It would have been impossible to know it was in the attic without actually going there. So it was a lie. At least one of them, besides Donnelly, had climbed that ladder. It might be a harmless fib but it was one of the few pieces of incriminating evidence he had.

More interesting, though, was the comment he'd picked out of Spurle's transcripts of the first lot of interviews they'd had with them. "You'll get the same story from all of us as far as Floyd's concerned. Didn't belong here. He was a bastard." The remark had been made on Friday evening, long before Donnelly's body had been discovered, and yet he was spoken of in the past tense. It had struck Carston when he'd first read it, but he'd let it pass as perhaps a sign that, despite their apparent coolness, they were feeling the stress of Simpson and Mitchell's visit or that they were just assuming that Donnelly would be moving on from the squat very soon. Now that Donnelly's death had been so clearly linked with items he'd taken from Forbeshill Road, though, the comment might prove to be less innocent.

It still wasn't enough to fill the gaps which Hilden's confession had left, but it did give him something else to look for. He went down to the basement, where older records were kept, and began to sift through some files. He was interested in one case in particular and suddenly, on a page giving details of probation arrangements, he saw a name which made a new set of connections, confirmed the value of his previous discoveries. When he'd finished reading, he went back upstairs, grabbed his coat and left straight away for Forbeshill Road.

He decided to walk. If he went up the hill and then round through Macaulay Park, it'd be exercise of a sort. He needed a little time to think and it wouldn't be a bad idea to shed some of the flab forming as a result of nightly doses of wine, cheese and pâté.

He noticed the change as soon as Will let him into the squat. The security precautions were less stringent than they'd been on the previous visits, and there was no one in what seemed to be the communal room at the front. The place was dustier; magazines and sheets of paper were scattered on the floor. The bloodstains from Will's altercation with Jez were still clearly visible. In just a couple of days, the squat had begun to degenerate towards a stereotypical squalor.

Will sat in an armchair, leaving Carston standing in the doorway, and picked up the book he'd been reading when Carston arrived. The impression he'd given before was one of detached self-sufficiency; now, there was a moody antagonism which he made no attempt to hide.

"I need to talk you and your ... flatmates," said Carston, irritated once again by the fact that he still didn't know what to call them.

Will didn't look up from his book. "Fran's ill," he said. "She's upstairs but she won't want to see you."

"And the others?"

Will's shoulders hunched very slightly to signal that he didn't know where they were. A noise behind him made Carston turn. It had come from the kitchen across the hall. He went to look in. Liz had just put on the kettle.

"Want some?" she asked, holding up a tea bag.

"No, thanks. If you've got coffee, though …"

She nodded and Carston watched her as she opened a cupboard to take out a jar of instant. She, too, looked different. She'd worn a little makeup before; now she had none. It made her look younger. She'd left off the tinted glasses and her eyes looked red and tired.

"How're things?" asked Carston.

She gave a short laugh, looked at him and tilted her head to indicate the room in which Will was sitting. "You're the detective. What do you think?"

"Seems a bit subdued."

"Aye. Burchill's going to get his way."

"What d'you mean?"

"I can't see us stayin' here much longer. It's no the same. He's beaten us." The tone of her voice confirmed the idea of defeat.

"Sure it was him?" asked Carston.

The question made her turn to look at him again. They held one another's gaze for a moment, then her lips lifted into a small smile that made her look even younger.

"At the end of the day, aye," she said. "He was always bound to. The cards are stacked, aren't they?"

"How?"

"Everything. Criminal Justice Act—no, I know it doesn't apply up here yet, but it'll come. And you're on his side, too."

Carston began to protest, but she went on. "You know fine you are! Your specialist squads in Scotland Yard, every one of them, know what they're aimed at? Protecting property."

Carston knew that she was right.

"Can't do without laws," he said, lamely.

"'Unthinking respect for authority is the greatest enemy of truth.' Know who said that?"

Carston shook his head.

"Einstein. No bad for a role model, eh?"

Her light cynicism was still there; so were the arguments she could skillfully marshal to justify her position. But the fire had gone. The passion she'd shown in her defense of the squatters during their trip to Aberdeen had faded. Where Will's broodings had turned outwards and started impacting with the outside, Liz's zeal had shrunk and she'd retreated from confrontations. There was still confidence in her movements and defiance in her voice, but something had been lost. The silence between them had left her to savor her little victory.

"What brings you back?" she asked at last, switching off the kettle.

"More questions. Just checking a few things."

"Even though you've charged somebody already?"

It was intended to shock him. No one knew that Hilden had been charged. She was flaunting her inside information.

"How did you know?"

This time, she only half-turned and the smile was already there.

"Come on, Inspector," she said, her voice teasing, provocative. Her desire to shock had worked. For a moment, Carston was caught, unsure of his ground. He'd been wondering which way to approach the subject and she'd taken the initiative. Despite himself, he smiled back at her and even wagged an admonitory finger. She poured the water, stirred his coffee, and handed the mug across to him before sitting down at the table. He helped himself to milk and leaned back against the sink.

"He phoned you, did he?" he asked.

Liz nodded. "Last night. When he got back from your place. Poor Donald. He was in a terrible state."

It was the first time Carston had heard anyone say Hilden's first name. It made him sound even more vulnerable.

"Have you known him long?"

Liz looked at him. "You know that, surely?"

Carston smiled at her.

"Yes. But I'd like to have it confirmed."

"Two years, bit longer," she said, a softness in her voice.

"Tell me about it."

"It's no a time I like to remember much. Before I met him, I mean. But he made it different. He was ... kind to me. No, better than that. He was ... I don't know."

"He put up the bail for you when you were on that shoplifting charge."

Liz nodded. "That's not all, though. I knew him before. He helped me ... I was rock bottom. The only thing I hadn't tried was prostitution but that would've been the next step."

Carston knew that she'd go on in her own time, so he waited.

"Strange, isn't it? He's such a wimp, such a nobody, but he's so bloody kind."

Her voice broke with memories and Carston kept his stillness and his silence. She wiped her fingers across her eyes and told him how, when she'd first arrived in Cairnburgh, she was a drunk. Looking at her firm, strong body, Carston found it hard to believe that she'd ever been as low as she claimed but, calmly, clearly, she spoke of how she'd had to leave Aberdeen because the thieving she'd been doing to fund her thirst for alcohol was getting her noticed. She still had some small candlesticks which she'd stolen at an antiques fair and, by chance, the first place she'd gone to to try to sell them was Nostalgia. She knew they weren't worth very much, but Hilden had offered her more than she'd asked. Her first reaction was to suspect some ulterior motive, but it transpired that he simply felt sorry for her.

In the next few days, she'd gone back to him from time to time and they'd talked and he'd given her a little money.

"But it wasn't the money," said Liz, seemingly far away. "The thing was, he was ... well, like I said, kind. He listened and talked like nobody had for ages. He was interested in me. Not sex or any crap like that. Me. It made me interested in myself again. I began to ease off on the booze. Then I went to stay with him."

For an instant, Carston had the unpleasant thought that, despite her claims, there might have been some sexual component in the bond between this attractive young woman and the wretched antiques dealer, but her next words dismissed it.

"Father figure, I suppose. But gentler, not like my father at all. Christ, no. A million times better than him. He was all for the regiment, discipline, snap out of it, and all that shit. Donald *listened*. Cared."

She stopped, her memories now pleasant.

"Why did you leave?" asked Carston, lowering his voice so as not to break the spell.

"I was getting to depend on him. It was time to move on. And this place was empty." She spoke as if squatting were the most natural thing in the world. "I was off the booze completely. With Donald there, I didn't need it. So I put my energy into this place."

"But you still saw him."

"Oh aye. We were very close." Suddenly, she gave a bitter little laugh. "I was the one who sent Floyd round to him."

Carston's attention quickened.

"When?"

"The first time. When I realized he was taking stuff from here. Oh, don't look so shocked! Robbing Burchill is doing the world a favor. I told Floyd he'd get a good deal from Donald if he mentioned my name. He went round. At first, though, Donald wasn't interested."

"Why not?"

"He was frightened."

"Of … Floyd?"

Liz frowned at him. "Of course not! Burchill."

Carston wasn't sure of the connection and his expression showed it.

"He owns his place, too."

"Yes, I know."

"Donald's terrified of him. When Floyd told him the stuff had come from here, he knew it belonged to Burchill, so he didn't know what to do. If he handled it, Burchill might find out. And that'd be more trouble. More little visits from Burchill's SS." She stopped. "Aren't you going to take notes?"

Once again, she'd surprised him.

"Should I?"

"How should I know? It's your job."

"I mean, d'you think I need to?"

Liz allowed herself a little smile again, but it disappeared quickly and once more Carston saw the fragility underneath. As she'd spoken of her father and the contrasts between him and Hilden, she'd seemed like a very young girl. Now again, for the briefest of moments, her eyes widened and she looked scared. In spite of the apparent control she was exercising over their talk, he saw the extent of her vulnerability. The stresses that had originally led her to seek relief in a bottle were still unresolved. Hilden may have soothed them but they were deep. She was lost and she needed help.

"I don't think I need any notes," he said gently. "Not yet, anyway. Let's just talk."

"What about?"

"Whatever you like. What did Donald do about Floyd, for instance?"

"I went round. Just … talked with him. Told him it was OK. Made a sort of deal."

"A deal?"

"Aye. He knew how much it cost to keep this place goin'. I said we might as well get Burchill to pay for some of it. And Floyd had no idea of values, he was askin' peanuts for the stuff he'd brought. Donald reckoned he could resell it for plenty."

"And give you what he made?"

"Some of it. Profit sharing, see? It was the nearest I'd come to the enterprise culture since I'd been engaged."

She'd chosen the corporate terminology deliberately but, for a change, seemed not to have done so with the usual sharp intention. She told him that there'd been many more visits by Floyd and that she and Hilden had had a laugh about it all. He trusted her, saw her as an ally against Burchill, and took enormous delight in the thought that he was deceiving him.

"And what was in it for you?" asked Carston.

Liz thought about the question only briefly. "I've told you. He's generous, giving. You've seen him. He looks like such a poor wee soul. Folk've walked all over him for years. He was so chuffed when I went to see him. Every time, he tried to give me presents from his shop. I felt sorry for him but I knew I didn't need to. He's ... OK. I owed him everything. Without him, I'd've ..." She stopped for a moment, remembering Hilden, then shook herself out of it. "And then there was the money."

Carston was sure that she realized she was admitting being an accessory to theft and reselling stolen goods, but he was more interested in the fact that the coldness and hostility she'd shown in their previous meetings had all but vanished. As they talked, her fondness for Hilden made her relax. She no longer had to justify living in Burchill's house; she could speak instead of personal concerns and private impulses. Her bond with the antiques dealer, her need to protect him, allowed her to operate as a human being rather than as Liz the Squatter, symbol of all that was wrong with society.

They finished their drinks. "It's me you came to talk to, isn't it?" she said.

"Yes," said Carston quietly.

Liz nodded. "I thought so." She stood up. "Can we talk somewhere else? I don't want the others coming in."

"Of course."

"Let's go for a walk."

She fetched her green coat and the two of them left the squat. There was no warmth in the sun and at first they said nothing as they walked briskly across the road, then down and through the gate into Macaulay Park. As they climbed towards the children's swings which hung still and empty, with a scattering of frost along their edges, Liz stopped suddenly and turned to him. "How did you know?"

"What?"

"About me."

"To be honest, I wasn't altogether sure. Just a vague suspicion. There was the link between you and ... Donald in your shoplifting case notes."

"Ah." Liz smiled. It made her face look very pretty.

"And you said you hadn't been in the attic—but you had."

She nodded.

"And that first night we came to the house—the phone call? You answered it, then, when it was your turn to make a statement, you talked about Floyd in the past tense. You *knew* he was dead. It was Hilden on the phone, wasn't it?"

Liz nodded again. "Aye. Complete panic. He told me he'd just … you know."

Her voice had broken at the memory and she stopped as she sucked in her breath to stop herself crying. Carston talked to give her the chance to recover.

"I only remembered the call because I thought you were all wasters and didn't deserve a phone."

"You read the *Daily Mail* then?"

"How did you guess?"

They went on in silence for a while, past the swings and towards the bare earth of the memorial rose beds and the severe black skeletons of their bushes. As they turned to walk along beside them, Carston was suddenly alarmed to feel her slip her arm through his. He looked quickly at her but her face showed nothing. It wasn't a cynical tactic; there was no coquetry in the act. It was simply the latest impulse of her self-revelation. Perhaps she was remembering her quasi-filial contact with Hilden and repeating it with Carston; a reaction against real parents whose Victorian strictures had constituted a different but no less damaging form of parental abuse. She was opening up, ridding herself of stresses which had made her role as spokesperson of the group even tougher. Carston was a sympathetic figure who had found his way into her secret but had the sense to tread softly. He was embarrassed and yet flattered by the contact. He knew that it was unprofessional but, equally, he recognized that Liz needed the small reassurance it gave her.

"Fran's cracking up," she said at last. "Will doesn't know what to do. Dawn and Jez never say a word. There's nothing left." She stopped speaking and watched a Highland terrier buzzing past, nose to the ground, smelling something that excited him no end.

"You must be used to aggro," said Carston.

"Aye, but this has been … It all comes back to Floyd."

"Liz," said Carston, "we need to talk about him. About what happened."

"I know," she said simply and began to tell him of what had happened on Friday evening.

Donnelly was not long dead when Hilden called her. She'd had to wait for Spurle to finish taking the statements and, as soon as he and Carston had left, she'd gone round to Nostalgia and found Hilden sitting on the floor in the passageway beside the body, in a slick of blood. Her own first reaction had been one of terror, but the state of Hilden didn't allow her to indulge it. He was almost catatonic, turning over and over in his hands a glass stopper sticky with blood. It was she who'd heard the sirens and the news of the fight at Macy's, and it was her idea to use it as a screen. The two of them had driven into the town center, manhandled Floyd under the steps, and disfigured him with the glass. Again, this was Liz's idea; Hilden was still acting on automatic; simply obeying orders. They'd driven back and she'd helped him to clean up the mess. It was when they'd poured away the last bucket of pinkish water that Hilden began to wake up. He handed her the sword.

"You need to hit me," he said.

Liz thought he'd actually lost his sanity.

"What?" she said.

"There's still blood there. We need to cover it. Hit me. Make me bleed."

Liz was appalled at the idea. "I can't," she said.

Hilden looked at her, screwed up his features, lifted the stick, and struck himself first across the left arm then on his thighs. He'd split the skin on his arm quite badly and he held it over the floor, let the blood drip on the area they'd just been cleaning. For the first time, she'd started crying as she saw the person who'd done so much for her squeezing his thin forearm, forcing the blood to flow. Her tears seemed to cause him more distress than the wounds he'd inflicted on himself. He tried to comfort her, then told her he could manage and that she should go home.

The whole story had been told in a quiet, unemotional tone, but Carston had felt the pressure from her arm increase as she described her first sight of the body. She was telling it all to him not as a confession but as a strange anecdote, removed from reality, whose significance she hadn't yet understood. Guilt and responsibility weren't in the equation.

"I think he's got a sort of death wish," she said. "He's been a victim so long, it must feel normal for him to be punished. Poor Donald."

It was a creative insight into Hilden's life and one which Carston shared. He'd seen so many examples of it; proofs that if you abuse people long enough they take on the appearance of someone who deserves it.

She shivered and pulled herself more tightly into his side.

"That guy Simpson beat him up very badly, didn't he?"

"Yes. But you could say he asked for it. Phoned him up and more or less invited him round."

"Aye, he told me. Part of his stupid plan. Poor Donald."

"I suppose he told you that Simpson's dead, too?"

She stopped, forcing him to do the same, and turned him to face her.

"I thought that's why you came," she said.

"What d'you mean?"

She looked at the trees that bordered the path, then back to him.

"Of course I know that Simpson's dead. I killed him."

Twelve

Carston looked at Liz, trying to formulate an appropriate reaction. The fragility was back with a vengeance; the cold had pinched her cheeks, made her eyes look even wider. He turned away to look across the roofs of Cairnburgh, piled up over all their Christmas preparations. None of this was official, but he needed to know what had happened. He turned back, offered her his arm, which she took gladly, and they continued their walk.

"I didn't know that, Liz," he said. "And I haven't got any evidence, so you'd better think carefully before …"

She interrupted him. "It's OK. I'd already decided to come and tell you. Fran and the others have put up with too much already. I don't want them to have any more pressure. And I couldn't let Donald take all the blame."

Carston said nothing, reluctant to let her incriminate herself so blatantly, yet unable to suppress his curiosity. And she told him, in the same flat tones as before, about the call she'd got from Hilden on Sunday evening. Simpson had been on the phone to him, threatening him again, asking for more money—this time not for Burchill, but for his own nasty little protection scheme. Hilden had promised to pay up; Simpson would be coming to collect that evening. The problem was that Hilden didn't have any money and was terrified that, when Simpson found out, he'd give him another beating.

"I knew what he meant when I went round to see him," she said. "He was so low. Never seen him like that before. Sort of broken." She laughed without humor. "Almost made me feel maternal. He needed putting to bed with a mug of Horlicks. That was my mother's answer to everything, from colds to AIDS. But I didn't put him to bed. I took him to find Simpson. Went to his house. But he wasn't

260

there—the place was in darkness. I didn't know where else to look for him. Then Donald said he worked at Enderby's, so we tried there. It was just a long shot, really. But when I saw the broken lock, I knew he was inside.

She paused and took a deep breath.

Carston was afraid to say anything. He couldn't use any of this, but Liz clearly needed to talk. It was her story, not his interview. He let her tell it her own way; he'd work out the consequences later.

"We were supposed to be there to talk with him, but we'd both put gloves on, so I suppose we knew what might happen. He was just lying there on one of the carpets. Asleep. Donald looked at me. He had no idea what to do. Neither did I. Then Simpson snored. One big, long snore. What a din it made. I picked up a baseball bat that was there and hit him. More than once." She was clutching his arm hard. "Donald was in too much of a state to do anything, besides, he was sore from his battering. We were there to solve a problem. Getting rid of him … Well, that was one solution, wasn't it? He wasn't the sort of guy you reasoned with. We rolled him in the carpet and went home."

Gradually, her grip slackened. "I suppose you get into a sort of spiral. You do one thing, the rest just follows," she said. "And then it's too late to go back." And at last, with the story unlocked, her weariness and fear began to well over in the catharsis of tears. Instinctively, Carston unhooked her grip and put his arm round her. He hugged her protectively as they turned to go back to the squat.

"Simpson was a real bastard," he said.

At eight-thirty on Monday morning, the incident room was packed. As well as the usual team, there were twelve uniformed constables and two sergeants, all sent by Superintendent Ridley. The rumble of their conversations died as Carston went in.

"OK. Thanks for coming, all of you, but you can relax and stand down."

All the faces were turned towards him; each one showed surprise.

"Developments over the weekend," he explained. "It's all been tied up. I appreciate your cooperation but you can get back to your sections. Sorry for the inconvenience."

Slowly, uncomprehendingly, they got up and filed out, leaving the regulars behind. The only one missing was McNeil. Carston sat back against a desk and looked round at them. "You've done bloody well," he said. "If you hadn't got all those interviews done and brought it all together, we'd still be wondering where to start."

"So what's happened?" asked Fraser.

Wearily, with no real enthusiasm, Carston went over the week-end's developments. He'd brought Liz back to the station, taken her statement with the assistance of a duty constable, then charged her and driven her back to Forbeshill Road, where she'd given them some of her clothes for forensics to start on. He'd been in early that morning, starting to get the papers together to send to the procurator fiscal. He gave them the details of the remaining paper-work and told Spurle to organize the team to deal with them. There were reports to type, statements to collate, and set procedures to follow. It would make a pleasant change for them all to sit in the warm room, doing things that needed little effort.

Back in the office, Ross picked up the typed manuscript of Liz's confession and shook his head.

"Wish they were all this easy," he said.

Carston's expression was grim. "It wasn't *easy*, Jim. It was bloody awful. That kid's been completely destroyed. And all she was doing was helping the person she cared most about." He pointed at the sheets in Ross's hand. "It's desperate stuff. Just made me furious when I re-read it this morning. Bastards like Burchill and Simpson—"

There was a tap on the door and Spurle stuck his head round it.

"Any idea where McNeil is, sir?"

Carston looked at Ross, who shrugged his shoulders.

"Only, it's deciding who's going to do what."

"Leave it with me. I'll chase her up," said Ross. "Meantime, just do what you can."

"Right, sir. There's always the checkered skipper butterflies. That's one for the ladies."

He sketched one of his gruesome smiles but Carston wasn't in the mood for his leaden humor.

"This is a serious case, Spurle. I'd appreciate it if you gave it your full attention."

His tone was enough to warn Spurle away. He went out and Ross picked up the phone to start his search for McNeil. He called various departments and tried her home number and her mobile without success. There was no answer from her radio and he was beginning to feel anxious about her when, just after ten, she walked in and forestalled their questions with an immediate apology. Almost simultaneously, Carston's phone rang and he had to field a furious phone call from Ridley.

"It's bloody chaos," said the superintendent. "Schedules are shot to pieces."

"Sorry, Ridley," said Carston, careless that he was addressing a superior officer in a way which amounted to insubordination. "We solved it ourselves. Maybe we should have waited for your reinforcements to arrive but we just cracked it. Happens sometimes."

"Maybe, but seven different rosters have had to be reintegrated and …"

Carston slammed down the receiver. It was an action he'd have to explain later, but in his present mood he couldn't tolerate Ridley's petty inhumanity.

McNeil stood waiting.

"What the hell's going on?" said Carston, still hot with the anger Ridley had provoked.

"Sorry, sir. It's something I've been on since last Monday. Couldn't tell you about it. The—"

"What d'you mean, couldn't tell me about it? You running some separate department here?"

"No, sir … You remember I asked for your authority to get stuff checked at the labs?"

Carston had a vague recollection that she had. "So?"

"It was in connection with this other case. I've just come from her."

"For God's sake, McNeil, stop playing around. What's it all about?"

"Rape, sir."

She stopped. The word had the effect she'd wanted. Carston's temper ebbed quickly away. "Go on," he said.

"Monday night. I got a call. An Isobel Beattie. She'd phoned the station and refused to talk to any male officers. Wanted a female who knew something about rape. I was here. It got put through to me."

"We're not running a private service here, McNeil. Not yet anyway," said Carston, his tone more reasonable. "Whatever state she was in, you should have told me. I'm not completely useless. I can be discreet. Thought you'd know that."

"I do, sir. And I did try," replied McNeil, the strain of the whole experience obvious in her voice and face. "I told her you'd understand. Tried to reassure her. But she wasna havin' it. The guy ... she was terrified of him. Scared that ..."

She stopped. Carston noted her distress.

"It's OK, McNeil," he said. "Just tell me. There's no problem. You've done a good job."

McNeil nodded. "She was scared to trust another man, she said. Said they're all the same. She said if another man knew she'd gone to the rapist's place willingly, they'd only judge her, label her a slag. She wouldna budge. At first, she wasna even sure she wanted us to arrest him. Just needed to talk."

"Why didn't she ring the Samaritans?"

"It was more than that. It was like she was ... well, sort o' hedgin' her bets."

"How?"

"She wanted him caught, wanted him put away, but was still too scared to go right through with it. Getting the police involved sort o' kept her options open."

"Sounds a bit calculating for somebody who's supposed to be hysterical."

McNeil shook her head. "Oh no, sir. She wasna hysterical. That's the strange thing. She was scared to death, angry as well, but she was ... sort of in control. Hardly let it show. She knew what she wanted, she just needed another woman to show her the way. That's why I didn't push too hard to get you involved. I was afraid she'd just ... well, withdraw from me, too, call it all off."

She went on to tell how Beattie had asked whether there was a female police doctor available and, when she was reassured that there was, she cooperated in getting swabs taken and having a full examination. She gave McNeil the clothes she'd been wearing and made a detailed statement which she'd signed with McNeil and WPC Ellis as witness. But it had all drained McNeil's resources. The work she'd had to do to bring it all together without breaking her confidence had brought her close to exhaustion and she'd been on the point of telling Carston about it several times.

"I wish you had," he said.

"Aye. But you understand, don't you, sir? I mean, she could've clammed up any time. She still doesna leave her flat. Thinks he's waiting for her. He's a powerful man, I can understand why she'd think that. It's going to take her some time."

Carston looked at Ross, who was nodding his own understanding of what McNeil was saying.

"It's nearly all there now, though," said McNeil. "There's a heap o' evidence. She's no been at her work for a week, the swabs were all positive, we've got photos of the marks on her. And at last she's said it's OK for me to tell you."

"What changed her mind?"

"A piece o' evidence that'd be quite handy."

"Meaning?"

"He raped her at his place. On the carpet. There'll be bloodstains there. I told her if we could get a sample of that, we'd have enough to be pretty sure of a conviction, but that I didna have the authority to order it on my own. That's what swung it. She wants him out o' the way. Some place he canna get at her. We need to get a shift on."

"Right. Where is this place, then?"

When McNeil told him the rapist was Burchill, it took a moment for the information to register and then a lot of self-control to stop him shouting in triumph and conducting himself in an unbecoming manner with a WPC. Just as suddenly, his mood changed back again.

"He'll have cleaned it up."

"Aye, maybe, but you didna see the state she was in. There'll've been quite a bit of blood there and he canna shift all of it. I tried asking DCI Baxter to authorize a warrant on Wednesday, but he didna want to."

Another flash of anger hit Carston. "Do it, McNeil," he said. "Then come back and tell me all about it."

She turned to leave. Carston's voice stopped her.

"I haven't finished." She turned back. "Bloody good job," he said. "But next time, tell me. Even if they say not to, tell me. I can be discreet, I promise you. And we can't take chances."

"Yes, sir," said McNeil.

As the door closed behind her, Carston looked at Ross, who gave a small nod.

"Aye, DCI Baxter, too," he said.

As Carston had suspected, Baxter was another of the rolled-up trouser brigade. Even in the face of a crime as despicable as rape, their cohorts tightened and set the solidarity of their ludicrous brotherhood against the feeble crying of wronged individuals. On the other hand, maybe he was being unjust; maybe there were simply a few rogue examples who diverted an honorable intent to serve their own greed. Whatever the truth, the news that McNeil had brought helped to lift some of the dankness that had seeped into his soul from the weekend's discoveries. In the end, Burchill's acquisitiveness had rebounded on him. He'd tried once too often to grab what he wanted at the expense of someone else.

"We'll nail the bugger, Jim," he said with enthusiasm. "If McNeil's done her stuff properly, we'll put him away."

"I hope so," said Ross.

"I know it." His mouth formed a wide smile. "Who said there's no justice?"

As Carston spoke, the ten-twenty was leaving Perth railway station for Inverness. It was seventeen minutes late and the driver was trying to make up the time.

Twenty-three miles ahead up the track, a figure was walking slowly along between the rails towards him. Fran had no idea when she'd meet the train. But she knew it was bound to be along soon.